Questions of Guilt

and other stories

First Published in 2008 by;
Red Kite
PO Box 223
Walton on Thames
Surrey
KT12 3YQ
www.redkitebooks.co.uk

Illustrations by Mark Postlethwaite   www.posart.com

Also by this author;
Flight into Darkness
Published in 2006 by Red Kite   ISBN 0-9546201-7-8
Limited edition author-signed copies of both books are available directly from the publisher.

ISBN   978-0-9554735-7-9

Printed and bound in Great Britain by
CPI Antony Rowe, Chippenham, Wiltshire

Questions of Guilt

and other stories

by

Wing Commander Thomas F. Neil DFC* AFC AE

For my loving parents, now long since gone,
who spent five years of war, worrying, hoping and praying
for the safety of their only son.

Contents

Author's Foreword

This book of three individual stories, follows my previous book 'Flight into Darkness', which marked something of a departure in that, for the first time, I wrote of my experiences as a fighter pilot during the Second World War in fictional and somewhat more dramatic terms. I adopted this method, believing it to be the best means of more truly reflecting the excitement and horrors of the times and in order to get away from the more pedestrian descriptions of aerial combat and the parade of statistics and aircraft performances. In short, I wanted instead to dwell more on the effect on those many young people, men and women, who were caught up in the exuberance and thrills of battle but also encountered the many stressful and heart-rending aspects of war.

As in my previous book, the stories here describe many incidents and events I myself experienced or of which I had first hand knowledge. However, in order to broaden the scope of my tales, they also involve the activities and recollections of some close colleagues and friends with whom I flew or served. On all occasions, although the stories may, and indeed should be regarded as fiction, all the situations described are based broadly on actual events and many of the places mentioned are authentic, particularly some airfields which are readily identifiable today and remain in use as I write.

Similarly, names will arise from time to time which are those of former friends and colleagues. Should they perchance be recognised even now by distant relatives and perhaps others, despite their aliases - and the passing of more than 50 years is a long time now by any measure - I hope and trust that I will be seen to have dealt with them fairly and without malice.

Finally, these stories are, I believe, a true reflection of how events appeared to a young man flying a fighter aircraft in times of war, and later. Many of the situations described are exactly as I remember them. Moreover, the memory of some of the splendid young people with whom I became associated, although their names have been changed, will remain with me for ever. And, though perhaps difficult to understand now, it was painful at times for me even to write about them.

Tom Neil
Suffolk, July, 2008

Questions of Guilt

Questions of Guilt

The business of going into battle, whether in a bomber or a fighter aircraft, inevitably resulted in stress, both physical and mental. So much so, that the effects of combat during the Second World War very often remained in the memory of those who took part for years; for some, for the rest of their lives. The wounds, injuries and burns were the more obvious reminders of desperate times, but the effect of battle on minds, although less obvious, was sometimes more deeply felt.

The Royal Air Force and the German Luftwaffe, although experiencing the same problems relating to stress and morale, tended to deal with them differently. It was the German practice to keep their aircrew in the same units for lengthy periods but move their squadrons to and from zones of varying combat intensity, thus affording them at least some respite. The RAF instituted a system of 'tours of duty' in both Bomber and Fighter Command, each tour involving about 250 hours of combat flying.

In Fighter Command this resulted in a pilot serving in an active fighter squadron for about nine to twelve months. This assumed he was not shot down or severely damaged in the meantime. He was then posted away to some less taxing job, either as an instructor in an Operational Training Unit or to some minor staff appointment. In Bomber Command, an operational tour usually involved 30 sorties over enemy territory, followed by a six-month period of rest. Very few aircrew members in either Fighter or Bomber Command completed more than two tours of duty, although there were some notable exceptions.

In order to alleviate the stress of combat, aircrew were granted an annual leave entitlement of 61 days. They were encouraged to take up other pursuits away from flying, although war conditions generally often made this difficult. 'Questions of Guilt' is the story of a successful young officer who, for reasons of his own and the whim of a senior officer, remained on operational flying duty for far too long, with sad consequences for him and for many around him. Although based on fact, this story and the characters portrayed are imaginary. However, the names of the airfields involved and some of the personalities described are real enough.

CHAPTER ONE

Until that fateful morning of Wednesday, 7th January, 1942, Flight Lieutenant Marcus Wyndham Rayne had always regarded himself as normal, rational, and undemonstrative, even in circumstances amounting to crisis. However, if pressed, he would have admitted - albeit reluctantly - to being a trifle unrestrained when confronted with what he considered to be inhumanity or official stupidity.

Few, however, regarded him as normal in the sense that he was ordinary. To his doting parents in far-away England he was the greatest of heroes, whose survival they prayed for every day. To many of his contemporaries and colleagues he was a young man to be honoured and admired. After all, which other RAF fighter pilot, not yet 22 years of age, had already been awarded three Distinguished Flying Crosses? He had fought with notable success throughout the Battles of France and Britain and later in Malta, been credited with close on 20 victories in aerial combat, and had been obliged to bale out twice and crash-land his crippled fighter on three other dire and memorable occasions? Clearly, here was a young man of merit who had been granted a charmed existence, having taken part in some of the most intensive air battles of all time. Here, indeed, was a person for whom the future held considerable promise.

Privately, however, Marcus Rayne's mind had increasingly harboured doubts about his ability to survive or even to continue. In short, how long his morale and luck was likely to last. In particular, he had hated the A.O.C Malta's most recent instruction, requiring his squadron to seek out enemy aircraft supporting the Axis armies in North Africa, by flying endlessly at low level over the waters of the Mediterranean in inadequate and poorly maintained Hurricane fighters equipped with unjettisonable long-range fuel tanks.

His log-book would reveal that he had flown operationally for four months in France, during the so-called 'phoney war' of 1939/40, 141 times during the 16 weeks of the Battle of Britain in England, 50 or more over France and Belgium in the bitter winter of 1940/41, and a further 102 sorties fighting in the defence of Malta.

Finally, having quite recently survived - miraculously - five engine failures in eight weeks over Malta's inhospitable rocky terrain, he had quietly rejoiced when it had very recently been announced that his tour of duty had finally come to an end.

In the silence and solitude of his monk's-cell bedroom in Torre Combo, the ancient building accommodating the officers' mess and sleeping quarters at RAF Ta Kali in Malta, after hearing the news, young Rayne had flopped onto his bed, closed his eyes, and breathed an audible prayer of thanks to the Almighty for the respite. Where their 'Airships' were likely to send him now he didn't know, nor did he very much care. The important thing was to relax and rest; above all for there to be a end to the feverish take-offs, the straining climbs, and the tensions of combat. Yes, lots and lots of glorious rest! Because, after more than two years of constant, mind-bending effort, he was exhausted. Physically and mentally spent. Too tired to go on. Thank God!

He awoke in an instant, which was unusual for him, his mind racing. It was dark and silent, too dark for him to consult the luminous hands of the RAF's two-guinea watch still on his wrist. Even so, he sensed the approach of dawn. Burton, his bedroom companion, would have already left. He glanced across the room through his draped mosquito net but could see nothing.

For a time he lay on his back, listening. Waiting. Staring up into the blackness of the ceiling, his head tilted, his mouth open, to catch even the slightest sound. But, nothing. Deafening silence. And stillness. Unusually, however, he felt strangely aware. That sixth sense he knew he possessed more than almost anyone else he had ever known. The awareness of an enemy's presence. Almost like an odour, a smell, a prickling of the skin.

He sat up quickly. Yes, this was the morning they would come. He knew it! Sensed it with his whole being. They would come - attack! - as soon as the light was sufficient. In fact, they would already be on their way. Impulsively thrusting aside his mosquito net, he stepped out onto the cold flagstones of his room and walked quickly in bare feet to the open window space.

The shutters pushed back, he looked down onto the dim, dark square of the courtyard beneath. Nothing. No movement. No sound. Then, turning, he reached for a towel, hitched it around his naked middle, then walked by instinct through the bedroom door into the open and to the elevated walled passage that led to the mess and ante-room. Outside, the night was damp and cool. He shivered, looking towards the north and into the darkness. Behind him the first glimpses of dawn lightened the eastern sky.

Yes, from the north was the way they would come, directly south from Sicily. Any moment now. He strained his eyes and senses. Shivered massively once again. And waited. Then, in moments, as though at the flick of a switch, it all started.

First, and to his distant left, the cough, splutter and roar of a Merlin engine starting up. Then, another, after which three more, as a group of Hurricane fighters came to life. In his mind's eye he could see the clouds of dust rising in the wake of their fast revving airscrews as they began to move off, turn, then taxy quickly to the point of take-off. He was right. They were off! The alarm had been sounded!

Simultaneously and out of the northern darkness, came the hum of many approaching aircraft. A crescendo of noise followed by a mass of swift-moving black dots, all in a gentle dive. After which, lines of glistening beads as the guns of the attacking force sent their lancing, lethal streams towards the ground, tracer that streaked and curved then bounced as the bullets and cannon shells struck or ricocheted into oblivion.

The dark shapes, larger now . . . 20? . . . 30? . . . many of them anyway, racing overhead, the clamour of their engines a shrill, deafening scream.

As they streaked away, the defending guns responded: the rapid 'tonk-tonk-tonk' of the two 40 mm Bofors guns in their emplacements just beyond the airfield boundary, and the coarse, tearing chatter of several machine guns and 20mm cannons. In desperate curving lines, the glistening balls and tracer rose - oh, so slowly! - in pursuit of the enemy, now racing eastwards down the island and out towards safety. Finally, and little more than a defiant gesture, the roar of five . . . six . . . seven Hurricanes as they clawed their way into the air in fruitless pursuit of an enemy now rapidly disappearing into the greying darkness.

As the noise died away and lines of tracer continued to rise silently into the sky some miles away to the east, Marcus Rayne was suddenly aware of the cold. He turned wearily away with a shiver, and sighed. As per usual. Too little and too late! Much too late! God! What a way to fight a war!

Twenty minutes later, and fully dressed, Rayne walked the half-mile to the airfield he knew so well - the undulating square of impacted yellow earth, sparse brown grass and dust, from which he had flown for more than seven months.

Several of the Hurricanes he had earlier seen taking off in the half-light, were in the circuit preparing to land. He stopped to watch them briefly before walking towards three other fighters parked with their 'chore-horses' and starter batteries set well apart in the distance, and the single, low, oblong building built of ochre-coloured sandstone that was the dispersal hut, squadron office and crew room. There were still obvious signs of confusion. An ambulance and fire-tender was still in attendance and figures were moving about in haste, gesticulating and conversing.

He was some 50 yards away when a figure he recognised as his replacement, Flight Lieutenant John Davenport, came into view. Turning, the man saw him before coming in his direction. Even from a distance Rayne saw excitement and concern on his face. As they grew near, Davenport shouted, "Come back to give us a hand? What a bloody business!" Then when they had fallen into step. "Is this what normally happens around here?"

"Every day of every week," Rayne lied with a grim smile. Then, "How badly were you hit? I saw it all from the mess."

"Strangely, very little." Davenport was pointing. "One Hurricane damaged superficially and three airmen hit by spent bullets." His voice still tense, he went on. "I'm not even sure they were going for us as only some of them fired. I think they were aiming for Luqa and perhaps became confused in the dark. Gave us a hell of a fright, though. I was sitting in my cockpit when they arrived and really thought my number was up."

"Did you see who, or what, they were?"

Davenport nodded. "There were two groups. The first, Macchi 202s - Eyeties, about ten of them. The second, the escort presumably, a dozen or so Hun 109s. And not just the old 'Es' but the new 'Fs', with their ruddy great painted noses.'

Having reached the dispersal hut they stopped and Davenport was pointing again. "The Bofors boys over there say they hit one of the Macchis, which seemed to come down somewhere between here and Luqa. Luqa confirms this though they say they haven't been out to see it yet. They lost two Blenheims, by the way, which kept them pretty busy." He turned. "You can still see smoke from them rising in the distance even now."

Rayne stared towards the eastern horizon, only mildly interested. Suddenly he felt tired and utterly superfluous. This wasn't his fight any longer; he was going home - he hoped. It was now Davenport's show; he didn't want to get involved. He ought to get away.

On impulse he asked: "You wouldn't lend me the squadron buggy, would you? I'd like to find that Macchi and see what's what. Perhaps Terence Burton could come with me and bring the car back - if he's free, that is."

"If he's free!" Davenport's frustration was obvious. "Half the ruddy squadron's free; we've only got five serviceable aircraft left." He turned away, muttering. "Malta! What a hell-hole to come to."

Rayne walked towards the ancient ochre-camouflaged Austin 16, which was the squadron vehicle used by whichever senior officer was on duty. He was hailed by Flying Officer Terence Burton, for the last seven months one of the senior members of his former flight and Rayne's roommate.

Burton, a few years older than himself, was a quiet, resourceful Rhodesian. As short-service commissioned officers since 1938, they had both joined the squadron in England at about the same time in late '39 and knew each other intimately. In the air he was reliable rather than flamboyantly successful, having less than five shared victories to his credit in more than two years of fairly intensive combat. Rayne had flown with him a hundred times and knew him to be utterly dependable. An uncomplicated man but not a natural leader, Burton was, even so, an asset to any squadron.

As they neared the car Rayne said, "You drive. It's your car now. I'm just a guest." Then: "D'you know where to go?"

Burton shook his head. "Haven't a clue, except that they said that the Macchi came down somewhere between here and Luqa." He turned the car into a minor lane and sped away. "I suggest we drive in the general direction of Luqa and keep an eye open for a small crowd of Malts and a few whisps of smoke. Which'll probably be all there'll be to see."

Rayne nodded and, saying nothing, scanned the rocky path ahead and the passing tiny stone-walled fields.

They had barely driven two miles when Rayne perked up and pointed. `There! Over there on the right. As you said, a crowd of Malts and smoke." Then, as the car was obliged to slow to a crawl, "We'll have to get out here and walk."

Parking their car in a slight widening of the narrow lane, they clambered over an adjacent stone wall and plodded across a field of furrowed grey dust barely fifty paces wide. Then another stone wall and a further tiny field, after which, to their left, a huddle of dust-stained chattering locals and a rising haze of blue smoke.

Immediately, Rayne detected the noisome odour of fuel, burning rubber and aircraft paint. It was a poignant reminder of an earlier occasion when his own aircraft had been set on fire in the air, compelling him to bale out in haste.

The grey, dust-caked crowd, observing their uniforms, parted obsequiously to let them through. Rayne saw that they were mainly farm workers - women mostly - and road labourers, all with leathery brown parchment faces and arms. They were clad in the ubiquitous Maltese country garb of sweat-stained flannel shirts, shapeless pantaloons and skirts. The proletarian wide flat cap was much in evidence and there were many bare feet. And all around were wandering animals, a few skinny pi-dogs, and a clutch of bleating Bethlehem sheep with trailing, milk-heavy udders - referred to by Rayne and others at Ta Kali as either `Geep' or `Shoats', because of their similarity to the all too numerous Middle Eastern goat.

Halting in front of the crowd, Rayne saw that the Macchi had struck the ground at a fairly sharp angle, so that the shattered debris was spread over an area of less than 30 yards.

There was only a small crater - the island of Malta was almost entirely sandstone and rock - and much of what had been in the crater itself had burnt away. The tail of the Italian aircraft was almost whole and lay to one side, as though lonely and unbelieving of what had just occurred, and there were unidentifiable twisted pieces of the aircraft everywhere.

The pilot, too, had been pulverized except for a few recognisable remains - several yellow snakes of the man's intestines and one hand, pathetically spread out, with all five fingers intact, everything obscenely visible. And all around was the stench of fuel. And of burning. And of death. For some moments both Burton and Rayne surveyed the scene in silence, their noses wrinkled in distaste. Burton said quietly, "Poor sod! Someone's darling son." Then, turning. "Still, that's what we look like when we go in!"

Rayne making no response, Burton glanced in his direction to see a look of burning intensity on his companion's face. Continuing to stare, Rayne said tightly and in a low voice, "Watch that character over there! The one bending down! Picking something up!"

Burton eye's followed his gaze. A burly man in his mid 20s had just retrieved something from the side of the crater and was carrying it to a point where he could sit on his haunches and examine his trophy, like a monkey with a nut. To Burton's frowning horror, he saw it was the dead pilot's hand. Then, after glancing hastily round, the man drew out a knife and began to chop away at one of the fingers.

Immediately, Burton heard Rayne utter a cry and saw him launch himself in the man's direction, grab the fellow by the neck and throat and lift him bodily into the air, screaming abuse. Instantly, the severed hand and knife, released in the fury of the assault, flew into the air and fell among the ashes.

Everyone, including Burton, stunned momentarily by the suddenness and violence of Rayne's attack, was transfixed and silent. Then Burton took several swift paces forward, pinioned Rayne's arms as they were lifting again to beat the man into the ground. Rayne's face was contorted with rage, his eyes wild as he struggled to free himself. He almost screeched. "The bastard! The scum! He was trying to cut the ring from that man's finger. Did you see him? Did you? The bastard! I'll kill him!"

His victim, meanwhile, overbalancing, fell on his back and stared wildly up in Rayne's direction, terror on his face. Then, perceiving that Burton was preventing a further attack, he looked around before grinning sheepishly and shrugging his shoulders in the familiar Latin manner.

"For God's sake control yourself, Marco!" Burton's voice was a harsh whisper, his powerful grip on Rayne not slackening. "He's not worth it. Come on, lighten up. It's all over. Alright?"

Feeling Rayne's body hesitate, then slacken. Burton released him slowly and there was a brief period of several seconds, during which the whole crowd, Rayne and Burton included, sank back into a state of quiet, heavy-breathing sanity. Meanwhile, the man with the knife rose and melted into the crowd.

There followed a sudden parting of the onlookers as a small group in RAF khaki and blue, headed by a sergeant then an officer, walked into view. Rayne, still seething but now completely under control, noted their arrival before inviting them forward with a jerk of his head. The officer in the new party explained breathlessly, "We're from Luqa. I'm the doctoring man. Our ambulance and fire tender are just back there." Then, looking from face to face, "Have we just interrupted something?"

Rayne responded tersely, "Not really. I just had to prevent that Maltese oik from mutilating that Eytie corpse. All over now though." He nodded towards the crater. "The pilot's still in it, although there's not much of him left to pick up." With Burton, he began to move away. "We're from Ta Kali incidentally. But it's all yours now." He gave the ghost of a smile, "Okay?"

They had driven back in silence more than halfway to Ta Kali when Rayne stretched out a hand and patted Burton's knee. "Thanks for intervening back there." Then, with a touch of emotion, "When that character began to hack the ring off that bloke's finger, something snapped. I just wanted to kill him. With my bare hands I wanted to kill him!" He shook his head, then exhaled deeply. "Strange really. I've seldom felt like that before."

Burton gave him a glance and raised his eyebrows. "It certainly showed in your face, old sport. For a moment I wondered who you were." Then, after a pause, "The Malts can be excused, you know. They're not a warrior race and it's not really their war. They've been bombed and shot at for more than two years now and the ordinary chaps working in the fields are as poor as church mice. Why shouldn't they pinch the rings off those who have been knocking hell out of them from dawn to dusk and whose bits will just be dug into the ground anyway?"

Rayne, not agreeing, curled a lip but remained silent.

When they had reached the Ta Kali officers' mess, Rayne dismounted and Burton drove off to return to his squadron. Rayne glanced at his watch. Just after 10 am - he felt already as though he'd been up all day. In the distance, came the sound of Hurricanes taking off again. He thought with a trace of nostalgia and bitterness, "never ending, all day, every day". He was tired of the sight and sound of aircraft - particularly Hurricanes! He turned and wearily climbed the stone steps that led to the walled passage and his silent bedroom. Nothing to do, he would get in a few hours kip before something else cropped up. He'd miss his lunch, of course, but, what the heck?

He was wakened from a light and troubled sleep by a voice shouting his name.

"Flight Lieutenant Rayne, sir! Flight Lieutenant! Are you there? Telephone! Sir? Can you hear me?"

Rayne, his mind still foggy, roused himself, climbed out of bed, and walking to the open window space, looked down into the courtyard. The Maltese telephone receptionist, a small man in khaki drill, was shouting up at him. Rayne had always quite liked the little chap - small and dark with a thin moustache, shorts always immaculately pressed and his English perfect but heavily accented.

"Air Headquarters, sir!" He was still shouting up in Rayne's direction. "They want you to telephone quickly. I think you are to go home, sir. It is very important".

Rayne immediately came awake. Home! The magic word. But how and when? It looked as though he would soon know.

The terse voice the other end of the telephone was brief and to the point. "Can you get yourself down to the Sliema dock area by five o'clock? - which gives you about two hours. With all your kit, of course."

Rayne responded briefly, "If I'm going home, I could be at the South Pole by five o'clock. I'm going by sea, I take it? Which way?"

"Eastwards, unfortunately. To Egypt initially. There are four of you, two from Ta Kali, two from Hal Far. I'm sending transport up for you within the hour, so you'll have to look slippy. One of my chaps will brief you on the dockside. Okay? But, don't get too worked up about getting home. Things being what they are, you may not even get as far as the Middle East. Best of British, though."

Rayne took a deep breath and smiled grimly. Such comforting optimism.

Rayne stood alone beside the rail of his ship and surveyed the scene through slitted, streaming eyes. It was about noon the following day.

They had slipped out of Valletta harbour at around 5.50 pm on Wednesday, 7th January, and had been sailing for some 18 hours now and were well clear of Malta and on course for the Middle East. The weather, unlike the generally supposed notion of the Mediterranean scene, was most unpleasant. It was dull with occasional curtains of fine rain. There was complete cloud cover at around 2,000 feet, and the sea in every direction was a glistening, heaving expanse of molten lead.

The S.S. Canberra Star, of about 5,000 tons, was one of four frozen-meat vessels which normally traded between New Zealand, Australia and England. At present the four were in a line-ahead formation, the Canberra Star being third in the group.

Rayne had gathered from the Captain, who had joined them for dinner the previous evening, that they would be sailing at about 14 knots. This speed, accidents barred and the enemy permitting, would enable them to reach Port Said and the Suez Canal in a little under three days.

It had also been hinted rather sombrely that this particular trip was a 'death or glory' break-out. Besieged Malta was desperate for food - of that Rayne was well aware. It was vital, therefore, that this small convoy reached the Middle East in order that the ships should return, suitably provisioned.

Nothing much had happened thus far, but they would shortly be in 'bomb alley'- the area south of Crete which, since the previous May, had been in the hands of the Germans. There they could certainly expect some action. Some very nasty action, too, it was thought.

The Royal Navy - the 'Grey Funnel Line' - were clearly expecting the worst. Slightly to the rear of the Canberra Star and about 400 yards to port, the light cruiser, H.M.S. Dido, sailed along serenely. Its sharp prow dipped and rose gracefully in slow motion, creating a most impressive creaming bow wave. Its main armament, 6 dual-purpose 5.75 inch guns, raised to maximum elevation, appeared to be pointing straight up, presenting an unlikely, almost comical picture.

The Dido, Rayne knew all too well. As part of Force 'K' based in Malta, it spent most of its time on secret, violent enterprises somewhere in the Med. These necessitated the RAF to 'find it' now and then. And on almost every such occasion when Rayne had been involved, the Dido (and others) had shot at him unhesitatingly.

No, the Navy certainly didn't like aircraft, friend or foe. Moreover, if they hit the wrong chaps, they were never in the least apologetic or penitent.

There were also seven other ships forming the escort, all lean, low-in-the-water destroyers. Like the Dido, as they were all normally Malta-based, Rayne knew most of them by name, although their identities didn't interest him that much at that particular moment. One was about 1,000 yards ahead of the leading merchantman, another away to the rear, at about the same distance. Two each were on either flank on parallel headings and the seventh appeared to have a wandering brief, requiring it to rush about now and then in most impressive, leaning surges, white foam streaming from its bows. In all, a convoy of twelve vessels. All radiating awareness and concern.

Rayne was eating his midday meal when the 'Action Stations' siren began sounding its strident message. Leaving his lunch unfinished, he rushed up on deck just as a series of violent and deafening cracks from the Dido's dual purpose guns heralded the sighting of some unidentified aircraft.

Within moments, he recognised a German Junkers 88 bomber at less than 2,000 feet and at about two miles range, turning to avoid a clutch of ack-ack shell-bursts, even then some distance behind the aircraft. Rayne grimaced in frustration; the gunners were clearly not allowing sufficient deflection when sighting their weapons so that the intruding aircraft ran little risk of being hit.

For several minutes, the German 'plane flew parallel to the convoy before turning away in a leisurely fashion, apparently unscathed. And all the time, the guns continued their ear-splitting barrage, scattering dark puffs of smoke into the heavens seemingly at random, long after the 88 was a mere dot on the horizon.

Rayne sighed in exasperation. A reconnaissance 'plane obviously. Now they had been discovered and the convoy's speed and track noted, the fun was bound to follow. All they had to do was wait.

The period of waiting was all too short. At about 3.30 pm, when Rayne was resting in his cabin, he again heard the 'Action Stations' alarm and went racing up to the main deck.

The guns were already in full voice. He saw another Ju 88 bearing down on them, running the full length of the main line of ships. Then, as he watched, four bombs detached themselves from its fuselage and curved in his direction.

Fascinated, he followed them down with his gaze, sensing rather than believing they would miss his ship. Which they did - but not by much! The noise of the guns and cannons on the Canberra Star and escorts drowned the thunderous reports of the bombs exploding, sending up towering plumes of water barely 50 yards away, causing Rayne to duck instinctively.

The Hun aircraft, as if disdainful of the curving streamers of shot and shell, then continued along the entire length of the convoy before turning off to the right and drifting into the distance. And all the time, the barrage continued until, by degrees, it petered out as though exhausted by its efforts and ineptitude. There were no more attacks that day.

At the Captain's table that night, several seats were ominously vacant, some senior members of the crew, clearly believing that the enemy's activities signalled a period of extreme drama to come. The Air Force contingent of four, however, were inconsiderately light-hearted, hinting that their seamen companions were overly pessimistic. None of the bombs had thus far caused any damage, they pointed out, in spite of the defending gunners' total and obvious incompetence. So, with more effective shooting, who knew? - the enemy might yet be repulsed.

The Captain, a small wizened man in his 50s, was in no mood for levity, however, still less for any well-meaning advice on the simple rules of deflection shooting. With a sour face, he rose unexpectedly from the table, clearly stung by their caustic remarks. Blotted his lips with his napkin, he then departed with a final riposte that if the Air Force felt they could any better, they might like to man to the two gun positions on the bridge when the next attack threatened.

The subject - and threat - was further discussed at length and with some amusement before Rayne and his three Air Force companions, having nothing better to do, retired for the night - the ship was a cargo vessel and did not cater for passengers, still less for their amusement. Later, having committed himself to the rock-hard bunk in his tiny, claustrophobic cabin and being unable to read as the ship heaved, rolled and creaked its way towards Egypt, Rayne, uttered a silent prayer that any nocturnal torpedo might keep its distance. Finally, shuddering at the thought of himself floundering in a black, cold sea, clad only in his pyjamas, he extinguished his light and tried to sleep.

The following morning the weather was marginally better although there was still a sullen and continuous cloud base at around 3,000 feet. The dozen ships ploughed ahead, maintaining their original positions, seemingly unconcerned. Even so, there remained a constant and obvious air of tension and suspense.

Rayne, his hands in his pockets and bracing himself against a constant chilling wind, paced around the deck for an hour, his head bowed, his mind unfocused, before going below for his midday meal. His worst fears had not been realised as they must be somewhere south of Crete. He had expected the enemy to have launched some major attack before now. Greatly surprised, he wondered why.

He was lying on his bed, reading, when at about 3 pm, there came a series of violent thumps on his door and a voice strident with urgency.

"Captain's compliments - please come to the bridge at once!"

Out in the passageway in moments, Rayne collided violently with one of his three RAF companions and together they raced aloft, to be met half-way by an officer he recognised as the first mate. The man, wild eyed, shouted briefly, "Up here!" and led them, at the double, up several steel-edged stairways towards one extremity of the bridge. In the glass-enclosed control centre, Rayne observed the Captain in animated conversation and pointing.

Almost immediately, the cruiser Dido beside them fired a broadside. Its six elevated guns vomited smoke and recoiled like snakes with reports of such violent intensity that Rayne, unprepared, blinked with the shock of it and visibly jumped. God Almighty! Then, more thumps and cracks from far and near as the destroyers joined in with their 4 inch weapons, sending shells screaming overhead. They seemed so close that Rayne had to control his immediate impulse to duck. My God! What were these lunatics doing and at whom were they firing?

Meanwhile the ship's officer was waving Rayne and his companion towards a cupola on one end of the bridge. Clambering in with ungainly speed, they found themselves confronted by a single machine-gun and belts of ammunition, with scarcely space to breathe far less move.

The ship's officer's face was over Rayne's shoulder and he was mouthing instructions above the din.

"Know anything about the Marlin?"

Rayne shook his head. "Nothing at all."

"Right! It's a .303. Okay? Load it here and cock it, so. Trigger here. Then just fire the bloody thing. Okay?" After that, and with a further nod, he climbed briskly down and disappeared.

For a moment, Rayne and Flight Lieutenant Peter Rawlins from 185 Squadron at Hal Far, eyed each other questioningly, each with a single thought in mind. Rawlins was a bulky youth and he and Rayne, both more than 6 feet tall, were clearly more than the tiny gun position could accommodate.

Rayne without thinking, assumed control. "Look, Pete, we'll get in each other's way. I'll fire the gun, you feed in the ammo. I suggest you get outside and do it from there."

Rawlins needed no encouragement, scrambled out like an eel and, leaning over, began to sort out the ammunition - yards of it! Across the other side of the ship and on the far extremity of the bridge, the remaining two members of the RAF contingent were busy sorting out their own small turret. During a brief lull in their preparations, all four stood up at once and waved to each other cheerfully, like children on a Sunday School outing. Only then did they relax to the point when they could look into the distance and take stock of what was happening around them. The guns meanwhile had ceased firing.

With the main armament on the Dido all elevated skywards and pointing towards the north, Rayne scanned the horizon carefully in the direction of Crete but saw nothing. Clearly, the radar boys in the cruiser were seeing things hidden from everyone else. There was an electric air of suspense and tension abroad.

With all 12 ships ploughing ahead, lifting and dipping in slow motion, Rayne decided to keep his eye on the Captain. When he began to get excited, something was bound to be happening, as the little man seemed an edgy and irascible little fellow. At that moment, he was pacing about anxiously on the bridge like an expectant father in a maternity ward, bringing a flicker of a smile to Rayne's face.

After some minutes, the man suddenly came to life again, pointing and moving about almost at a run. At the same time, the Dido loosed off a deafening salvo amid tongues of flame and clouds of smoke, the whole ship appearing to wilt beneath the recoil. And at that point and as though on cue, all the bigger guns on the destroyers began to go mad.

Away to the north, the dark flowers of bursting shells began to pockmark the horizon in silent clusters - and Rayne immediately saw why! Barely above the line of the horizon, about a dozen large aircraft were parading back and forth, flying parallel to the convoy. In his ear, he heard Peter Rawlins's shrill and anxious voice above the clamour of the guns.

"D'you see what they are?"

Rayne was shading his eyes. "Not clearly . . . but I'm pretty sure they're Eytie 79s. And if they are . . . they'll be torpedo bombers." He turned with a grimace, baring his teeth. "It looks as though we are just about to be tin-fished, old mate!" Another grim smile, "How's your breast stroke these days?" Then after a time and as the Italian aircraft still paraded about on the horizon, "I reckon they're grogging up with Chianti to bolster their spirits."

"Well, they're on the port side, anyway." Rawlins gave a brief and unconvincing laugh. "Only that side is likely to catch it and sink!" He gave a wolfish grin, "How lucky can we get?" Rayne returned him a pitying glance.

In the eerie serenity that is sometimes a feature of the prelude to combat, the guns of the convoy suddenly fell silent. The enemy aircraft flew back and forth on the distant horizon and Rayne let his gaze wander over the decks of his own ship and beyond, to the other merchantmen and escorts sailing steadfastly behind, ahead, and beside them, all apparently unconcerned.

Finally, in that strangest of intervals, he found himself looking straight down on the sea some 40 feet beneath his cupola, perched precariously on the extremity of the bridge. It was a racing, foam flecked tide, that streamed to the rear before finally losing itself in the frothing disturbance of the ship's wake. If they were torpedoed, would he be killed instantly? He had seen many such tragic occurrences on the newsreels and in photographs. Or, if he were lucky enough to survive the devastating explosion, would he find himself struggling and gasping in the water's chilling embrace? It seemed incredible even to contemplate such an outcome, but in minutes - moments even! - it might very well happen. To them! To him! Suddenly, the awful consequences of such an attack made him shiver instinctively and turn away to swing his gun and check the drooping belt of ammunition.

Almost immediately, he observed the Captain become animated again, shouting silent commands behind the glass of the bridge, and pointing. Following the man's arm and gestures, he saw that the aircraft in the distance had separated and at least six were making off to the west before describing a distant detour behind the convoy, no doubt having decided to make an attack from the south. From the starboard side! His side! Suddenly, the whole affair began to take on a more personal and threatening aspect. And, as if to corroborate the fact, he saw and heard the

Dido's main armament swing about with almost frightening swiftness. And begin to shoot.

For the rest of his life, the events of the following five minutes were to remain indelibly seared, as though by fire, on Rayne's mind and memory.

As more and more of the heavier guns began to fire, setting up a din that was almost indescribable, the smaller 40mm Bofors and 20mm cannons joined in, sending streams of red balls aloft and white lines of tracer skidding and dipping across the surface of the sea. Realising his own gun was useless at so distant a range, Rayne, tense and silent, squinted down his open sight, but held his fire. What did they say - the whites of their eyes?

In the far distance, he watched the Savoias - he now recognised them as such - turn in his direction, sort themselves out, then approach some 50 feet above the waves in an orderly, frightening phalanx. Still more than a mile away and their wide line-abreast formation complete, they aimed themselves at the convoy and began their approach. Determinedly! Relentlessly! Splendidly brave! Shell and shot splashing, bursting and streaking all around them amid a bedlam of ear-numbing sound. On and on! On and on! Until Rayne felt that at last they were within range of his gun. At which point, as tense as a bow sting, he began to fire.

When he at last pressed the trigger, the Marlin gun began to jump and clatter, the stink of cordite pungent to his nose. He was looking then, directly at one Savoia, the fourth in the line of six, its three engines and canopy now so close as to be easily recognisable. The attacking aircraft, still some 50 feet above the water, Rayne watched his tracer streaking towards it, apparently without effect. Now no more than 200 yards away, it was heading straight for him. Within seconds, if it loosed its torpedo, without doubt he would a goner!

And as the thought flashed through his mind, and as his gun chattered and shook, hot and hysterical, he watched the torpedo fall   Splash!. . . rear up for a moment . . . then splash down again. Before disappearing . . . to begin its run, straight in his direction!

For a moment, sheer horror! He had just five seconds to live! He felt himself beginning to cringe. But firing still. He was going to be killed! Within seconds he would die! But he'd die fighting!

At which point, he caught a glimpse of two small aircraft, streaking in pursuit of the nearest Savoia He recognised them immediately as Grumman Martlets or Wildcats, of the Royal Navy - he couldn't remember their current name. They were shooting, he could see. And closing rapidly, oblivious of the mass of defending fire, his own included.

Caught up in a savage blood lust and deafened by the almost overwhelming din of the guns and cannons all around him, he continued to swing his weapon around and follow the bomber, now merely feet above his head. He was aware, too, that one fighter was racing straight into his stream of bullets. He would hit it! Hit it! His mind screamed Stop!! Stop! But he couldn't. And at the same time, there was the torpedo. The torpedo! Five seconds running time, that was all!

In his subconscious, he began to count. Four!. . . five!. . . six!. . . He half-closed his eyes, waiting for the catastrophic bang and the pain of violent death. Then a moment of agonised waiting . . . but no explosion! No bang! He wasn't dead! He was alive still! And firing! And screaming incoherently to relieve the tension of the moment.

To his right, he caught a fleeting glimpse of the Captain, gesticulating and running wildly up and down the glazed bridge, his mind obviously in torment for the safety of his ship. Then, his own mouth agape, Rayne, still man-handling his juddering gun, saw with amazement and - ridiculously, mild amusement - his bullets magically create a line of holes in the ships funnel Oh, my God! What on earth was he doing? Suddenly shocked into immobility, he stopped and, for a moment, stared.

All around him the battle raged - smoke, bedlam, scores of red balls sailing aloft in groups, all amid white and glowing lines of whipping tracer. And the Savoia he had been shooting at, now staggering like a wounded animal. Finally rearing up out of control, until he could see the whole of it in plan view. After which it toppled over and began to fall. Fall and twist in slow motion. Before plunging into the waves in a huge ball of flame and black smoke.

Rayne closed his eyes for a moment in horror. Oh, dear Christ! A ghastly, awful sight! Death in its most instant form. And further afield, the tiny naval fighter. It, too, was falling towards the sea. Like a crippled bird - staggering, tottering, then dropping into the water in a sudden flurry of spray and foam. And, in an instant . . . disappearing.

He watched, horrified. Stricken! Appalled! He had shot it down! His own man! He had just killed a friend! An ally who had come to help. Oh, dear, dear God! What had he done? What had he done? He turned about in his cupola almost demented Then, aghast and sobbing, stared into the distance.

The remaining Savoias, hugging the sea, were jinking and weaving their desperate way towards the north and safety. There was no sign of the second naval fighter. Was that down, too? He hoped to God it wasn't but he couldn't see it. And all the time, the noise of the guns continued unabated, the red balls soared into the sky and the tracer scythed its way across the waves. Meanwhile, and as though unconcerned, the prows of ships rose and fell majestically as they ploughed their stately way eastwards. Apparently untouched. Unscathed.

At which point, an incident developed that Rayne could hardly credit, one which left him in anguished dismay and screaming protest.

As the remains of the Savoia still blazed fiercely on the water beneath billowing clouds of black smoke, the single itinerant destroyer curved its way dramatically towards it at full speed. It then drew up beside the inferno with an impressive white churning of screws thrown violently into reverse. And there, for a full minute, it stopped. Stopped! And searched! Then, when there was clearly nothing to rescue, it turned and headed off at full speed - back to its former position in the outer screen.

For some moments, Rayne watched silently in impotent astonishment then in protesting agony. Why the enemy aircraft, for Christ's sake? He and others had just been trying their damndest to shoot that Savoia down. After which, the Navy had chosen to stop their ship right in the middle of a violent engagement, putting their own destroyer crew in jeopardy, to look for the enemy, then leave without searching for the remains of their own fighter and its pilot?

Why? Why? Why? They were mad! Criminally mad! Lunatics all of them! Rayne heard his own screaming cries of protest, his eyes blinded by rage and tears. The fools! The blind mistaken fools! Why? Why?

Then in the passage of a moment, he suddenly felt infinitely weary. His mind blanked out even the circumstances of his own escape - the torpedo that should have killed him, but hadn't, the attacking enemy; the blazing Savoia. Even the Grumman Martlet and that poor, poor boy he had so recently killed. And amid all the action, the mind-numbing noise continued - would it never stop, even now?

Finally, as the ear-splitting din gradually died, down, he found himself relaxing. He was alive! Still alive! But how, and, why? Suddenly, he neither knew nor cared, was just thankful. He closed his eyes. Dear God! Overwhelming relief. Nothing but total, overwhelming relief. And infinite weariness.

He was wakened by silence and the absence of movement. For some moments he lay on his back, staring into the darkness - his cabin had access neither to light nor fresh air - before concluding that they had arrived at their destination. Egypt, probably. He didn't know where exactly. Snapping on a light, he saw it was just after 5 am. Then, scrambling out of his bunk, he dressed hurriedly and went aloft.

On deck, it was the coolest and most beautiful of mornings, an endless expanse of translucent mist and diffused pastel shades. Above, strands of cirrus were stationary in an inverted bowl of the most delicate pinks, blues, and the palest of yellows. There was not a sound, a quiver of movement or a zephyr of breeze. The Middle East, at dawn! Positively at its loveliest.

About a mile away, was the low curving line of a jetty, and beyond, some flattish buildings which looked like aircraft hangars, outlines etched against the horizon with a fine sepia brush. Everything was quiet. No movement anywhere. Only the occasional sea bird in the distance, wheeling but silent.

The four merchantmen were at anchor; lying within 500 yards of each other but pointing in different directions. In the far distance, two destroyers moved slowly back and forth, like hyenas patrolling an encampment. There was no sign of H.M.S. Dido or the other naval vessels.

Hearing a voice, Rayne looked up and saw the Captain shouting down at him through an open window of the bridge. Irritated again.

"They won't let us into the Canal, the silly buggers! Just waiting for us to be torpedoed."

Rayne shouted back. "Have you heard what's happening to us?"

"Not much, except that you 'll be getting off here at Port Said. Someone will meet you to take you on to Cairo. They'll come on board"

"When? Do you know?"

"Search me! This afternoon probably. If we're not sunk in the meantime."

Rayne acknowledged the message with a smile and a wave. Then turned to gaze into the distance - reflecting.

The previous day had been hectic but without major incident. The weather rather better, for several hours the destroyers had gone mad, racing about like demented hares, dropping depth charges. But no submarines had appeared, or presumably been sunk. And no torpedoes either, thank God! Then a Sunderland flying boat had turned up and had floated around for the rest of the day, suggesting that the north coast of Africa was not far away to the south. As it looked as though they were finally going to make it, everyone had begun to breathe more easily, even the Captain.

That night, Rayne had slept fitfully, his tortured mind full of aircraft, large and small, crashing unendingly into the sea. All amid flames and smoke. He awoke many times before finally sinking into a deep sleep just before dawn. And now, at mid-morning, here he was, feeling like a piece of chewed string. Even fully conscious and in his most rational frame of mind, the picture of the little Martlet would not go away. Had he really shot it down? Someone had! He hoped fervently it had not been him.

Later that day, having been put ashore with their piles of luggage, the RAF contingent travelled by lorry, first alongside the Suez Canal to Ismailia, then beside the Sweetwater Canal and via the RAF Station at Abu Sueir, to Cairo - in all, an excruciatingly uncomfortable journey of more than eight hours.. Although they had never before been in Egypt, Rayne and his three companions had lost interest in the place long before their transport had trundled into the outskirts of Cairo. Sand, stinks, and bloody camels! Egypt had them all in abundance. What was more, they were now a further 1,500 miles from England. God what a war!

Rayne was to remain in Cairo for three weeks. Finally he and the others went by train to Port Suez, at the southern end of the Suez Canal. Then on one viciously cold dawn - who said the Middle East was warm! - boarded the commandeered Dutch liner New Amsterdam and sailed towards the south.

Months later, after many adventures and seeing half the world, Rayne landed in Liverpool during the latter part of April, 1942. The sea voyage from Malta had taken more than three months and he had been abroad a full year.

CHAPTER TWO

Rayne had been on leave at his parents' home in Northwood, on the northern outskirts of London, for less than a week, when an official letter arrived instructing him to present himself to the 'P 2' Department of Air Ministry, Adastral House, Kingsway, London , on 13th May - which was a Wednesday.

He read the letter with frowning dismay as he had already arranged to spend that week walking in the Lake District. A pox on the Air Force! Where was the month's leave they had promised?

He arrived at Adastral House in a none too friendly frame of mind. He filled in the customary pink form and was escorted by an elderly ex-serviceman along lengthy corridors before being led into the outer room of a set of offices. A middle-aged woman with glasses on the end of her nose, read his accompanying note and smiled in his direction.

"Flight Lieutenant Rayne? You're a bit before your time. I'm just making a cuppa. Would you like one?" She then turned her back on him and busied herself with a kettle.

Rayne removed his hat and sat down. "Thank you. That would nice." Then, "Who am I supposed to be seeing?"

The woman poured hot water unhurriedly into a pot.

"Squadron Leader Merriman. Do you know him? He posts Squadron Leaders."

Rayne gave a pale smile. "That's encouraging news, anyway. Yes, I do indeed. We were commissioned together in 1938. I had no idea he was here."

The woman handed him his tea. "He's got someone with him at the moment, but he won't be long. Do you take sugar, by the way? No? Good for you! Very patriotic."

She sat down with her cup and smiled again. "You've been away for quite some time I hear. You're in great demand, I would have you know. When did you get back?"

Before Rayne could respond, a door opened and John Merriman appeared, his hand outstretched, his face beaming.

"Marco! As I live and breathe! Come into my parlour and tell me all"

Rayne raised his eyebrows in thanks in the direction of the tea lady and followed his companion into an inner office, where he was waved to a chair. He sat down again - and waited.

Merriman consulted some papers before him, then smiled.

"First, the good news. You are to be promoted to squadron leader with immediate effect. Acting, of course, but the money's just as good. Okay?"

"Second, I'm sorry to have had to call you back from leave, but the top brass has been leaning heavily on me. The AOC 9 Group wants you for one of his two Spit. squadrons which has recently taken a bit of a beating"

Rayne frowned. "I don't believe I know the AOC 9 Group."

"Ah, but he knows you, that's the difference. Naturally, I pointed out that you'd been on the go since the beginning of the war and that you were entitled to at least six months' rest.

He was not in the least impressed, however, and went over my head. Which is the reason you're here today."

Rayne remained silent, prompting Merriman to put on an enquiring look.

"You not pleased, Mister?" he mimicked ; "Spit Vbs after those dreadful Hurricanes? With just the prospect of being further re-equipped in the near future with something really juicy? I'd take the offer like a shot, old son. But, anyway, why don't you tell me what you have been up to since you left Malta. Three months ago wasn't it?"

"Rather more than that. But it's a long story "

Merriman settled into his chair. "We have the whole morning, old sport " He suddenly looked round. "Keen for another cuppa? No? Whatever you say."

Rayne collected his thoughts, then began to speak in measured tones:

"We had a pretty hairy three day trip between Malta and the Suez Canal, culminating in a nasty torpedo attack by twelve Eytie Savoia 79s." He halted for some moments, remembering the burning Savoia and the poor boy in the Grumman fighter, but could not bring himself to mention the incident. Instead, he merely added, "We survived, but not with much to spare."

"Then, after three weeks hanging about in Egypt, four of us left in the New Amsterdam, which was taking 2,000 Italian PoWs to Mombassa in Kenya. After that we took another week going straight down to Durban in South Africa, where we waited for a Bibby Line ship coming from Singapore."

"It arrived - finally - with 1,000 women and children on board, who had managed to escape the day before the Japs took over in Singapore Poor things! They were all in a sorry almost pitiful state, most of their menfolk having been left behind as prisoners of war. So, we joined them - four of us RAF crammed into a single small cabin - before taking off for Cape Town."

"After Cape Town, we 'rounded the 'Horn', but had only gone for half a day when the ship developed propeller trouble. So, back we went and were delayed for five days whilst repairs were carried out."

"After that, completely unescorted and with the horde of wives and kids beginning to become very fractious, we zigzagged up the middle of the South Atlantic for ages until we began to run out of food and water, requiring us to put into Freetown in Sierra Leone to take on fresh supplies."

"From there, and still on our own, we wandered about in the North Atlantic at a steady 12 knots, dodging the U-boats, until we were within shouting distance of Canada. At which point we ran slap-bang into a Hurricane - or something - which came up quickly from the West Indies area and hit us like a thunderbolt."

"John . . . I have to tell you now that that was the most unpleasant part of a very long and trying voyage." He paused in unhappy recollection of the event. "The waves were so high and so brutal that we lost about half our lifeboats and two American destroyers were apparently swamped within 100 miles of us."

"Our ship was forced to tread water, so to speak - just point its nose into wind and stay put - for a terrifying three days, during which we lived in our clothes and life-jackets, had not a single meal other than scraps, and simply prayed that we would stay afloat. They were ugly moments, I can tell you."

"After that . . . well, it was comparatively easy. We trailed up to the coast of Greenland, freezing to death meanwhile, turned right towards Iceland, then down into the Irish sea and eventually to Liverpool. And it was in Liverpool, unbelievably, that I caught the ruddy 'flu and had to spend an extra three days on the ship before the doctor would release me."

A brief silence.   "So there you have it. Kids' stuff, really. Just over three months at sea. A complete rest cure, as you will gather. All of which you have my permission to describe in detail to the AOC 9 Group!"

For a time nothing was said, before Merriman observed quietly, "That was quite a trip." Then, after a further moment's thought; "Look Marcus, if you feel you would like to take your full entitlement of leave or even ask for a six months rest interval, I'm willing to dig my heels in. I could wangle you a Chief Flying Instructor's post at some OTU, or even find you a hole in this place for a spell. To lend strength to my arm, however, can you say how many operational hours you have done thus far?"

Rayne shrugged indifferently. "The last time I counted it was something over 440, so I would guess it would be nearer 550 now."

His companion gave a quiet whistle, "That's well in excess of two tours of duty on fighters without a single break. With that sort of record and your gongs, you could demand permanent retirement."

But Rayne was shaking his head. "John, there's a war on, for Pete's sake! My name would be mud if I asked for preferential treatment. No, there must be many others in the same boat, and worse." He smiled, "So, just tell me the whereabouts of this squadron you have in mind."

Merriman brightened. "West Wales. An unpronounceable Welsh name somewhere between Barmouth and Harlech. On the coast, with the sea in front of you and mountains to your rear. Lovely spot, I believe. First though, I'll have to set up an appointment for you to see the AOC. Nice feller I hear, with a future, apparently. But stubborn!" He winked, in Rayne's direction as he picked up the telephone. "You've made the right decision, old sport."

To which Rayne, with a wan smile, thought but did not say, "I hope you're right, John Merriman. I really hope you right!"

Rayne travelled by train to Wales a week after his interview at Adastral House. The journey took eight hours. The number of coaches on each of the four different trains he was obliged to use, became progressively fewer until he finished up a single passenger sitting in a single coach pushed from the rear by a panting locomotive which looked - and sounded - as though it had originated in 1850.

He had recognised from the outset that he had mixed feelings about this new appointment that had so suddenly been foisted upon him. On the one hand, he was elated by his promotion and the prospect of command and flying a decent aircraft again. On the other, he felt oddly lacking in enthusiasm for the considerable challenge of the task that no doubt lay ahead. But, as the Welsh hills and the green of the countryside drifted endlessly past his carriage window, his feelings of uncertainty were to some extent soothed and blurred. Even so, there was still that vital something lacking, he knew. He just wasn't himself. But, for the life of him he didn't know what, exactly - or why.

His train finally limped to a squealing stop at the final minuscule station platform, the tiny engine behind breathing and hissing heavily with relief. He stepped down with his baggage - the solitary passenger. The adjutant and engineer officer of his new unit, who were awaiting his arrival, moved forward to greet him with cautious and unsmiling formality. Both men in their early 40s, they eyed their new commanding officer - who couldn't be a day over 21, for God's sake! - with a mixture of surprise, curiosity and indifference.

The adjutant said, "Welcome to Wales, sir. We have your car in the station yard." He picked up two of Rayne's bags. "The officers' mess is up the hill a mile or so away. D'you want to drive or shall I?"

"You drive, Adj. I seem to have been travelling for a week." Rayne's voice betrayed his weariness.

Later that night, lying in his bed, he was to remember the deafening silence of the hills all around his primitive hutted room, a brief period of rain lashing against his window, then the bleating of sheep in the quiet of the early morning. Wales! And the weather! He might have known.

He called upon the Station Commander early the next morning. Squadron Leader David Wynn-Jones was a Welshman from the valleys, but a Welshman with a difference. A temporary officer, in civilian life he had been a wealthy and successful businessman with a ruthless streak. A member of a family whose affluence was founded on steel, Wynn-Jones was 52 years of age and a polished and urbane manipulator, who had long since decided that as an administrative officer in the RAF was the best possible way of surviving the war in comparative comfort and with a whole skin.

Not being a General Duties officer, he was in fact subordinate to Rayne. But as the latter's squadron was not permanently based on the airfield, as Squadron Leader Administration, Wynn-Jones had taken upon himself the title of Station Commander and had accepted without a qualm, every benefit that went with it. He lived out, unaccompanied, in a splendid commandeered house further along the coast, ran his own private car on Government petrol, and had a batman (personal servant), to which he was entitled, and a cook and driver - to which he was not. He was, in short, a glossy, plausible, entertaining rascal, besides being a very able administrator,

Rayne had met him several times before when Wynn-Jones had held less exalted appointments in one of the several Group Headquarters under which the former had served He had enjoyed his company in the past, and, with an inward smile of recollection, looked forward to meeting him again. Wynn-Jones greeted him warmly, embracing him in a bear-hug, exuding powerful odours of aftershave and expensive pipe tobacco.

"By God, Marco, it's good to see you again!" He waved an arm towards a chair. "More than a year isn't it? I knew you were coming, of course; the AOC told me a week ago. Park your bum, dear boy!" The Welsh musical lilt was only faintly evident and attractive.

"You were clearly better informed that I was," Rayne retorted peevishly as he sat down. "I was dragged back early from a month's leave and presented with an ultimatum. I only arrived last night and thus far have met one or two of my chaps."

Wynn-Jones rolled his eyes expressively. "Ah! Long story!" Then after a pause. "Your squadron's in a bit of a hole at the moment , old son. And as you've probably not yet been told, I ought to explain."

"First, your being here is all the AOC's doing, you should understand that. You're his blue-eyed boy at the moment although I understand he'd never met you before last week. Your immediate predecessor, incidentally, was killed a fortnight ago when on his first operational flight over France. Hit by `flak' (German anti aircraft fire) on a low level sortie and went straight in. They were operating from Tangmere at the time."

"Then unbelievably, having returned here a few days later, one of your flight commanders, leading four others, flew into the top of one of the mountains behind us. They were letting down through cloud preparing to land having finished a training exercise out to sea. Four killed, one by a miracle missing the top of the hill and living to tell the tale. And before all that, another C.O. was removed on the orders of the AOC, having put up a black I'd prefer not to discuss here and now. So, four commanding officers in less than four months Small wonder that some of your blokes might be looking a bit sideways at you. And not only that but there has been a constant drain on the squadron's resources as it is being asked every other week to provide experienced section leaders for service in the Middle and Far East!" Wynn-Jones spread his hands. "Can you wonder why morale has gone to the dogs?"

Then, as though getting his second wind, "And another thing, you have an aircraft problem."

At this, Rayne put up his hands. "Steady on, Uncle! That's enough for the moment. An-other word and I'll be back on the next train travelling east!" Impulsively, he stood up and Wynn-Jones rose with him and carried on talking

"Oh, and I forget to mention it The AOC wants you personally to go on this new course on high altitude flying he's been trying to arrange with the Institute of Aviation Medicine at Farnborough. Only three or four days. He has left it to you to fix it up. As soon as you can, that is."

Rayne stared, unbelieving "But I only arrived here last night, for heaven's sake! What on earth's got into the man?"

Wynn-Jones placed a comforting hand on his shoulder. "He's worried to death about one of his only two Spitfire squadrons, old boy. And his future! He's only human and he's relying absolutely on you to rescue his reputation."

Outside some minutes later and standing alone in a chilling wind, Rayne faced the middle-distance coastline and gleam of the sea, hands in pockets and sombrely pondering his future. Plus his ability to summon up the energy and enthusiasm to restore the morale of what was clearly a squadron in distress. He shivered. Perhaps he would feel better having had a few flights under his belt.   Suddenly, the prospect of flying a Spitfire again, after an absence of more than two years, brought a chink of light into a gloomy scene.

Later that morning, Rayne interviewed his engineer officer, Flying Officer William Birch.

Rayne seated at his office desk, did not invite his junior colleague to sit down; he was not feeling in that sort of mood. Birch stood uncomfortably in front of him, 'properly at ease' and blank faced, his forage cap tilted precisely at the right angle.

Rayne started without preamble, "Two things. One, I trust you have a decent Spitfire for me? Two, what is the state of the squadron's aircraft at this moment?"

Birch, a commissioned airman, wearing a long service and good conduct medal, signifying (it was often alleged) 20-odd years of undetected crime, fixed his gaze somewhere over Rayne's right shoulder and answered formally,

"Your own aircraft, sir? Well, I've been holding one back especially for you. Came in several days ago. Have given it a good once-over and I'm sure it'll fit the bill. As regards our aircraft in general; there are problems as we had to leave the best ones behind when we came up here from Tangmere You may also know that quite recently we lost another four which flew into a local mountain. Such replacements we have had since are usually those that other squadrons wished to get rid of. In short, we now have a load of cast-off, part-worn Spits and our serviceability state could be a lot better,"

"What in general is wrong with them?"

Birch shrugged. "Just the difference between new aircraft that stay serviceable and clapped-out ones that don't - second-life engines, ropey hydraulics, transformer drives that shear, leaks generally. And of course, general airframe problems; dents, squeaks, badly fitting panels and worn fasteners, popping rivets etc. You know the sort of thing."

"And, how many aircraft are serviceable today?"

Birch gave a faint smile. "A total of eight this morning but it could be less as I speak. Plus yours of course."

"Out of 18, I take it?"

"That's right, sir."

"So, as you see it there's no solution. Unless, that is, we qualify for some newer or different aircraft."

"That's about it, sir."

"And mine! I'm naturally interested as I've been flying junk in Malta for the last year and I want something better - much better! Is mine guaranteed?"

Rayne saw Birch hesitate. "As far as I know, sir. We've checked it over and there's nothing obviously wrong with it."

Rayne nodded with a grim smile. "You'd better be right! Otherwise . . ." He drew a finger across his throat with an ominous glance.

His engineer officer did not smile in return, prompting Rayne to ask, "You're telling me the whole truth, I take it?" To which his companion tilted his head, but remained impassive.

As they parted, Rayne detected both resentment and animosity in Birch's attitude, whilst Birch decided he did not much care for this new, toffee-nosed bastard of a commanding officer. In spite of all his bloody gongs!

The Spitfire was on its hard-standing about 100 yards from Rayne's hutted office. As he walked towards it humping his parachute and grasping his helmet, goggles and gloves in his free hand, Rayne experienced the first frisson of excitement. It was more than two years since he had last flown a Spitfire, which had been a Mark I in his first squadron. This, however, was a Mark V, with the same engine admittedly, but with extra boost, cannons and other minor improvements, a trifle faster at height and at wide throttle openings. Also, from a distance, it looked nice enough with one of the newer Rotol airscrews and elongated spinner, all bright and shining withal. So far so good!

Two airmen were waiting to greet him, their faces betraying cautious interest and unease at meeting their new squadron commander.

Rayne greeted them with a smile and addressed the nearest youth   "Good morning! What's your name? And are you the rigger or fitter?"

"Fitter, sir. My name's Steadman."

"And you?"

"Jones, sir. I'm the other one!"

Rayne grinned and held out a hand. " Alright, Jones 'the other one' , let's have the Form 700" Then as he was opening it, "Being Welsh, you aren't responsible for all those sheep bleating their hearts out outside my room at dawn this morning, were you?"

The boy shifted his feet and grinned in return. "I'm from Bristol sir, not Wales. And no, I've nothing to do with the sheep."

The ice broken, the two airmen waited and watched as their senior read the Form 700 with a developing frown.

"This is a new 700, but I see the engine has done more than 200 hours. Where's the original one?"

The two airmen exchanged slightly worried glances. "This is the only one there is, sir. The aircraft's only been here a short time and we haven't seen any other."

Silence. Then, realising that he was not going to be further enlightened, Rayne pulled a face and, after examining all the signatures carefully, signed the document as accepting the aircraft as serviceable.

After that, after making a brief circular tour of the aircraft and looking up with a further smile, he added "Okay, let's get this show on the road, shall we?

Five minutes later, as he taxied around the perimeter track, he experienced more than a trace of the delight and enthusiasm he had felt before his first solo in a Spit. those several years earlier - the long nose, which he was obliged to move about in order to see ahead, the raucous snarl of the exhausts as he adjusted the throttle, the sweet and pungent scents of dope and blue exhaust smoke, and the hiss and squeal of the brakes as he manoeuvred the aircraft around the turns. At the end of the 24 runway, he braked to a stop, ran up the engine to '0' lbs boost, exercised the constant speed unit - twice - and finally tested the ignition switches - one at a time. Then going methodically but quickly through his cockpit drill and finding everything to his satisfaction, he turned swiftly onto the runway and opened the throttle up to the gate in a single decisive movement.

With 9 lbs boost and 3,000 revs. showing on the dashboard, the Spitfire set off like a greyhound out of the traps. Rayne sat back and waited until the tail lifted itself so that he could see ahead, before gently easing the aircraft off the ground and retracting the wheels. The green light disappeared on the dashboard and he felt the clump of the undercarriage locking home. He climbed away westwards over the waters of Cardigan Bay, a thin yellow line of sand having flashed obliquely beneath his tilting wings. Keeping the speed at 180, he allowed the aircraft to lift itself steeply into the heavens, Mmm! Lovely! The engine as smooth as silk, he suddenly felt elated and deeply thankful he was back on Spits.

At 5,000 feet, Rayne throttled back and after trimming the aircraft carefully fore and aft and on the rudder, flew hands-off for a time until the Spitfire tilted slowly to the right and fell away. Not bad! A little adjustment to the ailerons and it would be fine - he'd get Jones to give it a few judicial whacks with his hide-faced hammer. Then, suddenly feeling in the mood, he decided to execute a few aerobatics.

Opening up again to 9lbs boost, he lowered the nose until he saw 330 on the airspeed indicator. Then pulling back on the control column, he brought up the nose until the aircraft was climbing vertically. There he left it until the speed fell off entirely, at which point he let the Spitfire topple over backwards and found himself looking straight down into the grey expanse of the sea that was Cardigan Bay. He smiled to himself. A rather special sort of a loop, that. No 'g' force, no pressure or slip anywhere, everything delicately and smoothly done. He felt quietly satisfied - he had not lost his touch.

Then, with the speed rising again, he brought up the nose once more and executed a perfect roll. Well . . . a roll just short of perfect, being sufficiently barrelled to prevent the engine cutting out. That was the eternal problem with the Merlin engine; negative 'g' followed by a rich mixture cut as the carburettor flooded. Lordy! How he remembered that in combat! And how the Hun 109s with their fuel-injection Daimler Benz motors had walked away from the Hurricanes especially over the years.

Feeling he had just one more trick to perform, Rayne increased the revs. to 2,850 and opened the throttle through the gate and beyond. Immediately the aircraft seemed to stiffen as more than 14 lbs of boost appeared on the dashboard. The speed rose rapidly to 350, then more slowly to 400 and beyond as Rayne slanted the nose of his aircraft down before levelling out. The engine was smooth but clearly under pressure; it should have achieved the upper limit of 16 lbs boost, but perhaps he was a bit too high for that. Anyway, that was enough for the moment - he throttled back and the Merlin sighed with relief. Then, turning back towards the coast and the line of mountains, Rayne went through the motions of joining the circuit and landing. After a curved approach and as he touched down with easy aplomb, he felt a glow of self-satisfaction. After more than two years, not at all bad, No, not bad at all!

With a final glance at the rising radiator temperature as he taxied towards his hard-standing, he saw Jones walking forward to greet him. As Steadman held the ropes to guide the chocks beneath his wheels, Jones climbed up beside him to help with his straps,

"Everything all right, sir?"

"As far as I can judge, yes - after a twenty minute flight, that is." Rayne was smiling in response,

"She's flying a bit right-wing low though, so it may take a flight or two to sort that out Got your hide-faced hammer handy?"

Jones was grinning back like a conspirator, "Just tell me what your want, sir, and I'll attend to it." Then, "Do you want me to put your parachute back in your office?"

"Thank you, if you would." Then, after a moment. "Would you also see if you can find the old 700 for this aircraft? I'd like to see it."

"I'll see what I can do, sir"

Back in his office, Rayne put his head around the adjutant's door. "Adj, where's that engineer officer of mine? Have you seen him?'

The man stood up immediately, 'Not this morning sir, no. Do you want me to find him?"

Rayne hesitated. "No, not really. I just thought he might be sufficiently interested to ask how I liked my new aircraft. Or should I say, my old new aircraft."

Then, with a smile that could have been interpreted as a grimace, he withdrew his head and closed his door.

The following morning, Rayne taxied his aircraft up to the 'A' Flight dispersal area. From here, by arrangement, he was to lead a small formation of four of the newer boys in battle formation turns at high altitude.

Violent turns in formation, even without using radios, were fairly easy low down. High up and well spread out - above 25,000 feet for example - they were a good deal more difficult. Moreover, with a lurking enemy often in the vicinity, they were manoeuvres that had to be learnt, practised, and executed automatically. And quickly! Otherwise - ! Having then explained in detail what he wanted, Rayne issued some concluding instructions.

"Right. We'll take off in twos on runway 24 and on Channel 'A' - that is, local control. Once airborne, I shall go over to our GCI frequency, Channel 'B', on which we shall conduct the whole exercise. Channel 'C', as you well know, is if we wish to use a neighbouring Sector, and Channel 'D' is our emergency 'Mayday' frequency. Okay?" There were nods all round - pretty routine stuff!

Five minutes later Rayne led his formation off the ground and turned towards the north over the grey waters of Cardigan Bay. There was only broken cloud in the local area and good visibility. Further north, however, he knew there was an approaching weather front with rain and complete cloud cover. But at more than 25,000 feet that was not likely to worry them unduly. Moreover, he would have the Ground Control Interception unit to advise him and keep tabs on their position and weather.

As all four Spitfires continued to climb up in a relaxed manner; by the time they had crossed out into the Irish Sea north of Anglesey, they were at 22,000 feet. Fifteen minutes later, from a height of 28,000 feet, Rayne looked down unconcernedly on a solid bank of white and grey some 10,000 feet beneath him. Slanting his flight towards lowland Scotland, he gave instructions to carry out the first of his intended turns. Not a sound or complaint from anyone. His aircraft apparently in good nick, everything appeared to be fine. So far so good.

But, things were about to change - rapidly!

Rayne and his section of four had commenced a hard turn on to a southerly heading, when his No.2, who had been wool-gathering, made an ugly dart in his direction. He narrowly missed his leader but caused the latter to take instant evasive action before muttering a holy word under his breath and resolving to have a sharp word with that young man when they had their wheels on the ground.

Bringing then his eyes back to his dashboard, he had an even more unpleasant shock when he noted that the coolant temperature of his engine, hitherto running at a steady 88 degrees, was now over the 100 mark - and rising! Almost unbelieving, he immediately placed the radiator flap to 'open' position, expecting, indeed praying, that the pointer on the dial would show signs of decreasing. But, to his dismay, the reverse happened. The pointer went slowly up to 115 degrees, the oil temperature rose in sympathy and the oil pressure reduced to below the minimum permitted.

Clearly he had an engine problem. Oil? He didn't think so. An external coolant leak possibly, although there were no obvious signs. Or, an internal one, which was even worse as it was one you normally didn't see. He closed his eyes in despair. "Jesus! Not again!"

His face screwed up in anguish, Rayne recognised his silent entreaty as a prayer and not a blasphemy. It couldn't happen at a worse time and in a worse place - miles from anywhere, in miserable weather, and over the sea. Keeping his voice level he began to issue instructions and to report.

"Ganer Red Section from Red Leader, I have an engine problem and we are returning to base immediately. Red 2, you are to stay with me at all times. Red 3 and 4, you are to proceed on your own if my engine packs up and I have to bale out."

Then: "Lumba control, this is Ganer Red leader. I have an engine problem. Give me a fix and a course for base. Also check the weather at our nearest diversion airfields."

Lumba responded immediately. "Red Leader. Your position is 124 miles from base or 62 miles north of Anglesey. Diversions in the Liverpool area and in the Isle of Man doubtful because of low cloud and poor visibility. Suggest you try for Valley in Anglesey, in which case steer 192 degrees. What are your angels and what is the nature of your problem?" (At this Rayne actually smiled - just in case you don't make it, is what they really meant!)

"Lumba, I am now at 24,000 feet and descending. It looks like a coolant leak so that I expect my engine to die on me within ten minutes. I shall bale out if it does, so alert the Air Sea Rescue Walrus and boats immediately. I have three aircraft with me, one of which will remain. Warn Valley and also my home base. Do you want me to issue a Mayday call on Channel D, or should I remain on this frequency?"

"Red 1, this is Lumba. Flash your weapon and stay with us on 'B'. We now have you 54 miles north of Valley. Keep broadcasting every minute. Steer now 190 degrees."

Rayne nodded and switched on his IFF equipment, which painted a `feather' on his radar plot. Then he coarsened the pitch of his airscrew to its fullest extent and reduced engine power to minus 4 lbs boost. All four aircraft were now in close formation, heading steeply downwards towards the cloud, still well beneath them.

Praying that breaks would appear before - and if! - he was finally forced to bale out, he began to busy himself around the cockpit. Being so engrossed, he had not worried too much, thus far. Suddenly, however, the prospect of abandoning his aircraft - this would be the third time!- followed by a breathtakingly cold dip and a life-threatening struggle to get into his dinghy, loomed large in his imagination. Blast and damn the wretched engine! And a pox, too, on Birch, who had talked him into accepting it! By God, he would have the tripes of that man if he made it!

Meanwhile, the Spitfire floated down calmly, seemingly in total ignorance of its likely fate. Towards the cloud. Towards the sea. Beside him, the pilots of his section formated on him closely. Down! Down! All three watching in silence and agonised sympathy. All metaphorically shrugging their shoulders, too. Poor sod! He'd be the fourth head man! And he'd only managed to get in two flights. Two!

The Spitfires were still in formation and among broken cloud at 4,500 feet when Rayne's engine shuddered to a standstill. It did so silently and with great dignity. There was no bang, noise or fire, it just died, refusing to answer to the throttle. Rayne warned everyone, especially his No. 2, then went methodically through the business of getting out.

First he trimmed the aircraft to fly hands off at 160 mph. Then he unclipped his oxygen tube and mask, pulled out his radio plug, and saw that his dinghy was well and truly clipped to his life-jacket. He carefully checked the fastenings on his Mae West, then pulled back the hood - never an easy task on Spits at any speed above 150.

As the wind roared around his head and shoulders, he decided not to remove his helmet, goggles or gloves. Then, after a quick prayer and a deep and shaking intake of breath, he lifted the nose and turned the aircraft over. As the Spitfire rolled onto its back, Rayne gave a slight push and simultaneously turned the small lever on his Sutton harness release box.

In a moment, he felt himself ejected into a maelstrom of rushing wind that was icily cold and took his breath away entirely. But, his senses remaining very much alert, he waited several seconds, rotating slowly meanwhile head over heels, until he felt assured that he was clear of the aircraft, particularly the tail. Then, falling feet first again, he felt down the buttons on his Mae West until his hand came into contact with the ripcord of his parachute. This he pulled firmly and was mightily relieved when after about two seconds, the canopy opened with a snap and he was jerked hard but not violently into the vertical position.

A deep and heartfelt sigh of relief. Thank God for that! He looked down beyond his feet towards the sea. It looked very grey and very cold. He shivered involuntarily.

When he finally splashed down into the water, he learnt later that he was 14 miles off Amlwch in Anglesey. He scrambled into his dinghy, which was anything but easy with the swell and waves smashing into his face and nearly choking him - it was nothing like those practices in the local swimming bath. He then lay there cramped and shivering for more than two hours before the Air Sea Rescue launch from Holyhead, guided by circling aircraft from his own squadron, found him and hooked him aboard like fish. By this time he was well nigh frozen, felt sick and exhausted, and in no friendly frame of mind.

He was taken initially to sick-quarters at RAF Valley, where he was given a quick once-over before being released to the Station Commander, a lively New Zealander, who, with his wife, insisted on taking him home for tea. After which there was something of a celebration in which a series of warming brandies played a considerable part.

Finally, Squadron Leader David Wynn-Jones appeared in his car a little before midnight, bringing with him messages of sympathy and congratulation from the AOC and others, plus a complete change of clothing. By this time Rayne was, on his own admission, feeling absolutely no pain.

The journey home - all 60-odd miles of it - at night and over the hills, he remembered little. Even the normally loquacious Wynn-Jones left him in peace, well aware that there would be lots to talk about in the morning

Rayne, seated at his desk, had just completed his accident report - RAF Form 765c - and was considering how best to deal with the rather unpleasant task ahead of him. Much discussion had taken place throughout the previous three days. The final outcome was in no doubt: it was just the manner in which the end was to be achieved. Rising to his feet, he put his head around the door to his adjutant's office.

"Adj. would you please have Flying Officer Birch call on me now."

The man looked up. "I think he's away for the moment, sir."

Rayne answered sharply, "I don't give a damn where he is, get him here in fifteen minutes, or else!"

Well within fifteen minutes Birch arrived, saluting briskly and looking animated. "You sent for me, sir?" Then with a grin which was almost impertinent added,

"You're looking rather better than when last I saw you."

Rayne nodded in acknowledgement. Then, sitting back in his seat, said quietly and un-smilingly. "I've just completed the 765c and there are one or two points I would like to discuss with you."

Birch, still standing, became noticeably less animated.

"First, when we originally discussed my having the aircraft, which is now in bits on the bottom of the Irish Sea, you said that you had had it only a few days and that you had reserved it especially for me. In fact, you had had it for more than a fortnight and had already offered it to each of my two flight commanders, neither of whom would touch it. I imagine they wouldn't accept it because they saw on the original Form 700 - which you took pains to conceal from me - that it had a long history of unserviceability, including overheating problems, and that it was shortly due for 240 hour major overhaul and engine change."

Birch lifted his gaze and stared woodenly over Rayne's head. "I'm not responsible for replacement aircraft sent to us by Group, sir. That was the only one available and there was nothing wrong with it when I first spoke to you."

"Oh, I accept that. But you knew of its previous history and you sought to palm it off on me by making out a new Form 700, which would not contain most of its many previous entries, and neglected to tell me anything about its past. In short, you knew it was a lemon, Birch, and you didn't give a damn, thinking no doubt that this young inexperienced sucker is not likely to be here for long, so let him take the risk of writing it off and possibly himself at the same time."

Birch's face exhibited outrage. "That's absolutely not true, sir. I never thought anything of the sort. I do the best I can with what we get. I'm not responsible for our aircraft being clapped out."

"That's not what I'm complaining of Birch. As I see it, and I admit I have been here only a matter of days, you do not strike me as an officer who at all times acts wholeheartedly in the best interests of this squadron."

"You are the only officer who lives out, I understand - you are certainly seldom in the officers' mess. And when I expect you to be around during the day, you are invariably missing. I would have thought, for example, that having given me a sales-talk on my so-called new aircraft, you would have been sufficiently interested to greet me after my first landing to hear what I thought of it. But no, not a sign of you. And whilst on the subject, I gather you obtained formal permission to live out after choosing carefully to time your request to Station Headquarters when every senior member of the squadron and the station was absent."

"In short, you are an old soldier, Birch. You have been in the Service long enough to know all the rules backwards and you have no hesitation in bending them whenever you can and always to your own advantage."

There was a brief and pregnant pause as Rayne sought to control his anger and Birch was frozen into swallowing silence.

Rayne then continued quietly. "I have to tell you. Birch, that I have no confidence in you and I have taken steps to remove you. You are to take a week's leave commencing tomorrow, during which time I suggest you rearrange your personal affairs. Your posting notice will be sent to you in a few days time. Meanwhile, your duties will be taken over by Flight Sergeant Bennett, your No.2, until a new engineer officer is posted in."

Birch, white-faced with shock but with eyes aflame said in a cracked voice, "But, you can't do that! I'll put in for `redress of grievance'. I've been in this squadron for eighteen months and I've always done my best, very often without help from anyone. You're not being fair, sir, and I shall protest formally."

Rayne responded quietly, "You can do as you think fit. However, you should know that I have studied your career and discussed your future at Station and Group level and also with the AOC. You have more than 20 years experience since you were a Halton Apprentice and technically you are a good man. But I note that you have never yet been overseas; indeed I learn that you've avoided it on several occasions. I suggest you stop ducking and weaving and, for a time at least, forget about the women and other diversions in your life and give the Service your full attention. You are a nine-to-fiver. Birch - at times not even that. And you exhibit a resentful smart-alec attitude. In war that simply won't do and in my squadron it certainly won't do. The Service demands much more from all of us; 24 hours a day, 7 days a week, 52 weeks a year." He smiled thinly. "And everyone in my squadron gives just that - nothing less! Which you don't!"

Two minutes later, Birch was in the adjutant's office, his face a mask of stunned disbelief. Almost to himself, he was muttering, "The bastard! The toffee-nosed bastard! He's shafted me! After a lifetime of service, a kid of 22 has shafted me!"

The adjutant, never one of Birch's wholehearted admirers, enquired wide-eyed, "What's he done?"

"He's posted me. That's what he done."

"When?"

"From now! Tomorrow morning!"

"To where?"

"He didn't say. But from the sound of him, nowhere closer than China!"

The adjutant's mouth-ends lifted in the smallest of smirks. "Well, if you will dunk your new commanding officer in the drink on his first flight!"

But Birch, with a venomous glance in the adjutant's direction, was stalking out of the office.

Marcus Rayne gazed without interest on the changing scene that drifted below the rear cockpit of the Miles Martinet in which he was a passenger. Most fighter squadrons not in the immediate battle area around London had a Martinet to tow the drogues used for air-firing practices. The wriggle of a river beneath he recognised as the Severn, which made their position, he guessed, somewhere north of Gloucester. He glanced at his watch. They had been airborne for what - 50 minutes? Another 35 would see them at Farnborough, their destination.

Rayne was supremely bored, which was surprising. Usually, having had an accident or a near miss in the air, he would be on edge for at least several flights thereafter. Now, however, for some reason or other, he couldn't care less.. At least the Martinet, which had an air-cooled Bristol Mercury engine, wouldn't spring a coolant leak. And the aircraft itself was almost new, unlike some of the squadron's Spits. Also, the pilot was one of his flight commanders and a pretty experienced aviator. So, as he sat there, his thoughts dwelt mainly on the events of the previous week rather than prospects of his immediate safety.

It was now five days since his ditching accident, which, he had to admit, had shaken him up considerably - even now he shivered when he thought of it. Also, his unpleasant interview with that wretched man Birch had disturbed him more than a little. He hated being cross with anyone and was beginning to question his decision to have the man posted. Had he been fair? Had he not been just plain vindictive, bearing the man's long service with the squadron and his record?

Then there had been that conversation with the head man. The AOC had telephoned him out of the blue. First with his congratulations, then an enquiry after his health, finally an instruction that he, Rayne, should take three weeks off to 'recover his composure'. Did his composure really need recovering? At that, Rayne had put on a silent grimace. If the wretched man had had his well-being so much at heart, why had he insisted on him being brought back from leave prematurely and dumped in never-never land with a fighter squadron that had problems too numerous to mention. And now - what was the man saying about Farnborough?

The AOC had spelt it out. "I especially want you to go for a reason that will become evident when you get there. I know you have been on the High Altitude Course before but this is more in the nature of a discussion about the future. Listen to what they have to say at the Institute and let me know what your views are in due course. That will only take you a day or two, after which enjoy your leave." And that had been that.

In fact, Rayne had not been too displeased. He had already been considering a private visit to Farnborough to discuss a personal problem that had been worrying him for some time and Squadron Leader Ian Murray, second in command at the Institute, was an old and valued friend. A brilliant and highly qualified chemist, physiologist and doctor, Murray was just about the best man to consult about anything.

When they had finally landed at Farnborough and were taxiing towards their dispersal point, Rayne saw Murray from afar, a solitary figure in a raincoat and forage cap, his hands deep in his pockets. He smiled to himself. How civil of old Ian to form a one-man reception committee. He might have known. Suddenly, everything seemed a lot better.

Rayne climbed down from his aircraft and stretched his legs to restore the circulation. Then as Murray walked forward to greet him, he held out a hand.

"Ian, how nice of you to meet me - an unexpected pleasure. And how's the good woman?"

"Hermione? Never felt better - or if she has, she's keeping quiet about it."
Murray waved an arm in the direction of a small Hillman staff car. "You're dining with us tonight incidentally and staying over - my spouse insists. What I suggest, therefore, is that we go to the mess later to book you in, after I've taken you home to freshen up." He grinned, "Note the American idiom. We've had some of their specialists here in a big way ever since the Japs knocked them for six at Pearl Harbour."

Then, as they settled themselves in the rear of the car, Rayne enquired, "D'you know what I am here for? Is it a secret or am I the only one who hasn't been told?"

"Not a secret exactly but something that's not widely talked about. But we shan't be discussing it until tomorrow morning when we meet in Michael Stewart's office. Michael is my boss man - as if you didn't know."

Rayne smiled as he shrugged. "The plot thickens. I hope I like what I'm going to hear." Then: "And where do you live now? Somewhere expensive I'll be bound."

Murray snorted: "On a squadron leader's pay? I see you still retain your sense of humour. The other side of Farnham, anyway. It'll take us about 20 minutes to get there." He leaned forward. "Right at the next set of lights, driver."

As the car wended its way through the traffic, Rayne found his mind wandering through the labyrinths of the past.

Flying Officer Ian Murray - as he then was - had been the doctor in his first fighter squadron at the beginning of the war. He had formed a close and easy relationship with Ian despite the difference in their ages - Murray would now be about 39 he guessed. Even then he had been highly qualified, having started off with a double first in chemistry before moving on into medicine and specialising in physiology. He also had earned a pilot's wings to qualify for his appointment with the Institute of Aviation Medicine, although his flying had not gone beyond the Tiger Moth stage. No, there were certainly no flies on Ian, despite his quiet and unassuming demeanour.

And it was whilst he was at Edinburgh University that he had met Hermione Robb, who was also a medical student. A rather plain though effervescent young woman, they had married some years before the war and now had two noisy and undisciplined boys. Rayne well remembered the occasion when he had gone to dinner at the Murray home, that during the meal, one of the young rascals had thrown a knife at him which had stuck quivering in the wood panelling behind his head. Stunned and expecting the child to be roundly chastised, he was astonished when his hosts had chosen to do little other that mutter, "Jonathan, that is really rather naughty!" He thought ruefully that Hermione, being a psychiatrist, had something to do with that!

They had almost reached the Murray home when Rayne turned and said offhandedly, "By the way, quite apart from what we shall be talking about tomorrow, I was intending to come and consult you anyway. I've a personal problem I would like to discuss with you - with provisos that is."

And Murray had turned, his eyebrows raised and half amused. "Personal trouble! I'm all agog!"

They had finished dinner and were sitting before the fire in the drawing room drinking their coffee. Rayne and Murray were in armchairs and Hermione was on the settee with her legs folded beneath her.

Murray said, "This personal thing you were talking about. Will Hermione have to go and wash the dishes, or is she old enough to be allowed to listen?"

Rayne smiled. He was not too sure but he couldn't in all conscience turn her out in her own house. He temporized, "If she's willing to stay, of course." Then after a long pause. "Ian, can I ask that you don't repeat a word of what I'm about to say to anyone in the Service? I can't have it becoming officially noised abroad, or anything like that."

Murray stared for some moments, slightly surprised, but said lightly, "Okay, if that's what you want."

Another pause, a long one. Rayne was aware of Hermione avoiding his gaze. He continued. "I honestly think . . . well, it's my belief . . . that I may be going odd in the head." A pause. "No, don't smile, I really mean it. Something is happening to me. From being a perfectly normal, rational being, I find myself at various times wanting to kill people. Losing all control. Absolutely. And when I say kill, I mean exactly that. Suddenly, something explodes within me and I become almost unhinged. In fact, on several occasions, only some external influence or circumstance has prevented me from committing murder."

He saw Murray and his wife exchange frowning glances.

"All right, give us some examples." Ian put down his coffee cup and his wife swung down her legs and added, "I'll go if you want me to."

But Rayne shook his head. "No, please don't. After all, two heads and all that."

Silence.

Then: "The first time I became aware of it was at the back end of the Battle of Britain. You may remember it, Ian, because you were around at the time. A group of us were involved in an engagement with German 109s off Dungeness. Most got away but we hung on to two of them, one of which we caught out to sea and managed to wing. Then, with a white line of coolant coining from its back end, we knew it couldn't get home. As of course did the Hun pilot, because he turned back immediately and, losing height, made for the airfield at Lympne, about five miles away".

"At this, naturally, we were all cock-a-hoop. We had got a 109, whole and almost untouched. What a triumph! At this stage, I was flying alongside it, a mere 20 yards away, so close in fact that I could see all the markings on the aircraft's fuselage and the pilot's head."

"With only another 500 yards to go and at less that 100 feet, I was willing that chap to succeed, the engine to keep going, urging him on. Until, out of the corner of my eye, I saw another Hurricane surge into the line-astern position and fire point-blank into the 109's back end. Immediately, the German fighter nose-dived into the ground and burst into flames, the pilot being killed instantly."

Rayne, obviously somewhat emotional for some moments, turned to Hermione.

"Sweetie, I want you to know, I was enraged, enraged beyond belief. Even now, after a period of several years, more than words can describe. Something just burst inside me. We had just killed quite unnecessarily another pilot - that he was a German made no difference - and also lost a perfectly good German fighter. I experienced a Niagara surge of adrenaline. I would kill the stupid bastard who did it! Kill him! Even one of my own side, I would kill him.

"I whirled about but in the act of so doing, lost sight of the culprit among the seven or so Hurricane pilots who were flying behind me. So that when I finally straightened up, still intent on murder, I couldn't pick out the halfwit among those who were circling the burning crash site."

"Well, you may recall, Ian, that after an investigation within the squadron, the chap involved was roundly reprimanded then posted away. Even so, it took me a day or two to calm down, even to think of the incident without flying into a black, silent rage. I don't think either you or anyone else in the squadron, was ever aware how deeply it affected me."

Hermione shook her head almost in disbelief. "How ghastly for you. I can quite see how much you must have been upset." Then quietly, "But, go on. Tell us more."

Rayne continued almost dreamily. "There were many other incidents, alas, and in each of them my rages began to become more violent and energy sapping. Until, finally, I went with the squadron to Malta in 1941."

"And - ?"

Rayne shook his head sadly in anguished recollection.

"In Malta, we were flying outdated Mark I Hurricanes which were totally outclassed by the Germans flying from Sicily. In those early months of 1941, we lost over 30 fighters whilst the Huns lost one Me 109 - and even that, apparently, was through engine failure!"

"Then later, when we got Hurricane Mark IIs, it became only a little better as the Hun had then re-equipped with the newer 109Fs. Until finally, by the late autumn of 1941, we were so useless, we were being chased off the island altogether, with the Germans circling our airfields - our own airfields, mind you! - in absolute triumph."

"It was galling as well as desperate as we had been pleading with the AOC for months to demand Spitfires from home, or some other aircraft, in order that we might better defend ourselves - which of course never happened, he being a chap with a bomber background."

"Then after one particularly nasty day, when we had been hounded off the island, we landed back having lost two experienced friends of mine. I well recall our discussing the events of the previous very emotional hour, when the AOC turned up in his golden hat, presumably to bolster our spirits. Instead of which, at one point and speaking directly to me as leader, he pushed his face into mine and told me sternly, "It isn't the aircraft, you know, it's the man!"

"That did it! I remember looking into his eyes and wanting to kill him. And very nearly did! But, because he obviously saw violence flare into my face and realising what he had said, he took a quick backwards step out of my reach. Which, I have to believe in retrospect, was Divine intervention as I was about to strike the man, for all his rank and gold braid – beat him into the ground for his crass insensitivity. What's more, others around me watching, plainly saw what was in my mind and were mutely horrified by the turn of events."

A long silence followed during which the only visible movement was of the flames of the fire flickering in the grate. Neither Murray nor his wife said a word. But waited. Now and then exchanging glances. For a long time.

Finally, Rayne went on, "Then, still in Malta, there was that time of the Eytie Macchi that had just been shot down and the dismembered pilot's severed hand and finger. I visited the crash scene within minutes and found one of the Maltese locals trying to cut off the dead pilot's finger in order to pinch the ring he was wearing. Well, once again, I completely lost control and attacked the wretched fellow and could well have done him some serious damage had not a companion not physically restrained me and indeed held me down until I recovered." Rayne gave a grim smile. "He'd said he had never ever seen me like that before, but . . . well, I knew that it had happened like that. Several times."

After a further lengthy silence, Rayne continued. "And then there was that business on my journey home. Via Egypt."

Murray prompted gently, "And what was that?"

Rayne then talked at length about the torpedo attack against his convoy in the Mediterranean and described the engagement during which the Savoia bomber and the Royal Navy fighter had been shot down. Both his listeners became acutely aware of the growing tensions in his voice.

Finally, and in quiet tones: "I know now that I killed that chap in the Martlet. I know it! He ran straight into my stream of fire. Perhaps it was not my fault, I don't know. I've relived the event many times ever since, but I'm now sure that I shot him down. I killed him! He died because of me and I was stunned and horrified at the time. But strangely, it was not that that caused me such agony of mind at the time, but the fact that that a Navy destroyer went back and searched for the crew of the Savoia and left our own pilot in the water, if indeed he was alive still and there to be rescued. But, they left him! They didn't even try! They just left him! There, in the water!"

"And I went berserk! Pointing and screaming abuse, and wanting to kill the Captain and everyone else aboard that bloody, stupid ship. Thank God, with all the other noise going on at the time, no one heard me. But I know I went off my head. I completely lost control. My God, it was awful! And I've dreamt about it so many times since." He shook his head in silent recollection.

Another silence. Then, as though temporarily exhausted by all the emotion and revelations, Hermione suddenly rose to her feet.

"Look, I think it's time we had a break. Who's for a drink or more coffee?" She caught her husband's significant glance. All deciding on coffee, when she had left the room, Murray enquired gently, "Any more horrors?"

Rayne gave the ghost of a smile. "Not really, although I dare say you know that I had an engine problem a few days ago on my second flight with my present squadron and spent an uncomfortable two hours in the sea north of Anglesey. Rightly or wrongly I put that down to negligence on the part of my engineer officer, as the result of which I had him posted. Since then, however, I've been having second thoughts. Was I too extreme? Was it just plain vindictiveness? Is it all part of the same pattern of mental something-or-other that I've got, or getting? Which is really why I'm here talking to you."

Murray studied him impassively. "All right, what do you think you've got? Why do you think you have, or are getting, some sort of mental problem?"

Rayne returned his constant stare. In silence. For more than a minute.

Then: "Some years before the war, when I was about 16, I was friendly with another family in our village. The father was a doctor - quite an eminent one - and there was a rather domineering mother, three daughters and a son."

"I was a pal of one of the daughters. We used to play tennis together and go to the flicks now and then, all very uncomplicated. The whole family was very pleasant in a slightly neurotic way - they were all talented, on-edge musicians and had played in the National Youth Orchestra at one time or another. The son was about four years older than me and having left school went on to Edinburgh University to read medicine. I knew him fairly well but not intimately; well enough, though, to know that he had already had one or two scrapes over the years when he had flipped his lid and assaulted quite violently various people with whom he had been involved."

"To cut a long story short, driving home from Edinburgh one night he crashed his car, resulting in someone's death. He then left the scene of the accident, stole another car - and vanished. Two days later the police found him holed up in an hotel and, taking him into custody, had him examined medically before informing his parents, who naturally were absolutely shattered."

"Later, he was diagnosed a schizophrenic, escaped a prison sentence and went through the usual course of treatment and rehabilitation. He took his pills for a time, then suddenly discovered God and went off to Malaya, or somewhere, in search of the meaning of life. After a time he returned home, married and had two kids, then refused to continue his treatment and finally ended up one day in the back of his father's car, where he committed suicide.

I have missed out some of the various stages in my story, but in essence, those are the facts." Rayne, paused for a long time then added quietly, "His symptoms, you see, and mine, are not too dissimilar and I . . . I, well . . . I'm frightened sometimes that one day . . . I may end up in the back of a car . . . somewhere "

At that point, Hermione returned with the coffee and, sensing the atmosphere, asked carefully, "Any important developments in my absence?"

Murray explained heavily, "Marco is worried he may have schizophrenia, as a friend of his who was similarly afflicted committed suicide. From what I have heard tonight, I think he is worrying unnecessarily but he needs to be reassured." Then as Hermione silently refilled the cups, "However, as he has had rather a wearing few days recently, I suggest he takes to his bed and leaves us to consider some suitable courses of action to set his mind at rest."

Which was how the matter ended that night.

The following morning at breakfast, the subject of the previous evening was not even mentioned. It was only when the two men were in the staff car taking them to the airfield that Murray turned and said, "By the way, Hermione and I discussed your problem long into the night. We feel that you should join us again this evening and stay overnight, at which time we can talk again. Is that all right with you?"

Rayne shrugged. "Whatever you say." Then with a weary smile. "Thank you! I hope I'm not being too much of a bore."

Half an hour later, all three were seated comfortably in Wing Commander Michael Stewart's office with mugs of tea in their hands and exchanging Service gossip, when Stewart rose and after closing the door, returned to his seat.

With some surprise, Rayne looked from one to the other and asked with feigned concern, "I thought I was just coming here on some Course or other. What are you two chaps cooking up for me?"

The other two exchanged conspirator's smiles, after which Stewart took over.

"Marco, you did this Course of ours many months ago so you know most of the facts and practical details of high altitude flying. What we are about to discuss now is something much more radical but in the same field. We will also touch on you and how you might become involved."

Almost involuntarily Rayne exclaimed, "Me! I don't understand."

More exchanged glances. "Well, you will in a moment."

Stewart cleared his throat. "At the moment, none of our fighters - or indeed any other RAF aircraft - operate much above 45,000 feet, the main limitation being engine power. Well, we now have it on good authority that in the not too distant future we will have new-fangled engines that will enable us to fly very much higher."

Rayne, mildly unconvinced, found himself frowning in disbelief. Stewart, noting his look of scepticism, ignored it and went on.

"As an organisation, we have been instructed to examine the practical implications associated with day-to-day combat flying at up to 70,000 feet, the equipment necessary in the aircraft, the safety measures required, and all the physiological problems likely to be encountered."

"In short, we are going into the space exploration business, because at those extreme heights, as you well know, there is virtually no air pressure or life supporting oxygen, and temperatures are very much lower than any the human body normally experiences. Apart from the provision of the aircraft and the engines - which are other people's problems - we have been charged with the task of planning the design and production of pressure breathing equipment generally, the provision of sealed environments and pressure suits for all crew members, incorporating all the highly sensitive valves and engineering associated with unplanned explosive decompressions. Everything, in fact, to enable aircrew not only to fight successfully but also to exist in emergency situations at extreme altitudes. In short, a mammoth task which will take us perhaps three to five years to complete."

Rayne was forced into a wary smile. "And - ?"

Stewart continued. "Most of the design and experimental work will be done in this Institute, in conjunction with industry - in fact, work has already started. Our decompression chambers here will, of course, be in great demand, and we are already in communication with the Canadians and Americans who expect to be working in the same field."

Rayne's face began to lose most its smile. "All fascinating stuff I agree, but where do I come in?"

"Well, it has been suggested . . . er, merely suggested at this stage, that you . . . you shall be the 'guinea pig' pilot in phase two of our plan."

An almost painful silence. Then, quietly, "Suggested by whom?"

"By us initially - Ian principally. Then our masters in Ministry of Supply. After them the Air Ministry, the Air Council, and not least, your own darling AOC, who thinks so highly of you."

A long pause and absolute silence.

"You blighters! You devious - !" Rayne could hardly find his voice. "And what am I supposed to do now?"

Murray smiled and put in, "Nothing for the moment, Marco. You will want to think about it naturally. Then we want you to spend several days with us here, listening to what we have in mind. After that, you can always say 'No'."

Rayne was silent. Then, "I'm stunned. Absolutely stunned. Dunked without warning in the Irish Sea and five days later, this!"

His companions smiled not too comfortably. "We thought you might be surprised."

After some moments, Rayne asked, "And these new engines you mention. What's so special about them?"

Stewart answered succinctly. "They'll be called jet engines. A new method of producing enormous power."

In the Murray household, as on the previous night, they did not attempt to discuss Rayne's personal problems until all three were comfortably replete and again taking their coffee in the drawing room.

Ian began to explain: "As I mentioned this morning, Hermione and I talked about you long and hard last night and agreed that your fear of schizophrenia has no real foundation. Split personality is a complicated mental disability but there is usually a heredity factor involved and the signs of such a problem are normally detectable over a longish period. Without going into details, from what you have told us, none of those critical factors are, or have been, apparent in your case, so we can rule out your own very sombre diagnosis.".

"Having known you fairly intimately over the years and taking into account your record of flying, I would put your problem down quite simply to war fatigue. You have flown more than 550 operational hours on the trot in single-engined fighters without a break – or so you tell me. That is getting on for three normal tours of operational duty. Had you been in the last war you would probably be classified as having 'Flying sickness D', the D standing for Debility - a fairly common complaint in 1918."

"In short, your reservoir of courage is slowly being drained towards the 'empty' mark and you are exhibiting the all the usual signs of mental and physical exhaustion - impatience, shortness of temper, unreasonable behaviour, explosive outbursts and reduced motivation. If you go on as you are, you will without doubt get yourself killed, kill someone else, or just plain totter to a standstill."

Rayne, who had been watching them seriously but with the faintest hint of critical amusement asked, "And the quick fix - ?"

"First, to recognise that you have an obsession. A real obsession, which is at present, your job, flying in combat, and, who knows? your need for recognition and success. Second, to refill your reservoir of courage by every means available to you and the Air Force. Third, to have proper alternatives in terms of physical exercise, a hobby - or hobbies - and, dare I say it, a pretty girl to claim your attention. And fourth, take your full allocation of leave which, as you are well aware because you sign other pilots' leave applications, is 61 days a year. Do all that and you'll be home and dry within six months or a year."

After some moments Rayne shook his head ruefully. "A bit like the curate's egg - I'm not going nuts but am just an operational invalid. And how does this affect the job we discussed today?"

"You haven't said 'yes' yet. But in any case, it needn't. You will not be required immediately except to monitor and learn our methods and procedures and in six months time, who knows? You could well be back to normal. And you'll always be the best judge of that."

After a brief silence, Rayne nodded. "Okay, you've made your points and I'm very grateful." Then a smile in Hermione's direction, "You've been very kind, sweetie, putting up with all this nonsense."

To which his hostess smiled in return and tilted her head in acknowledgement.

Rayne returned to his squadron in Wales some three weeks later He was physically more relaxed but in no easy frame of mind. He found a new engineer officer in post - another commissioned 'Halton brat' - and another Spitfire on his personal hard-standing. He was not in the least surprised to learn that it was a reconditioned Mark V with a new, second-life engine. He found himself shrugging resignedly - what the heck. It seemed that nothing was new these days.

Alone in his office on the airfield, he found himself gazing into space. Looking back, he had been relieved that Ian Murray had dismissed so lightly the possibility that he might have something vital happening in his head. On the other hand, and although he had long since realised it himself, the fact that he was at the end of his tether, both in body and mind, had come as something of a jolt. It was one thing recognising one's own innate failings and keeping quiet about them, but something altogether different when they became so readily apparent to others.

Also, about that other thing, there was the somewhat worrying prospect of being asked to operate at 70,000 feet in a single-seater fighter, and all the dangers that went with it. No, he was not at all sure about that - not sure at all! It seemed that he might be getting involved on a long-drawn-out and rather unpleasant experiment. He had no particular liking for flying at extreme altitudes and he had certainly never heard of any engine or power source that would take any aircraft he knew of to those enormous heights.

And then there was that eager beaver of an AOC who kept putting his name forward for these harebrained schemes - what was in it for him, for heaven's sake? No, life was certainly not easy. Not easy at all.

Chapter Three

It had been wet for days on end. A succession of fronts had come scurrying in from the west, bringing rain in penetrating, slanting surges. The clouds, dark and ragged, jostled and pummelled each other at little more than hangar-top height and the waterlogged airfield was deserted and silent, its runways slick and gleaming.

On their hard-standings around the perimeter track, the Spitfires crouched on spindly legs, tethered and hooded spectres, barely recognisable in the curtains of drizzle and mist.

For Rayne it was an especially frustrating time. Apart from the irritation of not being able to fly himself and the knowledge that his training programme was going to pot, he was all too aware that a fighter squadron was a bubbling, volatile organism which, kept idle for too long, rapidly became bored. If left unchecked, it was liable to turn its fertile mind to mischief. It was his job to keep 200-odd pilots and ground-crew on their toes so that standards were maintained, discipline enforced, and good spirits preserved and encouraged.

For several mornings, on arriving in his office, he had been dismayed to find himself faced with evidence of a growing number of petty misdemeanours. Fellows he knew normally to be sound in every way, suddenly appeared before him charged with bad time-keeping, insubordination and loss of equipment, even to the extent of someone negligently detonating one of the most important items in a Spitfire - an IFF set - costing hundreds of pounds.

The pilots, meanwhile, trooped dejectedly back and forth between dispersal and the Link Trainer, until that marvel of electronics, as though resenting the extra work-load placed upon it, finally dug in its heels and went unserviceable.

Then, to cap it all, the Station Commander, David Wynn-Jones, was called away for a week, leaving Rayne, the next senior officer, in complete charge. This meant extra chores each day at Station Headquarters and the unwelcome necessity of 'lording' it over an additional 800 officers and men.

With his hands in his pockets and from a window overlooking the airfield, Rayne looked out miserably over the dripping landscape and shook his head. Wales had certainly been on the back row when good weather had been dished out. He found himself frowning darkly. He would certainly have to take more exercise - find a mountain to climb, a cycle to pedal, even a horse to ride. Anything physical to rid himself of his frustrations and black spirits. There were, as he well knew, a dozen decent-sized mountains in the local area but, with visibility down to 200 yards and a persistent heavy drizzle, it wouldn't be easy finding them, far less climbing them.

And there was all that other stuff, wasn't there? Ian Murray's only half encouraging verdict on his 'problems' and the vision of that as yet unnamed and unpleasant high altitude job - he had lain awake for nights thinking despondently about that. No doubt, too, the AOC had something else unpleasant for him up his fertile sleeve.

And then there was Ian's advice to take up a hobby and get himself a girlfriend. Hobby? Girlfriend? He snorted to himself. There wasn't a billiard table in the mess or space in his tiny bedroom to write or build a model. And where the heck did one find a 'poppet' in Wales, surrounded as he was by mountains, slate quarries, rain, and thousands of bleating ruddy sheep? Anyway, girls were a distraction. They took one's mind off the job. There had been that girl at the beginning of the war; she was very attractive but had wanted to get her hooks into him and had insisted on following him around from station to station, silly creature that she was. And had so got in the way, that finally he had been obliged to end the relationship amid a lot of anguish and tears. The young lady had been terribly upset, needless to say. As indeed was his mother, who had registered glum-faced disapproval for weeks on end. In fact, everyone had thought him a whale of a cad at the time. But, they just didn't understand, did they? Had no idea. No, wartime flying and girls just didn't mix - not for him, anyway.

But, the fates were soon to relent and produce something of an agreeable surprise.

Having arrived at the mess for lunch one Wednesday, dripping and depressed, he had found three letters in his pigeon hole. One was from his parents (pleasant), one from his bank (not so pleasant), and the third, a great surprise.

This was from `The Officer Commanding and Officers of Royal Air Force, Valley, Anglesey', inviting him to a social function the following Saturday - three days hence! Attached to the invitation was a short hand-written note from Pamela Leggett, a friend since childhood and now the wife of the Wing Commander commanding the night-flying Beaufighter squadron based on the airfield. She apologised for the 'disgraceful lack of notice' but expressed her earnest hope that he would be able to attend.

Attend! Rayne had grinned to himself. Try keeping him away! Anything to distance himself from this wilderness of drizzle, mist, musical sheep and fossilized aircraft.   Pocketing his letters, his spirits rose immediately.

On the appointed day, flying being out of the question, Rayne drove the 'gutless wonder' that was his Hillman staff car, on its two-plus-hour journey northwards, setting off later than he had intended when an unforeseen crisis had arisen.

On the airmen's married patch, two senior NCOs and a husbandless wife were involved, the latter being renowned for her generosity in bestowing favours of the more personal kind. With two blank and sheepish faces before him on an indecency charge, Rayne had soon found himself out of his depth and in very deep water. Taking the advice of the Station Adjutant - an elderly and experienced officer – he had announced with admirable discretion that the Station Commander himself ought properly to be involved. Accordingly, he had deferred the case until the return of Squadron Leader Wynn-Jones, marvelling meanwhile at the virility and ingenuity of some members of the sergeants' mess and the stamina of the lady in question

The countryside en route to Anglesey, normally one of Rayne's special delights, was hidden beneath a depressing blanket of mist and rain. It seemed that he had Wales entirely to himself, his only companions being black-faced sheep - scores of them! - all congregating on the centre-lines of the mountain roads, hell-bent on suicide. After driving with commendable consideration for a thousand or more ovine delinquents, he reached the officers' mess at RAF Valley considerably later than even his revised estimate.

After a swift but much needed change in the bedroom set aside for his use, he returned to the mess proper and walked in the direction of a hubbub of noise and laughter. The party had clearly started without him. He stood at the entrance of the ante-room and cast an eye over the heads of the throng. After some moments, he saw Pamela Leggett bearing down on him like a frigate under full sail - tall, dark, leaning, determined, and frighteningly swift. He smiled in her direction as she gripped his arm with a set of red-tipped talons.

"You're late! Where have you been? We were beginning to think that something had happened to you."

Rayne gave her one of his helpless puppy-dog expressions. "We workers, you know. It is sometimes difficult to throw off the mantle of responsibility."

"Heifer dust!" Pamela Leggett's euphemisms were legendary. "Come and join the gang. You're my guest incidentally, which means you don't have to pay. Look, when you have said what you have to say, I want to get food over and done with so that we can get down to some serious dancing. I know you just love to dance!"

Rayne rolled his eyes. He and Pam, who was a year older than himself, had a rumbustious brother and sister relationship. He had known her since they were both in their early teens and dancing was one of their special areas of disagreement. She went about dancing as though digging a hole on the road - all sinewy violence and determination - whilst his attitude was one of suffering compliance. If hopping about was what the ladies wanted, alright, he would oblige, but only as a duty.

She dragged him through the crowd and Rayne saw that there was a lot of Air rank about the place. His bete noir, the AOC 9 Group, small and balding, was there with his wife, and two Air Commodores he didn't recognise. There was also the grinning gnome-like face of the Station and Sector Commander, the little New Zealander, Ramsbottom-Isherwood. Marcus was very fond of the man and the feeling was reciprocated. In fact, everyone liked the little chap. He it was who had taken the first Hurricane fighters to Russia the previous year and had come back shouting, "If that's communism, give me rheumatism!"

He heard Pamela introducing him to several officers and their wives, whom he had not already met, and suddenly conversation was in full swing. A drink appeared at his elbow and a Wing Commander from Group Headquarters, with a ribbon on his tunic denoting the award of three DFCs and just a trace of Australia in his accent, was remarking that he, Rayne, could expect to see him on a staff visit before too long.

"I'll be down with the Sector Commander", he had shouted in Rayne's direction. "We'll bring the Abbo-sticks' (boomerangs) with us and give them a whirl on the airfield".

Marcus said that he would look forward to it and smiled. It was a relief to indulge in a little childishness now and then - if there had to be staff visits, these were the very best kind.

He was about the congratulate himself that he had completed his conversational duties when one of the senior wives claimed him. Marcus explained patiently that, yes, he was from Llanbedr, that he commanded the Spitfire squadron there and, yes, he was the chap who had baled out the other day and dropped into the water. He agreed that it had been jolly cold - the water, that is - that the weather had been absolutely filthy of late and that they hadn't been able to fly for almost a week. In spite of that, he was very fond of Wales, although it was not exactly in the thick of things, was it? Given the choice he would much prefer to be down south and among the action. No, he was originally from the north. Liverpool, in fact, although he had not been there much since the war started. Yes, he supposed he was a bit young to be a Squadron Leader but, if his colleagues insisted on getting themselves bumped off, there was not much he could do about it, was there? (Why on earth did they all have to keep harping on about how young he looked?).

Throughout, Rayne had had some difficulty in talking to the lady, although she, God bless her, was trying her very best. The trouble was, he could hardly hear a word she had been saying; he being six feet three inches tall and she all of five feet nothing, he found having to keep bending down and cupping his ear, something of a trial. Still, he hoped he hadn't seemed rude, off-hand, or bored.

As soon as he decently could, he glanced over her head in the pretence of answering someone's query and caught Pamela Leggett's eye from a distance. She responded with a knowing lift of an eyebrow and came to his rescue.

"Marco, come over here and meet Charles." She latched her talons on to his arm like a sparrowhawk.

"Who's Charles?"

"There isn't a Charles, you half-wit!" Pamela's voice came as a hiss from the side of her mouth.

He allowed himself to be dragged away, casting a glance of apology towards his erstwhile companion. At a respectable distance and out of sight, she stopped, put her arms around his waist and, being tall enough, tried to rub noses with him, a gesture of affection he had experienced many times before and took urgent steps to avoid.

"Are you going to dance with me?"

"Pamela, behave! You're a respectable married woman Do you want me to finish up a pilot officer again? "

"There are times when I could think of nothing better."

"Alright, I promise," he conceded. "But after dinner. You know very well your dancing puts me right off my food. "

She stood on his toe none too gently and smiled at him fondly.

"Heartless beast! I don't know why I waste my time on you. Now, run along. I'm going to check with the mess steward that the grub's ready." After that, she planted a brief kiss on his cheek and set course for the door, cutting a swathe through the guests like that of a destroyer at speed.

Rayne, thankful for the respite, surreptitiously removed a smear of lipstick from his face before breathing out in grateful relaxation and looking around. One of the advantages of being tall, he decided, was that it afforded periscope vision.

He had just concluded that the guests seemed a remarkably undistinguished bunch, when his eyes were attracted to the auburn-red hair of a young woman in the far corner. She was standing between two lights so that the reflection from her nodding head was nothing less than arresting. Which surprised him rather as, in his opinion, red hair on a girl especially was usually too much of a good thing, being accompanied, more often than not, by skin looking like uncooked pastry and a rash of sovereign-coloured spots. This girl, however, was different. Her hair was like burnished copper and she radiated personality. He watched her, smiling unconsciously to himself. She was obviously mimicking someone, going through a pantomime of gesture and silent dialogue, so that her companions were laughing uninhibitedly. What a stunning creature! He felt himself being drawn towards her. Ignoring a few conversational remarks to him left and right, he returned a pleasantry or two and set off in her direction like an icebreaker.

She was one of a mixed party but he had eyes for her alone. A little closer now, he saw that she was dressed in a dark green full-length ball gown and that her eyes were green too, although that might have been her eye shadow, which was of some sort of matching colour. Whatever it was, the effect was captivating. A green Goddess, in fact! Yes, she really was something different. Really different.

About three paces away, he stopped and she looked up and saw him. After which, for several seconds, they stood and gazed in mutual appraisal. Then, as though triggered by some compelling impulse, the girl immediately put on a wicked look and crowed, "Aha!" before putting her fingers to her mouth and trilling a creditable imitation of a bosun's pipe. After which, in a masculine voice, "Prepare to repel boarders!" - all the time her eyes sparkling with mischief.

Aware that everyone was watching her performance, Rayne grinned a little stiffly, not entirely pleased with his reception. Then the girl was hunching her shoulders, knuckling her forelock and dropping into stage Irish. "T'e top 'o t'e mornin' to ye, sorr!"

Still wary but having encountered this little bit of Irish repartee many times in his native Liverpool, Rayne answered promptly and with a knowing grin, "An' the rest o' the day to yerself!"

At this the girl clapped her hands and shrilled, "Ah, a wit, begod! And handsome to boot." Then with a contrived stage bow, "And wot does yer honour have on his mind?"

"Merely a dance. Nothing more. Would you care to join me?" He held out his hand.

He saw the young woman hesitate, but taking her by the arm, Rayne pulled her gently but firmly towards the floor. She followed without a word and six pairs of amused eyes looked on with surprise and interest. As they pushed their way through the crowd, she walked ahead regally, very erect and with her nose in the air. Behind her, Rayne recognised her nervousness and smiled to himself. When they reached the dancing area, the band suddenly stopped playing. So they waited. Facing each other. Without a word.

Then, in a contrived Mayfair accent, the girl remarked, "You'll dance divinely, of course!"

He responded with a straight face. "Like a gazelle!"

Her eyes widening momentarily, she let out a squeal of approval which caused all around them to look in their direction in surprise. Then noting its effect, she issued another even louder squeal, which had Rayne looking about apologetically. What on earth had got into the woman?

At which point, the band started up again, his partner stepped forward lifting her arms, and they moved off sedately, her nose buried in his tunic. In moments, however, and in a voice muffled by his wings she hissed, "Mind me feet!"

He thought he had misunderstood her. "Your what?"

"Me feet! Me plates o' meat! With your great big clod-hopper boots!"

Before he could protest, the girl lurched and, clutching his lapel, uttered a loud and unladylike "Ow!", a cry which brought most of the surrounding dancers to a halt.

Bending down, she was examining the sole of a raised foot. "Will you luk at t'at, for God's sake! T' blood an' all!"

Rayne, looking down, exclaimed in surprise, "But you're not wearing any shoes!"

The girl, hopping about on one foot, cried, "It's a splintor, sorr! As big as a flamin' nail! And it's all your fault! Back there! You dragged me off before I could get me shoes back on again."

Rayne now reduced to helpless laughter, said, "Right, than let's go back for your shoes and we'll start again. With this floor and my dancing, you could well be a hospital case in no time."

But the girl shook her head, her magnificent hair bouncing. "No. I'm fine. Reely I am. Just bleed'n t' death, God save me." And they continued, her eyes darting about, moisture glistening on the white of her teeth and against the curve of her red lips. And with Rayne still amused and shaking his head in disbelief, they moved off again and quickly found a rhythm.

The girl danced well. She was light on her feet and, willowy and supple, she moulded herself easily into his arms and body. She smelt clean and fresh with just a hint of perfume and her glorious hair shimmered beneath his chin. No country bumpkin this, he decided. He had a thoroughbred in his arms and a sophisticated one at that, in spite of all her Irish blarney.

For some minutes Rayne steered the girl round the dance floor in silence, responding with a fixed and glacial smile to a succession of knowing grins. Envy would get them nowhere! What a stroke of luck that Pam had invited him. And that he had accepted. The Gods had indeed smiled down at him - at last!

Then, with something of a shock, he remembered his hostess. Oh, Lord! This was going to take some explaining away, particularly by a chap who was supposed to hate dancing. Then, as though telepathically guided by his misgivings, Pamela Leggett appeared in the doorway, her eyes searching.

Being tall, her dark head stood out above the shifting crowd and she picked him out immediately. He saw a look of surprise pass quickly over her face, followed by an over-dramatic frown. Then her lips formed the word "Pig!" and she aimed an imaginary pistol in his direction. Rayne grinned weakly in return and she responded with a swift jerk of her head, mouthing the words, "Grub up!" at the same time. He sighed inwardly, knowing that he would have to go. If he didn't, there would be a scene, that was for sure. Just when he was making progress, too.

He led the girl gently to the side of the room. "I'm sorry, I shall have to go."

The green eyes widened. "Go! Go where?"

"I'm the guest of the Leggetts tonight and I've just been given the urgent signal to parade for dinner - you know, AOC, duty, and all that."

For a second the girl looked bewildered. Then she caught sight of Pamela in the distance, and nodded. "Ah! Of course. I quite understand." She radiated disappointment.

"I'm sorry we couldn't have danced longer."

"Me too. But, not to worry."

"Look . . . let me take you back to your friends."

"Don't be silly! I know where they are." A slight defiant lifting of the nose.

He was suddenly aware that she was talking in an entirely new voice. "Before you go. I don't even know who you are, or anything about you."

She smiled and held out her hand. "Nor do you. But, thanks for the dance, anyway."

"But, who are you? What's your name?"

"You'll find out."

He looked blankly at her, then smiled. "Alright, then . . . I'll find out."

"Goodbye, then."

"Goodbye."

Rayne hesitated, touched her hand again, then left. Beyond the door, he turned and saw that she was still standing there, following him with her eyes. He smiled once more and she nodded almost imperceptibly in response. After which, he turned, feeling thoroughly deflated.

Pamela was waiting for him and, as he joined her, dug him painfully in the ribs. "Bum-faced rat! As soon as my back is turned you're off, poodle-faking."

Rayne said nothing and divining immediately his mood, she changed the subject.

"We've got a table for ten, which means that you don't get stuck with the same partner all night - even if it happens to be me!"

He glanced at her quickly and said gently, "Pam!", putting his arm around her slim waist.

"I've put you next to Mrs. AOC to start with. She's very nice but she does go on a bit. After that, you'll be on your own. But don't forget about our dance, will you?"

"I won't. And, thank you sweetie." He kissed her gently on the ear and whispered. "Why did you have to get married?"

The girl looked away with gathered brows. "Because you didn't ask me in time, that's why. And because. I was cold in bed at night. That's really what did it."

Rayne sat down to dinner with some misgivings. Pam was some way off to his right, a little on edge and clearly in one of her wicked moods. He hoped she would not make any of her show-stopping remarks at the top of her voice. Her husband, John, a nice man but ten years her senior, was deep in conversation with one of the older ladies. He was an even-tempered chap with endless smiling patience. With Pam as a wife, he jolly well had to be!

The meal started pleasantly enough with some pretty knock-about repartee, Rayne thought some of these oldies were really quite human. The Station Commander, especially, was in rattling good form, telling jokes about his former life in the outbacks of New Zealand and

Australia. Across the table from Rayne was a rather elderly Wing Commander fastidiously forking over a plateful of hors d'oeuvres and examining each piece carefully as though it had rising damp. He was referred to as Willie and Marcus had never met him before. About 50, he had a Duke of Wellington profile and, though quietly undemonstrative, had ears like a fox and from time to time produced some devastating responses in a drawling, rather pedantic sounding voice. Throughout, he never seemed to raise his head and forked away endlessly. Rayne, watching with frowning curiosity, could hardly keep his eyes off the man.

After some 30 minutes, with Rayne's guard well and truly down, Pamela launched her shaft.

"The Squadron Leader has been making sheep's eyes at your girl-friend, Willie."

Willie continued his microscopic examination of a dangling piece of herring. He drawled, "You are referring to the exotic Cee-Bee, I take it? What a thoroughly sensible fellow."

Rayne shot a hostile glance at his hostess and had it returned defiantly before giving his attention to Willie.

"Who, or what, is Cee-Bee?"

"Cee Bee?" Willie raised both his eyebrows and his voice. "Cee Bee is short for Siobhan. Her name, dear boy. But, as so few people in this primitive realm are able to pronounce the word correctly, she is referred to as Cee Bee."

"Cee Bee, what?"

Willie looked up slowly, a sardine in mid-air. What a pressing young man this Squadron Leader was. " Fitzgerald!" he articulated ponderously. "Cee Bee, or Siobhan Fitzgerald."

"Is she Irish?"

Willie produced a minuscule bark from down among the fish. "Irish! Good God, with a name like that she couldn't be anything else."

Pamela chipped in. "Come on Willie, stop playing hard to get. Extracting information from you is worse than pulling teeth. Tell us about the girl. Marco here is about to burst something vital."

Willie put on a pained expression. "God forbid! My dear Pamela, you are talking about the girl I love. My girl-friend! I do have a proprietary right, you know." He turned towards Rayne, still forking away meanwhile. "Cee Bee's father trains horses - or used to - somewhere in the south east of Ireland. Whether or not he does so now, I really don't know. Quite famous before the war." Then, registering mild surprise, "You've not heard of him?"

Rayne, who had had neither interest in, nor knowledge of, horse-racing, other than to be taken round the Aintree racecourse on 'Jumps Sunday' when he was a child, shook his head.

"But, if she's Irish and neutral, what's she doing over here?"

"She's a Wren, dear boy. A lot of them are."

"From here?"

"Oh, Lord, no! She's 'lower deck' and couldn't possibly be here at this party unless in disguise. No, she's from the Naval Station at Pwllheli. I believe she does things with electricity, or radio, or something equally obscure. Most unlikely choice in my view."

"Then she must be someone's guest I presume. Yours, perhaps?"

"Not mine, dear boy. But, I'm sure someone did invite her. On the other hand, it could have been an open invitation from the President of the Mess Committee, acting for all of us - six attractive and virginal maidens to meet the carnal needs of the many evil-minded young officers on this station. It's not her first time here by any means. She's very popular, naturally, and it's only my mature charm that enables me to fight off the unseemly swarm of young bloods constantly breathing down her neck. And now" - he directed a smiling glance towards Rayne - "it would seem I have yet another rival."

"Not a bit of it!" Rayne was surprised to recognise the stiffness in his response. "Pam's exaggerating as usual. I was allowed to dance with the girl for three minutes precisely before I was dragged away."

"I know, I know, dear boy." Willie was actually grinning. "Women are vicious predators at heart and quite ruthless."

Pamela hooted, "Round objects, Willie! Anyway, Marco's too young for that sort of thing. I was just protecting him."

Later, Pam and Rayne danced together in silence, for them an unusual state of affairs. She said quietly, "You're cross with me, Windy."

Rayne smiled. Other than his mother, she was the only person in the world to call him by his pet name, Windy.

"Not really. I would have preferred you not to have said anything, that's all."

"If I hadn't, you'd have spent a month finding out what you've just been told in two minutes flat."

"Don't you believe it!"

"You would, and you know it."

Silence.

"Are you really fond of her?"

In exasperation. "How on earth should I know? I've only spoken to the girl for five minutes and danced with her for three. Hardly an extended courtship!"

"Alright, miseryguts! Say no more. You're a goner, so why not admit it?"

"Don't be silly."

Another silence. Then: "Tell you what! Organise a party at Llanbedr. Invite her along and I'll come down and give you a hand."

"If I organise a party, Pamela dear, I shan't need a hand from you, thank you all the same."

"Pig!"

The following day, Rayne drove his 'gutless wonder' of a staff car down towards Llanbedr, deep in thought. The weather had improved; a cold front had raced through during the night so that the sky was clear, with a blustering wind and just a few scudding clouds. The countryside sparkled, the greens and mauves of the hills and distant mountains were tinted in brilliant tones and in sharp contrast to the ice-blue of the sky. If he had not been preoccupied with other more weighty concerns, he would have been intoxicated by the sheer beauty of it all.

Other than brief glimpses of her later in the evening, Rayne had seen little of Cee-Bee after parting from her on the dance-floor. After midnight, the guest population had decreased noticeably. Valley was a night-fighter station and had business of its own to attend to, so that it was likely that she had left earlier in the naval transport bound for Pwllheli.

For a moment, he even considered making a detour and dropping in on the Navy; he could dream up some plausible excuse. But, just as quickly, he decided that that would have been altogether too undignified. Much too short an interval! Rayne was a great chap for sleeping on issues that were likely to result in far-reaching consequences. He suddenly found himself smiling. He simply could not imagine the girl in a sailor-suit with that ridiculous white-topped hat, similar to the one he had worn ages ago when he was a kid in the Boys' Brigade.

He had left Pamela on good terms - on the surface, anyway. If she was really upset, she would soon forget about it. The trouble was, she had always regarded him as her personal property and had never made any bones about it. Right from the start, those many years ago, any outsider threatening their relationship, was liable to get the rough end of her tongue. And Pamela Leggett was more than just articulate! But, was he the only one? Rayne had never really been sufficiently interested to consider the possibility. Probably not. She had what he always termed a 'catholic taste' in boyfriends.

All the same, it was the engaging, vigorous openness of Pam he so admired. She knew exactly who, and what she wanted, and said so emphatically, defended her possessions with tooth and nail. No half measures about Pamela! Wham-Bam-Pam, they called her.

Moreover, she was disturbingly attractive, with her dark hair and eyes and all that vivacity and go. Probably a touch of Jewish blood somewhere, Rayne suspected. He wondered if John, her husband, really appreciated her and whether she was still happy about her choice of partner. They were so utterly different.

As he drove south, relaxed in body if not in mind, he was conscious of smiling to himself. No, he was very fond of Pam, always had been. But his policy was always to steer clear of married ladies and he saw no reason to change it now. Flying Spitfires and fighting the Germans was about as much as he could cope with, thank you very much.

But, the girl Cee Bee! Those mischievous green eyes and that shimmering copper-coloured hair! Yes, she was something altogether different. He would see how he felt about her after a few days at Llanbedr. Mustn't rush things.

As the mountain road climbed away ahead of him, he began to whistle, and even his car, the gutless wonder, gave all the signs of having had an injection of monkey gland.

Throughout the following week, Rayne and his squadron devoted themselves to night flying. Rayne thought flying a Spit. at night a waste of time, although he accepted that it was necessary to be able to take off and land in the dark, if only to involve themselves in dawn or dusk attacks on the enemy, when operating from the Channel coast, for example.

For intercepting bombers at night, however, he considered the Spitfire useless. With no radar in the aircraft, a pilot was dependent on instructions from the ground, and even when the enemy was very close, the long, black nose of the Spit., together with the unshielded glow from the six exhaust stubs left and right- which completely destroyed the pilot's night vision - made a successful interception very rare indeed.

Moreover, the Spitfire was a skittish aircraft to control on the ground, so that accidents were much more frequent than during the day. Also its sensitive elevator made flying on instruments a bit of a problem. Still, it had to be done, so the squadron's programme included many 'circuits and bumps' in the dark and cross-country flights of an hour or more at altitude.

Rayne was largely indifferent to the 'circuits and bumps', but quite enjoyed the cross-country flights. He normally flew at about 20,000 feet, on a course that took him north and eastwards to approximately Liverpool, then south to a little north of Birmingham, before turning west and letting down over Wales. On moonlight nights especially, the sight of the mountains drifting quietly below him, was a constant source of pleasure. Also, the long, silent legs of 30 minutes or more, provided ample time for thought. During such intervals, Rayne found himself thinking now and then of the girl, Cee Bee, their brief meeting at RAF Valley, and her quite stunning personality and appearance. And it was one such occasion that his mind focused on the Naval station at Pwllheli. It was not too far from Llanbedr, he reasoned. Why didn't he pay it a visit?

So, it was on his third night cross-country sortie that, on returning to base, he flew beyond Llanbedr and dropped in a steep dive onto the Naval base, situated on the southern edge of the Lleyn Peninsular. Coming down quickly from 20,000 feet to less than 1,000, he found himself with 450 mph registering ` on the clock'.

Aware that he must be creating a bit of a din up and down the coast at something after midnight, on impulse he pulled the aircraft up into a long loop, and despite the darkness and lack of a decent horizon, was quietly pleased when he completed the manoeuvre without frightening himself to death.

After that, and visualising Cee Bee listening to all the noise and wondering if it was one of his squadron's Spitfires, he did a vertical turn around the town before heading off across the waters of Cardigan Bay towards Llanbedr.

He smiled quietly to himself. Yes, he felt altogether better after that.

Some days later, Rayne was uncomfortably seated in the single wooden chair in front of the small table that served as a desk in his so-called office in the squadron headquarters hut. It was 10.35 am precisely as he sat there, physically weary, quietly depressed and staring blindly into space. Outside, the rain pattered on the sloping roof above his head and wriggled in streams down the window.

He had been there since 8 am, and had spent the intervening time in conversation with Wynn-Jones, the Station Commander, consulting independently his adjutant and engineer officer, reading and writing reports and official letters, signing forms and log books, studying the war situation and the most recent intelligence data, trying to absorb a long list of modifications affecting his squadron's aircraft, and dealing with defaulters - of which there had been three.

Finally, the weather putting an end to hopes of flying for the day, he had accepted his morning cup of almost undrinkable tea with just a nod of acknowledgement.

Next door was the adjutant's office and, further down the corridor, the orderly room. This was run by a corporal with the assistance of two airmen, one of whom was the occasional two-fingered typist, whilst the other airman's main duties, it seemed, were to keep the coke-stove going, make tea, and act as messenger boy and general dogsbody.

The adjutant's office also accommodated a desk (of sorts) used now and then by the flight lieutenant squadron doctor. He was a delightful man of 38 and highly qualified in civilian life, who spent most of his time on duty in Station sick quarters.

The squadron intelligence officer, an elderly squadron leader and a knight of the realm, also had a room adjacent to the adjutant, in which he lovingly displayed a mass of records and other documents and photographs, all of which he regarded as vital to the conduct of the war.

The main cause of Rayne's unhappiness, however - which he recognised all too clearly - was loneliness. There were other factors, too, not least of them, the programme for his future mapped out, apparently, by the AOC. Plus, the still nagging belief that, somehow, he was still not quite right in the head.

He had now been in command of his squadron for 33 days and although all his pilots and ground officers treated him with commendable respect and deference, he was keenly aware that he was younger than both his flight commanders, and indeed, to all the other non-flying officers on the Station. Moreover, at 22 years of age, was only marginally older than some of his younger pilots.

Thus far, he had not been other than on formally friendly terms with any of them, which was quite unlike his relationships with colleagues and friends in his earlier units. Not a loner by temperament, although naturally reserved, he found the isolation of command trying in the extreme. There was no one - neither the doctor nor the intelligence officer - with whom he could really let his hair down, or even talk. Ian Murray, he recalled all too clearly, had underlined his need for convivial relaxation - with a girlfriend if necessary! He had reflected bitterly, "Huh! If only!" But it was this final piece of advice that persuaded him that it was time to put theory into practice.

Which turned his mind again to the recent party held at Valley, his girl-friend of old, Pamela Leggett, and the red-haired young lady with the pantomime Irish act, who was the Wren stationed at Pwllheli.

For several days, mulling over the possibility, indeed the seemliness, of telephoning the girl, he decided to take the plunge and, in a state of nervousness which was quite foreign to his nature, he found, through Service sources, the telephone number of the Naval base. With a thumping heart, he picked up his office telephone, all too aware that someone at Llanbedr might well 'listen in' to what would be a private conversation.

From the outset, he encountered difficulties.

The male telephone operator at Pwllheli, whilst not positively obstructive, was certainly not helpful.

"Wren Fitzgerald! Do you have an extension number or the name of her department?" And when Rayne said that he couldn't let him have either, added, "This is a training depot, you understand, and with hundreds of Wrens here, I wouldn't know where to start. I don't carry a list of names, you see. You could go straight to the top - the Captain's office - and work down from there. Other than that I wouldn't know what to suggest."

Rayne, by now aware of the problem facing him, thanked the man, and rang off. Lord! What had he started?

Next, after giving the matter some thought, he decided to try RAF Valley and asked for Mrs. Pamela Leggett's married quarter – only to find Mrs Leggett out. However, he was able to leave a message, and an hour later, Pamela's voice, bright and breezy, sounded in his ear.

"Windy! As I live and breathe! What a wonderful surprise. Are you going to ask me to elope with you? If so, what train do we catch?"

Rayne shook his head and had to smile. What a girl!

"Pam, sadly, I'm not about to suggest we run off together. In fact, I'm going to upset you by asking for details of a rival." A small pause. Then: "Do you remember that red-haired Wren, Willie's friend, who I met when last I visited you? I've been trying to get in touch with her and not getting any joy. Can you perhaps help out? An address or something. Who invites her to Valley and how do they go about it?"

He heard a small scream of disapproval over the telephone.

"You naughty old thing! I'm going to cross you off my eligible list this very moment. It's just as I said; you've fallen for the girl! Come on, admit it! You have, haven't you, you wicked, wicked boy?" Then, more seriously, "Windy, I can't help you, I'm afraid. But, if you give me a little time, I'll get back to you. Will that do?"

She rang back the same evening. "Windy my love! You can reach your beloved on extension 249. So, get to it, dear boy."

Rayne said, " Thank you Pam. How did you find out?"

"That's a secret, my lad."

"No, tell me! Was it the elderly Willie? If not, who invites her to your parties at Valley?"

"I'm not going to tell you, so there!" Then, more gently: "Windy . . . what's wrong with you these days? You are always snappy with me. You're not the bright and eager young fighter pilot hero I used to know and love. Is there something troubling you?"

Rayne hesitated. "I'm a bit tuckered out these days, I'm afraid. Perhaps it's nothing more complicated than that." Then after some moments, "Between just you and me and not to be breathed abroad, I didn't want to be posted here in the first place. But the wretched AOC insisted, for reasons of his own, and here I am, nursing a squadron which is only firing on two of its four cylinders. I'm grateful in some respects for the promotion, but I've been through quite a lot these last three years and wanted a long rest - which I didn't get. Now . . . well, everything is just that little bit more difficult. I'm less keen. I'm not sleeping too well at night. But, more than anything, I feel terribly alone. There's no one here I can confide in. Talk things over with. And, Pam . . . I don't think I ever imagined telling you this, but I so wish you were with me. Here. Now."

Silence.

Then, in a small voice, "Windy, that's very sweet of you and very nice to know. And you think, perhaps, this red-headed charmer is going to fill the gap?"

Rayne gave a short laugh. "Subconsciously, possibly. I just don't know. It was suggested that I might try getting myself involved with someone, but there's no guarantee that she'll be the one."

A wan smile. "Remember, you only allowed me to dance with her for three minutes."

"Who made the suggestion? That you should get involved, I mean."

"Oh, a doctor friend of mine at Farnborough. An old mate, with whom I will be working in the future."

"And he was serious?"

"Very serious. He reckoned I had become too up-tight, too obsessed with my job, had overdone things and might end up killing myself. And that a steady girl friend might take my mind off things. A bit, anyway."

"Well . . . I just don't know what to say, my love. Except that I'm absolutely crushed, of course.' A little laugh the other end. 'But, I do so hope things work out for you. And if I can help in any way, well . . . you know Good Samaritan me!" Then, more lightly, "Anyway, I shall need a blow-by-blow report on your love-affair. But remember, no monkey business. Nothing I wouldn't approve of. My spies will be on the lookout from now on."

Another wan smile, "Thank you, Pammy. You're a very dear girl."

"No thanks required. But, just watch it!. And watch yourself, because I love you very dearly. But . . . as if you haven't known that for the last ten years!"

The female voice that responded to Rayne's request to be put through to extension 249 at Pwllheli was not at all like the voice he expected or remembered. Which prompted him to repeat, "Is that Wren Fitzgerald? The Irish girl?"

The voice came back, slightly peeved, "I'm sorry you're disappointed but, yes, it is. Anyway, who are you?"

Rayne smiled into the mouthpiece - this was the one all right!

"I don't remember telling you my name, but I'm the chap you danced with briefly, the last time you came, or went, up to RAF Valley."

A moment's hesitation. Then, "I danced with all sorts of . . . but, wait a minute, yes! Of course! I remember! You're the tall chap with all the medals. Who left me standing there when our hostess turned up and made eyes at him. And who trod on my toes when I was not wearing my shoes. Yes, I remember you all right! Anyway . . . to what do I owe this honour, good sir?"

Rayne, feeling somewhat tongue-tied, explained lamely. "Well, I felt, suddenly . . . well, that I wanted to see you again. A silly thought perhaps, but there it is."

Silence.

"Well . . . it's not that silly! But, you being you and me being me, it wouldn't be easy. Would it now?"

"Why not?"

"Well, you're a 'bleed'n orficer' and I'm 'lower deck', and all that. You couldn't come here and I would always have to be in uniform. So it would be difficult for us to meet, here or outside. Anywhere, in fact. Anyway . . . I don't go out with officers."

"You don't!" I hadn't noticed - you turning up at Valley regularly and dancing in the officers' mess. Anyway, what's wrong with officers? Me, for instance?"

Another silence.

"Come on? Don't be shy. Tell me!"

"Nothing personal. But, officers are out of court as far as I'm concerned. They let you down. They lead you on. You depend on them. You're mates for a time. Then, poof! - they're gone! Killed or wounded. Or they just plain disappear."

Rayne said quietly. "I see. It sounds as though you've had some experience."

"You could say that, yes."

"So, I'm wasting my time?"

Silence.

"Tell me! "

"For the moment . . . yes. I'd have to think about it, though. Later, perhaps."

Rayne gave a grim smile. "I'm encouraged anyway." Then, wishing to change the subject, "You 're not doing your Irish blarney act today."

A faint giggle. "No, my Irish act, as you call it, is having a day off"

Silence. A roaring silence.

Rayne struggled on. "By the way, did you hear us flying over at night, about a week ago?"

A squeal! "So, that was you, was it? In that case it would be better that you kept well clear of Pwllheli."

"Why so?"

"Well, our Captain here was sunk twice in the Mediterranean by aircraft, so he hates them with an almighty passion. Every time an aircraft comes anywhere near us at night, he rushes out in his pyjamas, screams 'Black out the Ship!' and every light on the camp is switched off. Last week, I happened to be in the bath when it happened and spent half an hour in the noddy trying to find my clothes. And not only that. The cinema went off in mid-picture and everyone in the mess halls couldn't see to eat their meals. Boy, you were certainly popular, all right!"

Rayne found himself laughing in spite of his earlier disappointment. This was clearly something to bear in mind for the future.

"From what you tell me, it couldn't have been me as I was over you at about 1 am. At which time, you wouldn't have been in the bath. Or having a meal. Or sitting to the cinema. I did a loop over your head, incidentally."

"What, in the dark? You must have been out of your mind!"

"You have that effect on me. And by the way, what do I call you? I believe Cee Bee is their name for you at Valley."

"Call me whatever you like."

"That doesn't help me very much, does it?"

"It's not meant to. But, thank you for ringing, anyway. And I'm sorry about the other thing. It was very nice of you to ask me though. So, I'm afraid it's just . . . goodbye!"

"Goodbye. I'm so disappointed."

"Oh, you'll recover. But, before you go. What do I call you? You know, just in case."

"My name's Marcus. Marcus Rayne. And I come from Llanbedr. I command the Spitfire squadron, there - here."

"Right. Marcus Rayne from Llanbedr. I'll remember the name. Again, goodbye . . . Marcus!"
"Goodbye!"

Rayne replaced the telephone - despondent. Crushed, almost. He was not used to being rejected. Which only increased his desire and intention to see the girl again. No, he wouldn't be put off! He'd be darned if he would!

The following day, he rang Pamela Leggett at RAF Valley.

"Sweetie, it's me again. I spoke to Cee Bee, as she's called, and asked her to see me. And d'you know what - ? "

"She turned you down, flat," interjected the girl.

"How on earth did you know that?" Rayne's voice had risen an octave.

"Female intuition, my love. I'd have done precisely the same had I been in her place. Her mother had probably told her not to go out with strange men. Most mothers do."

"But, I'm not a strange man."

"You are to her. So . . . pocket your pride and try again."

"That's what I wanted to talk to you about."

"I'm probably already ahead of you there, Windy dear. You want me to have another party and invite her along. That's what is in your mind, isn't it?"

"Pamela, you are positively clairvoyant. But, have you her details - her name and all that?"

"Marco, my sweet. Just fly your Spitfires and leave me to do all the brain work. And please be careful! I don't want you killing yourself."

Rayne heard nothing from Pamela nor about any party she had in mind until he received a formal invitation to an 'At Home' gathering at the married quarter of Wing Commander and Mrs J.G.R. Leggett .

Checking the weather, he decided to fly across to RAF Valley and took off in his Spitfire in the afternoon of the appointed day to make the 20 minute journey north.

Crossing Cardigan Bay at only several thousand feet, and making a slight detour to his left in order to look down on the distant coastal town of Pwllheli, his mind immediately focused on Cee Bee. With a spasm of sheer delight, he saw her red hair again in his mind's eye and the Irish mischief in her green eyes. He assumed she would be invited, of course, but would she know that he, too, would be present? Perhaps not. He never knew what Pam would get up to.

He did a slow circuit of Valley airfield and then a gently curved approach with wheels and flaps extended, before landing slickly and easily on all three points. Taxying towards the hangars, he saw in the distance what he imagined would be John Leggett's staff car. He smiled with satisfaction. It was nice to be met with the red carpet, to have such firm friends as Pam and her stolid husband.

As he levered his long frame with difficulty into Leggett's small Hillman saloon, John said, "I shall be taking you straight home. Pam says you'll be staying with us and not in the mess. Apparently, this do of ours is of some importance. So she tells me, anyway" He turned towards Rayne, his eyes amused. "Do you happen to know what it's all about?"

Rayne smiled a secret smile in return. "I've not the faintest idea."

As they drove out of the station and towards the officers' married quarters, he wondered how much Leggett knew of his problems; how much Pam confided in him; how, indeed, the evening would develop.

He remained in his bedroom for the next several hours 'out of the way', as Pamela put it. Downstairs, Pam's voice was much in evidence as was the telephone, which rang unendingly. Only once did Rayne hear John make some minor remark in a raised voice. He smiled to himself. Pam was not to everyone's taste.

It was something to seven in the evening when the first guests arrived. He heard the door bell ring several times and many voices and laughter in the downstairs hall. At which point he felt he should put in an appearance. With a noticeable quickening of heartbeat, he wondered whether Cee Bee had turned up, what she would look like, and how he should greet her.

When he reached the main drawing room, there was a short reception line, with Pamela resplendent in a full length maroon gown, which accentuated to great effect, her dark hair and eyes. Alongside her was John, in what was obviously his best uniform, and the Leggett batman, plus one other mess servant, holding trays of drinks. Scattered throughout the room were about a dozen guests, already drinking amid a hubbub of conversation. But no Cee Bee, he noticed.

He presented himself to Pamela as though a stranger who had just arrived.

She cried out in a formally strident voice, whilst taking his hand: "Squadron Leader Rayne! How fortunate we are! Welcome to our humble abode! I trust your health is blooming?"

And Rayne had gravely replied: "Ma'am, my blooming health will, I'm sure, bloom further as the result of this evening."

At this, they both fell into each other's arms, laughing, whilst John, alongside, rolled his eyes and indicated that there was at least one other lunatic in the house. Then, as Rayne was moving away, Pamela hissed into his ear. "She's coming by car but is held up. Give her another half hour."

After which, Rayne accepted a proffered drink and found an elderly matron advancing in his direction like a 74 gun battleship under full sail.

"Squadron Leader, I have been so wanting to hear your story of how you parachuted into the water quite recently. Do tell me. Wasn't it dreadfully cold?"

Rayne smiled and tilted his head, as though he were happy to repeat the story, even for the 100th time. Inwardly he sighed, "Lord! Would it never end?"

It was a good hour later when raised voices and laughter caused him to glance up and into the distance. Cee Bee and one other girl had arrived. He saw her look about quickly and when she had caught his eye, give the smallest of smiles and nods in acknowledgement. It took a further 10 minutes, however, before he found himself at her side.

She stood there, looking at him, smiling; her hair still the most attractive and shimmering red-auburn he had ever seen, her eyes still as green as ever, but now clad in a modest but beautifully cut plain, dark dress which hugged the contours of her figure. She was just as tall as he remembered.

He asked, warily, "You're not going to hit me with your Irish act again, are you?"

She replied quietly, smiling. "Not unless you insist."

"And your shoes are on?"

"Both in place, yes."

"Then, hello!"

The smile widened. "Hello yourself!"

"I'm so glad you've come."

"I'm glad I've come."

"In spite of - ?"

"In spite of everything I said last time. For which I apologise. I was so banjaxed and on edge when you telephoned that I said some very silly things."

He smiled. "We all do that from time to time." Then: "I so want to talk to you."

"You do? About what, in particular?"

"About you. About me. About everything. Such a lot of important things."

"You sound very serious."

"I am very serious."

He continued to look at her with smiling eyes. "You know . . . you are a remarkably beautiful young lady."

The green eyes twinkled mischievously. "More beautiful than Pam, for example?"

He smiled, but inwardly - the first hint of jealousy, perhaps. Aloud he said, "You are both beautiful, but in different ways."

A brief laugh, showing her teeth. "Ha! You wriggled out of that one pretty well, didn't you?"

He said, "Look, we mustn't monopolise each other completely this evening. So let me ask you one or two things now. Do you get time off - you know, a week-end, for example? And do you have civilian clothes? - although to go to and from Ireland, I'm sure you must have."

"How do you know I'm Irish?"

"You're joking, surely! Anyway, I was told."

"Ah!" The girl nodded. "Well, we have masses of courses at Pwllheli and at the end of each course there is always a short break. I started off being a student but I was retained as a junior instructor. Which means that I can get a weekend pass every now and then, in addition to which, I get one or two other perks being an instructor. And, yes, I do have civilian clothes, as you see" - she lifted a leg - "although I'm not allowed to wear them other than for very special occasions. And, of course, for going home to Ireland. But . . . having said all that, if you are thinking of asking me out for a dirty weekend, the answer's no! Sorry about that, but it's just not what I do."

The girl then smiled at him openly and without embarrassment. After which, there was a brief silence before, Rayne, on impulse and with serious eyes, bent forward and kissed her gently on the forehead. "Well said! You're obviously a nice, wholesome person. "

He straightened as a means of introducing a new subject. "Something else before we mingle. I have a telephone extension of yours. Is that private, or very public?"

"Well, it goes to a room at the end of my billet. Sort of public but it is only used by a few of us, especially in the evening. If you want to speak to me about something important, you'd have to ring in the evening. Otherwise it would be almost impossible to find me on the camp."

Rayne nodded. "Right. Next, I would like you now, or this evening, to write down your address at Pwllheli, because I intend writing to you. With some ideas I have about where and how we can meet, and why. Assuming you still wish to, that is." Then, flatly: " Do you?"

She looked up into his eyes, which were almost pleading, and felt both a joy and a sadness somewhere inside her..

"Not everything I said last time was untrue, though. I still have this reservation about going out with officers, or perhaps I should say, with officers who fly aeroplanes. I've seen so many of my friends hurt - desperately hurt! - when their boy friends disappeared for one reason or another, that I know what hell it can be. And . . . well, I don't want it ever to happen to me."

"It has happened before?"

The girl hesitated, then nodded, and he realised that to discuss it further would have been an unwelcome development.

"But, you haven't answered my question, have you? Do you wish to see me again, or not? Please be frank!"

She hesitated for some time, then smiled.   "I do, yes! I would like us to be friends. Because you're an attractive chap and because I feel we have something in common. Subject to the usual provisos, mind!" Suddenly the Irish grin lit up her face.

She went on: "But, tell me. I overheard Pam once refer to you as 'Windy'. Why so?"

Rayne sighed, closed his eyes, then gave a sheepish grimace. "It's a pet name, used only by my mother and Pam, whom I've known since I was 13. As far as I'm aware, no one else uses it. My middle name is Wyndham and my mother once told me that when I was christened as a tiddler - Marcus Wyndham Rayne - an uncle promised to leave me a legacy if I ever married a girl called April Showers or May Flowers. You're neither of those, I don't suppose?"

The girl stared then, clapping her hands, burst into laughter. "You're pulling my leg! You must be!" Then: "That's really killing! April Showers or May Flowers! Although, it does bring to mind a little story I have to tell you, when I know you better. Not now though. Some time in the future, perhaps."

"There you are, you see." Rayne was grinning delightedly. "We have lots of secrets to reveal. Lots to talk about."

His eyes shining and full of love for the quite extraordinary creature before him, he reached out and touched her hands.

"We should be mingling. But, don't forget, you'll be hearing from me."

After that, the evening developed along familiar lines. He heard himself telling his usual anecdotes and party stories whilst sipping his wine and sampling the wide variety of finger-foods tastefully set out on the large dining room table. He felt his eyes constantly straying in the girl's direction and caught occasional glimpses of her, animated and laughing, as she took part in the chatting exchanges among the various conversing groups. He felt strangely uplifted.

Quite light-hearted by her presence. Marvelling at her attractiveness, yet almost surprised that he should be so affected. How could it be happening? So quickly? And to him?

About halfway through the evening, he felt an arm slip round his middle and turned to find Pamela's face by his ear. She whispered, "Well?"

He responded with a conspirator's smile. "Very!"

She half-turned and muttered, "Huh! I shall now only be No.2 on your list, I take it?"

He squeezed her hand. "You'll always be No1 on my list, sweetie. In time, possibly No. 1, equal! Not just yet, though." Then: "Tell me, are the two girls going home tonight? It's such a long way."

"I believe so. At about 10 o'clock."

Later, and back in his bedroom, he was to wonder how two comparatively junior Wrens could be permitted such privileges. Obviously, influence in some quarter.

Wren Siobhan Fitzgerald at first waited for the arrival of Marcus Rayne's promised letter with keen anticipation. When it did not arrive within a week - two weeks - then three, she began to wonder whether or not it had been lost among those of the mass of the girls living within the camp or put in the wrong pigeon hole. Whether, too, he had lost the address she had written down. Whether, even, he had had any intention of writing at all.

After which, the thought struck her forcibly that perhaps it was Divine intervention, and that this new association was being frowned upon from above. A Catholic girl by upbringing, the Holy Mother still tended to figure large in her appreciation of events, if only subconsciously.

Finally, there always lurked in her mind, the horror of that earlier bereavement. A year ago now, was it? Something like that. She still saw his face. His youthful, laughing face - always his photograph in its place on her dressing table. Please God, never again! Never, ever again!

Then, it arrived. On a Friday. After almost a month. Delighted, like a squirrel with a nut, she slipped the letter into a pocket and fled to her billet. There, she sat on her bed. And read it.

He wrote:

Dear Cee-Bee,

I am unhappy having to address you as Cee Bee. It is a silly name which does no justice at all to your beauty and personality. I must dream up something more fitting, which we can discuss when next we meet.

I am sorry to have kept you waiting so long for my promised letter, but I have been away in Northern Ireland with my trusty Spitfires - Eglington, near Derry, to be precise. Where, true to form, it rained constantly for the whole week we were there.

Since my return, I have been giving some thought as to what we might do together, and have come up with the following:

First, that you get an over-night, or two-day pass, either at a week-end or even mid-week - all days are the same to us here.

Second, you take a 'bus to Criccieth, where I will meet you in my car.

Third, we then come back here to Llanbedr and you can stay the night with David Wynn-Jones, our station commander, in his official residence, which is off the station. You may possibly have met W-J in the past. He is 25 years older than me and therefore quite harmless!

Whilst you are here, you can visit my squadron and see how we poor Spitfire pilots exist. After which, we can walk the hills and coastline and eat cream teas - it is lovely around here - during which we can talk endlessly, enabling me to tell you how beautiful you are. And how jolly lucky you are to have me as your escort!!

You will have to come in your sailor's suit, but with a change of civilian clothing, plus some dark uniform trousers - I imagine you have some of those - or slacks. Plus some walking shoes.

As this will no doubt take you some time to arrange, I shall telephone you about a week hence, when you can tell me what success you have had, or suggest something altogether different.
No cards up my sleeve, I promise, or anything even remotely naughty.

Till then.

Affectionately,

Marcus

She read the letter several times, with mounting excitement. Gosh! Not exactly a love-letter, rather like something written by her bank manager, in fact; but a step in the right direction. Talk endlessly, he said. About what, and where? And Criccieth - she'd never taken the 'bus to Criccieth before. And what if someone saw her - them? Holy Mother of God! - she crossed herself devoutly - she really would be for the high jump!

Rayne sat in his car several hundred yards from where he knew the 'bus would halt. She had counselled him urgently during their brief confirming telephone conversation not to park too near her point of arrival. She could well have some unplanned companion on the 'bus, she had explained, and at all costs she didn't wish to be seen meeting an attractive RAF squadron leader; particularly when carrying an overnight bag! Oh, Lord! Her hand had gone up to her throat. The very thought of it!

From a distance, Rayne watched her dismount, a single, slim figure in dark blue uniform with a white-topped sailor's hat. Saw her, too, look about nervously, before picking up her bag and crossing the road in his direction.

Then, after stopping casually to look into a nearby shop, she cast another nervous glance up and down before lowering her head and almost running towards his car. Aware of what was going through the girl's mind, Rayne grinned openly to himself and, leaving off his hat, stepped quickly into the road and opened a door to let her in.

The girl almost fell into a front seat with a whoosh of exhausted breath, throwing her bag into the back with a swift cast of her arm. Climbing in beside her, he sat grinning in her direction.

"Young lady! You look nice enough to eat!"

She blew a nervous jet of air upwards, towards her tilted cap.

"Young man!" she announced with feigned sternness, "I didn't come all this way just to be eaten!"

After which, and another several moments of silence, they both giggled comfortably and touched hands, the ice broken.

Setting the car in motion, Rayne said briskly, "Tell you what! We'll just get out of town then we'll stop and I'll explain what I have in mind."

"Well, I hope you have food on your agenda, because I'm famished. I had to catch the 7.30 bus, which meant I missed my breakfast. So, the ball is in your court, good sir!"

A mile out of town, Rayne pulled into a large lay-by from which there was a clear view of the shoreline and the grey-blue waters of Cardigan Bay.

He began: "Right! First stop is Wynn-Jones's house, where his batman will no doubt feed you breakfast and you will change into your trousers - you've brought your slacks or uniform bottom's, I hope?

"Then, it's to the airfield at Llanbedr, where I shall introduce you to W-J himself and he, I'm sure, will be suitably astonished to meet his niece - his niece, I would have you know! - who is a Wren based at Pwllheli, paying her uncle a courtesy visit."

At this, the girl by stages looked baffled, then mildly outraged, before slumping finally into astonished silence.

Rayne continued, straight-faced: "It's our cover story, don't you see? This will enable me to show you my Spitfires and . . . wait for it, get you airborne in one of the aircraft we use for target-towing." Grinning mischievously and observing again the stunned look on the girl's wide-eyed face, he continued, "How'm I doing?" Then, a little anxiously: "You do approve, I hope?"

The girl could barely speak. She squeaked, "Fly! Me? But we'll go to gaol! Both of us!" Then, dropping into her stage Irish idiom: "Holy Mother o' God!" - she crossed herself yet again – "I've never flown in me whole life. T'at, I haven't!"

He laughed gaily into her face, "Not only that, but you'll also be forced into wearing a parachute. Which is why I asked you to bring trousers with you. You can't use a parachute in skirts - not without showing your next week's washing."

On that note, and humming some unidentifiable tune, he backed out into the road and drove off southwards at a brisk pace, with Cee Bee sitting silently beside him, stunned by surprise and apprehension.

The Station Commander's residence, a few miles north of the airfield of Llanbedr, was a distinctive large wooden building of modern design, spectacularly balanced on a mass of stilts, affording a broad and impressive vista of Cardigan Bay.

As Rayne led the way up the dozen-or-so steps to the entrance, he said over his shoulder. "W-J never stints himself. This is some millionaire's country retreat which he has persuaded the Air Ministry to rent for him. It comes complete with a couple of mess servants - misemployed, I should add - and, I hope, an ample supply of breakfast victuals."

They were met at the door by an RAF corporal in a white coat, whose bowed greeting left the girl in no doubt that he was expecting them.

"The Station Commander's niece has missed her breakfast and demands that she is re-fuelled immediately with eggs and bacon," announced Rayne in a commanding voice. "And, fried bread and black-pudding, too?" He cocked an amused eye towards the girl, who could only stare open-mouthed in return.

"Gosh! I seem to have joined the wrong Service!" was the only remark she eventually could manage. Then, walking to an enormous window which afforded a panoramic view of an endless expanse of sea, sky, and gliding sea-birds she added, "All this is quite beyond belief! Pure magic-carpet stuff, in fact."

"The day is yet young," was her escort's comfortable response.

Later, with Cee Bee successfully refuelled to the point of explosion and the girl clad in dark-blue uniform trousers, Rayne drove her to Station Headquarters at RAF Llanbedr and announced their arrival to the Station Adjutant.

Knocking on Wynn-Jones's door, a trifle obsequiously it seemed to Rayne, the elderly flight lieutenant ushered in the two visitors.

Rayne waved an arm. "Good morning, Uncle! Let me introduce you to Wren Siobhan Fitzgerald - the niece you didn't know you had."

For a moment bewildered, Wynn-Jones, because he was a man of infinite experience and one well acquainted with Rayne and his often surprising antics, kept a straight face initially, then held out his hand with a welcoming smile.

"Good morning! - niece I didn't know I had! How fortunate I am to have such an attractive relation." Then, to Rayne, "What else surprising do you have for me - up your sleeve, as it were?"

"Wren Fitzgerald is part of my course of rehabilitation, as recommended by the Institute of Aviation doctor at Farnborough. I intend taking her flying in the Martinet later this morning, so I thought you should be aware of my plan - and why."

Wynn-Jones nodded, debating quickly in his mind, whether or not he wished to be part of this rather doubtful subterfuge. Rayne, noting his momentary hesitation, put in quickly, "Your niece is in the radar/control-and-reporting business and has expressed a wish to be given a little air experience. It seemed to me that I could kill two birds with one stone."

Wynn-Jones smiled, "Ah! - and why not? I can think of no better person than yourself to provide the necessary." Then, to Rayne, "But, treat my niece gently, young man. I wouldn't be too happy about putting my signature to the 765c if you pranged."

Rayne winked in reply, "Nor would I, Uncle! But I have no intention of damaging her." To himself, he admitted knowingly, "I bet you wouldn't, Uncle, dear!"

When they were outside, Cee Bee asked, "What was all that about? And, what is a 765C?"

"A 765c is an accident report form, which would be made out by me in the event that we crashed, assuming I was still capable of so doing, and finally signed by W-J. There were clearly doubts in his mind about the wisdom of my flying you and his getting involved, hence his remarks."

"And you?"

Rayne grinned in her direction. "I have absolutely no doubts in my mind. You are an important part of my rehabilitation. Very important!"

The girl shrugged her shoulder and sighed. "I have no idea what you're talking about. But, whatever you say."

As they walked towards his Spitfire standing alone on its hard-standing, Rayne asked, "Would you like to sit in the cockpit?"

"Gosh! May I?" The girl's eyes were like stars.

"You may, and as my parachute is in the seat, you'll be able to see out."

The girl climbed in, not too elegantly, and sat with her hands in her lap, her face alight with interest as Rayne began first to explain the controls and their effect, then the various instruments.

Fingering the spade-grip on the control column she asked, "And what are these things?"

"Those 'things', dear heart, are the gun-buttons."

"Oh, Lord! And if I pressed - ?"

"You'd kill about 50 people standing the other side of the airfield! Our guns are always loaded."

Giving a little shriek, Cee Bee hurriedly pulled away her hands and tried in vain to hide them. She turned a little white-faced. "Would I really kill people if I did that?"

"That's what the guns are there for." Then, smiling, "No you wouldn't really as they are on `Safe'. You'd have to slip the safety-catch first."

The girl, however, continuing to look uncertain, said, "Gosh! Suddenly, it's all spooky in here. . I'd like to get out now, if you don't mind."

As he helped her from the cockpit, he said, "Look . . . if you're not too keen on - "

But, the girl interrupted him quickly. "It's not that. It's just . . . well, a funny feeling suddenly came over me when you mentioned killing people." Then, brightening, "Is that the aircraft you'll be taking me up in?"

Rayne turned towards the Miles Martinet which was standing on its concrete pad, 50 yards away.

"That's it, yes. But we'll have to go to my office first, to fit you with your special parachute harness. The passenger wears a different type of parachute in that aircraft."

In his office, and not unaware of the interest of his adjutant, orderly room, and others in his attractive Wren companion, Rayne went about the business of fitting the girl with an observer-type parachute harness.

With polite smiles and not a few giggles, when the two of them adjusted buckles and tightened straps in the more private of places, he introduced the parachute pack itself, demonstrating the manner in which it should be clipped on. Finally, he drew her attention to the rip-cord and gave her a little advice on how and in what circumstances it should be pulled.

"Yes, but how do I get out of the aircraft?" The girl's query was half jocular, half serious.

He said blandly, "I just turn the aircraft on its back and you'll be shot out! I'll tell you first though!"

She stared, then complained, "No, please! Explain it to me properly! I never know when you're joking."

A tilt of the head. "Lady, believe you me, I'm not joking!"

For some moments, each looked at each other, he gently smiling, she bent slightly and a little apprehensive in her unaccustomed get-up, but each with different thoughts in their minds.

He was thinking, "She's a wonderful, lovely young woman. A girl of character with whom I am beginning to fall in love. Could she be the wife I'm looking for?"

And she was thinking, "This boy is different. Attractive. Special. I think I would always want him near me. But am I already too close? And should I not be pushing him away? Because . . . Oh, God! - please help me?"

The moment of intimacy passing, however, he said briskly, "Right, you need a helmet and then we're off."

He took one from his locker and held it out, the wires and tubes dangling. "And all pilots in my squadron carry their own parachutes, 1 would have you know."

As she walked out towards the aircraft, she felt as though she were approaching her execution tumbril. Gosh! Her very first flight!

Then Rayne and an accompanying airman showed how to climb in. Then they fitted on her helmet and plugged in all her tubes and wires. Finally, Rayne, after a pat on her head and a wink, let himself down into the front cockpit and settled himself.

After some moments and amid a small cloud of blue exhaust smoke, the engine started up, and without any palaver, the aircraft moved off with a squeal of brakes as they turned. She breathed in deeply, her heart pumping. Lordy! All right so far!

As they taxied smartly around the perimeter track, Cee Bee actually began to enjoy the swaying ride although she thought they seemed to going jolly fast. Then the aircraft was turning again and ahead of her was the broad grey swathe of the main runway. Oh, heavens! Now for it!

Rayne's voice suddenly was loud in her ears. "Right! Are you quite comfortable and in good heart in the back? "

"I think so."

"Splendid! Then, we're off!"

The engine note rose and the aircraft straightened up. Then with acceleration that to Cee Bee seemed alarming, it raced down the runway and lifted itself into the air. They flashed first over the end of the airfield, then a narrow curve of beach and the water's edge. The girl, looking down, saw the lone matchstick figures of two people walking their dog on the sands. And, like a child on her first merry-go-round trip at a fair, she waved to them excitedly. Oh, this was super! Absolutely wonderful!

Rayne, hearing her squeaks in the rear, grinned to himself. "Right. We'll get above this little bit of cloud, where it will be less bumpy, then we'll fly northwards up the coast."

Then, after a minute or two he nodded his head. "If you look down to your right, you'll see Harlech Castle. About 1,000 years old and still going strong. No jerry-builders in those days. Those who were, went straight into a pot of boiling oil. You're not feeling sick, or anything like that, are you?"

"No, I'm feeling fine. And . . . oh, this is so wonderful! Quite marvellous!"

"Right. So, Snowdon . . . here we come!"

For more than an hour they flew at slightly more than 3,500 feet. When they circled the summit of Snowdon mountain, it seemed almost that she could reach out and touch the brown and slate coloured rocks and heathers as they raced beneath them. He then took her northwards to the Great Orme at Llandudno before turning left and flying along the coast, where she watched with interest as they raced a plume of white smoke that was the main-line train bound for Holyhead in Anglesey. After that, it was the famous Menai Straits bridges built by the equally famous Stephenson and Telford, before visiting another castle at Caernarfon, then crossing the Lleyn Peninsular, where he tilted his wing so that she was able to look down into the town of Pwllheli and the Naval station in which she lived.

All the time, he kept her enthralled with the history and stories of each place as it passed beneath them, so that as the trip progressed, she came to marvel at his erudition and be enchanted by the casual and amusing manner in which he kept her attention, so that the hour passed as though it had merely been minutes.

Finally, as the grey waters of Cardigan Bay gave way to the approaching mountains and shoreline and later their airfield of Llanbedr, she was able for the first time to relax completely into her seat. Lord! What a wonderful and exciting experience!

She looked ahead to the helmet and shoulders of the young man in the pilot's seat and a feeling she had never before experienced suddenly developed within her so that she felt gloriously and ridiculously happy and wanted to sing.

Having returned to Rayne's office, they divested themselves then disposed of their flying equipment. Still feeling on top of the world, the girl, on impulse, suddenly held out her hands. Surprised, Rayne took them, to be further surprised when she reached up and kissed him briefly on the cheek.

"A small thank you for my wonderful, wonderful hour in the air." Her eyes were shining. "Not only are you a brilliant pilot, but your knowledge of local history has impressed me to pieces." She grinned happily. "Now . . . what do you have in mind for the rest of the day?"

Recovering quickly, Rayne put on his thoughtful face.

"Mmm! My first thought was that I should take you to bed immediately. But, . . . " He stopped and grinned at her wide-eyed stare. "My alternative plan is to take you chez Wynn-Jones, where we shall pick up some lunch, change, then go by car to a place I know, and walk."

A feigned look of disappointment on her face, the girl put a dramatic hand to her breast. "Oh, pity me! Take me to bed! - what made you change your mind? Poor wretched soul, I am a rejected maiden! Ah, well. Another time, perhaps!"

At which they both laughed comfortably, and she insisted, "And what else?"

"Well, tonight we dine with the Station Commander, who says he wishes to share a much prized bottle of vino with us, and . . . well, the rest of your stay we can discuss later."

As they left the room and fell cheerfully into step, she slipped her arm into his, only to withdrew it quickly when she realised where she was and that they might be seen.

By 2pm, they had left Barmouth behind and were on the road to Dolgellau.

He said, "If we turn left again shortly, we shall be travelling north again and heading for the Snowdon National Park." He added in explanation, "This is an old stamping ground of mine. My parents used to bring me here when I was a child."

When earlier they had arrived at the Wynn-Jones house, they found that the Corporal batman had obviously been warned of their requirements and had their lunch, packed into two parcels with a couple of flasks, ready and waiting. Then, when the girl departed to change, Rayne donned a more appropriate, casual coat.

When finally she put in an appearance, Rayne could not repress a small but audible intake of breath. Her hair had been unpinned and had fallen in a red-gold cascade around her shoulders, she wore a white blouse and three-quarter length pleated tweed skirt, a loose but light pullover, ankle-length socks and 'sensible' shoes.

Noticing his smiling stare, she asked, "What are you grinning at?"

"Er . . . your legs, to tell you the truth. Do you realise, it's the first time I have ever seen your legs?"

She looked down, drawing up her skirt to knee level. "What's wrong with my legs?

He laughed, "Nothing at all. They're more than fetching. No, on all previous occasions you have either worn a ball-gown, trousers, or those passion-killer naval stockings which are about an inch thick. Now, you look like that girl who 'followed the yellow brick road' – what-was-her-name, Judy Garland?"

"Well, I've better legs than Judy Garland but, I have to admit, her bosom puts mine in the shade."

At which point, Rayne feeling himself skating on very thin ice, rolled his eyes and turned to leave.

As they climbed away northwards into the National Park along a winding country path, their only companions in the unending rolling expanse of green and brown were the scores of black-faced sheep, silently dotting the mountainsides.

They finally turned into a large, pebbled lay-by, near which was a single rustic table and benches. As he switched off the engine, the quiet of the surrounding mountains seemed deafening in contrast. Each stunned into silence by the beauty and isolation of the scene, they collected their luncheon packets and flasks from the rear seat and sat down to eat in smiling companionship.

Rayne watched the girl covertly as he unpacked his food. The sun shone on her glorious hair and he was amused to note that she opened her sandwiches and inspected them solemnly with the air of a child examining the contents of her Christmas morning stocking.

She broke the silence. "I've got cheese in mine! What's yours?"

"Mine's spam, but we can swap, half for half, if you wish. And you can have my bunloaf, too, if you want it."

"What's bunloaf - as you call it?"

"It's that brown currant-cake thing - we call it bunloaf in my part of the world. We refer to it in the mess as 'standard British slab'."

She nodded, engrossed in eating, then looked up, her face breaking into a smile. A smile so utterly bewitching, Rayne decided, that he could not take his eyes from her. This creature really was the most fascinating and loveable person he had ever met. He shook his head in disbelief. It was so unreal. A month ago, despair and disaster - then she comes into his life and everything, but everything, had changed.

By the time they had finished their lunch, the sun had broken through, providing an unseasonal warmth. With a hand to his eyes and pointing, Rayne said, "If we walk in that direction and up the side of that mini-mountain, the view at the top is quite breathtaking - to the west the whole coastline, and beyond, most of Cardigan Bay. Do you feel up to it?"

"Of course!" the girl agreed brightly. "I shall have to shed this woolly though, if I'm to go climbing. Gosh, it's hot!"

She immediately began to drag the pullover over her head with such childish abandon, that he stopped and could not help but stare as her shapely breasts were revealed in sharp outline through the thin fabric of her blouse, the curve and points of them delightfully tantalising.

Noticing him looking in her direction, and correctly divined his thoughts, she grinned back at him, quickly and mischievously. Turning away, embarrassed at being caught out, he strode off up the hill with the girl following.

For almost an hour they walked together, sometimes laughing and joking, now and then serious, occasionally separated by ten or more strides, but always in comfortable companionship. At one point she had shouted up to him. "Hey! Steady on! I feel like one of those Bedouin wives, walking behind their masters carrying the water skins."

And he had turned and laughed. "Not any more they don't. Since the war and all the landmines in the Libyan Desert, the women are pushed to the front in order to clear a path." He grinned. "Anyway, you are not my wife, but if you were, I would value you far too much to insist on such a thing."

When the top was reached and, tired and breathless, they looked towards the west, a wonderful panorama of coastline and sea stretched out before them. Each of them, shielding their eyes, was stuck dumb by the sheer beauty of what they beheld, the wind a mere zephyr in their ears.

She breathed, "Gosh! Just look at that view! Oh, I'm so glad to have come." And turning, "Thank you so much for bringing me."

He said gently, "You complement the beauty of it all."

To which she slowly tilted her head, her eyes soft. "If you go on saying things like that, you'll have me crying." And reaching out, she touched his hand.

Later, they walked down towards a fast running stream which let itself down in stages towards a far distant lake.

"The mountains around here are about 2,000 feet," he explained. "And I think that stretch of water over there is known as Llyn Bodlyn."

"You seem to know a lot about this area." She was clearly impressed

To which remark he remained silent. Not wishing to tell her that four Spitfires of his squadron had crashed on this very mountain top only weeks before, killing all four pilots. Instead, he silently led the way downwards.

When they had reached the stream, they found a flat area of short, sheep-nibbled grass. Immediately, the girl dropped to her knees and put her hand into the water.

"Gosh! It's freezing! I thought I would like to paddle a bit, but now I'm not too sure. D'you think there would be any tiddlers to see or to catch? What did you call them in your part of the world?"

Rayne looked down at her with smiling amusement.

"We used to call them Jack Sharps, or Sharpies, when I was a kid. But, no, I doubt there would be any up here and in these cold waters".

The girl stood up and dried her hands.

"Well, 1 don't know about you, but my bones would welcome a rest. Why don't you join me?"

With that she sat down heavily then lay back.

After a moment's thought he joined her, but more cautiously, and for a time they lay there without speaking, staring up into the now well-broken clouds that were sailing quietly above their heads. It was deliciously warm. And silent, the wind a mere breath in their ears. Heaven, in fact.

After some minutes of silence, the girl turned and asked, "May we talk?"

He answered cautiously, "Of course! About what in particular?"

"Well, when we were talking to Squadron Leader Wynn-Jones, you said that I was your rehabilitation something. What did you mean?"

Rayne stiffened. He didn't wish to embark on the story of his mind problems and the various talks that had resulted. Nor did he wish to be too revealing about his Service career and possible future. But, the girl was entitled to be given something of the truth, if not all. So, he decided to temporize.

"Well, for me the war started in September, 1939. 1 was sent to France early on and there followed the Battle of Britain, Malta, war in the Middle East, and a long and nasty trip home by sea. By the time I arrived home after almost three years of fighting, I was tuckered out and wanted a long rest. But, alas, it didn't happen that way. So I was obliged to speak of my lack of spirit and tiredness to a doctor friend of mine at Farnborough. He recommended the usual remedies - rest, bags of leave, lots of exercise, a variety of hobbies and new interests in life - a girl friend, for example. Anything to take my mind off flying, and myself."

The girl frowned. "But surely you could have had a dozen girl friends. You are a very attractive chap with lots of medals and things, there must have been someone."

Rayne nodded. "Yes, there was someone at the beginning of the war, but I couldn't cope with her at the time and had to put an end to it all."

"You mean you dumped her! Would I be right?"

"You 're making it sound a very heartless business. Actually, we parted very amicably, as she was able to see that war and an over-attentive girlfriend didn't really mix - at the time."

"And now you've picked me up?"

"My goodness! You are making it sound very mercenary. As though I were merely soliciting someone off the street for my own gratification. No, it just wasn't like that. Pam's party was the first I had attended for years, and when 1 set out, I had no idea 1 would be meeting someone as special as you. Certainly, I did not have the doctor's remedy in mind. No, I looked across the room and saw an attractive red-haired girl who interested me immediately. I wanted to meet her, and I did, if only briefly. After that, I wanted to meet her again, but it wasn't quite so easy. Was it?"

The girl grinned. "And where does Pamela Leggett fit in? Or, does she?"

"Pam? Yes, she certainly does fit in and has done for years. We've known each other for ages, since we were both about thirteen, in fact. I met her at a friend's home in Cheshire - we both come from that part of the world - and we became good mates. I grew very fond of her and we met each other from time to time and exchanged love letters when eventually she went away to school. Then, the war came, I went off, and she got married. Since when we've simply kept in touch."

"Did her marriage upset you?"

Rayne thought, then answered candidly, "Yes, I believe it did. A lot! But, as 1 was abroad at the time, there wasn't much I could do about it."

There was the briefest of pauses. Then Rayne challenged, "Anyway, why this inquisition? 1 know practically nothing about you other than what was revealed to me by Wing Commander Willie - I don't know his other name - who told me that your father trained horses in Ireland, that you were called Cee Bee because you had an unpronounceable Christian name, that you were a Wren from Pwllheli, and that you graced the Valley parties from time to time. Other than that, not very much. Except that you are apt to do a pantomime-Irish bit before speaking normally, that you dance well and have a lovely figure and nice legs. And, of course, that you are very nice person. So, young lady, you have a lot to tell me."

The girl grinned. "Your pantomime-Irish bit is a bit wide of the mark."

A deep breath: "My family has lived in Ireland since about 1600 - Queen Elizabeth's time, anyway. Before that, the Fitzgerald's go back to Norman times and the Doomsday Book, and we have a family tree to prove it."

"Yes, my father trains horses but he was in the Royal Navy in the last war. And other forebears of mine, going back to 1800 and earlier, have served in the Army or Navy. The family has always regarded itself as Anglo-Irish anyway, so it was natural that I should join the Navy when war came."

The girl turned and grinned again. "How does all that sound?"

Rayne responded with a smile. "Very impressive! But tell me more about your family and your early life."

"Well . . . my parents are approaching 50 and in good health, and I have a younger brother and sister, both of whom are at school. In the Navy, until very recently, I was still under training, learning all about radios, radar, electricity, and a lot of other complicated stuff. Now, I'm a sort of junior instructor."

"And early schooling?"

The girl grinned again and hunched her shoulders. "You may well ask! "

She paused, as if undecided. Then: "I was sent away to a prep. school in western Ireland when I was eight. It was very Irish - English was only our second language. The nuns were terribly strict and the Reverend Mother an absolute dragon. I didn't enjoy it awfully but I wasn't really unhappy."

"And as a student?"

"Not too bad - no one complained anyway. Added to which, I was pretty emotional and was consumed with love for pretty well everyone - except the Reverend Mother!"

"At about nine, I fell in love with Jesus and wanted to marry him. Then, when I realised I was in a long line of potential partners, I decided to become a Saint and became very holy. Then, I finally entered my romantic Irish phase and - this will interest you - I decided to change my name."

The girl then raised herself on an elbow and looked straight into Rayne's face, her eyes plainly amused. "You see, I was actually christened Annabel May - I was born in May - but that didn't seem to be Irish enough for me. So I decided to answer only to Siobhan."

"Good Lord! And how did your parents react to that?"

"Not very well at first. But, putting it down to female childishness, they humoured me, until it became the name by which I was mostly known."

"And what happened later?"

The girl suddenly giggled. "I was expelled! For being naughty! The Reverend Mother sent a letter to my father telling him to take me away. He went to see her, of course, but it didn't do any good. I had to leave."

It was Rayne's time to grin. "And what was so naughty?"

Cee Bee shrugged. "It wasn't really that bad. A few of us used to write little girly letters to each other - you know, what we would do if we were cast away on a desert island with Errol Flynn or Franchot Tone - that sort of thing. Until, one day, I wrote in my letter what I would do if I were marooned with the Reverend Mother. Unfortunately, my letter was intercepted and she was terribly upset and offended. So, I had to go!"

"And - ?"

"Well, as I said, Daddy went to the convent but his visit cut no ice, so he took me away and I was sent to a school in England - I was then about twelve anyway."

"Where was that?"

The girl hesitated. "Down south."

"Down south! Where?"

The girl smiled. "In a place called Cheltenham. Perhaps you've heard of it?"

Rayne's eyes widened. "But . . . Cheltenham Ladies! Of course! That's where Pamela..."

The girl interrupted with a wide grin. "I knew you'd tumble to that as soon as I mentioned Cheltenham. Yes, she and I were there together, although she was about two years ahead of me. But, as we were both sporty types and in the hockey and lacrosse teams at the same time, we came to know each other pretty well. And, of course, our parents met at Speech Days and on special occasions."

Rayne grinned almost triumphantly "So, the jigsaw pieces are failing into place. That makes you 21 and Pamela is the one who invites you to Valley. Right?"

"True, oh cleverclogs!' But, we each have to be discreet, me being non-commissioned, and all that. Pam has to make sure that none of the Wren officers and I are invited at the same time. It wouldn't really worry me, but - "

"And why have you never been commissioned?"

"I've never been particularly ambitious in that respect. I've never pressed my claim and the Navy seems to be happy to have me as I am. Anyway, I enjoy what I'm doing and I wouldn't be particularly interested in becoming a cipher queen or in admin, looking after paper, postings and ladies' lavatories."

Rayne smiled and was quiet for a time, studying the girl's face and marvelling at her unassuming beauty. But, there was still a question he felt obliged to ask.

He said, "I have no wish to intrude, but this person who was killed. The one you said you cared for. Was he someone very special?"

Immediately, the girl seemed to shrivel and he saw tears come to her eyes.

She nodded, wordlessly. "Yes, I loved him. He was very special." Then, her face beginning to crumble she whispered, "But I can't talk about it. I'm sorry, but I can't."

"Did he fly?"

Again the nod. "That's why - ! Oh, I just can't explain."

"Of course! I understand and I'm sorry." Rayne nodded and was quiet.

After a time, the girl came alive again. She sat up and asked, "How long have we got? It is all so wonderful here, I think I could stay for ever."

To brighten her up Rayne said quickly, "You'd be frozen to death if you did!" Then examining his watch, "We should start walking back any moment. Don't forget we have dinner with his nibs at seven o'clock and it's a good half-hour's drive."

Then rising, he helped the girl to her feet, delighting in the touch of her hand and the brief smile of thanks that lit up her face. Once again in the car, however, she slumped back in her seat and was soon asleep.

Rayne dropped the girl at Wynn-Jones's magnificent house on stilts and returned to his own mess to smarten up. He had a feeling about the event to come and decided to change into his best-blue - one of the only two uniforms he possessed. Officers in wartime were not required to wear mess-kit, so he determined to look the best he could. As he dressed carefully, he felt his pulses racing. Tonight was the night!

Arriving at the Wynn-Jones house, five minutes before 7 pm, he was ushered in by the Corporal batman with the quiet instruction: "In the drawing room, sir."

This caused Rayne's eyebrows to rise. He had only been to Wynn-Jones's house before on two occasions and had never been further than the large entrance hall and dining room. In the drawing room, he was greeted effusively by his host in expansive mood, wearing an outfit of plum-coloured smoking jacket and matching bow tie. With a well-filled tumbler in his hand, his host asked, "A little licorice water, I presume? And what is your choice?"

"Thank you. A small whiskey and ginger ale, would suit." Then, by way of explanation, "It's the only drink I can keep down. Alcohol doesn't suit me, alas."

"Your good fortune, dear boy. You needn't apologise. "

At which point he saw Cee Bee. Standing behind. Smiling. A drink in her hand.

Not for the first time that day, he was halted, almost open-mouthed, into admiring her. She was wearing the dark figure-revealing dress he had seen her in at Valley and, as he raised his eyes in her direction and smiled, she lifted a foot and cried,

"See? Legs again!" And laughed.

Handing him his drink, Wynn-Jones exclaimed, "My new niece is a wicked Irish flirt, I would have you know. You should beware of her. Not only that, she is a person of artistic sophistication." He waved an arm, "She's the only person I've had in this house who immediately recognised the watercolours around this room as being of the Norwich School - John Sell Cotman, circa 1800, no less. Plus, she also tells me, she draws and paints more than adequately herself Though only portraits in oils now, watercolours requiring too much skill and patience. An enormous talent, don't you think?"

Rayne listened in awe, surprised and absorbed. He had no idea! Clearly, there was very much more to learn about Cee Bee. Still fascinated, but in a quiet and composed way, he looked about.

One wall of the enormous room faced out to sea and was constructed entirely of glass, with a verandah beyond. Sumptuously carpeted, it contained an expensive suite of sofa, mahogany furniture and armchairs, plus a baby-grand piano. On the latter, was arrayed a group of what Rayne presumed were family photographs, whether belonging to the owner of the house or to Wynn-Jones was not readily apparent. The whole area, in short, radiated a atmosphere of quiet comfort and luxury.

As it was still fading daylight - double day-light saving time, by Government decree - it was still well before black-out time and the panorama to the west was a sight to behold - a setting sun, the endless proportions of the wide, flat empty beach, and the tinged clouds on the horizon, a positive artist's dream. Rayne sampled his drink and, aware of the girl's faint perfume and her immediate proximity, felt utterly relaxed and radiantly happy.

Then Wynn-Jones was speaking again:

"This house actually belongs to a friend of mine. A business associate who likes the good things in life. The Government didn't like the idea of my having it at first, but - " He tapped his nose, "there are always ways and means." Finally adding, "Ah! And here comes Corporal Williams with news of the victuals. And a great cook and bottle-washer the Corporal is, as you will soon find out."

As they seated themselves in the dining room, the Corporal appeared, once more in his white coat, proffering a bottle of Chablis encased in a tub of ice.

Wynne-Jones explained, "One of my last purchases in France before the balloon went up." He smiled. "So you'll understand the importance I attach to this very special meeting of ours tonight."

Then, the Corporal having dispensed three glasses of the wine, Wynn-Jones, raised his glass. "A toast! To my very new and attractive niece, and to the young man who will one day become Chief of the Air Staff!"

To this, Rayne frowned and a little embarrassed, responded, "I'll happily drink to half that toast, anyway."

The meal progressed; five courses of small but delightfully presented items, with mine host loudly proclaiming that it was all `stuff ' that was now being served that very evening in the officers mess, but having been transformed by the touch of a catering genius.

To which remarks, Rayne and the girl exchanged glances with briefly raised eyebrows and the Corporal accepted the compliment with a polite but concealed smirk.

Then, for an hour, Wynn-Jones spoke of his earlier life in the valleys; of the part his family had played in the development of steel in the area; of the strikes, the depressions, the struggles of the working man. Of the hatreds and the loves that had resulted, and finally, what he prophesied would be the eventual decline and disappearance of that, massive and magnificent industry in the face of cheap overseas labour and new materials.

Finally, and the port having been circulated, they all rose and moved into the drawing room. By this time, the sun had departed, darkness was descending and the heavy blackout curtains had been put in place.

An offer of brandy being refused by both the girl and Rayne, Wynn-Jones waved an airy hand towards the piano.

"Do either of you chaps play, I wonder?"

Then, to the slight surprise of both her male companions, Cee Bee moved slowly towards an ornate piano stool and settled herself as her host at once hurried towards her to move aside some of the photographs. Then, to the obvious delight of both Rayne and Wynn-Jones, who sank comfortably into armchairs and listened utterly bewitched, the girl embarked on a long, soft and exquisite rendering of the Moonlight Sonata, followed by lengthy excerpts from the works of Delius then Rachmaninoff.

At one point, Rayne was obliged had hide his eyes, which suddenly and inexplicably became full of tears, and was only prevented from being completely embarrassed, when Wynn-Jones after applauding the girl vigorously, exclaimed, "Bravo! Bravo! And are there any Welsh melodies in your repertoire? And what about you, Marco; what are your favourites?"

"I'll go so far as singing Danny Boy, if pushed and given another drink," grinned Rayne, blinking his eyes and saved by the bell. After which, Cee Bee smiled in his direction and immediately began to play the Londonderry Air.

Following a moment's hesitation, Rayne began to sing quietly but melodically, as he had done some ten years earlier in that never-to-be-forgotten church concert, aware that his parents were sitting, tense and white-knuckled, in the front row of the audience. Thereafter, there was a prolonged series of Welsh and Irish patriotic songs - the girl complaining from time to time that, without the music before her, she was only guessing at some of the tunes - with Wynn-Jones singing lustily and tunefully.

Eventually and quite suddenly the evening came to an end. Wynn-Jones, with a conspirator's glance towards Rayne, stood up and announced that he 'had work to do' in his study, after which would be going to bed. As Corporal Williams was a permanent resident in the house, he would continue to attend to their needs and give Cee Bee a waking call in the morning.

Then, walking forward and bestowing a gallant kiss on the girl's forehead, he departed, leaving his guests slightly bemused and in two minds as to what each thought appropriate to follow. The girl, however, took control. Rising to her feet, she held out her hands to him.

"Let's switch off the lights and draw back the blackout curtains. There's a moon I think, and it should be warm enough to stand out on the verandah. Good idea?"

Rayne agreed, wordlessly, and they ventured out and stood facing the beauty of an evening in which a silver sheen shone on a wide, endless expanse of sands and distant line of water, and a million stars trembled in a black and cloudless sky.

There was total silence and, for a time each with swirling, tumbling thoughts in mind, neither said a word.

Then whispering, she remarked, "I didn't realise you had such a nice voice."

Rayne grinned into the darkness, "You forget, I was a choirboy for three years. Handel and I are old mates. I've sung his oratorios a hundred times. Moreover, my Mum was a concert singer, a Kathleen Ferrier contralto. Quite a celebrity in the northern concert halls."

The girl slipped her arm in his and they stood for a time in silence. "And what is our programme tomorrow?"

Rayne explained, "I'm on duty again at about 4 pm, so I shall have to start taking you back to Criccieth around noon. Before then, perhaps we can take a walk together on the sands, weather permitting, that is. Would that suit?"

He felt the girl nod. Then she asked: "Would I be able to go to church in the morning?"

Slightly taken aback, Rayne said, "Of course! If you wish. But I don't know of any church of your persuasion in the village. Do you need a Communion service?"

"Anything. I don't really mind, provided it's a church. Any old church. And as long as there's a book of words telling me when to stand up and sit down. I just want to say a prayer or two."

Obtusely, he asked, faintly amused, "What about, particularly?"

She turned towards him, calmly and, raising her face, "I just want to thank the Lord Jesus for giving me such a wonderful, glorious day with you today. And another to the Holy Mother, to keep you safe. Now and in the future."

Rayne felt himself swallowing and the tears begin to cloud his eyes.

He turned to grasp the girl lightly. Then said brokenly, "That was a very lovely thought. Now may I kiss you?"

Taking a deep breath, she whispered, "I shall be very cross if you don't!"

Which they did. Lightly and brotherly at first. Then with great depth of feeling.

And it was at that point that Squadron Leader Marcus Rayne from Llanbedr and Wren Siobhan Fitzgerald from Pwllheli, each realised they were passionately in love.

Finally, and when they had drawn apart, she whispered, "And now . . . may I be allowed to call you Windy?"

And he had smiled down at her, "Provided I can call you Annabel May."

He allowed an extra hour to enable her to attend church, so that it was about 10.30 when he stopped his car outside the Station Commander's house. She was already in her naval uniform, her glorious hair pinned firmly into regulation style and place.

She greeted him with a smile but her face seemed unusually serene and quiet. They touched hands but did not kiss. He did not mention her church visit.

Instead, he exclaimed cheerfully, "Your prayers obviously had some effect on the weather man. I have seldom seen so beautiful a morning in Wales. Are you still in the mood for a walk on the beach?"

The girl merely smiled an agreement but did not speak other than to say, "I'll have to change into my walking shoes."

As they descended the wooden steps to the beach, and walked towards the far-distant waterline, Rayne said lightly, "We must be the only people north of Aberystwyth out on the sands this morning."

Without answering, she smiled again and held out a hand, and together they walked on in silence.

A little disturbed he asked, "You seem very quiet this morning. Is there anything wrong? Anything to do with last night?"

The girl shook her head vigorously and after a short time, threw back her head and pulled him into a run.

"Oh, the morning is so beautiful and wonderful, it's good to be alive. Alive! Alive! Let's run, and run, and run! Right down to wherever it is, to the place you mentioned - Aber-something!"

He followed her, laughing. "But Aberystwyth is 60 miles away, you goose!"

"Never mind!" She was running hard, like a boy. "We can both get there this morning."

Her legs flying, he then was obliged to follow, thinking, "We are out of our minds! What will people think?" A Squadron Leader and a Wren, both in full uniform, capering about like two kids on an empty beach, on a Sunday morning.

Within about 200 yards he was catching her up when she stopped suddenly and turned, panting. "1 can't really run properly in this skirt." And her face alight, she suddenly said, "Please kiss me! Hard! I so want you to kiss me! Now! Please?"

And they fell into each other's arms. There, on that vast, desolate sandy beach of Cardigan Bay. With Rayne thinking, "This is simply not happening. What are people watching going to think? Here, on a Sunday. In Wales!"

But laughing still, he did as she asked. And they remained. As one. For several minutes. Happy and content.

Then, feeling wet on his face, he stood back and looked down at her. "You're crying! Why? This is a celebration. This is no time for tears."

"It's because I'm happy! Oh, so happy! But frightened, too. And sad. There are so many unhappy people in this world. At this very moment! And I suddenly thought of them. Those who have just lost someone dear to them. Someone killed." She suddenly hugged him so tightly that he gasped. "Don't you ever get yourself killed. Will you? Ever! Because I would die, too, if you did. I just couldn't bear it a second time." She shook her head. "I just couldn't bear it!"

They set off shortly before 1 pm. She was wearing her sailor's hat which Rayne found so amusing, as she sat beside him in silence. From time to time, he glanced in her direction but she sat solemn-faced.

"It's just like going back to school, isn't it?" He tried to be jocular but apart from a little nod, there was no response

At one point, Rayne noticed tears in her eyes, but decided not to comment, feeling thoroughly uncomfortable himself and not knowing what precisely to say. Once she commented on the scenery but only in a sentence. Otherwise – nothing!

When finally they reached the outskirts of Criccieth she said, "Could you leave me well before the 'bus stop? "

To which he responded jocularly, " Ashamed of me are you? "

And she had shaken her head without looking at him or smiling. Then, when they had drawn up at their chosen spot, she remained seated, looking ahead.

She turned then and said brokenly, "I just don't want to leave you, you know that!" Her face was crumbling.

"You're not leaving me. We are just separating for a short time. Nothing dreadful is going to happen to either of us and we'll soon be seeing each other again."

"You'll write to me, won't you? And telephone now and then? Tell me what you're doing?"

"Of course I will. I'll keep in touch, I promise."

Silence. A long silence.

He stretched out a hand. " Annabel May . . . I love you !"

And she surprised him a little by replying, almost shouting, "I know you do! And I love you, too! Desperately! That's what so upsets me. Because I'm so happy, I feel guilty. It shouldn't be happening in so short a time, And I feel as though it can't last. Which terrifies me. I just . . . I just ache with love and I don't know what to do. It's so . . . ! Oh, I am so unhappy . . . being happy!"

Finally, with an effort she turned and suddenly smiled, blinking away her tears. "I have to go, now. So kiss me once. Just once. And leave. I don't want you to stay. Please?"

Rayne nodded and said quietly, "If that's what you want."

Then, bending forward, he kissed her gently, once more feeling the wetness on her face.

When she had left the car with her bag and begun to walk quickly away, he started up and left immediately. Neither of them looked back.

Chapter Four

Marcus Rayne would not see his Wren girl friend for more than a month. It was, however, to be a month of incident.

Having flown one night with elements of his squadron as part of their normal training routine, he had partaken of his usual night-flying supper - the traditional bacon, eggs, and rock-hard squares of fried bread - before retiring to his bed at about 3 am.

He had flown twice and endured a tiring night. Sleeping well beyond his usual 7.30 am, he would have slept longer, had he not been awakened by his batman with a hushed voice and some firm shaking.

He came to, slowly and irritably.

"The telephone, sir! You're wanted on the telephone!" His batman's voice, quiet but urgent.

In a peevish voice, Rayne grumbled, "Telephone! Telephone! Who on earth wants me at this time of the morning. Don't they know - ?"

The batman interrupted, "It's the Station Commander, sir. He wants to speak to you immediately. Something pretty important it seems."

Rayne stifled a holy word and getting to his feet slowly, he walked into the corridor where the telephone was located. Picking up the receiver, he persuaded himself to be civil - if only just!

Wynn-Jones's voice came on, loud, excited, and unusually Welsh. "Marco, old chap! Great news! Guess what? You've been awarded a D.S.O! Telegrams and signals by the dozen are appearing on my desk. From the CAS and AOC downwards. Your parents, too! In fact everyone! It's just been promulgated in the London Gazette, apparently. The national and even the local papers have had the news already. Have you been doing something you haven't told me about? Congratulations anyway, old chap. We're all delighted here and the telephone is red hot. When you've surfaced, come to my office as soon as you can and we'll break open a bottle of milk - or something."

Rayne stood there. In his pyjamas. Stunned. Then gradually decided he was pleased. Delighted! - but only by degrees. For a time, he could not attune his mind to the message that had been passed to him. Then, in an instant, he thought of the pleasure it would give his parents. Then, strangely enough, Pamela Leggett. And finally - Wren Annabel May!

How extraordinary, he later thought - Annabel May! Wren Fitzgerald! Why particularly her? Then, when his brain was functioning at normal speed, he realised why. Of course! And why not? She was special.

Later in Wynn-Jones's office, there were the usual celebrations, which Rayne bore with exemplary patience, although his inclination was to hide himself away and savour the pleasure of it all in solitude. That same afternoon, however, he was delighted to receive a call from Pamela Leggett.

"Windy, my dearest love, I've just heard! What a hero you are! John and I insist that you come to a knees-up at Valley. We'll throw a party especially for you but it will have to be about a month hence, as we are just about to take a holiday in Scotland. John is having some leave and I am going with him, otherwise he will probably run off with some beautiful and more mature poppet. Until then, keep safe - and warm. For me, of course. Who else?"

Rayne remembered smiling. Dear old Pam!

July approached and the days began to slip by. The weather improved and it grew warmer, the mountains behind, green and silently beautiful, were dotted even more with sheep.

Rayne quietly celebrated his 23rd birthday and now had the red and blue ribbon of his newly awarded D.S.O. - sewn on his uniform by a lady in the village - alongside his three D.F.C.s and below his wings.

The Leggetts were still in Scotland and he found he missed them.

He was calmer in mind now, and flew regularly. He was sleeping better, too, and felt more rested. Even the state and morale of his squadron seemed to be improving. He had made a point of writing to Cee Bee once a week. Strangely, he still thought of her as Cee Bee and not as either Siobhan or Annabel May. His letters, whilst both amusing and endearing, were always restrained. He could not bring himself to write anything passionate - he was just not that type of person.

The girl wrote back just as regularly. In a bold firm hand, not at all like a girl or woman's writing. She, too, always expressed herself in affectionate terms, but as though she expected it to be censored. Neither telephoned the other. For him it was sufficient to know that she was close at hand. For her, it was as though she were guarding a secret - which she was!

The second incident of that intervening month occurred on 23rd July, which was a Friday.

At 10.35 am that day, Rayne, with three others of his Spitfires, were engaged on an attack and evasion exercise at altitude. The controller at Sector came over the air.

"Ganer Red Leader1 This is Lumba. What is your position and angels?"

Rayne responded drily. "Lumba from Red Leader: You should know! You're supposed to be controlling us."

But the controller was equal to the occasion.

"Humour me, Red Leader!"

Rayne grinned at the riposte. "I'm at 23,000 and about mid-way between you and the Island (Isle of Man). What is your problem?"

"Red Leader. I have a 'bogy' (unidentified aircraft) - or think so. About 120 miles south of you and travelling north. Do you think you will be able to play?"

"What angels?"

"No angels yet. Uncertain anyway."

Rayne examined his dashboard and saw that he had been airborne 28 minutes and had sufficient fuel for about another hour. A little less if he had to fight.

He answered immediately. "Lumba from Red Leader. Yes. Use us. Don't scramble any more of my unit unless I tell you, or you have to."

"Okay Red Leader. Vector Two-one-Zero. Stay at altitude until we have further information."

Rayne finished by contacting his section. "Red Section. Did you all get that?"

His three aircraft acknowledged, each one by clicking his transmitter.

The four Spitfires, now well spread out in battle formation, turned towards the south. Rayne considered the possibility of the interception ahead of them and the various factors involved. First, the three pilots with him were totally new. The two young officers and the single sergeant-pilot, were straight from Operational Training Units. They had neither shot at any enemy aircraft nor even encountered one. For them it would be their first blooding, with all the excitement and apprehensions such a minor conflict produced. They would have to be wooed, instructed and properly led.

Second, unless Lumba came up with some decent height information, they could well fly over the top of a single enemy aircraft and not even notice it; for him it had happened several times before, particularly when the enemy was low on the water.

Third, the `bogy' - if it became a 'bandit' - was probably a Junkers 88 bomber on an armed reconnaissance sortie over the Irish Sea. It would be spotting ships or convoys, but also briefed to attack any single target. And Ju88s, he knew to his cost, could be prickly rascals to engage. They were very fast, as tough as boots, and well armed.

Similarly, the new Dornier 217s. The original Dornier 17 he had always regarded as something of a soft touch. But not now! The 217 was a formidable bomber which, like the 88, could hit hard in return during any fight. Used mostly at night, it could more than hold its own during the day.

No, things were by no means straightforward. And he, for one, certainly didn't wish to end up in the water again. Particularly when so far away from a coastline where they were such limited rescue resources. No, once in a dinghy was enough for him, thank you very much!

All these thoughts passed sombrely through Rayne's head as he looked ahead and to his left and saw the distant coast of Anglesey drift slowly by. Below, was a vast expanse of grey water with only a few isolated dumplings of cumulus cloud at around 10,000 feet. He noted they were still at 23,000.

After a time Lumba came on again.

"Red Leader. We now have a definite plot of a 'bogy' which will probably became a hostile. Still no height information which suggests it is low on the water."

"Lumba from Red Leader. I agree. I will descend to 10,000. Any further information?"

"No, but your new vector is now 230 degrees. Target 72 miles ahead of you."

Rayne acknowledged the information and put on his thinking cap. Above all, he didn't want to fly over the top of an aircraft flying low on the water. It had happened so many times to him in the Mediterranean. On a sudden impulse, therefore, he took his formation down to 5,000 feet.

After about five minutes, Lumba again. "Red Leader. Still no height information. Target 43 miles ahead of you. Vector 240 degrees."

Rayne nodded to himself and acknowledged.

About fifteen minutes later, Rayne reckoned he was in the centre of the Irish Sea and about half-way between Dublin and Waterford. He had never been to southern Ireland except to Dublin as a child, but he knew the geography of the place. Only a few minutes more!

Then Lumba once more, the controller's voice higher pitched now with excitement. "Red Leader. Target now 10 miles ahead of you. Still going north. Vector 257 degrees. You should be seeing him about now."

Rayne frowned and pulled a face beneath his oxygen mask. They had passed the damn thing! He turned his formation gently to the right and scanned the leaden sea beneath, his gaze moving left to right in regular sweeps.

A minute later he saw it. Right down on the wave tops. No wonder they did not have a height on the blighter. He pressed his radio transmitter button. "Lumba from Red Leader. Tallyho! We have it! It's a Ju88. At sea level, going north. So, let's both shut up for a bit while we deal with it."

From Lumba, "Well done, Red Leader! Well done!"

To his formation Rayne added: "Stay at 5,000 feet. Red 2 will come with me to the left. Red 3 and 4 will stay on the right. And don't jump about!! I'm pretty sure he's not seen us yet."

With the enemy aircraft well in sight beneath him, Rayne passed slowly and carefully over the top of it, until he was about a mile behind, to its left, and into the sun. Then he carefully went though his cockpit drill, adjusting his gunsight for range and intensity of display, and slipping the catch on his cannons and machine-guns from 'Safe' to `Fire'.

He then increased the revs on his engine to 2,850 and pressed the override device which allowed him all the boost his engine was capable of delivering. Finally, he quickly checked over his instruments yet again and, with a conscious effort, released his harness release catch before pressing his shoulders firmly to the rear and replacing the catch, so that he was properly tied back and into place again.

After which, he spoke to his formation in a quiet, deliberate voice.

"Now, listen carefully! We can put paid to this chap down there if you do exactly as I tell you. First, put 60 feet on the wingspan dial on your gunsight. Then 150 yards on the range wheel. The target is flying at a steady 200, or thereabouts, so we'll need a closing speed of at least 300. Fire all guns together and in bursts of not more than two seconds. Close to within about 50 yards before breaking away upwards and, above all, do not fire when out of range. Attack in pairs, Red 2 and Red 4 in wide echelon port or starboard to confuse the rear gunners. Only one at a time to do the firing."

"I will attack first to draw any return fire and for God's sake don't fly into the water as this chap is pretty low. I believe he still hasn't seen us, which is all to the good. So, the best of luck and let's get on with it!"

Rayne's first movement was instantly picked up by the 88, which began a slow turn to the left and increased its speed.

He then began to dive into the line-astern position and saw at a swift glance that his speed was already well beyond the 300 mark. Settling himself directly behind his gunsight, he grimly focused his attention on the enemy aircraft, which was growing, rapidly in his windscreen like some Walt Disney cartoon villain. At the same time, he became aware of his No.2 bucking and swaying, some 100 yards to his left. So far, so good!

He was about 500 yards behind the German aircraft, when the rear gunner began to shoot at him. The tracer came out like a child's streamer, twisting and curving, slowly at first then with lightning speed. Familiar as he was with return fire from enemy bombers, he could not prevent himself instinctively ducking as the white trace flicked around his face and head, so close that he half expected to hear and feel the impact of the bullets.

But none came - or none that he was aware of.

Forcing himself to wait until the wings of the bomber entirely filled the space between the horizontal pink lines of his gunsight, he opened fire.

Immediately the two 20mm Hispano cannons began to thump mightily, almost drowning our the coarse chatter of the four machine guns. White streams of spark-flecked tracer reached out to envelop the tail and fuselage of the aircraft in front. The effect was instantaneous. A shower of dark fragments burst from the German aircraft, which seemed to stagger visibly as the result of the onslaught. As it did so, a savage, primitive feeling of satisfaction surged like an electric charge through Rayne's whole body, as he pressed his Spitfire forward, ever closer, until he was presented with two immediate problems. The first caused him to break away violently, upwards and to the left, in order to prevent his airscrew from striking the 88's tail. Second, in the last moments of firing, the starboard cannon in his aircraft stopped abruptly, sending his Spitfire slewing to one side.

Climbing away steeply, he looked back to take stock; the bomber was still there, turning slightly to the left, a thin dark smear emanating from the starboard wing root. Otherwise, there appeared to be little other damage. Then, in those brief intervening moments of watching, the second pair of Spitfires launched their attack.

The success of Rayne's most recent instruction was immediately evident. Red 3 was within 100 yards of the German aircraft's tail before Rayne saw the tell-tail black ripples of smoke emerge from beneath the Spitfire's wings as the pilot began to fire.

This time the effect was instantaneous. A sudden bubble of red appeared around the starboard engine and the 88 began to straighten up and lose speed. By the time his young officer colleague had finished his attack, the German bomber was clearly heading for Ireland, no doubt intent on an emergency landing there.

Without instructions from their leader, the four Spitfires reformed their battle formation and watched the efforts of the stricken bomber to maintain height and seek the safety of neutral territory.

All four watched it go. Silently. The bomber losing height and speed, the bubble of fire now increasing to a raging inferno of the most vivid crimson with a developing tail of black, billowing smoke. The German aircraft was dying. Soon it would be no more, either lost beneath the waves of the Irish Sea or shattered and burnt in some Irish pasture.

Rayne looked on. With both satisfaction but also with sadness. He disliked witnessing death in any form, either of an aircraft or of its human crew.

All four then turned for home.

The rapid exchange of congratulations between Lumba, Rayne and his three companions, soon, however, turned to less pleasant remarks. Red 2, on Rayne's right hand, suddenly informed his leader that there appeared to be a thin, dark stain of smoke or oil issuing from the rear of his engine. Rayne's heart gave a jump. Oh dear Lord! Not another one! Not again!

Keeping his voice level he said, "Drop behind me Red 2, and see if there is any obvious damage"

Within a minute his partner reported, "You appear you have been hit underneath. Not very badly, but enough. It looks like oil. Your bottom panels are all black."

Silent for some moments, Rayne let out a fluttering sigh. God Almighty! Forty-odd miles from the Welsh coast and this should happen!

To Lumba Control he said with admirable restraint, "Red Leader to Lumba. It seems I've been hit and am losing oil. Give me an immediate course to steer for the nearest point on the Welsh coast. And get the Air Sea Rescue boys prepared."

"How bad is it, Red Leader?"

Rayne said simply. "I wish I knew! My instruments are not showing anything at the moment. But anything more than a small leak and I'm in the water again!"

"Red Leader. Stand by!"

To which Rayne responded with grim humour, "Don't worry I I'm not going anywhere!"

Lumba came back almost immediately, sounding concerned. "We have you 32 miles from the nearest point in Wales. Steer 085 degrees. This will bring you close to your nearest diversion airfield, Brawdy. What angels have you?"

Rayne thought, to hell with security! It would be plain language for him from now on. Aloud, he said, "I'm at 5,000 feet and intend to stay here. I'll keep my No.2 with me in case I have to jump out again. Suggest you take Red 3 and 4 back to base and keep scrambling others of my unit until I'm picked up."

Lumba acknowledged and fell silent. Rayne, on the other hand, briefly closed his eyes and began to pray. Perhaps Cee Bee's God would lend a hand. Or even her Holy Mother. Four minutes later, Rayne's engine began to overheat. With rising despair, he watched the oil temperature increase and the pressure reduce. It was said that a Merlin would keep going for a full five minutes with no oil pressure at all. He hoped to heaven that that was the case!

Lumba came on again. "We now have you 12 miles from the coast, which should now be well within sight. What are your intentions?"

"My engine sounds very tired. If it stops over the sea, I'll bale out. If I make the coast, I'll land, wheels up. I'm not spending valuable time looking for Brawdy." He gave a grim smile. "I've been without oil pressure for some time now and the temperature is off the clock. I'm just sitting here - with my fingers and legs crossed!"

Lumba said quite unnecessarily, "Red Leader. You're doing fine!"

He was within two miles of the coastline when the airscrew of the Merlin engine, which had shown increasing signs of lethargy, finally tottered to a standstill. For one wild, impulsive moment, Rayne considered baling out immediately - he was still at 5,000 feet - but for no good reason, other than he suddenly decided he didn't wish to drop into the water again, he aimed his aircraft at a broad patch of tilting green hillside somewhere ahead and began to stretch the glide. Maintaining 120 miles per hour which, he reasoned, would enable him to manoeuvre quite steeply without stalling, he looked quickly about to ascertain which way he might land With his wheels still retracted, he knew he would only skid about 50 yards. There were no large trees to obstruct his crash-landing, but there were lines of stone walls running in several directions. Above all, he didn't want to hit any of the walls sideways on. Nor head on, for that matter!

Now gliding quite steeply, for a few moments he was in a mild state of panic, wondering at the last moment, where and in which direction he should put the aircraft down. And as he drifted towards the ground, he saw that the fields were not cultivated but merely scrubland and anything but flat.

Concentrating fiercely, he came to a decision and tilting his wings as steeply as he dared, he flicked down the small metal disc which activated the high pressure air system which lowered the flaps - it was all or nothing on a Spit. As he did so, the aircraft wallowed briefly so that he had to push down the nose quite sharply to maintain flying speed. Suddenly, the area before him seemed to open out - the hand of Providence, surely! And he forced the aircraft towards the ground which was now fairly streaking past below his cockpit.

At the last moment he saw quite sizeable stones - rocks! - immediately beneath and suddenly felt anguish for his aircraft, which he knew was unlikely ever to fly again. The Spitfire struck the ground hard at about 120 miles per hour, a violent, scraping, searing, lumpy, leaping excursion, which started straight but which, for some unaccountable reason, began to drift sideways. Instantly his mind screamed, 'No! No! Anything but sideways! The walls! And fire! Please, please, no fire!

During those last few moments, he was conscious of being hurled forward violently towards the dashboard. After which there was only noise, a flash light and searing pain . . . until finally, like a switch being turned off - blackness!

He came-to by degrees. Like a bubble of air rising slowly in a stagnant pool. His eyes focused with an effort on the artificial horizon on his dashboard, the tiny aircraft leaning drunkenly to one side, the gyros having stopped. Also, the airspeed indicator, which was registering nil.

So . . . he was still in the cockpit! That much was clear enough. There was also the noise of aircraft above him and, raising his head painfully, he saw there were three Spitfires - circling. Members of his squadron, he presumed

.   His senses slowly returning, he saw there was a mass of red/brown blood on his hands, down his front, and presumably on his face. He had obviously struck his head on something - probably the gunsight. And the right side of his body ached abominably. Oh, God! He didn't feel like moving Also, and to his concern, he saw that the ignition switches were still on and, reaching forward slowly and gingerly, he switched them off. He should have remembered to do that earlier.

He looked about. He must have been there for quite some time - possibly up to 15 minutes - and his Spit. looked very bent. Moreover, no one had been near him. The whole area was that isolated. Then, in the distance, three people, who were merely dots. Climbing the hillside towards him. They would help get him out. He didn't feel he had the strength to do it on his own. Lord above, he was shaken! And tired. So very tired. And a long way from home! But, he was alive, wasn't he? Alive!

Later, having been lifted painfully out of his cockpit and taken to a local farmhouse, he was given a cup of tea. After that, he was driven back to Llanbedr, where he arrived close to midnight. There, twelve stitches were inserted to repair a nasty cut above his nose, and strapping was applied for some badly bruised ribs. Later, he was credited with half a German aircraft - destroyed!

This last point he had disputed, arguing that he was only entitled to a quarter. After all, the other two chaps who didn't fire, had attracted the attention of the enemy and were therefore entitled to something, as they had made a contribution. Also, it increased their morale! Didn't it?

The AOC 9 Group telephoned to congratulate him,

When the Leggetts returned from their holiday in Scotland, Pamela immediately devoted herself to the business of arranging a party to celebrate Marcus Rayne's recent award of the D.S.O.

Pamela Leggett was well versed in knowing whom exactly to invite, and why. Strangely, whilst she seldom thought of her own husband's advancement, she always felt that her young friend Marco was destined for high office. John, ten years her senior, she loved and respected as a staid and comfortable companion, but not as an inspirational leader of zeal and ability. Moreover, he was on night-fighters, wasn't he? Not in the glamour-boy, day-fighter business, flying Hurricanes, Spitfires, Typhoons and the like, and shooting down heaven knows how many Huns.

With considerable pains, she sorted out the possibles, the important, and the necessary. There would be about 30, she reckoned, the venue her own married quarter - after consider-ing and rejecting the officers' mess. The day would be a Friday, not a Saturday or Sunday. And, towards the middle or end of August would be as good a time as any. Then, for the few she didn't wish to see included, she could always argue that she had thought they would be on holiday. A glamorous but devious lady was Pamela Leggett.

Satisfied finally with her line-up, she sat and wrote the invitations. They included one for her hero, Squadron Leader Marcus W. Rayne, DSO, DFC**, RAF (of course!), and another for Wren Siobhan Fitzgerald of the Royal Naval Station, Pwllheli. The invitations reached them two days later.

He was sitting in his office when the telephone rang. Automatically he picked it up and said, "Rayne".

A female voice said quietly, "It's me!"

Rayne smiled. "I know it is. I recognised your voice."

"Where are you and what are you doing?"

"Doing? I'm sitting in my office - where you fitted on your parachute. And I'm not doing anything, just sitting and thinking. Because I'm very sore still. And because I can't fly."

"Why are you sore?"

"Because I had to crash-land my aircraft the other day. D id you not know?"

Her voice, now slightly raised and full of concern. "Was that when that German was shot down? It mentioned Spitfires in the papers, but it didn't say anyone crashed. I take it that was you?"

"I was there, yes. One of four involved.. The only one hit by return fire; the only one who had to crash miles south of here. I bumped my head and hurt my side - which is why I'm sore!"

A brief silence. Then: "Gosh! I'm truly sorry. I didn't know." Then another pause, "I'm so glad you're safe. You see . . . prayers do work!"

Rayne smiled. " Sometimes! Not always. But I'll give you the benefit of the doubt."

Another brief silence.

Then: "This is the first time I've ever rung you, you know that?"

"Yes, I know. For anything . . . special?"

"Yes. Well, several things. The first was I just wanted to hear your voice."

"I see. And the second?"

"To congratulate you on your medal. Which I read about."

"Yes?"

"The third was to say that I've had an invitation to Valley. Next month. I imagine you had one too. Have you?"

"Yes. It arrived this morning. And . . . ?"

"Well, there was something else I wanted to tell you. But . . . that can wait until later."

"No, come on. What was it?"

"No, it can wait. It's not that important, anyway." Then, in the same quiet voice, "Are we being overheard?"

Rayne smiled. "Could be. I really don't know."

"Then I suppose it wouldn't be proper for me to say, 'I love you'. Would it?"

"No, it really wouldn't be proper. And it would be quite improper for me to say, 'I love you', back. I suppose."

"Then, we'd better not say it. Had we?"

"I absolutely agree."

"Right. Then I'll see you a few weeks hence."

"I shall look forward to it. Oh, and I forgot. I have something to ask you."

"You have? What was it?"

"Like yours. It'll wait. Till then."

"Oh! So . . . it's really goodbye then."

"Yes. It's goodbye! For the moment. And thank you for ringing."

He was fit enough - just - to fly up to Valley on the occasion of Pamela's party. His ribs still desperately sore, fitting on his parachute harness was very painful.

John Leggett was there with his car again when he landed and greeted him with a friendly smile as Rayne threw his kit in the back seat and climbed painfully into the front.

John said, "Pam was afraid that you might have lost your good looks as the result of your prang. But you look alright to me, although you can still see the stitches a bit and the wound. Are you in good heart otherwise?"

"Apart from not being able to fly regularly and take part in anything, yes. I'm afraid I'm not a very good patient."

John nodded. "Right. My instructions are to take you home, where you'll be staying the night. Where Pam is also waiting to give you tea and comfort. However, I'll have to leave you there as I have something to do. Okay?"

Rayne smiled in response. "That'll be fine. How lucky I am to have friends like the Leggetts."

When Pamela Leggett opened the door of her quarter, she planted a firm kiss on his mouth before standing back and examining his wound.

"We heard it was very much worse, so I naturally thought your beautiful profile would be seriously damaged. Still it was nasty old cut and it has left quite a dent in your head, dear boy. That's what comes from fighting, isn't it? Turning, she led the way into the kitchen calling over her shoulder, "We'll have tea in here. Around the table. I want to have a serious talk with you."

Having sat down, Pamela poured the tea in silence, then pushed across to him some scones, butter and jam.

"Muck in! And not a word if you don't like my cooking because that's all my fat ration for a week!"

Rayne did as he was instructed. And waited.

Pam started. "And how did your meeting with Cee Bee go down?"

Rayne frowned. "I don't remember mentioning it to you."

"You didn't, but there's not much goes on around here than I don't know about."

Rayne shook his head. "Well . . . it went down very well indeed. I met her at Criccieth, took her flying at Llanbedr, walked the hills in the afternoon, had dinner with Wynn-Jones that night, and all in all had a very pleasant time. And!" - he rolled his eyes accusingly - "I learnt a lot about her, and you! I now know, for example, that you and she are old school chums - which explains a great deal. And that she is an enormously talented young lady. She is a musician, plays the piano beautifully, knows a lot about art and is an artist to boot, and is also something of a linguist. In fact, a whole raft of accomplishments."

Pamela nodded. "And is she the one? For you, I mean. In short, do you love her?"

Rayne, for a moment, was taken aback by Pamela's directness. Then, after a second or two: "Yes, I think I do. In fact, I'm sure I do."

"And does she love you?"

Rayne shrugged. "She says she does and I believe she means it. But, there is - was - a hiccup in her life apparently, which makes it difficult for her to completely let herself go. It seems she loved someone else before, a pilot who was killed, and she is always in fear of it happening again. That's why I get the feeling she wishes, sometimes, to keep me at arm's length."

Pamela nodded, but said nothing.

Rayne went on, "Did you ever meet her boyfriend or know anything about him? If you did, it would help if I knew a little more than I do."

Pamela shook her head. "No, I knew of her love for someone but we never met. And, anyway, I think that is something you will have to sort out with her; I don't think it would be right for me to get involved - even if I knew anything, which I don't."

There was a silence until Pamela stretched out a hand to take his across the table.

"Windy, my love. Listen to me! I have loved you all my life, and still do. When you were about 18, I used to pray that you would make love to me - take me to bed. But, I don't think the thought ever crossed your mind, did it? You were so preoccupied with your bloody aeroplanes that you never thought of me except as a mate. A chum. Someone who would play tennis with you when needed. Or football. Rugby even. When, all the time I wanted to be loved "

"Then, of course, the war came and off you went. And I was obliged to go my own way and finally married John. Because he was there, and because he was nice, and comfortable, and paid me compliments. But all the time, I wanted you. And there you were, sitting in a flippin' desert somewhere, shooting things down by the hatfull and not giving me, or anyone else, a thought."

"And now this Siobhan girl has turned up - two years my junior - and you've fallen for her, because she young and beautiful and talented. And I'm terribly envious, I admit it. Not jealous, mind you, because I have made my choice and am stuck with it - till death do us part, and all that. And because I want you both to be happy and be together. Which I'm sure you will be, provided you don't make the mistake of regarding her merely as a chum, but someone to be loved. Ardently. With a passion. "

"So, sweep her off her feet! Make love to her, if you haven't already done so. Because then you will really know. If it's right for you both, the knot will be tied and you'll know it. If it isn't, you'll know that too, and your affair will come to an end with little harm done "

Rayne responded mildly, "Pamela, dear heart! I've only seen the girl on three occasions and been out with her for one. Hardly a reason or excuse for me to take her to bed."

"Well, them's me views, so see that you bear them in mind." She stood up. "And now, let me show you to your room and suggest that you make yourself scarce until the guests arrive. Okay?"

The party was in full swing and Rayne was listening to a senior wife telling him how brave he had been to shoot down that German aircraft and end up wounded. He was about, to disagree with both assertions when he looked across the room and saw Pamela greeting Cee Bee, who had just come in.

His heart missed a beat. The girl was in the green ball-gown she had worn when he had first seen her. She was smiling, talking animatedly and looked stunning. After some moments, Pamela looked in his direction and motioned him across with a jerk of her head. As he approached, in her formally mischievous voice she said, "You'll remember this copper-haired hussy, I take it?"

To which Rayne, holding out his hand, lied pleasantly, "No, I don't believe we've met.' Then, in a sideways hiss, "Is this the one I have to kiss passionately and sweep off her feet?"

Pam, feigning outrage. "Don't let it even cross your evil mind, my lad!' Then, with a wink, "But, if you do want to kiss her passionately, take her into the kitchen later on and I'll guard the door!"

As Cee Bee's glances went from one to other in wide-eyed surprise, Pamela went on: "By the way, I've asked the Station Commander, Ramsbottom-Ish, to say a few words about your gong, and so on. So don't be surprised." Then, making to leave, "And don't you two go holding hands all the time, will you? Someone is bound to notice and think there's something naughty going on."

When Pamela had departed, Cee Bee asked, "What on earth was all that about?"

Rayne smiled a little sheepishly, "Our irrepressible Pam! This afternoon she was counselling me to sweep you off your feet, be passionate with you, then whisk you off into bed." He grinned. "But I said I'd speak to you about it first."

"I was going to say! Don't I get a say in all this?" Then, feeling around a little for his hand, "Not a bad idea, though. All at the right time, of course!"

A little later, Pamela's head appeared above the throng, a wine glass and spoon in her hands. Tinkling one with the other she raised her voice. "Friends! As this is in part a celebration of something, I am going to ask the Station Commander to say a few words."

Amid a thin round of applause, Group Captain Ramsbotton-Isherwood climbed onto a small stood, announcing in a broad New Zealand accent, "I'm such a short bugger, I have to stand on this stool to be seen. You'll have no trouble hearing me, though."

After renewed, more hearty applause, he them began to eulogise about a certain very young squadron leader in his Sector who had recently been awarded the D.S.O. And had even more recently, added to his fame by shooting down a German bomber which had so rudely ventured into their part of the Irish Sea.

On and on he went, with Rayne, a glacial smile on his face, listening to it all. He was profoundly embarrassed, his only respite coming when Cee Bee, who was standing beside him, dug him in the ribs and whispered in her pantomime Irish, "Who's t'is fella he's talken about?" Which so reduced him to giggles, he couldn't stop and obliged him to turn aside and hide his face.

Finally it was all over and Rayne, with Cee Bee in tow, departed to a corner to recover.

He started. "Now, young lady, what's this thing you wanted to tell me? No shenanigans this time!"

The girl gave a resigned shrug. "Only that I'll be leaving Pwllheli shortly. I'm being commissioned!"

Rayne could not prevent his mouth from falling open. "Commissioned! When? And where will you be going?"

The girl shrugged, "It's not official yet, but I've been through all the interviews and things, and I've been told I've been selected. Now, I have to go to some training place or other and become an officer, tricorn hat an' all!"

The humour of the situation struck him immediately.

"So you'll lose your lovely white sailor's hat! What a tragedy! And those tricorn things are useless in the rain, you know that?"

The girl's smile was forced. "I wasn't frightfully keen I'm afraid, and I rather put their backs up. I said I didn't want to do cyphers or admin, but they pointed out the there were many other openings, in Intelligence, Personal Assistant appointments to Admirals, and even jobs in the newish Fleet Air Arm Fighter Control Centres they are organising. Anyway, the die is cast and I'm off - sooner or later."

For a time they were both silent. Finally, she said, "So there! And now, what was it you wanted to ask me? Do you remember mentioning it?"

Rayne smiled wanly, "I remember only too well." A pause. "I was going to ask you to come to London with me on your next few days off. Not a naughty week-end or anything like that, but just to see the sights, do a show or two, and have a few meals." He then took a deep breath. "I would also like you to meet my parents. They live on the northern outskirts of London. But now . . . well, how it all fits in with your new arrangements, I really don't know. If it fits in at all So . . . how do you feel?"

Rayne watched the girl's face - serious, sad and cautious in turn, but still with a faint smile in her eyes. Watched her swallow. Then breathe in and out deeply, several times.

Finally she said, "Would you leave it with me for a bit. You know what my problem is. So you'll understand I need to think about it. But . . . it's a lovely thought and you're very kind." Then she grinned, her face lighting up. "My hero!"

Feeling somehow crushed and disappointed, Rayne realised they had not been mingling. As the party had been mainly for his benefit, he suddenly recognised that he had an obligation to mix and talk. Obviously feeling much the same, the girl, too, turned with a wan smile and joined an adjacent group.

The evening proceeded. For both Rayne and Cee Bee, the party had suddenly flopped. From time to time, each looked at the other in the distance - and smiled. Another hour passed. Rayne felt he hadn't the heart to utter another sentence or drink another drink. For him the night was over. Then, all at once, he had Pamela at his side, her face bright, her eyes understanding.

She asked briskly, "Have you taken her into the kitchen yet?" Then when his face revealed his despondency, she punched him hard in the arm, "Come on Windy, pecker up! Give the girl a big hug and a kiss and snap out of your misery." She winked. "You go in now and I'll bring her to you in a moment."

Somewhat encouraged but still with a long face, Rayne slowly walked off and soon found himself leaning against a crowded works surface in the empty kitchen. This was all a waste of time, of course. But . . . Then, after a time, another door was opening slowly, and there she was. Smiling. A little apprehensively, he thought.

She said in an uncertain voice, "I've come to be kissed and swept off my feet!" A deep breath. "And Pam says she not going to let me go home until you've had your wicked way with me." Then, with tears in her eyes she moved forward quickly and wrapped her arms around him. "Oh, Windy, I do so love you. I'll come to London with you. Of course I will. Anywhere! Anytime! So . . . please?"

And she held up what to Rayne was the most beautiful face in the world. To be kissed.

Almost three weeks were to pass before they were able to plan their trip to London. They made their arrangements over the telephone. They would go by train - the Irish Mail - from Holyhead in Anglesey. On a Friday. This would give them two nights in London and leave them Sunday to call on Rayne's parents, before making the return journey to Wales.

"I've booked us in at the Piccadilly Hotel," Rayne announced, "Which is right in the centre of pretty well everything." Then, when Cee Bee made no comment, he went on a trifle hastily, "I've stayed there before and it's rather grand."

At this, the girl had declared loftily. "I would have expected no less!" Then, with a nervous giggle, "Do you realise that this will be the first time I've been to London since the war. And, of course, since all the bombing. D'you think the Germans will know we're coming?"

"I'm sure the Huns will have it all marked down in their diaries. Anyway, just as long as you've got your gas mask and tin hat - ."

"Oh, Lord! Do you really mean that? Seriously? Because I haven't got a tin hat!"

"Cee Bee, I'm pulling your leg! Forget about the bombs. Forget about the tin hat. Forget about everything - other than me, that is!"

As they crossed London on the rattling, clanging, jerking tube-trains, Rayne watched Cee Bee's wide-eyed amazement as she surveyed the underground station platforms, crowded with the thousands who had already taken up their night-time positions on make-shift beds and blankets in anticipation of the almost constant bombing visits by the Luftwaffe. And, above ground, by the hundreds of stationary, silent, 'blimp' balloons which, trailing their curving spider-web wires, appeared to be holding London firmly in position.

And finally, the teeming thousands of servicemen. With their inevitable gas masks. Walking! Talking! Laughing! Pressing to and fro. On the pavements and in the roads and streets. Every uniform - Army, Navy and Air Force - not only British, but also from every nation, it seemed, on earth. Gosh! She was stunned into silence. So much going on. So much noise and bustle. And stinks! Oh, Lord! The red double-decker London buses, and taxis, everything, each with its distinctive cloud of blue, acrid smoke. And all the suppressed excitement. No, there was nothing like this in Wales. In the north even, including the bigger cities of Liverpool and Manchester.

Her introduction to the Piccadilly Hotel also produced some merriment. As Rayne solemnly signed the hotel register in the company of three reception clerks, Cee Bee, with a straight face and in a voice purporting to be a whisper, asked: "Do you want me to put the ring on now, or wait till later?"

Everyone within hearing distance, went silent. Some feigned polite horror, a few produced quirky smiles, one or two, managed to keep a straight face.

Rayne, however, rose admirably to the occasion. Continuing to write without interruption, he eventually favoured the female receptionist with a tolerant smile. "Extraordinary what one's Irish cousin comes out with from time to time. Don't you agree?"

And with a twinkle in her eye, the woman tilted her head knowingly, whilst, alongside, Cee Bee struggled to keep a blank face.

When they had ascended to their second floor suite and their bags had been delivered, Cee Bee gave a squeal of delight and pirouetted around the room.

"Gosh! This is super! And so large! Is this my room or yours. And isn't it all going to cost a mint?"

Rayne grinned. "The bathroom is next door - en suite - and there's a similar bedroom the other side. Yours or mine, it doesn't matter."

The girl went to the tall windows and looked down into the street below. Then she wandered back and put her arms around his waist.

"Two rooms! You needn't have gone to all this trouble, you know. I wouldn't have minded. Really. Just as long as I can put my nightie on in private. Shades of my old school dorm, and all that."

Rayne smiled. "We agreed. So this is how it will be. Okay?"

She broke away suddenly. "I shall need to change. Then I want to go out and feed the ducks in St. James's Park. My parents brought me when I was very small."

"All right. As long as we can fit in tea and cucumber sandwiches at the Mayfair."

At this the girl gave another squeal and reaching up, kissed his cheek. "Gosh! This really is living!"

The visit to the ducks was a simple joy. Rayne noted that the girl threw athletically, like a boy. Earlier, she had gone down to the hotel dining room despite his protests, and had come back with two bags full of bread and cake.

After that, the Mayfair, with Cee Bee silent, her eyes on her cheeks.

She said roguishly, "I have a feeling you've done all this before. With someone else. Have you?"

To which Rayne had answered mysteriously, "We all have our secrets. "

"All right then, Mystery Marc, what are we doing next? "

"We're going to the flicks. In Leicester Square. To see Henry Fonda and that French girl, Annabel, in 'Wings of the Morning.' I chose it especially because of her name. It was either that or Charlie Chaplin. Which I thought would be a bit low-brow for you. Does it suit?"

"Of course! Anything!" The girl gave a little jump of excited approval which made her escort smile again. She really was a child. But a beautiful, talented child. And as bright as a button.

Later, they walked down Piccadilly and into Leicester Square, arm in arm and through the seething crowds. Each caught up in the excitement and the press of all the people after the isolation of their stations in Wales.

The girl said brightly as she clung to him, "See? If I were in uniform, I wouldn't be able to do this, would I?" Then, as they passed Austin Reed's at the end of Regent Street, among other uniforms they were displaying, was that of a junior Wren officer.

She crowed, "There! That's what I shall look like when next you see me. I've decided I really quite like that silly hat."

In the scented darkness of the cinema, they were led to their seats by a nodding flashlight. She hissed, "Lets have one of these double ones, should we? Where we can hold hands."

To which Rayne replied. "Hands! Is that all?"

And she had looked up at him and grinned - but said nothing.

About half-way through the main film, the then fairly commonplace notice was displayed on the screen:

An air raid alarm has just been sounded
A further warning will be issued if danger is considered
imminent and this programme may be discontinued.

Feeling no response from his companion, Rayne looked down. Cee Bee, her head on his shoulder, was fast asleep!

It was close on 11 pm when they emerged from the cinema. The streets were still crowded and there was the mutter of guns in the distance. Overhead, the thin drone of enemy bombers could be heard above the subdued chatter of the multitude. There were no lights anywhere.

When a clutch of searchlights again moved quickly across the undersides of the clouds, the girl stopped and looked up. "Is there an air-raid on?"

Rayne squeezed her hand. "It was announced on the screen in the cinema, you chump, but you were fast asleep."

"But no one seems to be taking any notice."

Rayne stopped to watch the searchlights again move across the clouds. "When you've been bombed by day and by night for more than two years, you tend to treat air raids fairly lightly." Then, when the staccato 'tonk-tonk-tonk' came from fairly close at hand, he went on, "Those were the guns in Hyde Park, I imagine. It's too far for us to walk up there tonight, but perhaps tomorrow we can go and look at them." Then, glancing down into her face, "This is all rather new to you, isn't it? Are you frightened?"

"Frightened! No, not frightened. Just interested. Anyway . . . with you around, how could I be?"

As she squeezed his arm, he smiled in her direction to see if she were joking. But her face quite straight, he saw that she wasn't.

Once in their hotel, they went immediately to the room they had decided was his. Quietly. Without speaking. There, they stood for a time, hand in hand, facing each other, their minds considering similar thoughts, thoughts neither of them felt they could mention.

Presently, he leaned forward and kissed her gently on the forehead. "It's been a long day for both of us. I think you should have a bath and go to bed. Then we both shall be bright-eyed and bushy-tailed in the morning. With a full programme ahead of us. Don't you think?"

She smiled. A little sadly, he thought. "Whatever my hero says!"

Then, closing her eyes, she held up her face to be kissed.

There were enemy bombers overhead for most of the night. As he lay awake, listening, the guns kept up their occasional response to the louder bangs he thought might be bombs exploding in the distance.

But they were sounds he had heard a hundred times before, so that he was neither unduly interested nor perturbed. He knew that shortly after midnight, the raid would be over and London could sleep again in peace. People in their homes and their tenement blocks. In their bomb shelters. Stretched out in grotesque postures on the scores of underground platforms. Everyone. Everywhere. Asleep or talking in subdued voices.

By dawn, the 'All Clear' had sounded and London had become alive again. To deal with the casualties and take stock of the damage caused in the night.

He rose early and, after knocking on their adjoining door, he entered to find the girl sitting up in bed, looking rumpled and sleepy still.

He said, "I see the air raid didn't worry you unduly last night."

"What air raid? After that long day yesterday, I could have slept through the invasion of Europe!"

She stretched like a cat, yawned, then pushing a hand through her magnificent hair, smiled up at him. He smiled in return, thinking how beautiful she looked and how important she was to him. He suddenly wanted to tell her precisely that. To explain how much he loved her, that he wanted to touch her tenderly, and for her to be part of his life for ever. But the thoughts and even the words seeming so inappropriate for that time of the morning, he simply added, "The weather being wonderfully fine, I thought we might walk up to Hyde Park and visit the guns that kept me, if not you, awake all last night. After that, we can have lunch at Claridges."

To this she had responded shrilly, "Claridges! What on earth! Have you come into a fortune?"

And he had explained patiently, "By Government edict, all meals cost five shillings, whether you eat at Claridges or Lyons Corner House. And as Claridges offers the best five-bob's worth anywhere, we won't be breaking any bank."

He went to the window and drew back the heavy blackout curtains. "After that, perhaps we can have tea at the RAF Club and discuss what we might do for the evening. I have a yen for an Ivor Novello play somewhere. I've always loved Mary Ellis, who is usually in one or other of his presentations, but you can choose. The theatres are not usually full at this time of the year, particularly during the bombing."

The girl, suddenly galvanised into action, threw back the bed-clothes. "Right! In that case, if you'll hop it for a moment, I'll get dressed." Then throwing him a quick grin. "Unless you want to stay and watch. Although I don't think there'll be anything on display that other girls haven't got - if you'll pardon my Shakespearian English!"

After breakfasting well, they walked out into the morning sunshine, both of them happy and light-hearted. He, because of the beautiful and garrulous partner who clung to his arm; she, because of her handsome and highly decorated escort, clad in his best uniform. And the prospect of a full and interesting day ahead of her.

Walking up Piccadilly, she suddenly insisted on making a detour into Bond Street, explaining that she loved expensive places and the sight of diamonds en masse! Rolling his eyes in apparent dismay, Rayne accepted the inevitable.

Hyde Park was full of guns between their associated huts, emplacements and moving soldiers. The girl eyed them solemnly and wonderingly. Thus far, she had encountered war only from a distance. Here it was a very tangible reality, with the long snouts of the clustered 3.7 inch anti-aircraft guns pointing menacingly and obliquely into the heavens. Somehow, they made her feel vulnerable and physically uncomfortable, a sensation she experienced but did not mention. Instead, she remained silent but showed no reluctance when he stayed only for several minutes before leading her away.

Walking down Park Lane, he pointed out the various nationally known hotels, commenting once, "That's the Grosvenor House over there. There used to be an Officers' Sunday Club tea dance which was held there each Sunday. Run by a group of blue-blooded ladies as a sort of war work, it was a popular gathering spot during the early part of the war. I used to go there pretty regularly when I was flying from North Weald during the Battle of Britain."

And the girl had grinned. "Where you picked up some nubile daughters of Duchesses, I'll be bound?"

And he had answered with a smile. "I came across one or two, I have to admit But they all had tastes far too expensive for me, alas. Don't forget my salary in those days was 11 shillings and 10 pence a day. Which hardly got me beyond the liveried doorman in any of the hotels in this area."

Later, they took a taxi to Claridges.

Luncheon was laid out on an enormous central table in one of the lower dining rooms, a mass of a hundred or more plates and dishes of hors d'oeuvres of every type and description, which had them both silent with awe and admiration.

The girl whispered, "With rationing and all that, how on earth do they produce this sort of food?"

And Rayne had whispered back "I don't know and I'm not about to ask. All I do know is that they still charge five shillings a head - so tuck in and eat your five bob's worth!"

This she did, to the full, entertaining the silent, munching Rayne meanwhile with a flow of comment, patter and stories, related now and then in her 'pantomime Irish'. All the time her eyes were dancing and for ever on the move, the girl clearly enjoying every moment of the experience. The lunch completed, they walked out into the sunshine again.

She enquired, "Where now?"

"Well, I wanted to take you to the RAF Club for tea. But as you've eaten so much - !"

The girl interrupted him gaily, "Fret you not! I have an Irish navvy's appetite. Tell you what, though, let's take a 'bus to Westminster Abbey. I want to see Poet's Corner again." And as she pulled him by the arm, he followed with a resigned smile and a shake of his head.

In Westminster Abbey, she once more became a changed person - solemn, wide-eyed and serious - examining in silence the slate and marble tablets underfoot, and the inscribed panels.

All the time, he followed in the wake of her faint perfume, fascinated by her uniqueness and attractiveness, being overwhelmed by her aura and very presence. She was so utterly different. Unlike anyone else he had ever met before. This girl, he knew . . . yes, he positively knew, he loved. Above everything, he loved her!

It was almost 5 pm when, seated in a taxi en route to the RAF Club in Piccadilly, Rayne found himself uncharacteristically on edge. He had been a member since 1940 and was well aware that it was a 'gentlemen's establishment'. Ladies were only admitted occasionally and on sufferance, being 'let in' usually through the tradesmen's entrance at the rear. But how on earth could he explain this to his attractive guest, who was sitting alongside, brightly interested in everything around her and clearly with every expectation of being royally entertained. In the event, however, his misgivings were unfounded.

On entering the portals of 128 Piccadilly, they were met by a grave and impressive looking flunkey who cast an immediate and critical eye over Rayne, his attractive guest, Rayne's youth, rank, and array of decorations, and the young man's obvious uncertainty. He anticipated Rayne's unsaid question with a polite gesture and some quiet advice.

"On the first floor, sir, if you are thinking of taking tea. You will have to hurry though, as it's getting rather late."

Vastly relieved, Rayne led the way up a wide flight of stairs, whose flanking walls were covered with magnificent oil paintings of aircraft of the present and former generations, all in vivid settings of war and peace, being aware of Cee Bee's fascinated and silent appraisal.

In the elegant Sitting Room, he was relieved to see that there were several small mixed groups still surrounding tables laid out with the paraphernalia of tea. They sat down and ordered, whispering together and listening meanwhile to the subdued conversation and laughter in the far corners of the room.

Behind him, Rayne was aware of a tall figure in uniform bending over and in conversation with a lady in one of the distant groups. He noted, too, that Cee Bee, was looking in the man's direction with a knowing smile on her face.

Their tea and food arriving, whilst offering a plate of sandwiches, he allowed her to pour the tea, aware that the girl's glance was straying now and then over his shoulder, the smile still on her lips. After some moments, he could no longer restrain himself.

"What, or who, is amusing you?"

His companion's voice was a whisper. "That chap over there! I've met him before. Some years ago. No, don't look round! In a minute, he'll come in our direction."

Now consumed with interest, Rayne waited until he saw the girl's smile broaden and her figure tense and about to rise. He turned. Bearing down on them was the massive figure of a gentleman in full uniform. Wearing the rank stripes of a Marshal of the Royal Air Force! Lord Trenchard! He recognised him at once and instinctively rose to his feet, the girl with him.

The Air Marshal approached, smiling, a craggy hand outstretched. "I seem to recognise your face. Has it been in the papers recently?" He glanced at Rayne's decorations. "Your D.S.O. perhaps?"

Rayne smiled in return. "My name's Rayne, sir, and I command a Spitfire squadron in Wales. And yes, I was recently decorated and my picture did unfortunately appear in the newspapers. My friend here is Miss Siobhan Fitzgerald from Ireland. We are both snatching a quick week-end in London."

The old man smiled knowingly in response. "You are both very young, my goodness! I sometimes think it is cruel to involve people as youthful and as beautiful as you both are, in the brutal business of war." Then turning towards the girl, he went on, "And your face, young lady, is vaguely familiar. Or perhaps it's the colour of your hair which strikes a chord. Have we met before? I believe we have."

Cee Bee answered easily, "We have, sir. When I was about 15 and still at school. I came to London in 1937 with my father and family to an official function to do with the Coronation, and met you then. But my father knew you very much earlier. He was in the Navy initially, then the RAF when it was formed in 1918. He met you then and several times later. In fact we speak of you often at home."

Trenchard's face wrinkled in thought. "Fitzgerald! Fitzgerald! Of course! Yes, I'm sure I remember him now. He was in Naval 9 as I recall, which became 209 Squadron. Yes, 209! The Camel squadron just north of Amiens, that put paid to that German rascal, von Richthofen, in the April of 1918. Well, well! What a small world it is! You both ought to be very proud, not only of your own success but also the prowess of your forebears. I am proud to have met you both."

Then, after a few further pleasantries, he shook hands with them both and moved away. A vast man of 6 feet 5 at least. None too steady on his feet though, and enveloped in a powerful odour of pipe tobacco.

When they were seated again and had recovered their composure, Rayne said with a grin, "My goodness! You are a dark horse. I shall learn next that you are related to Royalty!"

To which the girl replied quickly. "Oh, but I am! Although we don't often talk about it at home! Me being 'pantomime Irish' and all that!"

At the theatre that evening, the girl, having changed, was looking her best. Dressed in a plain dark dress which contrasted sharply with her shining titian hair, Rayne was aware that they - she in particular - were attracting the attention of everyone as they moved into their seats in the stalls. As they waited for the performance to begin, she reached down and felt for his hand and they both shivered with excitement in anticipation. After which, the curtain was raised and they both enjoyed an Ivor Novello experience - including the winsome Mary Ellis - which they felt at the time would remain with them for ever.

Two hours later, they went out into the night again, among a slow-moving, garrulous crowd, absurdly happy and ridiculously at peace with the world.

Outside an air raid was in progress with the searchlights moving in clusters across the few clouds there were, whilst the guns muttered and barked far and near. High above, bursting shells `crumped' away in series in a vain attempt to deter high flying bombers, whose thin droning was a constant background to the cacophony of distant thuds and explosions as the bombs fell and the guns replied. Both Rayne and the girl stopped and raised their gaze. But they didn't pay much attention. Nor did anyone else.

Holding her to him, he spoke quietly into her ear. "Are you scared? Too much to walk?"

And she had answered equally quietly. "No. Not with you around. So, yes, let's walk. On the Embankment. Along the river."

Later, they stood silent and alone at the junction of the Embankment and Westminster Bridge, their arms entwined. It was a dark night and the only light was from the searchlights which waved their tentacles in the far distance, producing faint oily reflections on the black water beneath. It was shortly after 11 pm and the place was quiet and almost deserted.

A few cars and 'buses hissed their way slowly across the bridge, their headlights filtered and diffused.

Overhead in the blackness and among the stars, single bombers droned their way across the sprawling metropolis and from time to time guns, far and near, thumped and barked as though in anger, the bursting shells `crumping' distantly, minutes after the shells had been launched. And, at intervals, there came the flare and muted bumps of bursting bombs as they fell somewhere in the direction of the City and beyond.

The girl was tired. They had walked all the way from Leicester Square and she was wearing shoes more suited to an indoor salon. Also, there was a chill in the air causing her to shiver now and then and bury herself more closely into his uniformed embrace. Rayne, sensing her discomfort, bent down and kissed her forehead tenderly.

"Sorry you came?" Then, when he felt her head shake a negative reply, "Let's walk back a little to that 'bus shelter. It'll be warmer there."

Huddled incongruously together in the shelter, somehow they felt less chilled and more secure, and as they stood there in silence, a single bomber, seemingly lower than the rest, droned its way overhead. Immediately the guns in Hyde Park and others barked their response with such violent reports that both of them jumped.

Rayne said comfortably, "Wait a few moments, then listen for the `crumps' as the shells burst."

When they did, the girl enquired, "What happens to all the bits that fly off everywhere? Do people on the ground get hurt?"

Rayne answered with a grim smile, "The one's that do don't usually complain." At which she punched him playfully and said, "You make a joke of everything, don't you? Can't you ever be serious?"

As she spoke, there came the faint whistle of other descending bombs and he felt the girl's body tense suddenly.

He said gently, "Not to worry. If you can hear them, they won't hit you. It's the one's you don't hear that are the killers."

After that there came a lull, during which she asked rather plaintively,. "Tomorrow. Can I go to church before we go to see your parents?" He felt the girl looking up at him.

"Of course! Westminster Cathedral is very close to where we are and is a Roman Catholic church."

"And will you come with me? Please?"

Rayne hesitated. He was not much of an institutional Christian. Then: "If you wish me to, of course I will. Provided you can guarantee they don't sprinkle anything on me with those pastry brushes they keep waving about."

He felt the girl smile in the dark as she admonished him, "You should show more respect."

Then: "And tomorrow. Will your parents approve of me, d'you think?"

"If they don't they'll be both blind and biased!"

"Mothers don't usually, you know. First go off, that is. They resent any girl who appears to be taking their son - particularly their only son - away from them."

Rayne gave her an added squeeze. "Let's wait and see, should we?" Then more seriously he added, "And your resistance to officers and pilots. Has it gone now? Or is it still a factor?"

The girl was silent. Then, after a full half-minute, followed by a sigh,

"I still have this horrible feeling. Of it all happening again. It's nothing personal. When you mentioned coming to London, most of me jumped for joy. But there remained a little bit of me that said 'no'. So, I admit, I had a bit of a struggle and I suppose it's still there. In fact, when some weeks ago you crashed after shooting down that German, my heart turned over, and for a short time I was back to square one. I was almost hysterical with grief and fear. Because I didn't know what had happened to you. You see, if all that happened again, I would die. I really would! I simply couldn't go through it again."

Silence.

Then Rayne said. "You've never told me, you know. Who it was and how it happened."

Silence again.

"I know. And I shall - in time. But not just now. The wound is still open and sore and I don't want to speak of it."

"Very well. I understand. But I feel it's a barrier I somehow have to surmount. You see you have been my saviour. The antidote to a refined sort of madness. I was in a pretty bad way before you came along. But you have made all the difference. You see, Annabel May . . . I need you! Desperately! But more than that, I'm now very much in love with you. Really in love! That is why I asked you here this weekend. To meet my parents. Because I hope we have a future together. Not this week nor next. Perhaps not even whilst this terrible war is going on. But sometime. Sometime I want us to be together. For all time."

The girl looked up earnestly into his face, her eyes glistening with tears. "And I love you, too, Windy Rayne! So much that it hurts. So much, that if anything happened to you I would die. That's what frightens me so. Oh, I know I'm being terribly Irish and over sensitive, but that's how I am. That's . . . well, that's just me!"

Later, they were walking up Whitehall in solitary state and arm in arm, when they were overtaken by a lone taxi returning from a late fare. Waving it down, Rayne found the driver in an uncooperative mood.

"I'm on my way home, guv. Where d'you want to go?"

When Rayne explained, the man reluctantly pulled down the hire flag without a word, and the two tumbled gratefully into the back.

When they reached the Piccadilly Hotel, it was a quarter-to-one in the morning - Sunday morning. As they entered, the foyer of the hotel was quietly deserted and only dimly lit. At the reception counter, two male clerks only remained in attendance, one of whom smiled mechanically in Rayne's direction as he led the girl towards one of the bank of lifts.

Upstairs on the second floor, the corridor was illuminated only by the meagre glimmer of several five-watt blue lights. Rayne opened the door to his room and they entered to find the shaded bedside lights had been switched on, the bedcovers turned back and the heavy blackout curtains in place. Preceding him, the girl stopped with her back towards him and he sensed uncertainty in her posture and attitude. Then, she turned in his direction and holding out her arms, embraced him silently, her head against his chest.

After standing in silence for a time, Rayne kissed her forehead gently and said quietly, "It's been a long and wonderful day and you're very tired. Why don't you use the bathroom first, and I will come to your room in a moment and say a final good night."

After a moment's hesitation, the girl drew away without a word and moving towards the tall separating door, disappeared.

Sitting down on his bed, Rayne slowly undressed and waited. Dimly he heard the noise of running water in the next room and after a time, the flushing of the lavatory and a quiet shutting of the two dividing doors. When he had showered and changed completely, he quietly opened the door to her room without knocking and moved silently towards her bed.

He saw she was awake and looking up towards the ceiling, her glorious hair contrasting sharply with the white pillows and covers. Moving only her eyes, she smiled affectionately in his direction. He bent over her and whispered, "Do you realise young lady it's a quarter to two in the morning and that we're still on the go? Only a few hours and it's early Communion for both of us." Then, in an effort to lighten his remarks, "Am I allowed any breakfast before we set off?"

At which, the girl grinned and lifting her arms said quietly, "Eat what you want! I'm sure the Holy Mother won't object."

Smiling, he kissed her slowly and lightly on the nose. Then equally lightly on the mouth. Finally, with added pressure and feeling, full on the mouth and with parted lips, feeling the girl's body tense in response and his own pulses begin to race. Then, when he finally had moved away from her, he turned and his lips formed the silent word, "Goodnight!" as he left.

Back in his own room, his mind was full of pleasant and exciting memories and thoughts of the beautiful young woman who was lying a mere ten paces from him in the next room. He took up a book he had brought and began to read, but had difficulty in concentrating. Tomorrow! What would his parents think of the girl? Would they immediately assume too much? Cee Bee was right, mothers always had doubts about someone they perceived to be a threat. His father would fall for her immediately he knew, but his mother . . . well, she might be a problem. He remembered the fuss about the girl at the beginning of the war.

Finally, he closed his eyes and laid down his book. Still thinking. His mind full of thoughts for the future, a future in which fighting at 70,000 feet in an aircraft he could not clearly visualize in his mind's eye, and the beautiful Wren, Cee Bee. Both occupied his mind in equal measure.

Minutes later - or was it an hour? - he awoke with a start to find his light still on, the book exactly where he had left it - and the silent and motionless figure of the girl alongside his bed.

In the moments it took for him to focus on her, he realised with a start that she was clad only in her white nightdress, a garment which left little to the imagination. Her pink-nippled breasts pressed almost eagerly through the flimsy fabric and lower down there was the faint shadow of her small pubic triangle.

Finding himself for a moment staring, he hastily covered his embarrassment with a hoarse whisper.

"Cee Bee! What's the matter?"

With a hand to her throat, the girl said urgently, "Can you come into my room? Please? There's something going on in the street below I don't like very much." Turning suddenly, she made to leave, her voice coming over her shoulder. "I haven't been to sleep yet and it's been going on for ages." She turned again, visibly anxious. "Please, Windy!"

Following behind her, he saw that her room was in darkness. The heavy blackout curtains had been drawn back and the sash window opened a trifle, presumably for the purpose of ventilation. Bending over the wide wooden sill, they each looked down into the darkness, from which direction there came the subdued sounds of movement, voices, and the occasional shout.

"Can you see anything? What are they doing?" The girl's voice was uncertain and trembling.

"Nothing much." He stood back. "Probably the police with a crowd of drunks." He turned and smiled reassuringly. "They certainly can't get at you on the second floor, old love. So, you're perfectly safe."

But sensing still the girl's uncertainty, he was, even so, surprised when she put out an arm in the darkened room and moving quickly in his direction, pressed herself against him, the firm curves of her bosom causing him to step back and producing in him a sudden flood of sensual pleasure. He then felt her damp lips against his face and her warm, whispering breath in his ear.

"Windy, darling! I'm afraid! Someone's walking over my grave. Windy . . . will you come into my bed? For tonight? I need you near me. I'm scared. Please? Just for tonight? Oh, I know I'm being silly, but suddenly I so need you with me. Will you? Please say that you will!"

Surprised to the point of confusion, Rayne's mind floundered as he considered a suitable response. He was actually being asked to sleep with this wonderful girl and he had neither expected it nor had he come prepared. Was this really the Cee Bee he knew? The beautiful but slightly puritanical young woman to whom the very idea of a 'naughty weekend' had been so repugnant?

Moreover, how could he possibly admit that he was not a practised lover and that the final act was as new to him as it probably was to her. Of course, there had been girls before - ages ago! - but there had never been any real intimacies with them, only youthful fumblings. Yet, here she was, apparently offering herself to him. Insisting, in fact. Despite the chill of the night, he suddenly felt himself hot and short of breath, his heart racing. Out of his depth, in fact.

Apparently aware of his thoughts and dilemma, she was whispering again in his ear.

"Windy darling! I know we've never considered this and you must think me terribly brazen? You do, don't you? But I love you so and tonight I need you. I suddenly need you, Windy darling, more than anything in the world. So, please say you understand. Please, Windy! For me!"

Her voice still in his ear and with her lips caressing his cheek, he heard her continue. "Please love me, Windy! Hold me! Please?" He felt her hand search for his in the darkness and lift it to one firm breast, squeezing it hard as she did so. And wonderingly and choking with emotion, he did as she asked.

Then, as though regretting her impulsiveness, the girl turned away suddenly,
"Look! I'll have to use the bathroom again. Please pull the curtains again and I'll switch on the light."

Feeling her move away, he felt in the darkness for the cord that pulled together the heavy curtains and a moment later, a light was switched on.

Moments later, her slim white figure disappeared through the door that led to the bathroom and he was left, his mind in turmoil as the reason for her sudden exit began to dawn on him. Cee Bee! The innocent and virginal Cee Bee! The girl he loved but knew so little about. Who would have believed it?

Later, when he was well enough to think about it, he realised he must have stood there breathing hard for three minutes at least, waiting for her to return. Hearing finally the faint sound of running water and the lavatory flushing yet again, he watched as the bathroom door opened slowly. After which, she was standing in the entrance, her eyes unnaturally bright and a smile on her lips.

He was to recall, too, that a moment later, a sight and sound that was to remain imprinted on his brain for the rest of his days ... which started ... then developed at a terrible, ghastly, slow-motion rate.

First there was a noise. A noise that was unlike any noise he had ever heard before. Not a bang, nor a clap, a thump, or anything resembling even a roar or a blast. Just a crescendo of what could only be described as prolonged thunder, accompanied by movement and violence.

The whole building shook and staggered as though struck by some primeval force and for the fraction of a second he saw a look of surprise and fear on the girl's face as she lifted an arm helplessly in his direction. He also saw - or thought he saw - her lips part and move in some silent and fearful entreaty.

Then, as the floor shifted massively beneath his feet and as he clutched wildly at the curtain which was even then falling and enveloping him, he saw the light flicker once, then go off completely, as the girl's white figure disappeared downwards as though at the stroke of an executioner's sword.

Though he did not see it or even be aware of what precisely was happening, the whole centre of the hotel collapsed inwards and the talented, chaste and beautiful person that was Wren Annabel May Fitzgerald was plunged into an abyss 50 feet deep, and crushed into oblivion by 500 tons of masonry and rubble.

Because he was by the wall and some twelve paces from the girl, and as the outer shell of the building remained largely intact, Rayne did not share her immediate fate but was pitched headlong into a vast pit that was already filling up. Momentarily aware that some dreadful catastrophe was happening around him, in seconds he was bludgeoned into black unconsciousness by his crushing fall.

In a matter of moments, all was quiet again, the whole area filling with a suffocating cloud of settling, stinking, filth and dust. The blast of a 500 kilogram bomb, fitted with a delayed action fuse of 30 minutes and dropped from a single Dornier 217 bomber from 14,000 feet - a bomber which had overshot its major target in the City area by mistake - had torn the heart and innards out of a major hotel in the centre of London's West End.

Rayne drifted to the surface of consciousness like a feather rising slowly in a breath of air.

His first appreciation was of light - dim and diffused light - as though seen through a heavily frosted window. Then he became aware of tubes and wooden gallows-like objects above his head, but was unable to comprehend either their use or what they were. Finally, there were quiet voices - many of them. - and faces, which looked down at him from time to time, some he half recognised but most were new to him - all of them moving away when he tried haltingly to articulate his thoughts and words.

And all the time, he was aware of being confined, of being unable to move, of pain and feelings of nausea, all of which flooded over him in turn, causing him to cry out often in protest and now and then call upon God to end his suffering.

Later still, when greater lucidity developed, he was told about the accident in simple words, about some of the casualties - not all! - and a given a brief description of his own injuries and likely future. It was only later that he learnt of Cee Bee's death, which had an immediate and devastating effect on his recovery rate and morale.

Thereafter, he descended into a trough of utter despair, a condition so marked that he became unable to communicate sensibly with anyone. The only outcome he wished for himself, he would sob endlessly, was that he might die. Die! Die! Die! He just didn't want to live and called tearfully and repeatedly upon Jesus and the Cee Bee's Holy Mother to end it all.

At the hospital's request, Pamela Leggett travelled by train from Holyhead to London. She arrived at four in the afternoon and took a taxi to St. Thomas's Hospital on the south bank of the river. There she was directed to the ward in which Rayne was recovering and was greeted by the senior ward sister, a woman of mature years and much good sense.

Having been offered, and accepted, some light refreshments and tea, Pamela sat alongside the sister's desk with great apprehension, waiting to be informed of Rayne's state of health.

The woman commenced. "I'm so glad you have been able to come Mrs Leggett because our patient, Squadron Leader Rayne, is causing us some concern. First, though, can you tell me what you already know, and what precisely your relationship is with the Squadron Leader? The reason we have invited you here is because our patient is in deep trauma and has kept mentioning your name repeatedly."

For all her normal aplomb, Pamela Leggett was obliged to clear her throat nervously.

"I'm afraid I`m not a blood relation but I have known Marcus Rayne since childhood. I am the wife a brother officer and, on a personal level, Marco and I have always been very close." She offered a wan smile. "It is unnecessary for me to tell you this, but I am happy to volunteer the information that I have been in love with him for many years."

She heard herself expel a deep and fluttering breath. "We heard of the terrible accident, of course, and I was doubly shocked to learn not only of Marco's injuries, but that the young lady he was with had been killed. She was an old school-friend of mine and was a Wren, stationed in Wales. Through me, he met her at my home in Anglesey and their relationship became very special and I believe it would have developed further into something . . . well, something permanent. She was Irish, as you probably know."

The woman nodded. "Yes, we know a little more about her now, but he kept on mentioned 'Cee Bee' in his confused state and for some time we wondered who, or what, the letters stood for." She smiled. "It took us quite a while to work it out."

"But, tell me? How is Marco at this moment?" Pamela felt herself leaning forward anxiously.

The woman paused, choosing her words carefully.

"He came to us in a very bad way more than a fortnight ago. He had a broken left arm and a badly mutilated left shoulder. Also there were terrible head injuries, which we thought initially signified a fractured skull. All these wounds were besides a mass of contusions all over his body, most of them, fortunately, fairly superficial. Also, he was in a deep state of unconsciousness, a coma that continued for more than ten days."

"So . . . initially we feared the worst. We were encouraged, however, when tests showed there was not a fracture in the skull and that, provided we could cope with the other less serious injuries, he would eventually recover."

" However . . . when he was sufficiently lucid and fit enough to be told of the death of his companion, it seemed to trigger a complete mental collapse. After that, he refused to cooperate with anyone, not even his parents, whom he barely recognised by the way, and went into a steep decline. Since then, he has totally lost control of his emotions and has sobbed and wept now for more than four days. In short, he is deeply troubled mentally, as he feels in some way that he was responsible for the death of his young lady friend. And - and this is the disturbing fact - unless he can be pacified and brought to accept reason, he will not recover; it's as simple as that! So, as your name was often mentioned during his fevered outbursts, we felt that you might be able to help in restoring some measure of mental equilibrium."

"You mentioned his parents. Are they here now?"

"1 don't know if they are here this very moment. But one or other of them has been at his bedside since day one, poor things. And if they are not around now, they will be back, I know."

"And other visitors?"

"There have been quite a few. Mostly officers of his own Service and one senior Wren officer, who has been several times. None of them, however, has been able to talk to him properly and will no doubt be back."

"And the girl?"

"Her body was brought here on about the fourth day, after they had found her. After identification and examination, I believe she was taken back to her Naval base in Wales for interment. That, I am not sure about, however."

Pamela nodded. "Yes, I know all about that as my husband and I attended her funeral at Pwllheli. Apparently, she left it in her will that she wished to be buried at sea. Which she was - in Cardigan Bay - although we did not think it appropriate that we should accompany her body on the Air Sea Rescue launch for the final act. It was a very sad moment for us and very moving. However, I don't think Squadron Leader Rayne will be aware of this."

The elder woman suddenly made a move. "Well, you'll be wishing to visit your friend. However, let me warn you that you may not like what you are about to see. He's still badly damaged from the bombing and looks like someone who has fallen off a cliff - which is more or less what happened. Also, he may not be very welcoming or cooperative. Mostly he is in a very truculent mood and is either sobbing his heart out or unwilling to talk. You see, he very much wants to die at this moment and he doesn't care who knows it."

The woman went on, after rising and shaking her head sadly. "One last point. How long can you stay? If you begin to have any success, it would help if you stayed on for a time."

Pamela nodded almost eagerly. "I shall be staying with relatives in Surbiton and will be happy to stay as long as I'm wanted."

Rayne was lying on his back staring at the ceiling. He did not move as Pamela and the nursing sister approached and for as moment she thought he was asleep. Then, when she was nearer and saw the extent of his injuries, her heart almost stopped.

The young man whose appearance she had so admired over the years, was a bandaged heap of heavily bruised and blackened flesh, his exposed face, arms and hands, liberally daubed with yellow antiseptic. Her heart thumping, she slowly lowered herself into a chair beside his bead, whilst the nurse stood aside and at a distance.

Laying a hand on his arm, Pamela said quietly, "Windy my love, it's me. Pammy! Pam Leggett. Can you hear me?"

Turning his head towards her slowly, Rayne's eyes slowly focused on her face. Then, his eyes showed recognition and came alive, if only slightly. His voice faint and almost a croak, he exclaimed weakly, "Pammy! It's you! I was so hoping you'd come. I'm very low, I'm afraid, and feeling terrible. I just want to die!"

There followed a lengthy, vibrant silence.

Then: "Pammy, you must have heard! Cee Bee is dead! She's dead! And I killed her, Pammy! She died because I forced her to come to London. She didn't really want to, but I made her. I wanted to show her to my parents. Because I was proud of her and loved her. And because I loved her . . . she died! Oh, Pammy! Pammy! Pammy! What am I to do?"

Suddenly overcome, Rayne began to sob, great gulps of breath choking the words in his throat and reducing him to silence.

Pam was mutely horrified to see Rayne, the cool, confident and successful boy she had known for years, reduced to such a low, helpless, and undignified condition. She clutched his arm and cried brokenly, "Windy, you didn't kill her! You didn't! The Germans killed her! She was just one of many who died that night when that ghastly, brutal bomb exploded. You weren't responsible for their deaths. Any of them. It wasn't your fault. Cee Bee came of her own free will. I knew her, remember? She was my friend. She wouldn't have come had she not wanted to. And Windy . . . she loved you. I know that she loved you. And she wouldn't have been happy to see you like this."

"But Pammy - !"

"No, listen to me! Listen! Windy . . . you have so much to live for. Your parents! Your friends! Your job and your country! And me! I love you Windy and I can't bear to see you talking and feeling as you are. It's just not right! You have to take hold of yourself, Windy. This is not you! Not the wonderful boy I have always known and loved. The doctors here can't help you unless you help them. So, you have to be brave, and strong-minded, and put your heart into recovering. Because so much depends on you! So many people depend on you! I depend on you, Windy! Do you understand? Tell me you understand?"

In the face of such prolonged and impassioned pleading, Rayne became quieter and his sobbing gradually subsided. To be replaced eventually by loud and exaggerated sniffs, . which by degrees lapsed into silence. But Pamela was continuing in the same vein, pleading, cajoling, instructing, explaining. All the time holding him and talking in a low voice that was shaking with emotion. And all amid tears.

And so it went on. For a long time. Until Rayne finally became quiet and turning to the girl, actually smiled and tried to raise his hand to touch her face.

Standing some yards behind them both and watching the minor drama being enacted before her eyes, the nursing sister, witness to a hundred similar scenes over the years, watched the tableau develop - the elegant weeping young woman, obviously very much in love, draped over the body of her friend, her arms enfolding him protectively, her voice shaking with emotion. And she seemed to be making an impression, too! She really did! The boy's swollen face, still raddled with tears and sorrow, was calmer now, his attitude visibly growing more resigned and submissive by the minute. The corner perhaps had been turned - she hoped and prayed so, anyway!

Hardened as she was to such incidents, the woman was obliged to turn away, her eyes glistening.

Chapter Five

Pamela Leggett stood on the platform of the Holyhead railway terminus waiting for the train from London to arrive. Somewhat on edge, she wondered how he would look. Having not seen him for almost four months, she was hoping for the best but preparing herself for the worst. Despite being the wife of a serving airman, the last time she had seen him on that terrible day at St. Thomas's hospital, had introduced her for the first time to the harsh reality of war and its sometimes terrible consequences. And it had happened to him! To Marco! The boy she had grown up with and still loved. She found herself cringing at the very memory of his appearance and his then state of mind.

These disturbing thoughts occupying completely her conscious mind, she did not notice the train, headed by a war-stained Royal Scot locomotive, slide gently towards the buffers in front of her and come to an almost silent stop.

Immediately, the passengers began to alight, mostly a mass of Army khaki but with a sprinkling of Air Force blue in evidence. Standing on tip-toe, she peered into the distance. She saw him, eventually, a tall thin figure, walking slowly, clad in his greatcoat and service dress hat, which, normally, he seldom wore. He looked very solemn.

When within hailing distance, she waved and, catching sight of her, he responded with a lifted hand. Meeting, they embraced silently, which saddened her somewhat as she was expecting something a little more affectionate.

Rayne said flatly, "It's nice of you to meet me. I was half expecting it would be John."

As they turned to walk off, she explained, "John's not here. He's taken the squadron down to West Mailing in Kent on a month's detachment. As you may have heard, they lost their Beaufighters two months ago and re-equipped with Mosquitos, which pleased them rather. As he's only there for a short time, it was thought best if I stayed here." She snorted derisively, "Marry a pilot and live on your flippin' own!" She turned, a mischievous look in her eyes, "So, you can now have your wicked way with me in the spare bedroom, any time you like!"

But Rayne did not respond as she had hoped, but simply gave the vestiges of a smile and said, "Ah, the opportunities I shall have to miss!"

They climbed into the family Vauxhall 14 and she attempted to lighten the conversation by adding, "Our own car, please note. Using some of my precious 10 gallons a month fuel ration."

Rayne responded with a wry grin, "Your sacrifice is noted. I will remember you in my will!"

"See that you do!"

After that, the 30-minute drive to the airfield passed mostly in silence, Pam willing to wait until they were around the kitchen table before she pressed him on what had been happening and his plans for the future. She had heard a little on the grapevine about the latter, not all of which pleased her. When they were finally seated around the table in the AGA-snug kitchen, Pam placed a tray of tea and scones between them and said decisively, "Now, young man! Tell me all! What has been happening to you since last we met?"

Rayne appeared lost in thought for a time before commencing to speak in a low monotone.

"I was five weeks in St. Thomas's before they shipped me off to the R.A.F. hospital at Halton. There they mucked me about for another month before sending me down to Torquay for physio and rehab. Finally, I had a series of medicals in London before spending a few days at Farnborough, where I managed to get in a couple of flights in an old Hurricane." He smiled reflectively, "It was nice to get airborne again, even in an aircraft I once fervently hoped I would never see again for the rest of my life!"

He paused, significantly, before resuming. "Then I was sent up to Preston in Lancashire to see the AOC 9 Group. He had always been very nice to me on the several occasions we had met in the past, and he was equally nice on this occasion. However, his message was not so pleasant. Apparently, he had insisted that I was not posted away to any other unit but that I should be sent back to Llanbedr when I was fully fit. The squadron, it seems, is to be re-equipped with a new mark of Spit. in the near future and he had demanded that I should be in charge when the new aircraft arrived and the unit was finally moved again down south."

Rayne paused again, as though considering the necessity or even the wisdom of revealing more about his future. However, after some moments, he continued.

"He then went on to say that he saw a great future ahead of me, which was why he had arranged that I should go to Farnborough and get myself involved in all this futuristic high altitude stuff. If things went as planned, he foresaw rapid promotion for me with nothing to prevent me going right to the top. Moreover, he would see to it that things proceeded as he hoped, unless something quite unforeseen occurred."

Pamela listened intently throughout, her eyes bright with interest. Then, she reached forward and clasped both his hands.

"But, Windy love, this is great news. It's a wonderful affirmation of your ability and success. Aren't you pleased? Aren't you proud? Doesn't the future look good to you?"

To her slight surprise, she saw Rayne return a pallid smile and shrug his shoulders.

"I don't feel at all excited, to tell you the truth. I've never regarded myself as a hero and I'm not too sure that I'm in favour of the plans the AOC obviously have in store for me. I don't want to come back to Llanbedr now. Wales is a desert for me since Cee Bee has gone, and a future in fighter aircraft rushing about at 70,000 feet just has no appeal for me. At the moment, anyway. No, I – "

But Pamela was squeezing his hands tightly. "But, Windy my love, you're right, Cee Bee has gone! She's dead! She's gone for good and more's the pity! But you can't live in the past, dear boy. Come on, there is so much ahead of you. So much you can do. You are young - only 23! You must stick with it and show them your mettle. Show them you can rise above a personal bereavement, no matter how deeply felt. Like the boy I have always known and loved over the years."

As she spoke with such passion, she watched Rayne's eyes surveying her calmly but with the faintest sign of grim amusement and disbelief, from time to time slowly shaking his head.

Undeterred, she continued. "And another thing, this trip to Ireland to meet her parents. Do you really think it's a wise move? Is it not raking over old coals? Because I rather fear it might result in your hurting yourself even more than has happened thus far." She nodded vigorously. "I really do think you should give it more thought."

But Rayne was also shaking his head. "No, I have to go. I have to meet them face to face and explain that their daughter's death was largely due to me. I want to tell them, too, that I really loved her and what she meant to me. Pammy, if I didn't I could never ever look myself in the face again. I just have to go."

Recognising that he was adamant, Pamela shrugged her shoulders sadly.

"Alright, go if you must. But I want you to know I have my doubts." Then: "Have you warned them and do you know exactly where they live?"

"I wrote about a month ago telling them of my intentions, although I couldn't then give an exact date. I take a train from Dublin to Waterford, apparently, then a couple of 'buses from there on. Their home is in the hills somewhere west of Waterford and north of Cork. A village I've never heard of but I'll find it."

"And for how long?"

"I don't know. Rather depends on how I'm received and how I feel. A couple of days anyway, I imagine."

Rayne took the night ferry to Ireland. It was a three to four hour journey, one that he had made some ten years earlier with his parents. Then, they had crossed from Holyhead to Kingston, but the Irish, with their anti-British republican sentiments, had since changed the name of their port to something Gaelic Rayne could not even pronounce .

It was close to 6 am when the ferry edged its way to the quayside, as Rayne, clad in civilian sports coat, slacks, light raincoat and crushed tweed hat, stood shivering on an almost deserted deck in the half-light. It was heavily overcast with a fine misty rain, the drab and angular buildings ahead shrouded in fog seeming to be in tune with his black feelings and spirits. At that particular moment, his visit to Ireland had suddenly become less important and something of a dark mission into the unknown.

Ashore, he wandered around for some minutes, seeking some means of transport that would take him to the railway station in Dublin some five miles distant. He eventually came across an old Austin 16 with the notice `Taxi' stuck on its windscreen, and a scruffy looking driver engrossed in what was presumably the racing section of some local paper.

Having been installed with his parachute bag in the rear seat, Rayne prayed that the man would not be one of the conversational kind. He was soon to be disabused.

"You just over from England?"

"Wales," was Rayne's monosyllabic response.

"Wales, England, same thing," replied the man obviously not dismayed. Then: "How's the war going on over there? "

"We're winning," replied Rayne dully..

"There's masses of us over there, y' know, giving you people a hand," informed the man, clearly eager to impress.

"I hadn't noticed," observed Rayne flatly, a remark he hoped, would put an end to the exchange - which indeed it did. Thereafter, the journey proceeded in silence.

At the railway station in Dublin, his train was already at the platform, coaches that were largely similar to those at home, although the hissing steam locomotive backing slowly into position at the front, looked strangely foreign. Selecting a compartment and seat, Rayne arranged himself comfortably, sat back, and waited. He felt himself a stranger in a foreign land, and somehow couldn't associate the girl he had so much admired and loved, with a place so utterly and drably different. Even the people around him and the spoken language, though recognisable, appeared strange.

Within minutes, the train started with a jerk and soon it was rattling southwards, his view of the local countryside obscured mostly by billowing clouds of smoke and steam coming from the panting engine in front. From what he could see, the passing fields and hills, though unremarkable, were very green, the whole area not unlike parts of Wales. He had been told that Ireland was 'a very ordinary picture in a lovely frame', suggesting that the more attractive parts of the country were in the coastal areas. As he was aware that he was heading south towards far-away Cork and Killarney and other well-known beauty spots, things - including his morale - could only improve.

It took more than three hours for him to reach Waterford, where he alighted and went in search of the first of the 'buses he had been told he needed. Having then been obliged to wait for more than an hour for it to set off, he was then borne in a direction his airman's instinct told him was roughly westward, all the time the countryside becoming more varied and attractive.

Then, another search and another more rural, time-scarred vehicle which could only be Irish, in which he continued his journey into what he gathered, from the sight of a local map, was taking him into either the Limerick or Tipperary countryside, an area of open, rolling hills. Finally, but not until almost 4 o'clock in the afternoon, he reached the village he had been told was adjacent to the Fitzgerald racing stables.

Stepping out with his bag, he looked about. This was the place Cee Bee called home. This was the area she had grown up in and must have known intimately. Suddenly he felt more at ease. Even the weather had improved. Yes, he could like it here. The rolling countryside, not exactly tidy in the English way, but orderly and lived in. Scudding clouds moved swiftly overhead and there was a fresh moist feeling to the wind in his face. Part of an ancient land! Cee Bee's country, where her family had lived for 400 years. He smiled. Absent she might have been, he so sensed her presence all around him, that suddenly he found his eyes filled with tears.

Rayne had been walking for almost an hour and the low-lying mound of buildings he judged to be the Fitzgerald home and out-buildings, was away to his left on a hill. He turned at the junction of the by-road he was on and the winding white path rising towards the farm, or whatever, and took a deep breath. Cee Bee's home and parents. He wondered what his reception would be. Whether even that he could control his emotions during the forthcoming encounter.

Then, as he was walking up the grass verge beside the prepared pathway, a figure appeared on a horse. Obviously fresh from the stables the horse appeared frisky and difficult to manage, the rider, dressed for the part, having his work cut out in controlling the animal. When the rider had it almost under control and it had come cantering towards him, Rayne stood aside to let it pass and was mildly surprised to see that the rider was not a male jockey but a young girl, who saluted his courtesy as she tried manfully to control the animal and its flying legs.

For a moment Rayne stopped, wondering if the rider could possibly be Cee Bee's younger sister, but the girl still with her attention wholly concentrated on controlling the horse, gave only a quick rearward glance before kicking the animal into a gallop and moving quickly away down the hill. Rayne watched it go, then turned again to walk up to the house.

It proved to be a substantial Georgian building of light-coloured stone, with a centrally disposed door of considerable proportions. Rayne mounted the several steps to the entrance and tugged the iron bell-pull, hearing a distant muted clang from somewhere within. After which he turned and waited, his heart beating marginally faster than normal. Would her parents be immediately available? How would they look and how would they respond to his visit? - because he had not telephoned his arrival date or time - and how would the encounter develop? For one heart-stopping moment, he wished he were somewhere else and found himself questioning the wisdom of his decision. Then the door opened and he was faced by a young woman - obviously a servant girl, clad in an apron - who looked questioningly at him, her face a mixture of surprise and interest.

Rayne said, "My name is Rayne, Squadron Leader Marcus Rayne, and I've come hoping to meet either Mr or Mrs Fitzgerald, perhaps both." He smiled and held out his card. "This will serve to introduce me, should either of them be available."

The girl hesitated for a moment then smiled and stood back. "Come in, sorr. Mrs Fitzgerald is at home I know, but I'm not too sure about Captain Fitzgerald." Her accent, noticeably Irish, she took the card, but did not examine it.

Rayne thought immediately 'Captain Fitzgerald!' A military title? Naval or Army? Or just a courtesy title bestowed by the household staff? Anyway, what did it matter? He removed his hat and stepped into the large hallway that had opened out in front of him.

The girl said, "If you'll wait here, sorr, I'll find Mrs. Fitzgerald. Do you wish me to take your luggage?" She held out her hand and he handed over his parachute bag which she placed on an adjacent chair before turning to leave.

A full minute passed. Then distant voices and footsteps. Finally, a woman of about 45 appeared who Rayne immediately recognised as Cee Bee's mother - the face was vaguely familiar and the hair similar, though chestnut-coloured rather than the more pronounced Titian shade of her daughter. Her hand outstretched, she welcomed him in a cultured English voice with just the faintest Irish intonation.

"Squadron Leader Rayne! How nice to see you and how clever of you to find us tucked away here in the wilds of Tipperary. We knew you were coming, of course, though not precisely when. Did you come across on the overnight ferry? You did? Then you must be dog-tired and also famished, poor thing. So, come into the kitchen and let me give you a bowl of our traditional Irish broth which is always on the hob in this house. I've sent Bridget to find my husband who is in the paddocks somewhere, so I suggest you keep all your news until he arrives."

She suddenly clasped both her elbows. "Oh, it is so good to see you at last! Poor dear Annabel wrote about you many times. She told us that you were the young man who shot down that German bomber some months ago - the one that came down a little north of here. As you might imagine, it created a tremendous fuss at the time. Here, let me take your coat and hat and do sit down whilst I'll get you something to eat." The woman prattled on not giving Rayne time to utter even a word.

Suddenly weary and his spirits dipping, Rayne sat down in the proffered chair with a sigh. Such an unexpectedly pleasant welcome. Especially given the nature of his visit and the message he knew he had to pass on to them. Were they still affected by their daughter's death as deeply as he was? Or was their courteous reception of him a typically British stiff-upper-lip facade? Well, he would soon find out. Then the steaming soup was set before him and as he tried manfully to eat, the pleasantries continued.

To Rayne it is was almost unreal. He had caused their daughter's death and here he was being treated by her mother as a hero and a family friend. He had a horrible, ghastly feeling that the atmosphere would shortly change - and soon!

He had almost finished the soup when Cee Bee's father arrived at the kitchen door. Discarding his cap and boots, he slipped his feet into a pair of indoor shoes - obviously a well practised routine.

Christopher Fitzgerald was a solidly built man of about 50 with dark hair and smiling grey eyes. Exuding quiet physical strength, he moved with silent strides towards Rayne, who had stood up to greet him, and held out his hand.

"Welcome to Ireland, Squadron Leader. We have heard a lot about you these last months and weeks. Have you quite recovered from your injuries? As you will understand, Annabel's death came as a terrible shock to us both, from which we are only now recovering. From what I hear, it affected you deeply as well, so it is a tragedy we share. We are so glad to see you because I hope we shall now learn in detail how it all happened. As you will understand, it will help us come to terms with our loss. You probably know that our darling girl was only 21 and it is very hard for any parent to lose a child of that age, particularly in such terrible circumstances."

Rayne found himself swallowing. Where did he start and what and where were the words he might use? Suddenly the enormity of his task reduced him to silence, so that it took him a full half-minute to recover.

Sensing the young man's obvious discomfort and distress, Christopher Fitzgerald said quietly, "If you have finished eating, perhaps we might go into the sitting room where we will be more comfortable. Would you care for a whiskey? We might all find a drink or two helpful. Mother?" He exchanged glances with his wife, who led the way through an adjacent door.

Seated comfortably in the sitting room with a glass of amber liquid in his hand, Rayne felt marginally more relaxed. His hosts sat opposite, their faces friendly, but anxiously enquiring.

Rayne started off. "I note that you refer to your daughter as Annabel. Over the other side, she is known as Cee Bee, as not many people know how to pronounce Siobhan." He smiled wanly. "Being a very privileged person, she told me of her Christian name and the reasons she felt it necessary to change it. I thought I'd better mention that as you may wonder why, and if, I keep lapsing into Cee Bee, although I try to think of her now as Annabel."

Rayne hesitated, considering where to begin.

Then: "At the risk of boring you, I have to tell you a little about myself, as I want you to know why Annabel became so important a person in my life."

A pause. "I had been flying at home and abroad since the beginning of the war and had reached the stage when I was completely exhausted. So much so that I began to fear that I might perhaps have a mental problem."

"However, I was assured by the RAF doctors that there was nothing wrong with me other than I needed to recharge my batteries completely. To do this, I was to rest, take lots of exercise, and if it were possible, find myself other sources of interest - including a girlfriend!"

"Stupidly, I had so focused on my flying, fighting and the need for success, that I never had any time for affairs of the heart. There were lots of other challenges, too, arranged for me in the future by my seniors, all of which lay heavily on my mind" - here a deep breath - "so that life for me became almost unbearable."

"It is against this background that, when attending my first party for ages at RAF Valley in Anglesey, I met Annabel, who, from the first moment I saw her, struck me as being very special and the possible answer to at least part of my rehabilitation programme. I didn't know until later that she was a school friend of Pamela Leggett, a senior officer's wife at RAF, Valley. She, I understand, you have met, and I mention her as she was responsible for my meeting Annabel."

"1 was so attracted to you lovely daughter that 1 later rang her up at her Naval station at Pwllheli and suggested that we met. To my surprise, she kept me at arm's length initially, hinting that she did not 'go out with officers and pilots' because they were always 'unreliable' By way of further explanation, she kept referring to a love affair she had had with a pilot who had since been killed."

"Well . . . I persevered and invited her to Llanbedr, which is where my Spitfire squadron is based, and she somewhat reluctantly agreed to come. In the event, she stayed the weekend, lodging with the Station Commander - a good friend of mine - so that we were able to go flying together and to spend a very happy day walking in the mountains."

"It was during that weekend that, despite our knowing each other for so short a time, we both realised that we meant something special to each other, and I found how talented and exceptional a girl she was."

Here Rayne was obliged to pause again.

"And . . . and, it was at that point that I fell in love with her and, I think, she with me, although there was always the single nagging impediment - her constant reference to the former pilot she had loved and had been killed."

"Well . . . things progressed. I was damaged in a crash when that German aircraft you mentioned was shot down, an incident which proved to me that she cared, because she was terribly upset about it."

"For my part, I was keen to show that I was made of pretty indestructible stuff. She knew that I had already experienced an engine failure some weeks earlier over the Irish sea, followed by a ducking when I had to bale out, so that I felt she was beginning to understand that I was not likely suddenly to disappear."

Another pause. A longer one, this time.

"At this stage, I was so in love with her that I wanted my parents, who live in London, to meet her. Again, she was reluctant to agree at first, but suddenly was persuaded."

"Well, we went down by train and stayed at the Piccadilly Hotel. And here I want to explain that it was not just a 'naughty weekend' - she was dead against that - and I went along, absolutely, with her decision."

"The following day, Saturday, turned out to be a joyous occasion. We had lunch at Claridges, then tea at the RAF Club in Piccadilly, where we met Lord Trenchard, whom apparently she knew. Finally we did a rather special Ivor Novello show."

"I know Annabel enjoyed herself enormously because she told me so many times as we walked together later that evening on the Embankment. She was so gay and light-hearted throughout and it was a lovely night; dark but clear, with the searchlights waving about and the sound of guns in the distance. There was an air raid on at the time, although not in our part of London."

"In fact, it was an evening of pure enchantment whose memory I shall treasure for the rest of my life. We walked for ages so that when we returned to the hotel it was well gone midnight and we were so weary, we went straight to our rooms and retired."

"Some time after, it must have been about 2 am, I found her standing by my bed; our rooms had adjoining doors separated by a bathroom. She was obviously in a very nervous state, explaining that there was something going on in the street below her room, and would I reassure her that everything was alright."

"I followed her into her room and we each looked down from her window - we were on the second floor - but could see very little in the darkness. So, I explained rather lightly that the commotion below was probably the police sorting out some drunks. That seemed to satisfy her and she left me standing at the window, suddenly saying that she needed to go to the bathroom."

"Minutes later, she reappeared and was standing in the doorway looking in my direction. When . . . when it all began to happen. And it was . . . well, it was something quite terrible, horrible, and unforgettable."

"Although I was not aware of it at the time, a delayed action bomb was about to explode in the basement. It caused something like an earthquake amid a terrible unearthly noise, during which the whole hotel seemed to rise into the air. At the same time, all the lights went out but not before I had a fleeting glimpse of Annabel as she disappeared through the floor which had opened up into a black hole as though by magic. And immediately after, I, too, found myself pitching forward with everything falling on me. After which, nothing! Just oblivion!"

As Rayne explained the circumstances of that tragic week-end, he listened with something akin to amazement to his own voice which he heard almost as a third person, a voice so levelly devoid of emotion that he hardly believed it to be his own. Also, Annabel's parents' faces, whilst showing tenseness and sombre concentration, had remained impassive throughout, although her father had lowered his gaze now and then and had shaken his head in disbelief, whilst her mother's eyes had filled with tears occasionally and her hands had clenched from time to time.

As he faced them directly, whilst marvelling at their composure and controlled response, he was somehow bitterly disappointed. Was it not the death of their much loved daughter he was describing? Why did not they react more visibly? Moreover, what was happening to him? Here he was, speaking of the girl he loved so desperately and had lost, his whole inner being tied up in knots of anguish, yet somehow it all remained deep within him and showed no signs of exploding to the surface. Why, oh why, was he not able to cry it out aloud? Shriek out his horror, his agony and distress? Yet, even as these thoughts passed through his mind, he heard himself continue.

"You may know that it took me many months to recover, the first ten days of which I spent in a coma, so that I did not know of Annabel's death until some time after her funeral and burial at sea. This so affected me that the doctors almost gave me up. Thank God, I had Pamela Leggett to support me as, apparently, I went into a period of deep despair which itself became life threatening."

Feeling himself beginning to be overcome with emotion, he continued haltingly, "Which is why I am here today. You see . . . I had to face you and tell you directly . . . that I feel I was responsible for the death of your daughter. Had I not insisted on her going with me to London, she would be alive now. Had I not met her, sought her love, and persuaded her almost against her will to be with me, she would not have died. I'm sorry. Truly, desperately sorry. So very sorry that I can hardly put my feelings into words and I ask you to forgive me. Because I need your forgiveness. Forgiveness . . . to allow me to live with myself."

As Rayne haltingly and almost in tears, brought his confession to an end, Cee Bee's mother rose to her feet, hesitated for a moment, then stepped forward to take his head in her arms, pressing his face against her body. With her own face crumpling with emotion, she said brokenly, "You poor, poor boy! It was not your fault. You should not blame yourself. We knew Annabel sufficiently well to know that she would never do anything she did not wish to do. She agreed to go with you to London, and that's the end of it. You were not responsible. Please understand that." Turning, she faced her husband who had also risen to his feet. " Isn't that true, Dad? She wouldn't have gone otherwise." Then patting his head gently, "From what we have heard about you and having met you, you are clearly a brave, dutiful and loving young man and we are proud to know you as Annabel's close and intimate friend. And don't you ever think otherwise!"

Having also risen and now standing alongside his wife, Christopher Fitzgerald patted Rayne's shoulder comfortingly. "I agree, absolutely. There is nothing to forgive. We are your friends, now and always. Annabel's death was a terrible, horrible blow but we are getting over it now, although she will never be forgotten, and we must all look to the future. War hits families in many ways, some more than others. For us it has been especially hard but others have suffered more, of that we are well aware."

Then, in an obvious wish to bring the emotional nightmare to an end, he added, "And now, let's change the subject, should we? As you may know, I also flew with the Navy during the last war and after, though things were much different then. That was when I first met Hugh Trenchard, incidentally, then, and later when we all went over to England during the coronation celebrations in 1937. Annabel was about 15 at the time. Perhaps you would like to see some photographs of those times and events? Plus some aircraft and pilots of that period? In which case, let's go into my study."

As all three moved into the study, Rayne looked about, taking in the comfort and orderliness of a well-used gentleman's sanctuary - a centrally sited leather-covered desk, two comfortable armchairs, bookcases and filing cabinets and the walls covered with a wide variety of photographs.

Cee Bee's father walked in front, pointing. "These photographs are of my squadron in 1918. We flew the Sopwith Camel in those days with the newish Bentley rotary engine. After joining the Navy in 1916, at the age of 18, I was finally posted to Naval 9 squadron, RNAS, which became 209 Squadron on the formation of the Royal Air Force in April 1918. At the time, we were at a place called Bertangles, a farmer's field a little to the north of Amiens."

"We were then heavily engaged in the final battle of the Somme and were flying all day, every day. Also, you may possibly have heard that a pilot of 209 Squadron was responsible for shooting down and killing the famous German Red Baron - von Richthofen - although that is now disputed by some. That was on 21st April, 1918, a time when I happened to be on leave in England, otherwise I could well have taken part."

"The chap involved was a Canadian named Brown - that's him there. He is still alive today, I believe, although he was badly injured later and has had a very rough time ever since, poor chap. These other photographs are of some other members of 209 who also took part; Mellersh, here, who is still alive and in the Air Force, and May, another Canadian, who did quite well later on. These others are of me and other pilots, and this is the Sopwith Snipe, an aircraft which replaced the Camel and remained in the Air Force until I left in the middle 20s. Finally, this one is of Trenchard and me, with others, of course. He was quite a chap to look at. Very tall and with a figure and features like granite."

Rayne, supremely interested, went slowly around the walls, smiling and commenting now and then.

"This is a Bristol Fighter, isn't it? Did you fly one of those, sir? There used to be one in the corner of a hangar at Farnborough for ages but I never got round to fly it, more's the pity. And, goodness me! Here's the Bristol Bulldog! That was a bit after your time though, wasn't it?"

Finally coming across a photograph of what looked like a younger edition of his host, Rayne asked, "And 1 take it, this you at the end of the First World War?"

After a brief silence which caused Rayne to look up and see his hosts exchange glances, Cee Bee's mother said gently, "No, that was our son, Patrick." Another silence, then: "Patrick is, or was, Annabel's twin brother. Or, perhaps you hadn't been told." She gave a sad smile. "I suspect he was the one she was referring to when she said there was someone she loved dearly, who was a pilot and was killed. She never had a close boy-friend, you see. Or none that we knew of, although there were many young men who weren't, of course."

"She and Patrick were always very close. She was the stronger character, however, and mothered him dreadfully, as she was born two hours earlier. Poor boy, he was never allowed to forget that, so I think he was almost glad to get away when he was 18 to join the Navy."

"He was killed when he was not quite 20, and Annabel for a time went completely to pieces. In fact, we became seriously worried about her health as she became what I believe is called 'clinically depressed'. But she recovered - she was pretty tough in every way - and immediately joined the Wrens saying that that 'bloody man Hitler' was not going to get away with killing her brother!"

As he listened, Rayne began to feel an icy hand begin to grip his heart, so that it was only with great difficulty that he managed to ask, "When and how was he killed?"

Christopher Fitzgerald took up the story. "It was more than a year ago now. He was flying fighters on a carrier which was damaged in the Med – H.M.S. Formidable, as I recall. Whilst their ship was being repaired, his squadron was deployed along the North African coast."

"One day, several of them were scrambled to go to the assistance of a convoy that was being attacked by Italian torpedo bombers about 50 miles north of where they were stationed. Patrick was one of a pair which made an interception but was shot down. By whom it is not known. Sadly, he just disappeared."

Rayne stared woodenly into space and was unable to speak. Finally, he was able to whisper, "Do you happen to know what he was flying at the time?"

Christopher Fitzgerald answered almost off-handedly, "Oh, yes! They had Fairey Fulmars initially but had just been re-equipped with American aircraft - Grumman Martlets, I believe. Nice aircraft, apparently, but not up to much as fighters , I'm told. Have you had any experience of them?"

Rayne, stricken, could only swallow with difficulty. Then shake his head, ashen faced.

When Caroline Fitzgerald returned from her ride, she took her lathered horse back to the stables and handed it over to a groom. Then, still in her hard hat and riding boots, she hastened to the family home and strode into the kitchen to find her mother at the sink washing glasses.

She almost shouted, "Mum, was that chap I saw walking up the drive Annie's boyfriend? You know, the one who was with her when . . . well, you know? I wanted to stop and chat but the bloody horse ran away with me and galloped off before I had a chance to open my mouth."

Her mother, still engrossed with her washing, nodded silently then added, quietly, "Don't swear dear! At 16, you're much too young."

"Oh Mum! Really! Anyway, what sort of chap was he and what happened?"

Her mother turned and for the first time Caroline saw her tear-stained face. Instantly, her attitude changed. "Mum, you're terribly upset! I'm sorry. Tell me what happened. And anyway, where was Dad? Was he not with you?"

Her mother nodded. "He was here most of the time, yes, but was called away when he heard that one of the horses had badly damaged a leg."

"And - ?"

Her mother continued almost dreamily. "He was a lovely young man, dear. Brave. And so penitent. He insisted on coming to see us as he believed he was responsible for Annabel's death. I was desperately sorry for him because it wasn't his fault and he was so badly injured anyway." Her eyes suddenly filled again with tears. "He said he had come to beg our forgiveness as he could not face the future without it."

"Well, Dad and I said there was no question of forgiveness, that we quite understood his feelings of remorse, but in our view they were quite misplaced."

"Anyway . . . after a time, he brightened up and we were looking at some photographs in Dad's study when he saw the one of Patrick. When he learnt that Patrick was Annabel's twin brother, which apparently he had not known before, and that he had been killed, he came over all strange and for a time couldn't speak. He seemed terribly upset and suddenly said that he was sorry but he had to leave . . . and, he just went!"

"But Mum, for heaven's sake! Didn't you ask him to stay? To talk everything over?"

"We did! We both did. Several times. And I was still insisting, when he decided in an instant to go. I thought about asking Dad to follow him but he was than called away."

"Well it's too late now," her daughter added almost fiercely. "I saw him from a distance on the main road when I was coming back and someone was picking him up in a car. He'll be long gone by now. Oh, heck! What a shame! And I did so want to meet him. Mum . . . d'you think he would have been too old for me?"

"Caroline Fitzgerald! You ought to be ashamed of yourself! What an absolutely outrageous thing to say!"

Pamela Leggett was in the garden gathering flowers when the telephone rang. The batman came to the door at the rear of the house and shouted, "For you ma'am. I think it may be the squadron leader."

Pam hastened in, almost running, and picked up the 'phone. "Windy? Where are you? You had us all worried to death, you half-wit. You've been gone more than a week - or hadn't you noticed?"

Rayne replied flatly, "I've just arrived in Holyhead, and sweetie . . . I'm not in the mood to be reprimanded."

"Alright, sourpuss! But tell me where you are and I'll come and collect you."

"I don't need to be collected." Rayne's voice was almost sharp. "I'll find my own way back to the airfield. I'm just ringing to see if you were still around."

"Well, I am. So hurry up and get back here as soon as you can. You've a lot of explaining to do. Did you meet the Fitzgerald's, incidentally?"

"I'll tell you when I get back." Rayne just didn't want to chat.

An hour later, Pamela opened the door to him and beheld a stranger almost, in civilian clothes still and wearing his battered hat.

She greeted him with, "God Almighty! You look awful! Come in and change into uniform, for heaven's sake, so that I recognise you." Then, over her shoulder as she led him towards the kitchen, "I'll make some tea and cut a few sandwiches, just to tide you over. During which time, you can tell me what happened. Alright?" After which, she turned and, straight faced, clutched him to her body and gave him a welcoming kiss on the mouth.

Later, he was sitting at the kitchen table and slowly chewing a sandwich as she watched him anxiously, a hand to her throat. Thus far, he had not uttered a word but had just gazed into space.

She broke the silence. "So . . . ? You found the Fitzgerald's it seems. What then? How did they receive you?"

He remained silent for a time. Then: "They were very civil. For parents who were entertaining a guest who had not long since been responsible for the death of their daughter, very civil. In fact, they were charming. And understanding. Even forgiving. Which was the hardest to take. Had I blown up the house over their heads, they would probably have taken it with nothing more than a sad shake of their heads. It was uncanny. Frightening, in fact."

"Windy, please don't! You're hurting yourself unnecessarily." There was anguish in Pamela's entreaty. But her words seemed to have no effect, as Rayne went on levelly and seemingly without emotion.

"Did you know that Cee Bee had a twin brother?"

"I knew she was one of four children. But I never met any of them. Why do you mention it?"

There was silence as she watched him slowly eating, his eyes vacant.

"Cee Bee had two brothers, one of whom was her twin. He was the boy she loved, it seems. He was the one she was always referring to when I thought she meant some previous boy friend. He was the one who was killed. The pilot who was shot down and lost. Her twin brother."

Another silence, as Pamela watched, fascinated but dreading what she was half expecting to hear.

"And do you know what, Pammy? I was responsible for his death, too. I was! I killed both of them, Pammy. Not one, but both of them!"

Pamela, unbelieving, screwed her face up in disbelief. "Marco, for God's sake! What are you saying?"

But Rayne went on quietly as though he had not heard.

"That beautiful girl, whom I loved, and also her twin brother! Beloved children of those caring and wonderful parents who stupidly regard me as a valued friend. I was responsible, Pammy." Then, with crumbling face, "I killed both of them and I don't know what to do."

Horrified, Pamela Leggett, a hand to her throat, listened and for a time was speechless. Then, in a voice that was almost a cry, "But you don't know Windy, love! It's all in your imagination!"

"But I do, Pammy. I do! D'you remember me telling you about the torpedo attack on our convoy when I was returning from Malta? And the two fighters who came to help us? Well, I was firing one of the defending guns and I shot one of the fighters down. I know I did! I didn't mean to, but I did! I saw it! And now I learn it was Cee Bee's twin brother."

Pamela, her hands over her ears in an unconscious gesture of disbelief, burst out vehemently, "But, Marco, even if you did, you were not to blame. You didn't mean to! There's a war on! These things happen. You can't go through life like this." She was shouting now. "Blaming yourself for everything and being a bloody martyr, for Christ's sake."

But Rayne was looking in her direction, his eyes in a bitter smile but speaking quietly and seemingly without emotion.

"Pammy, everything I touch, it seems I destroy. I destroyed our association when we were kids because I didn't understand, and I now know I hurt you terribly. I've killed God knows how many Germans, all of whom had parents. And now I've killed these two, one of whom I loved desperately. Added to which . . . well, something is happening to me. I know it! Every now and then I find myself losing control. I'm not myself. When things upset me, something snaps and I just want to kill people. With my bare hands, I want to kill people! I am unstable, Pammy, and at times I hate myself. And, well . . . I just don't know what to do. How it's all going to end."

Pam, now deeply distressed, walked around the table and held Rayne's head in her hands. "Marco! Marco, my love! What am I going to do with you? You can't go on hurting yourself like this?" Then after some moments and in a calmer voice, "Did you tell the Fitzgeralds about their boy and what you believe you did?"

Rayne shook his head wearily. "No, I couldn't. I couldn't bring myself to add to their misery. Or to my own."

"Didn't they ask you to stay with them?"

Rayne nodded. "But I had to get away. As far as possible from them - and quickly!"

"So, where did you go for almost a week?"

"Cork. I first had a lift from almost outside their house, then I caught a bus to . . . well, I didn't care where. And ended up in Cork. Where I walked the streets for hours on end, lived in some crummy lodgings, and ate next to nothing."

There was a long agonising silence.

"And what now?" Pam's voice was merely a whisper.

Another silence. Then, after Rayne found his voice, "Go home, I suppose. There's nothing else I can do. I've still got some leave to take. If my parents can put up with me, that is. And if I can maintain some sort of composure in their presence. First though, I have to get back to Llanbedr to pick up one or two things." He sighed. "I'll get on to Target Towing in a moment and see if they can fly me across."

"Marco! You won't be silly enough to go flying again in the meantime, will you? In your present state, that is? Please, please, promise me that you won't!"

Rayne gave a grim smile. "I doubt by now that I have an aircraft to fly. The squadron hasn't seen me for almost five months. They are certainly not expecting me."

In the back seat of the Miles Martinet, Rayne surveyed with detached interest the distant shoreline of Wales as it slowly approached. As it passed over the water's edge and sands, the Martinet banked towards Llanbedr airfield to its left and reduced power so that it drifted downwind and turned in the direction of the 24 runway. Then, lifting its nose gently, it touched down with scarcely a bounce and taxied ahead.

In front the pilot said, "Where do you want me to park, sir?"

Rayne said, "Turn right at the end of the runway and go towards that blister hangar over there and the two huts next door to it. There's a hard-standing in front of the hangar."

As the Martinet slowed and slewed around, two airmen came out to greet it and Rayne said, "Don't stop your engine if you don't wish to stay. I'll get out immediately. And thank you for the lift, by the way."

One of the two airman who had scrambled onto the wing, recognised him and his face lit up. "Welcome back, sir! It's been a long, long time!"

Rayne handed down his parachute bag and wriggled out of his parachute harness. Then, climbing down from the cockpit he added, "Thank for those kind words. I was afraid you might all have forgotten me."

"After what you have been through - not likely, sir! "

As Rayne walked into the adjutant's office, the man looked up and did a double take.

"Good Lord! This is a surprise. We were not expecting you for at least another fortnight. Welcome back, sir! It's good to see you back on your feet again."

"And active in all respects," added Rayne with a warning smile. "I didn't see any aircraft about, incidentally. Who's at home, or is everyone on leave?"

"We're night flying tonight so most of the chaps are resting up in preparation. Except for the pair on `Standby', that is."

Rayne nodded. "Could you find Douglas Hayward for me and ask him to have a word? I ought to report to him as acting CO, I suppose. And the engineer officer, too, if you can find him."

Walking into his vacant office, Rayne threw off his hat and sat down with a sigh. It had been about six months since he had last sat in his seat before the now empty desk. Six months and more, since Cee Bee had stood in front of him in her ridiculous white-topped sailor's hat, climbing into her parachute harness, before that flight they had made together. Such a long time ago . . . but, so very close in memory. Cee Bee! It was impossible to think of her, dead. Her voice not any more at the end of a telephone in Pwllheli. Gone! For all time! He found himself shaking his head and near to tears. Then, on impulse, he took up the telephone and asked to be put through to the Station Commander.

To his surprise, the Station Adjutant answered.

After registering surprise followed by a hearty welcome, the man explained. "I'm afraid Squadron Leader Wynn-Jones is away - on business! He said for two days but he has already been gone four. He's in South Wales somewhere." An old-fashioned chuckle. "His old stamping ground. You know how he is."

Rayne smiled and he rang off. He did indeed know how he was!

It was more than 30 minutes before Hayward and the engineer officer turned up, by which time Rayne, his mind on the past, had descended into a deep melancholy. After the congratulations, the excuses for their late arrival and comments and pleasantries had been exchanged, Rayne asked about his aircraft.

"Ah! When we knew you were returning, sir", the new engineer officer explained, "We put it aside. Since when we have flown it twice a week to keep the juices circulating. In fact, it was flown only this morning, if you are thinking of giving it a quick whirl, that is."

Rayne nodded slowly. "Well . . . why not? In fact, I was thinking myself of getting airborne tonight. Would that upset your programme, Duggie?"

Hayward, surprised, registered concern. "Would that be a good idea, sir? With your injuries and a lay-off for more than five months, I would have thought a short daylight flight would have been more appropriate. But, no . . . I could put you on the list without any difficulty - that is if you are serious."

"Right, then!" Rayne was decisive. "I'll take off around midnight and do an hour's cross-country. Around the usual circuit. I did a couple of trips recently at Farnborough, so I shouldn't be too rusty, even at night."

When they had gone and he was alone again, Rayne closed his eyes for a long time and thought about the past . . . and about the future . . . but, mostly about himself. And others! Almost everyone! And decided that . . . yes, it would be appropriate. Most appropriate!

Rayne taxied his Spitfire briskly around the perimeter track in the direction of the runway, all too aware that the Mark V, with its offset radiator, overheated on the ground very quickly.

It was 15 minutes before midnight, very dark and with no moon, but with a sprinkling of stars in an unclouded sky. In front, the exhausts of his engine rippled out lines of magenta-coloured flame and spat out the occasional glowing fragment of carbon.

At the 24 runway, with its row of glim lamps stretching away into the blackness, he stopped and went through his cockpit drill in a manner rehearsed many times over the years - Trim, Mixture, Pitch, Fuel, Flaps, Instruments, Oxygen, Harness, Hood. He then checked around the cockpit again with questing fingers in the rose-tinted darkness, before opening the throttle so that the boost gauge registered '0' lbs boost, at the same time switching off each of the two ignition tumblers in turn. Ahead of him in the darkness, the engine faltered momentarily but well within limits, so that, satisfied, he closed the throttle before moving forward onto the runway, and noting that the compass between his knees and the direction indicator on his dashboard, each showed exactly 240 degrees.

Then, not attempting to look over the long nose but sideways down the line of glim-lamps, he opened the throttle again to about '0' lbs boost, to get the aircraft rolling straight. Then, he pushed the lever right forward decisively so that '9' lbs showed on the boost gauge, causing the Spitfire to surge ahead, the exhausts in front a blue and orange blow-torch flame.

At about 60 miles per hour, the tail rose slightly of its own accord, and the aircraft left the ground smoothly at around 90. Keeping the nose depressed, he stopped the rotating wheels with his brakes, before raising the undercarriage and feeling the 'clump' as the two legs locked into the `Up' position.

Then he was up and away into the darkness, over the coast and out to sea, the engine raging away in front and 3,000 revs registering on the rev. counter.

As he watched the speed build up to 180, he throttled back slightly and reduced the engine speed to 2,850 revs, at the same time turning slowly to his left and climbing steadily. After two minutes or so, he was back over the airfield again at 6,500 feet, aware that to port was the black and unseen water of Cardigan Bay and to his right, mountains rising to 3,000 feet.

Still climbing steadily, he turned onto a heading of 013 degrees, knowing that he was aiming for about Llandudno on the north coast of Wales, after which he would turn right and head approximately for Liverpool.

The exact position of each in the blackness below him was not important; he knew he was flying simply an approximate rectangle of courses which would eventually take him over the Midlands of England and finally the mountains of Wales on the final leg. In all, he would be airborne for about one hour and 15 minutes - well with the endurance of a Spitfire with its 85 gallons of fuel.

At his first turning point, Rayne was at more than 23,000 feet. He did not have any particular height in mind, but decided that it was unnecessary to go any higher. So, after turning on to a course of 090 degrees, he throttled back to 2 lbs boost, set the revs, at 2,000, and carefully adjusted the fore and aft trim, then the rudder, so that he was able to fly the aircraft with one finger, if not completely hands-off.

In front of him, the airspeed indicator registered 210 miles per hour which, he quickly calculated in his head, gave him a true airspeed of about 280. After that, he checked his oxygen flow by blocking off the tube to his face-mask until he felt the throb of the oxygen as it forced its way to his nose and mouth. Satisfied, he sat back and, when he was not glancing regularly at his instruments, gazed around at the starlit blackness of infinite space. In front, his gently throbbing engine now produced merely a line of pink and blue flickers of flame which caused the exhaust stubs to be tinted a dull rust-red.

When he estimated he had reached Liverpool approximately, Rayne called up Sector Control on channel 'B' of his radio.

"Hello Lumba. This is Ganer 14. I am at the half-way point on my circular sortie. Now turning onto 185 degrees. Request you check my position."

Sector Control came back immediately. "Ganer 14, this is Lumba. We have you four miles east of (they gave the codeword for Liverpool)."

Rayne acknowledged with a click on his transmitter.

Turning onto 185 degrees, he was aware that he had a 20 minute leg ahead of him. He checked around his cockpit - oil pressure 70 lbs, oil temperature 65 degrees, radiator temperature 90 (about), fuel, bottom tank still full - then sat back and, after a minute or so, allowed his mind to wander, as he became half mesmerized by the beat and throb of his engine, the hypnotic glow of the exhausts, and the pin-pricked vastness of the stars and blackness around and above him.

His mind turning to the past, he thought of the many flying incidents over the previous several years, and his so-called successes in the air, particularly at night. He had done only moderately well in Malta, by his own standards. He had been obliged to fly the old Mark I Hurricane, which was by that time obsolete and no match for the current German fighters and Italian Macchi 202s. He had, however, shot down two Savoia 79s at night over Malta, but had been involved in at least several less successful interceptions, one of which had lived on in his memory.

Having had an Italian bomber illuminated over the island by the searchlights one very dark night, and at the point when he had just been about to open fire, the searchlights below had mistakenly turned their attention to him, so that he had been blinded absolutely by their blue-white glare at the critical moment.

After screaming obscenities at the fools beneath, he had chased the bomber half-way to Sicily, only to find that he could not overtake it, and finally to conclude that he was following, not the exhaust glow of the bomber in front, but a bright star that was low on the horizon.

Smiling to himself in bitter memory of the incident, his thoughts then turned to the unfortunate crew members of those two Savoias he had earlier shot down. Two men from each, he recalled, had baled out but the remaining members had been killed in horrible circumstances when their aircraft had crashed to flaming oblivion on the rocky ground beneath.

He had never given the deaths of those in the many aircraft he had vanquished very much thought in the past, but since Cee Bee's horrible demise, somehow things were different. And particularly when he thought of the occasion when that Navy Martlet had been destroyed before his eyes, flown by - of all people - Cee Bee's much loved twin brother, he was suddenly stricken, not only with the enormity of what he had done on that terrible occasion, but also over the months and years he had been a so-called successful fighter pilot.

What was his tally of deaths, he wondered, 20, 30, 40? Something like that anyway. All presumably young men like himself, with parents, girl-friends, and, possibly, young children. Gradually, as his Spitfire ploughed its way southward through the blackness of the night, the heavy weight of responsibility for his actions of the past, began to settle on his shoulders like an insupportable weight

He came-to sufficiently to recognise that he had reached stage three of his circular cross-country flight, and turned right onto 276 degrees. He didn't bother to speak to Sector Control to inform them - they would have his plot anyway. No . . . he would simply wait until he was within 50 miles of Llanbedr, before changing on to Channel 'A' on his radio, either to seek assistance or simply to inform them of his intentions.

Aware that he was now over the higher hills of Wales, invisible in the blackness below him, he continued with his sombre thoughts, thinking particularly of that persistent man who was the AOC, with his grandiose plans for him in the months and years to come; the somewhat now unconvincing assurances of his doctor friend, Ian Murray, at Farnborough; and always, his own wretched tiredness, lack of enthusiasm, and guilt. Yes, his guilt!

Then, too, there were his parents. His dear, loving parents! His father, who wished always to parade his virtues and successes to business friends and acquaintances at work and at his club, so that he often felt little more than a prize exhibit at a county fair. And his darling mother, whose love for him admitted absolutely no imperfections. Together, they both loved and were proud of him to the point that he felt positively smothered by their affection.

And then there was Cee Bee. That lovely girl he had so worshipped. With her beauty, her wholesomeness, her talents - and even her pantomime Irish chatter! How could he ever go on living without her?

Suddenly, the blackness of the night all around him and the stars above seemed full of her presence. Particularly, that one up there ahead of him now. He stared at it as though mesmerized. That bright one, so low on the horizon. Similar to the one in Malta - that one ahead which now seemed to be transformed, even as he watched, into Cee Bee's smiling features. That impudent, often naughty face, that so expressed her feelings - and doubts. And, oh yes, how she had misled him when she had spoken of the boy she had earlier loved, the boy who had turned out to be her own twin brother. The young man he had shot down and killed! Ah! . . . how much he had been so put off by that remark of hers, and so unnecessarily.

As he flew on, he became more and more submerged in a terrible melancholy. So that when a voice came up at him from below, he hardly comprehended its meaning.

"Ganer 14. This is Lumba. Please change now to Channel 'A' and call Llanbedr."

Then, when he not acknowledged Lumba's message but silently pressed his radio button for Channel 'A', Llanbedr came on immediately.

"Ganer 14. This is Llanbedr. We now have you 30 miles east of base. Do you require a course to steer? And do you need a QGH (a controlled descent). Finally, what are your angels?"

In response, Rayne said tiredly and very briefly, "I'm at 23,000. And no . . . I don't require any help. Of any kind! From you . . . or anyone! Now or ever!"

The Spitfire crossed over the top of Llanbedr airfield at 23,000 feet and headed roughly west over the waters of Cardigan Bay. Suddenly aware of the aircraft's position, the duty controller below, urgently conveyed his findings.

"Ganer 14. You have passed over the top of us. Your new course to steer is now 104 degrees. Are you receiving us? I repeat, are you receiving?" Then again, "Ganer 14, are you receiving?"

High above, Rayne heard the urgency in the man's tone, but made no response.

Then, in a state of quiet, almost dreamlike deliberation, he leaned forward . . . and twisted slowly the small knurled wheel in front of him . . . that switched off his oxygen supply.

After that, he sat back with a half smile on his face. Breathed deeply. And . . . waited.

At 23,000 feet, at which height the outside air pressure is less than half that at ground level and the oxygen content proportionately reduced, it takes about two to three minutes for a normal, healthy person to begin to succumb to the loss of life sustaining oxygen. First the critical faculties are affected, then the subject often becomes confused and incoherent, before unconsciousness gradually and finally takes over. More than anyone, with his experience and training, Rayne was aware of the likely consequences of his action. Even so, he did not ever remember pressing his transmitter and talking into his face mask.

Now in tears and as his mind grew ever more confused, he talked randomly about 'his problems'. About 'Pammy'; about Cee Bee and her brother and how he loved her; about the AOC, his feelings of guilt, and how he was unable to continue. Then finally, in hardly recognisable gibberish, he appealed to the Lord Jesus and Holy Mother for forgiveness - as Cee Bee might have wished him to - before finally and tearfully apologising to his own parents.

When he at last slumped forward into unending sleep, the Spitfire gently fell away into a left hand spiral, righting itself initially and lifting itself into an uncontrolled climb, as though protesting at the treatment of its apparently wayward pilot. Then, finally, and as though in anguish, dropped its nose and beginning to dive.

At something after 1.20 am, those awake in the area of Bardsey Island on the edge of Cardigan Bay, heard the scream of an aircraft descending in a spine-chilling terminal dive.

There was no explosion, merely a sudden silence as the Spitfire hit the water in the darkness. And disappeared.

In seconds, it was as though nothing had happened. Squadron Mark Wyndham Rayne, DSO, DFC**, and Wren Annabel May Fitzgerald of Ireland and the Naval station, Pwllheli, were at last united. To rest within yards of each other.

Chapter Six

Air Vice Marshal William Hawtrey, CBE, AFC, the Air Officer Commanding No. 9 Group, RAF, put his head around the door of his Personal Assistant's office. "Jimmy, try and get me the CAS on the telephone, there's a good chap."

Flight Lieutenant James Watson, somewhat surprised by the instruction to locate so important a personage, echoed, "You mean the Chief of Air Staff?"

Hawtrey returned him a bleak, tolerant smile, "That's what CAS usually means. You may have difficulty in finding him at this time of day, but leave a message with his ADC or office, asking him to telephone me when he has a moment."

An hour later, the CAS returned the call.

"William! You asked me to ring. What's the problem?" - most Air Rank officers were, with a few exceptions, on first name terms with their colleagues, no matter how exalted.

"John, I would like to call on you to discuss something I think important."

"You mean now? Today?"

"I had in mind tomorrow. If I came down to London, could I give you lunch at the Club?"

"I suppose so. I could probably fit you in. But, what's this all about?"

A slight hesitation. "It's about the recent death of that boy Rayne. I have something I want to tell you."

"Ah! A terrible tragedy. I was very upset. But isn't it something we can discuss over the 'phone?"

"I'd rather not. It's rather a delicate matter."

"Whatever you say. One o'clock tomorrow then. Will you be flying down or coming by train?"

"By train I think. One o'clock then, at the RAF Club. Tomorrow!"

The two senior officers met in the entrance hall of the RAF Club. After shaking hands, the CAS observed, "You're looking well, William. The Lancashire air seems to be suiting you." He glanced at his watch. "I'm meeting the PM in the House at 3 pm, so I shall have to leave here a little after 2. I suggest therefore that we go in for lunch immediately."

In the large dining room, the two sat down at a small table and were immediately surrounded by waiters.

The CAS waved away the wine list with the remark, "Can't meet the politicians smelling like a brewery. Although it never seems to worry Winston!" After which, he looked Hawtrey directly in the eye. "So . . . what's all this about the young Rayne and his accident?"

Hawtrey asked, "Did you see the Board of Inquiry findings?"

"No, but I had a note spelling out the result and some of the detail. A tragic accident, as I understand it, caused by either oxygen failure or an oversight by the pilot. Either way, very upsetting. I've seldom seem such obituaries in the 'Times' and 'Telegraph.'"

Hawtrey hesitated, carefully considering his words.

"I'm afraid neither cause was the case. Rayne died by his own hand. He committed suicide, and I fear I was partially responsible. Which, really, is why I am here today. You see . . . I am considering resigning."

His senior colleague looked across at him in frowning, perplexed disbelief.

"Are you serious? Because you can't resign and you know it! What on earth are you talking about?"

But Hawtrey's face was set. "In my view I made a serious error of judgement and . . . well . . . I feel I can't continue in my present position."

There was a silence of several seconds, before the more senior officer said quietly, "As you are so obviously upset, perhaps you'd better tell me about it."

Hawtrey, hesitated, then shrugged his shoulders minutely, before starting.

"Some days before Rayne lost his life, I had already arranged to visit Valley in Anglesey to have dinner with Ramsbottom-Isherwood, who is the Sector Commander there. Well, the day following the boy's death, the dinner took place. There were eight of us around the table that night, including a very attractive young woman called Leggett - Pamela Leggett - the wife of the Commanding Officer of the Mosquito squadron normally based there but temporarily away at West Malling."

"Because of the very recent accident, conversation around the table was very muted, and it was not until afterward that the young Leggett woman took me aside and into a corner where she imagined she couldn't be heard. There she then set about me, tooth and nail! She said quietly, with her eyes full of tears, 'Air Marshal, I think you are nothing more than an unprincipled and insensitive shit! You have just been responsible for the death of a gallant and wonderful boy, who has been a close friend of mine since childhood. Over the past six months you have goaded young Marcus Rayne into taking on a job he was too tired and worn out to perform, and one which he only agreed to do under protest. But you went on pressing, pushing and insisting on your hair-brained schemes, and now he is dead. He died, I suspect, by his own hand, because you pushed him over the edge. He took his own life, I know. He killed himself! And I want you to know that you are responsible and I hope you live the rest of your pathetic little life regretting it'."

"Well, I was so stunned, I couldn't reply. Which didn't matter anyway as the girl walked off and I have not seen hide nor hair of her since. After that, of course, the Sector Commander was apologising to me profusely, although it didn't make me feel any better at the time."

"Well, as you can imagine, this set me thinking, as I had believed until then that Rayne's accident had, in fact, been the result of some ghastly oversight. However, having arranged for the Commanding Officer at Kirton in Lindsay, Group Captain Tomlinson, to head the Inquiry, I decided to await his verdict."

"He took almost three weeks to come to a conclusion, because he found himself obliged to involve about 30 witnesses, from doctors at Farnborough and elsewhere, Sector and Watch Office controllers, 'P' staff at Air Ministry, station and other personnel from Llanbedr, Valley, and beyond, and finally, the redoubtable Mrs.Leggett."

"He finally concluded that Rayne had embarked on a quite unnecessary night-flight in an unstable state of mind. That he had quite successfully completed his cross-country and had passed overhead at Llanbedr at 23,000 feet, with the full intention of taking his own life. Finally, he had then purposely switched off his oxygen supply and in a state of confusion brought about by partial annoxia, had broadcast his problems and anxieties to the world, remarks overheard in horror and disbelief by the two chaps in the Watch Office at Llanbedr."

Hawtrey took a deep breath before continuing. "Realising the very delicate position he had on his hands, Tomlinson brought his draft conclusions to me to discuss before finalising them. I then told him to alter his report and make out that it may have been a failure of the equipment or simply pilot oversight. I had no wish to cause additional pain to the parents of a brave and honourable boy by revealing that their son had taken his own life. Nor would it add to the sum total of our knowledge of the accident's primary cause and, of course, of my own misjudgement. Furthermore, with the Spitfire at the bottom of Cardigan Bay, it would never be possible to prove that it was other than an accident."

Hawtrey looked up to find the CAS eyeing him curiously.

The latter said, "I am interested to hear why you have taken such an interest in this young man. It seems to be something close to an obsession. He was, I agree, an extremely gallant young officer, but there seems to have been something more than that. Was there?"

Hawtrey returned his senior's gaze squarely. "Yes . . . I believe there was. Something that I've since come to realise was simply a form of love. The love of a father for a son. We were more than a generation apart, I know, but from the moment I first saw him, I now realise that . . . that as a man with only teenage daughters, I felt greatly attracted to him."

He drew a long breath before continuing.

"I first saw him at Tangmere in the late June of 1940. He had been a member of 73 squadron in France when the Huns broke through and pretty well destroyed our fighter force on the Continent. Some members of 73 were forced to burn their aircraft in the retreat and Rayne was one of a few who managed to escape in a ship from, of all places, Nantes, on the west coast of France. I was Group Captain Plans at Fighter Command at the time and just happened to be visiting Tangmere when the remnants of 73 turned up, having just landed in England."

"Rayne, I know now, was only 19, a very tall and attractive young man. I saw him first in the ante-room of the officers' mess, and his attitude and general demeanour on that single occasion impressed me enormously. Although so young, he was so articulate and persuasive that he seemed to be in charge of those other officer members of his squadron who were clearly older and more senior to him. I watched from a distance and was greatly impressed. So much so, that I made a special note of his name."

"Later, of course, he did extremely well throughout the Battle of Britain and was, as you well know, decorated at least three times. After which, I became aware he had been sent to Malta with his squadron."

"Following his career, I then learnt of his additional successes in Malta and that he was being sent home by sea via the Middle East, deciding at that point, and having moved up to

9 Group, that I would ask for him to be installed as commander of one of my two Spitfire squadrons when he arrived home."

"'P' Staff put up some strong objections to my request, arguing that Rayne was too tired and worn out to continue operational flying, but I put pressure on them and he finally joined me. I also had another motive. Having heard of the advent of the jet engine and the possibility of having a wing of high-flying jet fighters in as early as late '43 or '44, I saw Rayne as the obvious leader and made arrangements for him to go to Farnborough to discuss the matter with the Institute of Aviation Medicine there. And . . . . well, I make no secret of the fact that I visualized him going from strength to strength, given that he was spared in combat. In short, John, I saw him one day in your seat - an eventual Chief of Air Staff. Fanciful you may think, but that was in my mind. He was that sort of quite exceptional, gifted young man."

The CAS lowered his head and nodded. Then, waving briefly in the direction of their now rapidly cooling food, indicated that he wished them to continue with their meal. Which they did, exchanging the usual Service gossip, comments on the progress of the war, and their personal views on a variety of subjects. Until the CAS, wiping his mouth with his napkin, changed the subject yet again.

"About that other thing, William. It seems obvious to me that you pushed young Rayne too far. And, it would seem, that is the view of others. However, I think you are making altogether too much of a drama of it all. To talk of resignation is obvious nonsense. Those of us in high places have the blood of thousands on our hands every day of every week. Arthur Harris of Bomber Command sends 20 crews to their deaths over Germany every night and I doubt that he loses very much sleep over it. You have taken this boy to your heart and I wouldn't criticise you for that. But, keep it in perspective. This is war and young Rayne is just another very sad war casualty. Feel guilty if you must - if it will help. Eventually, we all will have to live with the consequences of our actions."

Then, glancing at his watch, the CAS said, "And now, I must go and do battle with the politicians. There may not be much blood on our carpets, but many more of us die in offices than you imagine. Particularly with Winston in charge!"

Then, with a final handshake and nods, the two men separated.

Immediately following Rayne's death and her confrontation with the AOC, Pamela Leggett fell victim to the deepest of depressions. She had lost Windy, the love of her life, and also her school friend, Siobhan Fitzgerald. And she had so tried to see that he did not fly, as she thought he might, on that fatal night. The Sector Commander, Ramsbottom Ish., having been absent that weekend and without her husband to consult, she had telephoned Wynn-Jones at Llanbedr, to find him, too, away 'on some business visit', as his Station Adjutant had half jocularly described it, Why, in God's name, did people have to be away when she wanted them so desperately?

Then, when her darkest fear had been realised and she had heard of Rayne's death, she knew instinctively what had happened. He had taken his own life and that bastard, bloody AOC was largely responsible!

That night, and every night for a week, she had cried herself to sleep. Finally, when Wales seemed nothing more than an arid wilderness, she had packed up and joined John, her husband, in Kent. Vowing never to return.

Sixty miles south of her, Squadron Leader David Wynn-Jones sat in his office, head in hands. Outside the rain came down his window in steady, streaming lines, as it so often did in Wales. Why oh why had he been away when that boy had returned unexpectedly and decided to fly? And at night, too, for God's sake! If only he had been around to dissuade him - Marco would have listened to him!. If only he had been available, too, to talk to Pamela Leggett. What a tragedy! And that beautiful child, Annabel, as well. Such a lovely, delightful pair. So suited to each other.

Standing up on impulse, he began to walk about distractedly. If only he had been around! If only! If anyone was guilty, it was he! Well, he was, wasn't he? And now he would never forgive himself. He looked up and towards the window and swore mightily. Bloody rain! Bloody Wales! Bloody business! Bloody everything!

In far away Farnborough, Ian Murray was dining with his wife, Hermione. Without the children and in silence.

Forking up his fish pie slowly and with scant relish, he asked her: "What do you think? Did we make a mistake?"

"About whom? Marco Rayne?"

Her husband nodded. "He took his own life, you know. The Inquiry says he didn't, but he did. I know he did! As he said he might. Was it because of that girl? Or, something more fundamental, as he suggested? So hard to know exactly." Then after a silence he added. "All that's crystal clear is that he's now gone for good. That brave, brave boy, with such enormous talent and potential! And that, perhaps inadvertently, we made our contribution towards his going. Sad, sad old me! Sad, sad old fallible me!"

His wife added quietly, "Not just you, love. We both made a mistake."

An Escape to
Tragedy

An Escape to Tragedy

In this story, my aim was to illustrate several important aspects of the Second World War: air combat itself over France between 1941-43, the methods adopted and the trials encountered when escaping after being shot down, and, finally, the human problems that often arose when families were torn apart and scattered all over the world. In particular, I wanted to focus on the sad incidence of illegitimacy, when children were born out of wedlock and spent the rest of their lives wondering who they were and how they had come about. And as something of a garnish, I also wanted to introduce a small, little known piece of British history, which has always fascinated me.

That said, the main characters in this tale are imaginary and the story line contrived, dramatised, and is fiction. However, all of the events described are soundly based on fact and relate to my own experiences and those of two close friends of mine (one being still alive as I write), each one of whom finished the war with a most distinguished record of success.

As to the escape sequences, scores of aircrew who were shot down over northern France and Belgium and evaded immediate capture by the enemy, finally escaped by following the route and the methods described in this account. Indeed, I spent many hours discussing this particular incident with one gallant and distinguished colleague and the effect it had on him. He was also especially anxious to pay tribute to the bravery of the many young Frenchmen and women who helped him, at least one of whom was later arrested and executed by the Germans.

Again, there may be some readers who recognise themselves or their friends and acquaintances in the following passages and once more l ask for their indulgence, as it was never my intention to mislead, offend or denigrate. I merely wished to paint a true picture of a piece of history in which I took a minor part and its place in the broad canvas of war in the air.

Chapter One

It is a sad indictment of our present education system that so little attention is paid to the broader history of our nation or to its heroes. Rather do we now hear little more than the naughtiness of Henry the Eighth, the wickedness of Adolph Hitler, together with tales of 'social progress' and the emancipation of 'the downtrodden masses', concocted and proclaimed by such politically motivated historians as A.J.P. Taylor.

I was reminded of this unhappy state of affairs, having given a lengthy address on the 'Battle of Britain' to the seniors and staff of a major public school in the Oxford area. During my talk I had especially emphasised the contribution made by the leader of Royal Air Force, Fighter Command, Air Chief Marshal Sir Hugh Dowding.

Dowding, an austere, unsmiling man, was a Lowland Scot, born in Moffat. Bereaved early in life when his young wife died prematurely, he became deeply religious and a spiritualist. His main claims to fame, however, were a series of major decisions made at critical moments before and during the fall of France. These decisions proved to be right in spite of considerable pressure put on him by Government and a number of Service colleagues, to take more conciliatory lines. He also made evident his deep affection for, and loyalty to, the young fighter pilots of his Command, more than a thousand of whom were killed or horribly damaged during the sixteen weeks of that epic struggle in the air, later called the `Battle of Britain'.

Following his devoted service and many achievements to the nation, he was then shamefully removed from office when victory had been assured, the outcome, many felt, of the disgraceful machinations of a cabal of ambitious underlings.

Later, during question time following my talk and on a sudden whim, I asked my young audience if they had ever heard of the term 'Border Reivers', and recall standing there in slightly dismayed silence when there were only blank looks of complete incomprehension and I did not receive a single reply.

As I drove home that evening, I reflected sadly that not only did my grandchildren's generation appear to be ignorant of so many of the facts and romantic events of the past, but also of the injustices perpetrated by our nation on scores of its loyal and patriotic servants. My mind dwelt, particularly, on many of those, like Dowding, coming from the Border counties of England and Scotland - dour, sometimes rebellious people who nevertheless were strong in spirit and religion and tough and reliable in battle.

Especially was I reminded of one youthful friend of mine who came from those northern parts. A unique person and splendid fighter pilot during the Second World War, he achieved almost everything. However, in the first days of peace in late 1945, he died needlessly and tragically as the result, it appeared, of a few moments of recklessness. Or . . . was it perhaps for other reasons?

This story of my gallant colleague started in the autumn of 1996, on one Wednesday afternoon in September. My wife and I had finished lunch and she had just walked off up the lane to the village church - it was her 'flowers and brasses day' - allowing me a welcome quiet-hour in our sunlit conservatory to read the 'Daily Telegraph' and drink my coffee.

I had barely seated myself when the telephone rang. We have an extension hidden away among the flowers and, on answering it, I had a cultured male voice in my ear, the caller wishing to know, almost apologetically, if he was speaking to Group Captain Tom Burgoyne.

Wary of such enquiries, having long been irritated beyond reason by mainly Asian voices wishing to sell me double glazing or congratulating me on having just won a major cash prize, I answered somewhat facetiously that if my communicant was from the Inland Revenue, the Group Captain was in Australia and not expected back for at least a year!

I heard a quiet chuckle the other end of the line. My unnamed caller, no doubt believing he was speaking to the right person, added that he was nothing to do with the Revenue but merely wished to be granted a half hour's conversation with the Group Captain to discuss a matter of some importance involving a mutual friend of the Second World War, a Wing Commander Ian Graeme-Scott.

At the mention of that so familiar name from the past, memories came flooding back, persuading me to add rather grudgingly that I would be happy to entertain him and asking when he was likely to make his visit.

His reply was immediate and a little startling. "I had thought in about fifteen minutes' time, sir. I have already taken the precaution of being in your local area."

Bounced out of my afternoon reverie, I exclaimed, "Good God, man! Having enjoyed a hearty lunch, I was expecting to have a quiet nap. Is your journey really that important?"

Again, the quietly persistent voice, "It is, rather, sir. And I would be so grateful.".

So, after a moment's hesitation, I agreed and gave him directions how to reach me. Then, folding my newspaper with a sigh, I tidied away some local debris and went into the drawing room, shaking my head. Another quiet afternoon bit the dust! What it was to be a Battle of Britain 'hero'!

I was at the drawing room window when my guest swept in between our open gates in a very smart maroon-coloured Range Rover. Having executed a smart right hand turn on our brick-paved forecourt and braked to a squealing standstill, I watched the man inside straighten his clothing and put on what my mother used to call derisively a rat catcher's cap. He then patted a dog that was jumping about in the front seat beside him and, pushing open the door, stepped out.

I saw immediately he was a tall man and fairly heavily built. Wearing a well-cut tweed suit, he looked about 50 and rather 'prosperous'. As he moved in the direction of the house, I opened the front door and called out to him, "If you'd like to bring your dog in, please do. Provided he doesn't piddle on the carpets."

Smiling, the man returned to the car and let the animal free before approaching and extending a hand. "Actually, he's a lady and very well brought up." He added, "Her name's

Abigail, by the way, but she won't mind you calling her Abbo. And of course, she's very grateful because she's young and hates being shut in."

As I bent down to pat the creature - a black Labrador - it began wagging its tail furiously and frisking around in circles, before suddenly jumping up and lathering my face with a bright pink tongue. I led my guest through the drawing room into the conservatory, the dog grinning all over its silly face and sniffing everything in sight with obvious relish. Then, waving my hand towards a chair, I instructed, "Park your bustle - to use the immortal words of David Atcherley, a much loved Air Marshal senior of mine in ancient days." Which he did, settling first his dog then himself, as I sat down opposite and spread my hands. "Now, what's this all about?"

My guest cleared his throat with a somewhat nervous cough.

"Well, to kick off with, my name is Richard Cadwallader and I'm a solicitor with offices in Gloucester. For the past five years I have been researching the life and Service career of Wing Commandeer Ian Graeme-Scott. As I understand you were a close acquaintance of his, you will know that he distinguished himself greatly during the last war. However, he was killed tragically in August 1945, a matter of days after the Japanese surrender in the Far East. For many months now I have followed every twist and turn of his career - all his postings, promotions, his recorded victories in air combat, what he did and where he went, even to the point of accounting for pretty well every day's leave he took and how he occupied his time when away from his flying duties. In short, sir, there is very little I don't know about him".

I found myself regarding the man with mild amusement "I'm very impressed. But, why all the time and effort? Is this a personal thing?"

Cadwallader returned a calm stare and for a moment there was silence between us. Then he said quietly, "It is. Very much so. You see . . . I believe Ian Graeme-Scott was my father. I honestly think I am the son he never met or even knew about."

At this point, I'm bound to admit I did not know how to respond. Then, I heard my own voice commenting gently, "I must say, I'm surprised. Really surprised. Knowing Scotty as well I did, and for about a dozen very good reasons, I find what you have just told me almost impossible to believe."

At that juncture, our conversation was interrupted by my wife returning. I heard the front door close with a thump and then her voice calling out for me. Then she appeared and was somewhat taken aback when she saw first the dog then my guest. But after introductions had been made, a few pleasantries exchanged and she had fussed the grinning, capering animal, she declared that cups of tea were in order and that after his long journey, Cadwallader surely needed something to eat - a sandwich or a piece of cake, perhaps. At that I shrugged helplessly in my guest's direction and he politely rolled his eyes but said nothing.

After an interval of about ten minutes, our guest continued. "As you may have gathered, I was born "the wrong side of the blanket" in the late autumn of 1944 to a young woman who gave birth in the John Radcliffe Hospital in Oxford. My birth mother offloaded me immediately, after which, it seems, I was fostered for several months. I was then adopted by Anne and George Cadwallader. Later, of course, I was christened in their name"

"The Cadwalladers lived in Oxford. He was an academic who taught in one of the colleges there, and his wife, Anne, was a nursing sister somewhere in the same local area. Both were in their late 40s. They had no children of their own and they lavished all their love and attention on me, plus a good deal of their money. I was sent to a good prep. school, then on to Radley, finally moving on to King's College, Cambridge, where I read law. I couldn't have been better treated or with more affection and, until the age of 22, I had no idea I had been adopted, although, when in my teens, as I was fairly large and with fair hair and matching complexion, there was always the family joke that I was a bit of a throwback - both my parents being of Welsh extraction, were dark and fairly small. Cadwallader, incidentally, is an ancient Welsh name, as you may know."

"When I was in my early 20s, however, and making nesting noises, my parents, who were then 60-plus, thought it time to tell me who I was and how I had come about. This was somewhat to their embarrassment, I may add, and very much to my shock. They explained that my mother had been a single girl of about 20, that her name, as far as they could recall - it being 20-odd years earlier - was Walker, or something that sounded like that. Furthermore, that the father of her child had been a famous fighter pilot in the Air Force. The information about the father, incidentally, came to light a little later when the girl had apparently spoken very admiringly about him to her Social Workers, mentioning that his surname had been Scott and his Christian name, Graham. I should add that the Cadwalladers never met my birth mother, but it was the policy at the time for Social Workers to pass on as much information as was available about the mother and the infant for whom they were arranging a future."

"Anyway, for a time I did nothing, being in something of a state of shock arising from the news of my origin. Then I married and later both my wife and I came to the conclusion that it was important that I should know more about my antecedents."

"Information about my father - assuming he was my father - was fairly simple to discover. I was confused at first as he was placed under the letter 'G' in the Air Force list, his name being the hyphenated Graeme-Scott, and his Christian names Ian Malcolm. The name of my birth mother, however, proved to be a problem; I finally managed to find the register of births in the Oxford area for the approximate date on which I was born, only to find that the girl had given her name as Walkden, not Walker. The other information was that she was 20 years old, her Christian name Janet, and that her occupation was shown as 'Airwoman' of the 'Women's Auxiliary Air Force'. The father was not named, understandably, and there was no indication of where the girl was stationed. She obviously wished to keep the whole affair as private as possible."

"Thus armed, I then found, rather to my surprise, that there had been three 'Walkdens' in the WAAF at the time - it is not a familiar surname - all of whom I attempted to contact by letter and telephone. One, unhappily, had died, one was married and lived in South Africa, and the third was also married and resident in the United Kingdom."

"The lady in South Africa was very relaxed about my enquiry, saying that she was not my mother but adding that she would have been delighted at the time to have had the opportunity of sleeping with so distinguished an airman. She ended by wishing me the best of luck in my search. The remaining woman was very huffy, however, and refused to take part in any discussion or answer any of my questions, other than to say that she was certainly not my mother!"

"So, I am left with only my birth mother's word, first that her name was indeed Walkden and not something else, and that she did have an affair with Ian Graeme-Scott. After all, it may just have been the fantasy of a love-stricken young woman admiring a hero from afar - he was very well known at the time. Moreover, there are a number of further details of Ian's life-style and flying career I need, plus some very pertinent points about the manner of his death and even the reason why he died. Which is why I am here today and why I need your help."

I paused for a time then cocked a frowning eye in Cadwallader's direction. "It looks, dear boy, that not only are you here for tea and dinner, but you may have to spend the night with us as well."

I then embarked on the story of my association with Ian Graeme-Scott - and it took me a long time!

I started. "I first came across Ian Graeme-Scott quite by accident in the last days of June, 1940. At the time, I was a 19 year old Pilot Officer in a fighter squadron flying Hurricanes, based temporarily at Sherburn-in-Elmet, which is, or was, a small grass airfield a little to the south of York. We were a First World War unit which had recently been reactivated and had just been declared 'operational' and defending the nation for the very first time."

"At about 4 pm on Thursday, 27th June, I was in one of three Hurricanes scrambled to intercept a `bogy' (unidentified aircraft), which was flying south, some 25 miles out into the North Sea. At that stage of the war, the Huns were in the habit of sending reconnaissance aircraft and single bombers to look for our shipping convoys and to bomb small targets of opportunity. The weather, I remember, was fine with about 5/10ths cloud at around 12,000 feet - we later quoted cloud amount in 8ths not 10ths."

"All agog, as it was our first interception sortie in earnest, we climbed hot foot to around 20,000 feet and sped out eastwards, praying for a sight of the enemy and thirsting for success."

"After receiving several vectors, we spied the Hun, a Ju 88, about 30 miles off Flamborough Head. It was around 1,000 feet below us, which enabled us to work up a fair turn of speed before we sorted ourselves out into the approved line-astern attacking formation."

"We were within a mile of it and closing fast, when the enemy aircraft saw us and veered off towards the nearest cloud. However, we caught it before it disappeared temporarily into the murk, each of us firing a single two or three-second burst before it vanished into a quite small cumulus, to appear again in clear air beyond within seconds."

"After that, the poor Hun really didn't stand a chance. Although the rear gunner shot at us for a time, his tracer twisting and streaking in our direction, he was soon silenced. Then as one, then both engines began to stream thin trails if black and white smoke, the 88, still tilting and weaving, finally turned towards the Yorkshire coast and began to slow up and let down."

"Eventually, recognising that the enemy aircraft was in real distress, we stopped firing and formated on it in a wide, shepherding vic, by which time I saw that we were all within ten miles or so of the coastline a little north of Hull and that the bomber was likely to crash-land a mile or two inland. Which it did, remaining more or less in one piece but gouging a long, dark furrow in the earth and looking very forlorn and defeated."

"We circled the wreck several times during which two figures emerged and wandered about, no doubt recovering from the shock of being shot down and the crash. They looked up at us but didn't wave, which I suppose was not surprising given the circumstances. We then flew back to Sherburn to a riotous reception, it being the squadron's first victory. Later, we sent across some airmen to cut off the Nazi emblem and a black cross from the battered fuselage and tail, trophies that decorated our dispersal hut until we moved on shortly after."

"News of our victory reached the papers almost immediately and appeared the following day in a small paragraph beneath a minor heading. Feeling that our success had not properly been recognised, we went to the cinema in York hoping to see a report of it on Movietone News, being raised to noisy fury when the commentator alleged that our Hun had been shot down by `Spitfires from a northern airfield!' "

"A few days later, I and several others flew up to Acklington - an airfield just north of Newcastle - for some practice firing against drogue targets. Apart from the Gunnery School, a Spitfire squadron, members of which had claimed our Hun, was also based there."

"In the Officers' Mess that night, I asked for the names of those who had been involved in the recent engagement off Flamborough Head and was told that 'Scotty, the chap over there reading the paper', was the leader of the section of three Spitfires. This, incidentally, was the first occasion I had encountered the young man who was to become a friend of mine for life - his life, anyway!"

"As I walked over then sat down beside him, he looked up and put down his paper. I saw that he was a Flying Officer and appeared about two years old than me."

"I said pleasantly enough, 'Hello! My name's Tom Burgoyne from down south and I wanted to meet the chap who a few days ago shot our fox - or said he did!'"

"For a moment there was a look of surprise on his face, immediately replaced by a bright, almost mischievous grin. 'So, that was you, was it? We heard that the Hun had come down somewhere near Hull and that some other chaps had had a go at it. Actually, we thought we had done enough to have put paid to the blighter, but clearly that wasn't so. We intercepted it flying north about 20 miles out from Berwick and after a few attacks; it turned south and kept disappearing into cloud. We kept at it, however, getting in a few juicy hits now and then and causing some obvious damage, but it was still on its feet, so to speak, when we had to break off east of Flamborough Head when we began to get a bit low on fuel. Added to which one of our chaps had been hit by the rear gunner. So, we were glad to hear that you had finished it off. Even so, I think we deserved a good half, don't you?'"

"I responded grudgingly, 'I think our half was much bigger than yours. Anyway, it crashed, which is all that mattered I suppose, and that we claimed the trophies to adorn our dispersal hut. So, I reckon honours were about even, although I must add that none of us saw any of your Spits at the time.'"

"Again the grin. 'Ah, we might just have gone home, old boy. Either that or you couldn't have been looking properly. You Hurricane blokes are always shouting the odds about how you can see out of your aircraft better than we can from Spits.' Again the cheeky grin, although there was no malice in it."

"I did not see Ian Graeme-Scott again for many weeks. Shortly after our shared Ju 88 incident, my squadron moved from Yorkshire down to the Southampton area, where we became involved in the first real action of the Battle of Britain. We then moved up to Essex at the end of August and were stationed at RAF North Weald, staying there for almost 12 months."

"Meanwhile, I had heard that Graeme-Scott with his squadron had been travelling up and down between Acklington and Hornchurch at almost fortnightly intervals. Like me, he had apparently been heavily involved in the Battle, his name and exploits appearing regularly in the 11 Group Intelligence summaries. It was written there that he been credited with at least eight confirmed victories, that he had baled out once, crash-landed twice, and had been wounded on at least one other occasion, if only slightly. So that by the end of November 1940, he had become well known, if not a famous name. All this I read about with enormous interest but it was only on Christmas Day, 1940 that we finally met again at RAF Hornchurch and were able to speak together at length. I remember it well for all sorts of reasons."

"It had snowed heavily during that Christmas week of 1940 and it was only on 23rd that our new AOC, Leigh-Mallory, sent round a signal saying that he required the squadron and flight commanders of all 35 fighter squadrons deployed around London, to meet him on Christmas Day at RAF Hornchurch, where we were to discuss policy and tactics for the future."

"I remember especially driving down in the station Humber, through an Essex countryside a white wilderness of snow and iron hard with frost. We hardly encountered a single other vehicle on the 30 mile journey, my breath steaming like a kettle in the rear seat of that frigid car - heaters were an unheard of luxury in those days, scorned as decadent by the manufacturers of British motor vehicles!"

"The Officers Mess ante-room at Hornchurch, a venerable establishment of the early '20s, greeted us with paintings of Sopwith Camels and SE5s of the First World war, roaring coal fires, and a crush of welcoming faces, all in lively conversation. The sight of bent arms, tankards and wine glasses by the score and the deafening noise of laughter and good spirits was such that I found myself silent and awe-stricken by the sight of so many uniformed officers whose names I had read about and whose deeds had so inspired me over the previous months. And in the distance and amid the crush, I spied the animated face of Ian Graeme-Scott. Catching my glance, he raised his eyebrows and grinned in my direction, signalling that we should meet after lunch."

"The meal in that bright but tastefully lit dining-room, though formal and lasting for more than an hour, was excellent by any standard and loaded with good cheer; a full Christmas menu with wines, coffee and port to follow. As I ate, my eyes wide and wandering, in my mind I pictured my parents, 200 miles to the north, eating alone, quietly and frugally, their thin fare obtained via their two slim grey ration books."

"Finally, the meal concluded, we all trooped back into the ante-room and found seats - most of us anyway. At the end of a slow moving queue of around 100, I was finally obliged to sit on the floor in front of the fire, almost at the feet of the Air Marshal, Leigh-Mallory, who at one point smiled down in my direction and nodded - in approval I hoped."

"From this cramped and uncomfortable position, I sat and listened for more than an hour and with growing concern as the head man addressed us like a father telling a story to children. The Battle of Britain had been won, he said. The RAF, as 22 years earlier in 1918, had triumphed over the German enemy. But now, it was time not to defend but to attack! Attack, with escorted light bombers! Attack, with wings of fighters, drawing the Huns into the air before shooting them down like pigeons! Attack also, in small formations of two - 'Mosquito' sorties, so called - operating at low level in favourable cloud conditions against targets of opportunity such as airfields, gun positions, trains, anything of a military nature!. Attack! All the time and everywhere. We would take the fight to the enemy and beat him into the ground! And amid a silence that was of pin-dropping intensity - the new programme would start . . . tomorrow. Boxing Day!"

"My immediate feeling, I recognise even now 50-odd years after the event, was of instant, stomach shrinking dismay. What a terrible time to be killed - the day after Christmas, for heavens sake! And with my mind still on the meal we had just enjoyed, what a terrible waste of all that good food. Because I knew in my bones that we in Hurricanes would get all the miserable, low level, bomber-escort jobs. In short, the mucky end of every stick."

"After that there were lengthy opinions offered on tactics, heights, speeds, the effectiveness of the likely enemy response, including fighters and low and high level `flak'. Because of my 'juniority', however, and sad to relate, I listened to it all in tongue-tied and apprehensive silence."

"When, after an age we all stood up to leave, a chattering and on the whole excited group, I saw Ian Scott pushing his way towards me through a crush of senior officers, his face alight."

"Hello again! I was rather surprised to see you see here. Until I saw the two stripes on your arms, of course. Congratulations! When did it all happen?'"

"I pulled a dismissive face. 'About four weeks ago. After we had had several fatalities and a clutch of injuries in the squadron. I was selected, it seemed, as I was the only chap still standing.'"

"He smiled, his eyes disappearing into friendly crinkles 'And your two DFCs had nothing to do with it, I suppose. And, before you ask, I was promoted last July, just after our Ju 88 incident. Anyway, enough of all that. What do you think of the new plans for the future?'"

"I pulled a face. 'Not very much! Because I know who are going to be the bottom squadrons doing all the escorting and catching all the low `flak'. Not you in Spits, waltzing around at 15,000 feet and above, but us in our poor lame-duck Hurricanes, flying alongside the Blenheims at little more than walking pace. If the Hun fighters are able to get to us in time, we'll be slaughtered. No, I think the AOC was talking through his hat - my hat anyway, because it's more than likely I won't have a head to put it in.'"

"But Scotty was laughing. 'You're being altogether too pessimistic. I bet you chaps will soon be shooting down the 109s in droves. Cheer up! It'll be good fun, flak or no flak. You'll have a couple of D.S.O.s to your name in no time, mark my words.'"

"Well, all that was on Christmas Day, 1940. At Hornchurch, amid all the snow and ice. Happily, more bad weather intervened so that the Boxing Day show was cancelled. I went on leave for a few days over the New Year but was back when the first escorted bomber attack took place on 10th January, 1941 - against an ammunition dump in the Fôret de Guines, just behind Boulogne."

"And I was dead right in two important respects. We North Weald Hurricanes found ourselves as close escorts to the bombers and flying aimlessly around France at less than 5,000 feet. All the time, being shot at. I had streams of red balls and tracer floating and flashing around my ears for what seemed like hours. One of our chaps was shot down by something - or someone - and although able to cross the Channel, baled out before his Hurricane flew into the cliffs at Dover, and three others of us were hit by flak, I in the tail - nothing really serious - another pilot in the airscrew, and a third somewhere, I can't remember where."

"And of course, virtually no damage was done by the six Blenheims involved, the whole business being, in my view, a dismal and expensive waste of time and effort. I looked in the Intelligence Summary later for Ian Scott's name and that of his squadron, but neither was mentioned. So, like me, he presumably survived."

"After that I did not see Ian Scott again for about five months, although I read about him from time to time. During that period we at North Weald went about our business, escorting bombers attacking docks along the Belgian and French coastline, bombing German shipping in the Channel, hitting railway marshalling yards at Lille and elsewhere, and, now and then, on specified days, taking part in low level 'Mosquito' sorties against any suitable target we could find within 20 or 30 miles of the Channel coast."

"I found those low level sorties rather stressful, dangerous, and pretty pointless. With only eight rifle-calibre machine guns in our Hurricanes, we could not do much damage to anything other than the few thin-skinned vehicles we occasionally caught on the roads. And - very rarely this, as it was always a highly dangerous exercise - transport and aircraft on the Hun airfields, which were always dauntingly well defended."

"Now and then we were intercepted at low level by 109s but, provided we saw them in time, we were usually able to nip up into cloud and escape. Very few of us were keen to take on German fighters in their own backyards, as they were so much nippier than we were in all departments."

"No, I well remember, I didn't care for those low level attacks, not one little bit! Nor was I very much happier escorting the slow-motion Blenheims higher up when we were never at full fighting speed. I was a defending fighter, for heaven's sake, not just something to be shot at over enemy territory, particularly when it was for no obvious purpose."

"Then, in about June, 1941, as I recall, we had a very costly engagement when escorting the usual force of six Blenheims. They were bombing harbour installations at Dunkirk, an engagement which resulted in quite a change of faces in our squadron."

"At this point I ought to explain that we had been re-equipped with the Mark II Hurricane in March, 1941. This newer version incorporated the more powerful Merlin 20 engine, which had a two-speed supercharger, enabling us to fight with greater confidence above 25,000 feet.

Even so, our new mounts could not match even the old 109E in terms of speed, rate of dive and climb, much less so when the more modern 109F came into being during later that year."

"It was, however, because we felt more at home at the higher altitudes, that my squadron was, on that particular occasion, providing top cover at 18,000 feet. There were four Hurricane units involved that day, with me leading the final four aircraft of the rearguard of our own squadron, at 20,000 feet."

"Everything went swimmingly at first. I was looking down on Dunkirk far below and watching the bombs burst within the harbour and the rising columns of dark smoke, when to my astonishment, tracer began to flick past my cockpit and at least a dozen 109s swam silently past me with vivid yellow noses and black-crossed tilting wings, all engaged in an almost vertical diving attack on my group and other Hurricanes spread out beneath us."

"Immediately, of course, there was violent reaction as I and my immediate colleagues whipped into avoiding turns, the air filled meanwhile with almost incoherent shouts of alarm and warning."

"After that, there were whirling wings everywhere and much diving and twisting in pursuit of a rapidly disappearing enemy group, all of which were now dropping away like stones towards the sea. Then, with 'G' forces having dulled our sight as the blood drained from heads and eyes, I and others breathlessly circled and took stock."

"The action had been for no more than 20 violent and unnerving seconds. During this very brief period, the horizon had hurled itself in all directions and we had all felt our bodies cringe in expectation of the thud and stink of cannon strikes, the horrifying reek of leaking fuel, the numbing paralysis of body wounds, and the need perhaps to bale out in haste from a burning aircraft into the freezing sea far below."

"Amid groups of Hurricanes turning beneath us in apparent disorder, further afield I caught sight of the formation of Blenheims heading away from the shoreline in a slow turn. Still mightily concerned about my own naked and vulnerable backside, I looked about agitatedly for any of my three former companions. There being none to be seen and feeling totally isolated, I dropped down steeply to attach myself to a formation of about six widely spread aircraft, most of which I recognized as belonging to 56 Squadron, also from North Weald, who appeared to be heading back in the direction of England."

"Once in their company and feeling a good deal safer, I fell to speculating how it was that, without warning, we had been so dramatically bounced by the enemy and what had happened to the other members of my section. Had any of them been able to fire and with what result? I had been absolutely surprised and had been unable to shoot at anything. It had clearly been a typical fighter engagement - sudden, vicious, and over in seconds. And I - we - had been caught out like novices. Moreover, there was still much RT chatter suggesting that several members of formations lower down had also been hit and needed help and possibly rescue. It had all been very unpleasant and I realised how lucky I had been to have come away with a whole skin. Finally, with the coast of Kent approaching slowly, among friends and with my aircraft apparently undamaged, I suddenly felt much better. Thank God for that!"

"I taxied in at North Weald and parked my aircraft on my usual hard-standing. There were obvious signs of concern among our now scurrying ground crews. One of the South African members of my small group had been badly hit around the cockpit, the side of which was a shambles. However, he appeared to be unhurt though shocked and protesting noisily. My rigger also reported excitedly that I had sustained two deep gouges in my own fuselage where I had been struck glancing blows by 20 mm cannon shells, fired, it seemed, from directly astern. The fourth member of my section - one of our experienced NCO pilots - was apparently missing."

"What was also soon revealed when heads were counted, was the loss of our 'A' Flight commander, Flight Lieutenant Robert Rutter. He had apparently just disappeared. Furthermore, another squadron member had been forced to land his damaged aircraft at Mansion. All in all, a thoroughly miserable and unprofitable day."

"Then, two days later, when in the evening I was I the act of going into the Mess dining room, the Adjutant stopped me in the doorway. He had just received a signal. A new Flight Commander was being posted in as Bob Rutter's replacement. His name was Graeme-Scott, and did I know him? I recall standing there, stunned into silence. What an extraordinary turn of events!"

"Ian Graeme-Scott arrived two days later. Being told of his arrival, I drove up to the Officers' Mess to welcome him and found him unpacking in one of the rooms of our wooden First World War huts. We pilots were considered expendable and did not normally qualify for rooms in the Mess proper, which were infinitely warmer and much more comfortable, being reserved (we always alleged) for `important people', such as Equippers, Accountants, or Education Officers."

"He looked up when I entered and gave me one of his bright and mischievous grins."

"After shaking hands, I said, 'It's nice to see you again. But, what a come-down for you. Lame duck Hurricanes after your beautiful Mark II Spits'"

"He shrugged. 'Oh, it's not that bad. With the two-speed blowers of the Merlin 20, your Hurricanes should have a little better performance at altitude than even our new Spitfires. No, I'm not worried or in the least depressed. Anyway, I also hear that some of your kites have twelve machine guns and others four cannons.' Again the grin. 'How lucky can I get?'"

"After that we chatted for a time and I was turning to leave, I noticed a large crucifix on the wall. Without thinking, I asked in surprise, 'Is that yours?'"

"'Mine? Of course it is! It's the last thing I pack and the first I unpack. It's a very important part of my luggage.' And he smiled his bright mischievous smile again."

"As I left, for a moment I felt a little uncomfortable. Was he one of those 'Holy Joes'? If he was, it was surprising as he looked remarkably normal.".

"For the next several days, the squadron carried out a number of fighter sweeps over Northern France at 30,000 feet, uneventful as it proved. Although we saw several large formations of Huns in the distance, none of them showed any signs of belligerence."

"Ian Scott did not accompany us on those occasions, electing instead to fly off on his own on what he termed familiarising flights - he had never flown a Hurricane before, apparently, not that that mattered very much as both the Spit and the Hurricane were childishly easy to fly."

"He had selected a newish Mark IIb as his personal aircraft, one mounting twelve Browning guns, and apparently had shot off a few thousand practice rounds at the ground targets at Dengie Flats on the Essex coast."

"On one occasion I came across him at the butts, his aircraft on trestles, supervising the re-harmonisation of his guns. I stopped as I drove by and spoke to him about it. He explained that he liked to have all his guns focused at a point 150 yards ahead, which was rather unusual as the normal harmonisation range was 250 yards. He laughingly added that he was such a bad shot he had to get that close to have any chance of hitting even the largest Hun bomber, an admission I greeted with a disbelieving smile because of his considerable record of success and tally of victories. Clearly, here was a man who thought quite a bit about weapon effectiveness and his own personal methods and failings. I felt a little humbled, being well aware that few others in the squadron - me included - gave such details more than a passing thought. But the thing that really stuck in my mind about those early days of his in the squadron, was his quite remarkable ability as an aerobatic pilot."

"Aerobatics never figured large in the repertoire of any squadron member as it was never a requirement in combat; in fact, anyone who indulged in perfect loops, rolls, etc. within sight of the enemy, usually became a battle casualty pretty quickly. Moreover, practice flying, alas, of any sort since the early summer of 1940, had been almost none existent as pretty well every flight since then had been an operational sortie. So it came as a surprise one afternoon to hear, and witness, a Hurricane turning itself inside out at fairly low level over the airfield."

"As we all trooped out of dispersal to see who the `show-off' was, it became clear that the pilot was none other than our newly arrived flight commander. Then, as we watched, our admiration grew with every manoeuvre; his loops were perfect, the slow rolls immaculate and his upward 'Charlies' and rolls-off-the-top precisely and smoothly executed. Then, after about ten minutes, when we thought the exhibition over, his Hurricane lost speed and having turned on to the downwind leg of its landing circuit, to our astonishment, Scotty turned the aircraft over and flew upside down, holding it there for a full two minutes, and in that position, lowered the undercarriage. Then, as we watched in open-mouthed silence, he made a flat turn on to his final leg, still in the inverted position, before continuing to lose height and flipping the aircraft back right way up at less than 500 feet and within 400 yards of the airfield boundary. Finally, with the flaps emerging and the tail of the Hurricane fishtailing left and right, the nose rose and the aircraft touched down in a perfect three-point landing. At which point, most of us watching, first swallowed then closed our mouths in relief, whilst m the distance, small groups of ground crew began to cheer and clap. It had been quite an exhibition."

"In the weeks that followed, the squadron continued to fly over France and Belgium on a dozen ridiculous and comparatively ineffective sweeps, bomber escort sorties and two-aircraft low level attacks. The latter were particularly dangerous and, throughout the Command, resulted in the loss of many experienced pilots who had distinguished themselves greatly during the Battle of Britain and after."

"During his brief early period with the squadron, Ian Graeme-Scott had proved himself to be a capable and aggressive leader, shooting down at least two Me 109s during those several fallow weeks. This was a considerable feat when flying an aircraft whose performance was so much inferior to that of the enemy."

"In particular he was good at night; in fact we both had some success during the month of July, 1941, when at midnight one night, but with a full moon, I shot at and badly damaged a Heinkel 111, which fell into the North Sea some 10 miles off Clacton, while he shot down a Ju 88, which crashed in flames just south of Colchester, killing two members of the crew, the others having baled out."

"In those three months following his arrival, I came to know Ian very well indeed. We had much in common. Neither of us were what might be termed rowdy types and neither of us smoked or drank. We seldom went 'pubbing' with the others, being more inclined to sit around the fire in the Officers' Mess ante-room on the few occasions the squadron was released or granted a short respite, and either read, talked or played snooker. Even so, he was never noticeably stand-offish and always refused any invitation he felt unable to accept with good grace and a pleasant smile. In general conversation, I never once heard him swear, nor on the other hand, was he at any time ostentatiously pious. If asked, I would have described him as pleasantly wholesome."

"Physically, he was not impressive. Only slightly more than middle height, he was slim and wiry with straight dark hair and a fresh complexion. But he had about him a quickness of thought and action which made him stand apart. He was always lightning sharp when responding to any major, or even minor emergency, such as, for example, picking up with his bare fingers a live coal which had fallen from the fire and was burning a hole in the carpet, when the rest of us, undecided, had stood back and watched. This decisiveness was often repeated in the air when his reaction to difficult situations was always immediate yet seldom found wanting."

"By his own admission, he was a countryman at heart. He was an excellent shot with a twelve bore and enjoyed long walks in the Essex countryside, a pleasure he often shared with me on the few days off we had together. During such occasions, he was always an interesting and knowledgeable companion, often talking about his family, his home, and the Border areas of Scotland, which he clearly loved."

"Of his religious leanings he was quite open and never embarrassed or less than frank. During the war when Sundays were no different from any other day of the week, he usually managed to slip away to take early Sunday morning Communion - there were only several on the station who were practising Roman Catholics. And after a time, we all became aware that prior to every operational sortie, he would cross himself before closing his eyes and even kneeling now and then in a brief, silent prayer. Once when we were out walking, I broached the subject. I said, 'Ian, I notice you always pray before taking off on an interception or a flight over the other side. I'm very interested. What exactly do you pray for? For your own personal safety? For success? Or what?'"

"He thought for a moment before answering. 'None of those things. I just put myself into the hands of God, telling Him that I will do my best according to what I believe is His overall plan. I always find it a great comfort because I know then that no matter what, I shall then be in His hands. What is likely to happen to me, I can never foretell, of course. Except it will be for the best and that I need not worry - which I normally don't - although I admit, there are times when private doubts sometimes get the better of me, as I have no particular wish to die, because of the distress it would cause my family.'"

"I remember frowning. 'But, being God's instrument, so to speak, are you never uncomfortable when you shoot down a German bomber or fighter and kill the crew flying it?'"

"He gave an almost indifferent shrug. 'Normally, no, although I always regret the fact that people lose their lives. You see, I shoot at weapons of war, because they are attacking my family and my country and it's my duty to do so; and in the knowledge that the pilot or aircrew are part of those weapons - without them the bombs wouldn't fall and the guns wouldn't fire.'"

"'But Ian, those German pilots and aircrew, before taking off, probably said the same prayer as you did and to the same God. How do you reconcile that with your particular philosophy?'"

"'Ah, but God will then adjudicate. After all, I've been shot down a number of times and I have survived, which leads me to believe that He still has work for me to do. It's the same for them. Perhaps they are part of His overall plan, I don't know. If they are, then they will survive.'"

"Then I heard myself arguing, 'But that makes you sound something of a fatalist. Everything is pre-ordained. You seem to believe that God has it all sorted out and that Britain will ultimately win this war, despite the fact that we are now all alone against a massive and very efficient enemy. Is that really what you think? I've always believed we won't lose immediately, particularly after the fighting last year, but not losing a battle and winning a war are not exactly the same thing.'"

"'Ah, but you must have faith, Tom, because for us it is a just war and one we shall ultimately win. When and by what means, I honestly don't know. But it is God's wish, I am sure, that Britain and justice will prevail and that I am just one of his instruments. Even if I, and perhaps you, don't live to see the final winning of it. It is all in His hands. I know it will happen.'"

"I will long remember that discussion. It was the first, and indeed the last I ever had with Ian Scott on the subject of his religious convictions. It may have not been the most profound exchange of views as we were very young at the time - I was only 20 and he was but a year or two older. Moreover, we were no doubt constrained by the unwritten but long-held convention that officers, particularly young ones, were never to discus matters of politics, religion or ladies in, or beyond, the Officers' Mess."

"I remember it, too, because it was about a fortnight later that we were both engaged in an excursion into enemy territory that was to lead to far reaching consequences for both of us, but mainly for him."

At this point, having been speaking for close on two hours, with Cadwallader drinking it all in in utter silence, I called a halt and invited him to stay for dinner. After that, he fed his dog and took it for a 'comfort break' in the adjoining field before we all sat down for our meal. Finally, with a brandy in his hand and the dog asleep at his feet, my guest lay back in his chair and listened with rapt attention as I provided further details of my association with Ian Graeme-Scott.

"It was in early September, as I recall, when Ian came up to me one morning fairly fizzing with excitement."

"'I've just had a word with the C.O.,' he explained, 'and told him what I have in mind, to all of which he gave his consent.'"

"'Which is?' By then, I was becoming a little wary of Scotty's enthusiasms and bright ideas."

"'Well, tomorrow is our day for a low level jaunt over the other side, and I have suggested to him that you and I - we - both go together. A rather special trip, if you see what I mean.'"

"'No, I don't see what you mean, and before you go any further I think it's the worst possible idea. If I know you, it's bound to be dangerous and what happens if we both get bumped off? The squadron will have lost both its flight commanders at one fell swoop.'"

"But his enthusiasm knew no bounds and, leading me towards a map of France pinned on the wall, began to explain his plan with a moving finger."

"'Look! There's a railway line, here, between Arras and Amiens, which I want to visit, as a mass of trains use it each day, I'm told. Also, it has considerable significance for me as my father served in that area of the Somme during the last war, and here, at Corbie, close to Amiens, the rascal von Richthofen was shot down in 1918.' He turned to me his face aglow. 'Wouldn't it be great to clobber a really big train carrying a mass of Huns, with their tanks, vehicles and equipment? That would really be worthwhile. Make an enormous contribution.'"

"I remember being so appalled I could hardly speak. 'But Ian, that would mean a 70 mile sea crossing each way and flying into France for more than 50 miles. Then wandering about at nought feet within spitting distance of two Hun fighter bases, here at Abbeville and the other at Poix. Hoping - only hoping! - to find a train waiting for us to shoot at when, and if, we ever get there. My lad, you are out of your tiny mind. We wouldn't stand a chance if we were intercepted, and I couldn't give a hoot about where von Richthofen was shot down in 1918, because I have no intention whatever of getting myself killed in the same place!'"

"But, after much argument, my strident protests cut no ice and at 10 am the following day, we took off to fly down to Hawkinge on the south coast, in order to refuel."

"We took off again from Hawkinge at 2 pm and flew at tree-top height to Dungeness. The weather was just right, the cloud base about 900 feet and the top of the first layer at around 1,800 feet. Above that there were several further galleries and layers going up to 20,000 feet and higher, whilst low down the visibility was quite good - about two miles. I was still not happy with what we were attempting to do but at least the weather was cooperating and giving us at least a chance."

"Turning left at Dungeness, we dropped down to sea level and went into line abreast formation, our aircraft about 200 yards apart. Very early on in life, I had learnt that to fly behind anyone at low level over enemy territory was to collect all the light `flak' which had been directed at the bloke in front - and had missed! In that formation and height we crossed the cold grey waters of the Channel and hit the French coast about ten miles to the south of Le Touquet."

"Crossing the coast without incident, we continued at no more than 50 feet. The country-side was low lying at first but becoming somewhat more hilly some five or six miles inland. At this point, we were flying at about 260 miles an hour, at combat revs. - 2,850 - and with our throttles well advanced. Thus far, we had not been shot at, or not that I was aware of, but I knew that the tracer and red balls would soon be soaring in our direction and was already tensely preparing myself for that unpleasant development."

"We had reckoned that at 50 feet we would be reasonably safe initially. The German gunners would be unable to see us until we had passed over them at speed. However, in order to see a train, or any other small target in sufficient time to take aim and shoot, we had to be able to see at least two miles ahead, which at tree-top height was impossible."

"For this reason we had decided to climb to 250 feet when well into France. To climb to 500 feet, though desirable for purposes of navigation and recognition, would make us highly vulnerable and be simply asking for trouble."

"By now, we were flying a little south of east and I was looking anxiously to my left and into the distance for the first signs of Arras; by this time we had been well into the French countryside for almost ten minutes and the prospect of suddenly coming face to face with at least a brace of Hun fighters lurked like a spectre in my mind."

"Moreover, I was also scanning the ground ahead for signs of a railway line and of that there was absolutely nothing. Concern grew like a cancer. Were we properly on track? In the right place? I had expected to see at least something to shoot at by now but nothing suitable had presented itself other than cattle, trees, a meander of intersecting minor roads, a passing water tower and clutches of farm buildings. Even the enemy appeared to be asleep. Where was everyone, for heaven's sake? To my right and several hundred yards away, Ian Scott's Hurricane rose and fell in swaying unison with my own. There was no RT (radio telephone) and we flew on in tense and watchful silence. Overhead, the cloud seemed close enough to touch."

"Then suddenly, it all began to happen. To my companion's right and 500 yards distant, I saw several small aircraft sweep into view, approaching fast, their wings tilting. Then, before I had time to shout a warning, white streaks winged past my left ear together with the sound and impact of exploding cannon shells striking my Hurricane somewhere to my right and behind me, accompanied by the stink of cordite. At the same time I felt a numbing blow to my right thigh, not exactly painful but breathtakingly shocking, causing me to cry out momentarily into my face mask. Clearly, there were more than two enemy aircraft involved, with others obviously behind me - how many I never at any time knew, either then or later."

"Reacting instantaneously, I screamed a warning to Scotty over the RT and turning violently to escape the stream of bullets and shells, pulled up steeply to escape into cloud."

"Reaching the safety of the murk in seconds, I had trouble sorting out my bucking, porpoising aircraft. On the instrument panel before me, the DI (direction indicator) was whizzing round in a blur of motion and the artificial horizon was cannoning wildly around its circle of glass, both gyros having toppled with the violence of my manoeuvring. Also, I suddenly felt quite sick with shock, mostly I imagine from my leg wound - my thigh was still largely dead and I imagined I could feel blood trickling down my knee. Also, I had only a rough idea which way I was pointing, my DI unusable and my compass needle wandering around its bowl like a drunken sailor."

"Concerned that I might be flying into France rather than towards home, I cautiously climbed, using my airspeed indicator needle and my 'climb and dive' pointer as my main attitude guides, until I broke into clear air at about 1,900 feet. Then, bracing myself for another possible attack from behind, I immediately sank back into cloud again and, controlling my Hurricane with great difficulty and with my heart thumping like drum beats, began to gather my thoughts."

"My first concern was for my colleague - what had happened to him? There had been no RT - nothing. Had he been shot down? Suddenly the futility of the whole wretched exercise was borne home to me. We had achieved absolutely nothing - not even fired a bullet! - and if Ian Scott had been shot down and killed, what a stupid waste of time it had all been. No, Air Vice Marshal Trafford Leigh-Mallory, at that particular moment, was absolutely my least favourite person!"

"I flew ahead on what I hoped was roughly a northerly heading, after first being engaged with one hand in resetting my still wandering compass then caging and releasing my direction indicator. I then became conscious of a violent draught coming from my lower right side - presumably the result of enemy cannon fire - and began to worry that my hydraulic and coolant pipes might have been damaged, although at that point there was nothing to see or to smell. All the time though, I was worrying mainly about the fate of Ian Scott whilst struggling to keep my Hurricane on an even keel and remain in the safety of the cloud. Pressing my radio transmission switch, I called him several times using our prearranged call signs, but receiving no answers, concluded that he had been hit and had either gone down or baled out."

"The events of those last several minutes had occurred in a whirl of noise, naked fear, emotion and confusion. Until, after a brief period, I began to gather myself and felt able to take stock. At first, apart from the obvious damage to my side and rear, I could see nothing of what other damage had been inflicted on my aircraft by the enemy attack, until I noticed several jagged gashes in my starboard wing and felt my controls jarring now and then, suggesting that my aileron control rods somewhere had been hit. But, the engine sounded healthy enough, although still screaming its head off, persuading me to throttle back a little (not much!) and reduce my engine revs to 2,400. Then, with less noise and in a calmer frame of mind, I decided to drop down a little to see where precisely I was, whether even I was still in France."

"Letting down carefully, I came out of ragged cloud at about 800 feet to see green pastures underneath and a line of coast ahead which I did not immediately recognise. However, my presence was clearly anticipated by the enemy as two streams of red balls came drifting in my direction, to whip by in front of my Hurricane at what seemed to be the speed of light. Horrified, I climbed quickly back into cloud and flew on, my heart in my mouth, only coming down again a good five minutes later to be greeted by an endless expanse of cold grey water. The Channel, surely! Thank God for that!"

"Safe for the moment, I relaxed somewhat but suddenly felt both limp and terribly tired. My thigh was beginning to ache abominably, my whole body was shaking, and I felt very sick. What did I do? Press on to North Weald or land somewhere en route and have both my aircraft and my injury examined? With this in mind, I contacted Sector Control at Biggin Hill, spoke to them of my situation and asked for a course to steer."

"Still determined to press on to North Weald - I felt a responsibility to Ian Scott to give a first hand account of our disastrous trip. I crossed the English coast a little east of Beachy Head, and continued northwards until I felt quite faint and knew then I had to land as soon as possible. Which I did - at RAF Detling, near Maidstone. Greatly relieved when my wheels and flaps came down without hesitation, I brought my Hurricane in quietly on the main grass runway there and taxied slowly towards the hangers. Coming finally to a halt, I sat there breathing hard, wanting to vomit, and feeling completely spent."

"Presently, two airmen approached, one of whom pulled down the retracting step on the port side of my fuselage and clambered up alongside me."

"'What happened, sir? You're in a hell of a mess on your other side. Are you injured?'"

"When I said that I was and that I didn't think I could get out, he scrambled down saying he would get an ambulance and a doctor. Within minutes a group of vehicles arrived with screeching tires and people were leaning over me left and right. A face appeared on my right hand side, a young face scarcely older than my own."

"'I'm the M.O. (medical officer). I'm told you're injured and can't get out. Where've you been hit and are you in pain?' The young face was tensely concerned."

"I faltered, 'Down my right hand side, and yes, I'm hurting a lot and can't move.'"

"'Right. I'll get some morphine into you and then decide how we are going to get you out. The CTO (Chief Technical Officer) here thinks we may have to use a crane. Will that be alright?'"

"Which was a silly question, I thought at the time, but decided to let them get on with it, adding wanly, 'Just as long as you don't drop me.'"

"It took them about fifteen minutes to bring up the Cole's crane - used to lift engines in the hangar - after which they fixed a harness round my shoulders and arms before heaving me into the air and lowering me gently to the ground. I felt like a museum exhibit being settled on its plinth."

"Then the doctor again. 'Right, we're sending you straight to Maidstone Hospital to get your wounds seen to. I dare say they'll want to keep you for a few days depending on what thy find. Meanwhile, we'll get on to your home base and tell them what's happening.'"

"Thereafter, heavy with drugs, I was driven into Maidstone and ended up in a white hospital ward with doctors and nurses weaving around me like circling crows. Dimly hearing them say that they intended to cut off my trousers, I heard myself protesting weakly, 'Please don't do that, they are only one of two pairs I possess.' But I argued in vain; my trousers were cut off, after which I was injected again and remembered little else until the following day."

"I remained in that hospital for five days. After picking about 20 pieces of metal from my thigh and hip, they placed a massive wad of dressing and sticking plaster over my wounds and allowed me to walk about - in considerable discomfort, I may add - for several days. Then I was finally discharged and driven back to North Weald by car. I never saw my Hurricane again, incidentally, which, strangely enough, didn't worry me a scrap. Which sounds an odd remark to make until I tell you that on arriving back at North Weald, I learned that in my brief absence, the squadron had been ordered overseas, that I would not be going with them, and that I would be posted to 56 Operational Training Unit in Scotland after being sent on a month's sick leave."

"So, at the tender age of 21, I was promoted to Squadron Leader and became Chief Flying Instructor at RAF Tealing, which is - or was - a mile or two north of Dundee. And it was there, four months later, that I heard that my old friend Ian Graeme-Scott was alive and back again in Britain, having escaped from France after being shot down. My joy and relief at the news knew no bounds."

"I had been, I recall, about four months at 56 OTU and had just returned to my office after leading a formation of twelve Hurricanes around the sky for about an hour, when the telephone rang. Answering it, I recognised Scotty's voice immediately and after fairly scream-ing a near delirious greeting, asked him where he was, what he was doing, and what was his state of health."

"He responded with his usual light-hearted laugh, after which he explained that he was at his home in Scotland, having been given a month's leave to restore his morale and to 'fatten himself up'."

"Still bubbling with excitement and happiness, I heard myself crying, 'First, though, tell me your news! What happened to you on that ghastly, bloodstained day?'"

"But Scotty had other things on his mind. 'No, not just now. Look, I've really called to invite you to spend a day or two with me here at home. We're in the hills about halfway between Moffat and Hawick. Take a few days off and fly down to Annan where I'll meet you in my car - my family have collected quite a few petrol coupons in my absence - we can then talk our heads off.'"

"I responded gaily, 'But, where's Annan? I've never heard of the place'"

"I heard a chuckle the other end. 'These ignorant English! It's on the Solway Firth, dear boy. South of Dumfries. Find yourself a map!'"

"It took me a day or so to sort out my affairs at Tealing, after which I flew down to Annan in my own Hurricane - I never let anyone else fly it, a rather nice second-life Mark I."

"Scotty was already there, standing beside his car, a fairly modern Riley 9. Grinning all over our faces, we embraced, climbed in, then stopped for a moment facing each other in silence, each of us recognising, I'm sure, how lucky we were that fate had preserved us both and brought us together again. But the solemn moment passed in seconds and we set off on our one-and-a-half hour journey, talking animatedly."

"The Scott homestead was a large grey farmhouse sited amid a huddle of out-buildings and the centre of more than 800 acres of rolling hill pasture. Built, I was later informed, in the late 1700s, it was the last of a number of homes in that gaunt but beautiful area, inhabited by the Scott family over the centuries. As soon as I saw it I felt comfortable and enveloped in an aura of history; here was a root, a deep and firm foundation for a distinguished and ancient family. Even then I became aware of a powerful need to know more, not only about the place itself but also about the family who had lived in it for several hundred years."

"We had spoken of Ian's family during the journey. His mother and older sister, with the able assistance of a farm manager, ran the farm successfully. Apparently, Ian's elder brother, Douglas, a Squadron Leader in the Air Force, was never that interested in farming and was now serving in the Middle East. His father had sadly died some years before as the result of a riding accident when his horse had fallen heavily whilst jumping. It had then rolled on him inflicting severe injuries which later proved fatal. Prior to that unhappy incident, Graeme-Scott senior had been in the Foreign Service and, although based in Scotland, had lived abroad with his family for some years. In fact, Ian and his sister had both been born in India and had only returned to Scotland in order to further their education."

"On being introduced first to his mother and then his sister, I saw immediately the strong family resemblance. Slim and wiry in build and not particularly tall, both women had Ian's facial bone structure; a firm but delicate chin line, a mobile mouth that was almost sensual, and dark eyes that frequently sparkled with amusement. Also, the straight dark hair was a common factor, although in each of the women it was carefully parted and very fashionably worn. The sister especially was so attractive that for a time, and almost to my embarrassment, I found my eyes constantly straying in her direction. At that first encounter, I judged her age to be about 28."

"After my initial meeting with the distaff side of the family, however, Ian led me to a small room which he described as his private 'snug'. 'I like to get away from the ladies now and then,' he admitted with an almost sheepish grin. 'I find there's a shortage of men around here from time to time.' Which rather surprised me as the presence of his sister at any time would not have worried me in the least."

"Then waving me to a chair he plonked himself down heavily and said, 'Right. Time for a late debriefing, don't you think? Tell me, what happened to you on the fatal day?'"

"But I was adamant. 'No, I insist. You first. You're the hero around here.' After which, for the next hour he explained in a voice totally without emotion the manner in which he had been shot down and had then managed to escape."

At that point, I felt that I wanted to speak to Cadwallader exactly in the manner Ian Scott had related his story to me - in the first person. Although many years had passed, I remembered distinctly every remark, explanation and description he made at the time. His story as a whole remained indelibly printed on my memory. Also I reasoned that, although Cadwallader knew almost everything else about Scotty's career and record, it was unlikely that he had ever been given full details of Ian's adventure as an escapee in enemy territory. I even heard myself unconsciously imitating his voice.

It went as follows:

"I was looking ahead for signs of that railway line we had talked about and our intention to turn right and follow it down to Amiens. I then had a brief glimpse of two Huns to my right then heard a very abbreviated yell from you, followed almost immediately by several violent thumps behind me, at which point my radio went dead and my cockpit was filled with grey and white vapour, which was either escaping coolant or smoke from the engine. Intending to whip into a turn to face the enemy - I had a glimpse of four 109s but there may have been more - I found that my controls had been hit as the aircraft, without my bidding, went into a steep climb, so that I shot into cloud almost vertically. Even at that point, I knew I had to get out as I felt and smelt heat and decided that there was a fire somewhere, although I did not see any flames."

"By the tine I had come out at the top of that first layer of cloud, I had thrown off my straps and helmet and opened the hood, being then almost catapulted into space as my Hurricane turned over and very conveniently left me. Thoroughly disorientated for a few moments, I found myself turning head over heels but sufficiently compos mentis to search for, then pull my ripcord. My parachute opened without a hitch and I was jerked upright and found myself floating silently through cloud, stunned and quite breathless by the events of the last 30 seconds."

"Coming out of the cloud at about 900 feet, I saw at a glance that there was a wood slightly to my right, a couple of small country paths directly beneath, and green and brown fields to my left, with a few isolated figures working in them. Then, as I was drifting towards the woods, I tried desperately to steer my parachute away from the trees as I had a horror of falling into them and being injured. My efforts had little effect, however, and I plunged down into the top of one canopy with my eyes closed and my hands in front of my face. As I felt the initial impact and the branches tearing at my body, I thought for a moment I would be caught up and unable to get to the ground. However, I immediately fell free and dropped to earth with a crunching thud, bending one of my legs backwards instead of forwards. For some moments I lay there in absolute agony, my mind in turmoil, knowing full well that I could not afford at that point to be injured. Fortunately, too, my parachute had fluttered down beside me, so that when I was finally able to stagger to my feet and stand on one leg, I was able to hop around like a stork and gather up the canopy, with every intention of hiding it. Looking around, I saw no sign of my crashed aircraft nor even the smoke of a fire, which was a blessing. The further away I was from any crash site the better for me, as I knew the Huns would soon be looking for me and would head initially in that direction."

"Also, to my surprise, the few people in the fields about 200 yards away had carried on working, taking absolutely no notice of me - or so it appeared. That and the balmy silence all around was in a way very odd but most surprising and comforting."

"With some difficulty, because of my painful leg, I wriggled out of my parachute harness and gathered up the shroud lines and canopy of my brolly, hiding everything in a nearby ditch and covering it as best I could with leaves. Then I took off my Mae West and tucked that away under a hedge about 20 yards away. Finally, having straightened up, I realised how conspicuous I still was in my flying boots, Air Force blue tunic and slacks, and the round-necked white woollen jersey we had been issued with some months before. What did I do about them? On the other hand, if I was picked up in civilian clothes I could well be branded as a spy if the Huns decided to be nasty."

"I was standing there weighing up the situation, when I noticed a single figure waving to me from the side of the next field. Assuming that a Hun would not be doing that, I stumbled in that direction to be confronted by an elderly woman dressed in some very earthy farm worker's clothes, who mouthed at me in French, a message I could not at first understand. Eventually, I decided it was an instruction for me to get further into the wood, and hide, and not feeling I was in the position either to enquire or argue, I did just that. Crouching down, I then waited on tenterhooks for something to happen, for all of 30 minutes."

"I was getting to the point when I felt it was necessary to move off on my own, when a youth appeared pushing an ancient bicycle who, without words, motioned me to mount up and follow him. Which I tried to do, unsuccessfully, my leg giving me absolute gyp. Seeing that I was disabled, the lad pointed to the saddle then climbed on in front of me, working the pedals with his feet, so that we set off through the wood and down a nearby path, with me hanging on for dear life and almost crying out with pain as we lurched along over pot holes, stones, and roots. In this manner, we finally came into a wider more used minor road, down which my companion peddled furiously for almost a mile until, looking behind suddenly, he leapt off and pulled me off the contraption, pretty well throwing me and the bicycle into a deep ditch and signalling me with fingers and frantic grimaces to keep quiet. Which I did, wondering what on earth was happening."

"It took only moments for me to find out, however, as I heard the sound of an approaching car engine and a small four-wheeled vehicle came in our direction and inexplicably stopped merely yards from where we lay, my companion and I lying doggo with eyes closed and screwed up features, scarcely breathing. Then, cautiously lifting my head and opening one eye, I saw the straps and canopy of my parachute in the back of the open four-seater as the two occupants, German soldiers, looked about and spoke quietly together for about a minute. After which, to our enormous relief, they drove off and there was only breeze-blown silence and the occasional twitter of a disgruntled bird."

"When all appeared clear, my companion motioned to me to stay where I was whilst he climbed out of the ditch and surveyed the road and fields beyond. Then beckoning me to join him, we continued on our way, with me again on the saddle with dangling legs and him pushing on the rotating pedals. In this manner we rode for another mile or so until veering off along another even smaller path and ending up in the cobbled yard of a farm which can best be describe as having seen better days. Each of us dismounting stiffly - me positively aching with pain - my companion knocked on a door and after a moment or two, were both admitted by a middle-aged woman who immediately drew a very soiled curtain across the single window and lit a candle. Then, smiling wanly in my direction for the first time, she welcomed me in a subdued voice and asked in slow but quite comprehensible French, if I was injured or needed food and a drink."

"Here, I have to admit that having obtained credits in my Higher School Certificate examination in French and Latin, I could converse in simple French and understood it well enough, provided it was spoken to me slowly. The trouble was, regional accents usually floored me, particularly if the speaker was excited and conversation was rapid. With Latin I was more at home as, not only being taught it at school but with a Roman Catholic background, I was well versed in Church ritual. Later, as an escapee in France for more than ten weeks, I was occasionally obliged to speak to German soldiers, especially in trains, and although I was able to keep quiet most of the time, when forced into conversation, if I gabbled Latin at them, it usually flummoxed them so completely that conversation dried up immediately."

"Anxious that I might be putting my host's life at risk, acting as she was as a good Samaritan, in a laboured sentence I was able to make my concern clear, only to be told with a sad smile and Gallic shrug, that she didn't think so - the Boche, it appeared, seldom ventured beyond the main roads and that, anyway, a system of warning measures was in place should they ever come in her direction. I then asked her to tell me where exactly we were and she explained that her farm was about five kilometres south of Doullens, which didn't help very much as it was a place I had never heard of."

"We then spoke about my uniform and discussed whether or not I should get rid of it, her opinion being that I should not for the moment, but cover it with an old coat she would be able to provide. However, my flying boots would have to go but here too she probably had shoes of her late husband that might fit. Then, at the point of enquiring about the husband, I suddenly had second thoughts and remained silent, fearing she might have to tell me that had been killed in the recent fighting."

"Without another word, the woman left the room and returned with a bowl of thin cabbage soup, some bread and two cold, hard-boiled eggs. This, I ate with relish, washing the food down with some rather harsh red wine presented to me in a mug. As I ate, she watched me wordlessly then sat down beside me and explained quietly and slowly that I needed to move on to a place where I would be better cared for. This raised a problem as it was fifteen kilometres away, I would have to go by bicycle, and my damaged leg might not be up to the journey. However, there was no other means of transport and if I felt unable to cope at present, I would have to stay with her until my leg had recovered sufficiently. She was sure I would be perfectly safe in her attic bedroom, provided I kept quiet and out of the way. Meanwhile, she would sort out any clothing problems I might have."

"Which is what happened. I stayed in that attic for four days, where a young girl of about 15 appeared at regular intervals with food and also bowls of water, from which I washed and into which I relieved myself. And all the time, my beard grew and I looked steadily more scruffy and increasingly like your average French yokel."

"My leg improved also by the day, although I found time heavy on my hands despite busying myself cutting the gilt buttons from my tunic, one of which I knew was a compass, and pulling open the lining of my coat to extract an escape map, made beautifully of thin silk, which formed part of one shoulder pad. That map of northern France improved my morale enormously, although I was unable to identify the small town, or village, of Doullens."

"On the fifth day, I felt fit enough to travel and was introduced again to the bicycle I had used earlier. It was explained that I would be led by the boy who had brought me five days before and that we would travel by day, using the smaller back roads and footpaths - to travel by night after the curfew would obviously attract attention."

"When we were about to depart, the woman stood before me, her eyes moist. I asked her name but she said that names weren't important. When the war was over, I could come back and meet her again, provided the Boche hadn't shot her daughter and her, as they had her husband and son. Then, almost in tears, she brought me some bread and cheese to eat on the way, plus a sauce bottle of red wine. I was so moved, I could hardly speak. After that, with the lad leading, we pedalled away into a morning mist."

"I must say, I set off that morning in no very happy state of mind. We had no papers and although I may have looked like a Frenchman, I did not feel like one and doubted that I could carry off any convincing impersonation. It had been agreed that if stopped, the boy would do all the talking. I was supposed to be his gormless relative who was mentally impaired and did not speak very well, and that we were on our way to the Amiens area to look for farm work. However, after cycling for about three miles and encountering hardly anyone, my spirits began to rise and when we stopped about halfway to eat a little bread and cheese, I felt almost buoyant. My leg was standing up well and we could always see ahead so that we were constantly in a position to duck into cover if we observed anyone or anything that was in any way suspicious Several times small groups of Me 109s roared overhead, leading me to believe we were not too far from either Abbeville or Poix. On one occasion, I asked my guide where exactly we were going, but he couldn't, or wouldn't, say, except to add that we were on our way to meet someone 'very important'."

"At about four o'clock, we reached a series of low lying but isolated buildings and my guide signalled me to stop whilst he went ahead. Which he did, returning after about 15 minutes to say that the coast was clear and that we could proceed."

"Entering a large and well established house from the rear, I found myself being greeted by a neatly-dressed woman of about 40, who led me wordlessly into a small room which was obviously someone's study, and left me there. So I waited, alone and somewhat on edge, for another 15 minutes, my young guide and our bicycles having disappeared."

"When finally the door opened again, a man of about 50 appeared, smart, well appointed and looking like a professional person, possibly a doctor - which I later learnt he was. Offering me his hand, he bade me welcome in English and added that he could not speak to me now but intended to send me to another part of the house for the time being. Later, we would talk and I would meet some of his friends. Meanwhile, he would like to offer me some refreshments. All of which sounded very reasonable and succeeded in calming my nerves."

"The neatly-dressed woman again entered the room and words passed rapidly between them. Then she led me up two flights of wooden stairs and into a bedroom at the top of the house, better furnished than the last I had occupied, where I was invited to make myself comfortable. So, I breathed a sigh of relief, took off my threadbare coast and ill-fitting boots, and relaxed on the bed for the first time that day. It seemed at least a month since I had been shot down."

"It was not until the evening that I was asked to move to another room where I was confronted by four men who greeted me courteously but not with any noticeable warmth. I was then invited to sit down and prepare myself to be interrogated."

"The men were clearly aware that I was probably not going to give them anything more than my name, rank and number, so that the questions started off being fairly innocuous. Where did I live? What was the name of the nearest town to my home in Scotland and how far away it was, precisely? Did I speak any languages? And a dozen or so similar personal questions. Then their queries became a little more involved. What was the name of the statue in Piccadilly Circus? The full name of the AOC Fighter Command? The Christian name of Lord Trenchard? What the name was of the tunnel running under the Thames in London? The name of the Foreign Secretary? And many more. All of which I answered fairly promptly and I believe correctly."

"This whole question and answer session took more than 30 minutes and I was then asked to return to my bedroom while they discussed my response to their questions. Finally, I was invited back and sat on the edge of my seat, rather like a naughty schoolboy facing his headmaster. At that point, I began to feel a little resentful, being treated like a criminal and not as a chap risking his neck to save a wretched country that had so recently capitulated."

"This time, however, they appeared better disposed towards me and said that they would help me return to England with all the means at their disposal. However, there were enormous risks involved. The Germans were no fools. They were vicious and very vindictive and it was vital that, if captured, I should not reveal anything about what had happened to me thus far, or the details or methods of their escape organisation. I remember I kept nodding and when I stupidly asked what would happen if they believed me to be a German plant, they exchanged stony glances and replied quite simply that if I were, and they did, I would be executed within the hour. Which rather took the smile off my face."

"They then explained that, in a day or two, I would be introduced to another British escapee and together we would be taken to Amiens and put on a train to Paris. There, we would be met by a young woman who would lead me to a safe house in the City. It was important, however, that I should not at any time acknowledge her presence, speak to her, or become involved with her in any way, but merely follow at a safe distance. If I obeyed these instructions, there would probably be no trouble; if I didn't and was apprehended, I would be on my own and likely to spend the rest of the war in prison, if nothing worse."

"The following day, I rather reluctantly disposed of my uniform tunic and underclothes, but was able to hang on to my trousers which, although Air Force blue, looked fairly disreputable. I can only describe my new apparel as clean but grossly unfashionable."

"Later that night, well after dark, another man was brought to my room and was introduced as 'a further British escapee'. Still rather suspicious of everyone, I did not take to him immediately as he seemed morosely silent and if anything even scruffier than me. It was only after a time that he told me he was an Army officer - a Captain in the Royal Engineers - who had been left behind at

Dunkirk. After being picked up by the Germans initially, he had managed to escape and had travelled westwards fairly rapidly until he had reached Nantes on the west coast, at a time when there were still one or two ships leaving for England. He had then been persuaded, however, not to leave but to stay in France and, because he could speak French fluently, help others in the escape chain to evade. So now, having been in Northern France for more than a year, he felt fairly secure as he was familiar with most local accents and dialects and could convincingly pass himself off as a Frenchman. His cover name apparently was Paul - Paul Perrin (he never told me his real name), and, for the next day or so, I would be his half-witted relation from Lille, Henri Perrin. The fact that I had no papers was something of a problem but one that he could probably explain away. All I had to do was look stupid and keep my mouth shut."

"We then discussed our projected journey to Paris. We would be taken by car to Amiens where he would buy the train tickets and make the journey with me, answering any questions were we to be stopped en route. He would then lead me across Paris on the Metro, buying any further tickets and avoiding all likely hold-up points. The Germans apparently used the trains themselves in large numbers and regularly employed inspection teams, particularly following crashes of RAF aircraft in the area and airmen they couldn't account for. He would then point out our young woman contact, who would be there to lead me to the safe house. She would be distinctively dressed but on no account was she to be approached or spoken to. If I lost her in the crush, which was more than a possibility, I was to wait where I was and she would return to find me. Finally, having pointed her out, he would leave and return to base, so to speak."

"This was more or less what happened, except there were several occasions of real panic for me. As the train to Paris kept stopping, people, including German soldiers, kept getting in and out of our compartment and either looking at me strangely or engaging me in conversation. At these times, I either pulled a face and kept quiet or gibbered a few Latin phrases in their direction, which seemed to do the trick. On one occasion, the train stopped where there was no platform and an ancient crone attempted to climb aboard from ground level carrying boxes of chickens and live ducks, which presumably she was taking to market. As she struggled up, mouthing all sorts of what I took to be abuse in my direction, the birds were quacking and squawking their heads off, and everyone either laughing or wondering why I wasn't responding, as apparently all she was doing was asking me to help."

"Finally we arrived in Paris, a place I had never been to before. After quietly skirting one or two small groups of soldiers examining papers, we went down to the Metro and rattled across Paris, alighting at a place the name of which even now I can't recall. There the girl we were to meet was pointed out to me, a pretty young thing wearing a beret with a red feather in it. She seemed no more than 21 years of age, which set me thinking how indebted we were to such people who were risking their lives on our behalf."

"After that it was fairly easy. I stuck to her like a clam and we seemed to walk for miles, finishing up in a very seedy area of the City - the naughty place, I judged it to be - where the girl suddenly vanished into the front of a large rather drab-looking warehouse."

"Wondering if I were doing the right thing, I followed to find myself in a foyer of sorts, the girl in the beret having by this time disappeared. Presently, a man in shirt-sleeves turned up as though from nowhere, and nodding in my direction, motioned me to follow, which I did. He then led me into a vast and ancient luggage lift and pressed a button. The noisiest contraption I had ever heard in my life then whirred and howled into action, the lift ascending, drifting and shuddering through about five floors, before it finally ground to a halt. An iron-latticed gate then concertinaed itself open and I stepped out. I had arrived - wherever it was!"

"At that safe house, to my enormous surprise, I found at least a dozen other escapees, most of them officer and NCO aircrew. Several were survivors from Blenheim bombers recently shot down and there was a chap from 56 Squadron, whom I recognised, and another, a Canadian, of 242. They were all in good voice and it was a vast relief to be so cheerfully welcomed. There was sufficient food on hand to satisfy our immediate needs and more than enough brandy; furthermore there were places to sleep, although straw pailliasses on the floor were not my favourite type of bed. The real joy of the place, however, was that for the first time I felt comparatively safe."

"I was there in total for about three weeks, off and on. I never knew precisely who were in charge. About four local Frenchmen, who looked and sounded like educated artisans, professional people or ex-military men, came and went from time to time, whilst work of a skilled nature, such as the production of forged papers, was done elsewhere. My own documents, quickly produced, were masterpieces of forgery. I retained my cover name of Henri Perrin and was described as an injured railway worker from the Lille area. Neither the papers nor I would have stood up to detailed scrutiny by the Gestapo, but they seemed genuine enough to pass any casual inspection."

"We also spent time discussing how we might escape and get back to England. There were several alternatives; a long and tedious journey of more than 600 miles to the south, followed by a taxing climb over the Pyrenees into Spain. A slightly shorter journey to the Swiss border plus another difficult crossing operation. A lesser road or train journey to the north-west coast of France, followed by a highly fraught boat trip across the Channel to England, provided always that a willing fishing-boat skipper could be found. Finally, a pick-up by aircraft, normally RAF Lysanders, making nocturnal landings in France. All four methods carried enormous risks but, with local help, were possible and had been successful in the past. A further alternative was to capture and fly out a German aircraft, an option so wildly improbable as to merit little consideration."

"My first effort to get away occurred about ten days later when I was taken by road to a deserted area about 40 miles south-west of Paris. There, I found myself in the midst of a small group of sabo-teurs who were expecting a Lysander carrying some mysterious character from England, for which they had built a very sketchy flare path in a deserted clearing. Naturally, I was very excited and full of hope, expecting to he home within a few hours. So, for some time, I was one of about dozen chaps dressed like assassins and standing in the dark under some trees, with weapons at the ready, waiting for the aircraft to turn up. But it didn't, and although we heard a Mercury engine in the distance, either because the pilot couldn't find the flarepath, or for some other reason, he aborted the landing. Anyway, vastly disappointed, we were obliged to return to Paris. Because of the curfew, however, it was a journey we had to put off until the following day. And not without difficulty, I may add, as we were stopped on the way by a mixed group of Huns and French police, my minders managing finally, with a lot of arm waving, to talk our way out of what could have been a very nasty situation."

"Shortly after, there occurred two major developments in swift succession. The first was when, as a matter of urgency, we had to move to another safe house on the west side of the City. To our surprise, we found an additional dozen escapees already in residence, most of them aircrew. This brought our total number to about eighteen, some of whom had been hanging about for more than three months. This depressed me no end as I saw myself bottled up in France almost indefinitely, even assuming that I - we - managed to avoid capture."

"It was a complete surprise, therefore, when I was taken aside and quietly informed that arrangements had been made for two of us ex-fighter aircrew to make an accompanied journey down to the Spanish border, but only if we were willing and felt strong enough to make the journey."

"Again, although excited initially by the proposal, I soon had second thoughts and turned it down. I wanted a swift return home, preferably by Lysander, or failing that, a shorter journey to the north-west coast to take my chance on a fishing boat. When I made these points to our French contacts, I don't think they were any too pleased but they finally accepted my objections."

"There followed a period of about ten days which turned out to be the most frustrating and miserable I ever spent in France. With almost 20 of us cooped up in two small attic rooms, there was little opportunity for exercise and tempers often frayed to the point of violence when arguments developed. Moreover, I found our lack of toilet and washing facilities very trying. Soap was scarce and our few shared razors used blades so worn and blunt that we tore our faces to pieces when attempting to keep our beards in check, although we were advised several times to remain at least as scruffy as the average French worker. To while away the time, we played endless games of cards and read the handful of books that were available. However, on the positive side, we were able to practise our French for hours on end, so that I, anyway, became quite confident that I could carry on a sensible conversation if called upon."

"I recall it was a day or so after this very miserable period of inaction, that we were warned that eight of us would be going west by train to Nantes. After that, hopefully, we'd go up the coast to Brest and to one of several nearby coastal fishing-boat villages. However, the trip would present real dangers as the Germans had large naval, reconnaissance, and fighter forces in the area and the region was heavily guarded. Notwithstanding this dire warning, we began to prepare with enthusiasm, maps were eagerly scanned and plans discussed."

"Spreading out the silk map I still possessed, I saw that Nantes was about 220 miles away and estimated that the journey by train would take between five and seven hours, depending of the number of halts we made on the way. At that point I did not even consider the next leg of the journey northwards along the coast. We would be provided with tickets, money, and sufficient food for the journey and would be dispersed in pairs along the length of the train, each pair carrying a recognition article of clothing which would enable our contacts in Nantes to identify us."

"My companion was to be the pilot of a Whitley bomber which had been shot down at night by `flak' a month earlier. He had been dropping panniers of weapons to saboteurs in an area south of Paris and was on his return journey when his aircraft had run into a heavy anti-aircraft barrage and was hit in both engines, obliging everyone to bale out. The last to leave, he believed all his crew had survived but he did not see any of them again in the dark and assumed they must have been captured on reaching the ground. A nice, rather phlegmatic chap, he was several years older then me and turned out to be a steady and unflappable friend."

"Arriving at the station individually and in pairs, I noticed to my dismay that German soldiers were thick on the ground. However, carefully avoiding eye to eye contact, I became more relaxed when they did not appear interested in us, mostly being young men encumbered with heavy packs, steel helmets and rifles. Climbing into our seats, we made ourselves comfortable and waited, tense but not overly worried."

"The journey took us along the Loire valley and, had it been in happier times, I would have enjoyed the ride. My Whitley friend and I shared a compartment with about six French people of various types and descriptions, all of them friendly and generous as I think they saw through our disguises almost from the start and were soon pressing food and fruit on us. In so far as we could, we carried on a conversation with them but soon exhausted our vocabulary and then either feigned sleep or lapsed into silence."

"We stopped so many times that I cannot recall the names of any of the towns en route other than Orleans, which stuck in my memory because of the story of Joan of Arc. It was there that we were able to get out and walk about for a bit to stretch our legs, carefully avoiding any contact with the Germans. Thus far there had been no inspections of any sort and we gradually relaxed into comparative complacency".

"Before we finally reached Nantes, I found myself worrying about meeting our contact. What would we do if she, or he, didn't turn up? Our instructions had been to hang about until the person, whoever it was, appeared, which seemed to me a dangerous thing to do. The arrangements as a whole seemed so imprecise that I found myself greatly on edge. However, I need not have worried as, having alighted, out of a crush of people, a girl, not more than 19, rushed in our direction and greeted us effusively, kissing us on both cheeks and hissing at us out of the corner of her mouth, to try looking like two delighted members of her family. Which we did, though not very convincingly."

"Still chattering away, the bulk of which went right over my head, the girl led us down a series of mean-looking streets until we came to a cafe which she entered and waved us into seats. Then, obviously by arrangement, a man in an apron appeared with bowls of soup, some French bread and cheese, and the inevitable glass of red wine, to all of which we did full justice. Meanwhile, as we ate, the girl just sat there and, saying nothing, smiled in our direction, with me marvelling all the time at the courage of such people - children almost - who were risking their necks to help us. What did they get of this, for heaven's sake? Other than a pleasurable sense of carrying out a patriotic duty, the satisfaction of knowing they were defying a hated enemy, and of course, the enjoyment that came with the thrill of suspense and danger."

"Then, when we had finished our meal, the girl bent in our direction. She was going to leave us now, she whispered, but would return at 8 am the following day, when she would take us to the station and put us on the train to Vannes, which was a coastal town about 80 kilometres to the north. There we would be met again and once more holed up, for how long she didn't know. Tonight, however, we were to stay in this cafe, where the owner would look after us. In the distance, the man who had brought the soup, looked in our direction with folded arms, and smiled. I then asked about our other six friends, but the girl, standing up to go, added quietly that we should not worry as they were being taken care of. I then thanked her and asked her name, but she just shook her head and left. That night, my Whitley friend and I shared a large, soft, double bed in an upstairs room and enjoyed a blissful, undisturbed sleep, the first for ages."

"Our journey to Vannes the following day was both uneventful and interesting, despite the warnings we had been given. There were many soldiers and police about but none gave more than casual glances in our direction. It was clear however, that we were approaching a sensitive area as several times, single Ju 88 bombers flew overhead, and a least two formations of eight Me 109s roared above us at little more than 500 feet. Vastly interested in the aircraft, naturally, there was also a wonderful feeling of contentment that came from knowing that the sea, even the Atlantic Ocean, was but a mile or two to our left and an avenue to freedom."

"At Vannes, we were recognised immediately by another young woman of about 21. After greeting us with nodding courtesy, she shepherded us into a small 'phut-phut' Citroen and drove us carefully out of town and into the countryside. We stopped eventually at a series of rambling buildings which could generously be described as an ancient French farm destined soon to become a ruin. Stopping the car in a secluded spot, the girl led us towards the door of what we decided later was a large kitchen. It was an area more farmyard than human habitation, with pigs, cattle and chickens in a chaotic mix immediately outside, standing, chewing and pecking in a wilderness of mud, straw and manure, pungent traces of which were all too evident on the flagstones of the kitchen floor. But whatever the disorder beyond, there was great warmth within, as the farmer, a squat and grinning peasant in a flat cap, and his wife, a woman of enormous girth, greeted us silently but with the widest of smiles. As we went inside, ducking our heads to avoid being decapitated, my immediate thought was, here was absolute safety as no self-respecting German would ever consider crossing the threshold."

"After hand shaking and pleasantries had been completed amid many nods and grins exchanged, the farmer brought a stool. Climbing up, he reached above a heavily cobwebbed beam and brought down a small bottle of colourless liquid which he poured out into several not too clean glasses, handing one to each of us. After exchanging glances and offering smiles and the standard good wishes, we swallowed the liquid down - and immediately wished we hadn't! Although sweet, the spirit - neat home-brewed Calvados, as it turned out to be - had the all the throat-burning qualities of pure sulphuric acid. For some moments, all three of us were stunned into silence, before coughing and spluttering politely and steadying ourselves against the nearest wall."

"We were then encouraged to climb up a wooden ladder into the so-called bedroom area. This revealed itself as nothing more than a straw-littered hayloft. Here, the girl explained in English and with an apologetic gesture, would be our sleeping quarters, which we would be obliged to share with the three younger children of the family. Which confirmed my earlier belief that we would be able to rest at length and in absolute safety."

"We were to be at that farm for more than a week. Every second morning, the girl would appear, having driven out in her rickety Citroen to supply us with bread and vegetables. We found ourselves looking forward to her arrival, not only for the pleasure of seeing her but also because she was our only source of news. Again, I asked who she was and what she did, and she told me that her name was Martina Labouchere, that she was 22 years old, came originally from Paris, and that she taught English at the local school. She also apologised for looking so dowdy but she always especially contrived to look scruffy in order to ward off the attentions of those German soldiers who made a habit of accosting any attractive young woman they came across. I then assured her that to us she was positively beautiful and when the war ended I would return to find her and recompense her for all the splendid work she was doing. At this, she suddenly went silent with embarrassment before bursting into tears. Immediately, I tried to comfort her by taking her in my arms but as I did so, found a lump rising in my own throat, with the result that for a minute or two, we both were rather tearful until, pulling away, we cleared our throats and composed ourselves."

"Then, on the seventh day, she turned up with the news that arrangements had been made for us to take the train to Quimper, which was about 100 kilometres further north and not far from Brest. However, there were real dangers as she had heard that the Gestapo were known to be operating in the area and, as our destination was also only a little beyond the naval defences of Lorient, we were to be especially careful. We were to meet our next contact, probably another girl, at the corner of two streets, (which she then named), but were to leave the train immediately if there was evidence of inspections, particularly by the Gestapo. If we were obliged to do so, we were to walk to the nearest village and hole up in any church we could find, only venturing forth when the coast was clear. We might even have to walk the final few kilometres into Quimper, but our contact there would turn up at the rendezvous regularly at noon each day, until we finally arrived. We were to remember, though, not to greet whomever it was openly but leave it to her, or him, to make themselves known."

"The following morning, Martina arrived in her little Citroen and handed over our tickets and a small packet of food, after which we drove into Vannes without exchanging a word. When we finally dismounted in a quiet street, she kissed us both on each cheek and shook hands. Then she turned and left, with tears in her eyes."

"The journey to Quimper was slow and halting as the whole area was a military zone. There were masses of grey-coated soldiers everywhere, and we waited apprehensively as we travelled slowly north, expecting any moment to be confronted and searched. In fact, it became so frightening, that at a village stop a little before Quimper, we decided to get off the train and walk - I simply couldn't face being captured by the Gestapo or even the normal Hun soldiery, when so close to our destination and possible success."

"Walking off as advised towards what we perceived to be the local village, we found a church without difficulty and cautiously entered its bleak interior. We then went through the motions of praying, as it appeared at first to be empty."

"It was a wonderful but very frightening surprise, therefore, when two other figures materialised out of the gloom and we found them to be members of the group of eight who had left Paris with us in the train. After ascertaining we were indeed on our own, we compared notes in excited whispers and had more than a few carefully controlled laughs. After which one of our party ventured forth to spy out the land, returning immediately in a high state of excitement, to report that a group of Germans was marching down the road in our direction."

"In a panic almost, we found an exit which led down to a below-stairs vestry and, closing and locking the solid oak door behind us, we waited with bated breath as we heard, and felt, feet tramping about above our heads. One of our chaps then drew a knife and showed every sign of being prepared to kill anyone who tried to enter, so for some terrible moments, particularly when watching the door knob being turned and the door rattled, I thought that blood would be spilt and we would all be shot. However, behind the locked door, the sound of voices gradually faded away and, as we stood there, scarcely daring to breathe, eventually there was only a prolonged silence - a silence broken only by the sound of our thumping hearts."

"We were so unnerved that we might be seen and picked up if we returned that day to the railway halt, that we spent the most miserable night ever, sleeping on several of the hard wooden benches in that church. We awoke next morning weary, hungry, and feeling like pieces of chewed string, with me especially surprised that a place of worship should have been left open all night."

"Severely shaken by the incident of the previous day, we separated and walked back singly but within sight of each other to the railway line via several minor footpaths. We then formed up into our original pairs and walked warily to the next village. Here, to our surprise, there was another halt and a tiny stationary local train. As there were only a few passengers in evidence with their animals and birds, we climbed into the ancient coaches and sat down, comfortable in the belief that we were unlikely to meet any further soldiers or police."

"It was another half hour before we reached the station at Quimper. By this time we looked so bedraggled and worn out that we didn't have to pretend to be French workers and walked brazenly past everyone, without the station guards even glancing in our direction."

"With the guidance we had been given, we then began searching for the streets named as our rendezvous point. We found them without too much trouble but became concerned when the girl, or whoever, was not in position. So, not wishing to be seen hanging about, we walked around in circles for almost an hour before we saw a young woman who seemed to fit the description we had of her. She picked us out immediately and again, to our surprise, seemed a good deal less worried than we had been led to believe about meeting us in a public place."

"Being taken quite openly to a back-street café, we were provided with the inevitable bowls of hot soup and bread, which was something of a life saver as we had not eaten for a whole day. Then, another surprise; we were shown upstairs to a room above the cafe where there was a large bed and the softest of mattresses on which we collapsed and immediately went to sleep."

"Seemingly an age later, but probably only about midnight, there was much violent banging below us and the sound of raised voices as soldiers pounded on an outside door demanding entry. A woman's voice was screaming in reply and a man's shouts and further banging added to the turmoil. We scrambled out of bed in a panic and, rooting about for our clothes, each gathered up an armful. Then, after falling over each other in the dark, we pelted down the back stairs in flapping shirts and bare feet, the woman still screaming her head off but apparently making no effort to unbolt the door. Then, out in the darkness and still with howls and shouts in our ears, we found ourselves struggling through what appeared to be a hen run at the back of the house. Falling over fluttering, squawking birds and wading through all sorts of mire, we stumbled on until we ran into bales of straw behind which, breathing hard and scared to death, we crouched and hid, feeling very naked and very much part of a Laurel and Hardy comic film."

"Much later, and to our relief, lights came on in the house and the shouts and arguments gradually died away. Among the smelly hens and crouching down in muck and filth, I was still in bare feet and with only one leg in my trousers, my Whitley friend in more or less the same state. Suddenly we collapsed into giggles, albeit discreetly. Then, about an hour later and frozen to the marrow, we decided it was safe to move back into the house, which we entered timidly, stinking to high heaven, black to the thighs, and still clutching our clothes."

"Inside, the cafe owner and his wife began howling with laughter, not only at our appearance and state of undress, but also because the soldiers, apparently acting on a tip-off, had visited the right house but in the wrong street. Realising their mistake and being suitably embarrassed, they had only gently chided the cafe owner for not opening the door quickly enough, but had even apologised on leaving."

"Local people by the dozen then began to turn up to meet us and share what they considered to be a huge joke. It may have been a joke to them but their arrival and loud laughter seemed to us a very risky and frightening sequel to what had been a hair-raising incident. Later that day, and armed with information as to our next move, we left the cafe and caught another train, heartily thankful that we had not been discovered and arrested."

"We finally found ourselves in a local stopping train bound for a small fishing village called Camaret. This, apparently, was very close to Brest. I had never heard of the place and it was certainly not sufficiently large nor important enough to appear on my little map"

"As we trundled and clacked along in the train, with me half asleep, I allowed my mind to wander. Although so near to the end of our journey and within sight of success, I was so tired and dispirited that for once I felt myself almost indifferent to the possibility that I might be captured, betrayed, or even tortured. I had been on the run for more than nine weeks and during that stressful period, had hardly eaten a decent meal or enjoyed a good night's rest. I had clearly lost a lot of weight and was deeply unhappy at being perpetually in filthy clothes, walking around in worn and ill fitting boots that crippled my feet, and looking like the wrath of God, with unkempt hair and an unshaven face. Moreover, my shirt and underclothes were disgusting and I felt unwashed, flea-bitten and crummy. At that moment, too, I also had a nasty head cold and a streaming nose."

"We had been given information that we would be hidden away in the village bakery in Camaret and that provisional arrangements were already in place. We would then be taken aboard a fishing vessel bound for England when a suitable opportunity arose. We were also warned, however, that plans could always be changed at the last moment as the Germans kept a careful watch on the fishing fleet. They normally allowed only a single day's fuel to be carried. Furthermore, if a boat did succeed in escaping at night, the rest of the fleet was usually prevented from sailing for several months thereafter, with the result that many lobster-boat captains, although they might have sympathy for us, felt unwilling to jeopardise their livelihood by providing active support."

"Arriving in the village, we found the bakery without difficulty and were astonished to find at least ten other aircrew already there, including all six of those who had left Paris with my Whitley friend and me. Meanwhile, Ju 88s roared overhead now and then and formations of Me 109s were often seen in the distance."

"As almost all the boats were anchored in mid-stream, it would be necessary, we were told, to row us out in small groups of two or three, before hiding us away below deck. This in itself was a problem as the Germans patrolled the river and harbour regularly and kept a beady eye on all small rowing boats, dinghies and launches. We were also informed that there would be ten of us aboard one small vessel, a ten metre lobster-boat named the Francine."

"After hanging about on tenterhooks for three days, the night selected eventually arrived. I found myself, first in a bobbing dinghy, then scrambling up the side of the Francine, being then pushed unceremoniously down into a hold that was dark, wet, miserably cold, and stinking of fish. When all ten of us had finally been transferred and were gathered below deck, there was scarcely room to breathe far less move, as there was only a single cabin with one bunk. This allowed two people only to recline, plus a bench on which a maximum of two or three others could sit down. We were eventually to take turns in using the bunk; the rest using the bench or propping themselves up against the side of the vessel, and hanging on to, or sitting down on the wet plank flooring, as the boat wallowed, rolled, and dipped with sickening regularity. Our only toilet facility was a single lavatory bucket, which we were obliged to empty over the side at night."

"Having been taken aboard, for a time we had little to eat and obliged to sit or stand about, almost bent double and in the greatest discomfort, for five days and nights. The weather meanwhile deteriorated and became so thoroughly nasty that the fleet was unable to put to sea. Only at night were a few of us at a time invited to stand upright in the engine well and breathe cool, fresh air. It was a horrible, miserable experience for everyone, the more so as we were all aware that our circumstances were only likely to get worse."

"Finally, on the sixth day, the crew came aboard announcing that at last the fleet would shortly be moving off. And hot on their heels came two armed German sailors to inspect the vessel."

"Jammed into the hold, all ten of us held our breath as the sailors tramped all over the vessel, one of them loudly demanding to visit the hold. By the grace of God, however, the cover to the hold was littered with a mass of ropes, equipment and lobster pots, so that the inspection ended prematurely and the sailors eventually departed."

"Almost immediately, the fleet moved off and, setting a south-west course into a moderate sea, the crew of the Francine prepared to lay out their lobster pots. For the remainder of that day, the captain then allowed our boat to drift away from the main body of the fleet, so that when darkness fell, the engine was started and the craft set course for Penzance in Cornwall."

"When well and truly on our way, those of us below deck were able to come up again and take the air. However, all of us sick and miserable beyond belief, it was a mixed blessing. When daylight finally came, even the sight of German aircraft in the far distance didn't cause us much concern; many of us being too distressed even to care. Then, at one time in mid-Channel, we were suddenly confronted by a British destroyer en route for the Atlantic, which ploughed past behind an impressive bow-wave, without, it appeared, even noticing us. Later still, two Spitfires appeared and flew over and around us, suggesting that someone in England anyway, knew who we were and were at least moderately interested."

"Finally, within sight of land, we were met by a naval launch, which shepherded us into Penzance. Having tied up, I was offered food and wine but was too miserable to eat or drink. Nor did I feel able to take part later in the minor celebrations and hospitality that was later prepared for us. All I could think about were the trials I had experienced throughout those last ghastly 10 weeks, and the courage and bravery of those who had helped me in France, particularly the brave young women, all of whom were still there, fighting in their own quiet way - and suffering!"

Chapter Two

At this point in my account of Ian Graeme-Scott's Service career, and having repeated as best I could the story of his escape from France, I felt almost drained and in need of a rest. I had been speaking, I noticed, for more than four hours and considered that that was quite enough for the time being. So I suggested to my guest that he should stay the night, but he refused, explaining that he had already booked a room at the Maid's Head Hotel in Norwich. However, he would be happy to return the following morning and continue - if I felt up to it. He recognised, rather apologetically, that his '30 minutes chat' had been rather an underestimation of the time required for him to find out all he needed to know. Which was how it was left.

The following morning at 10 o'clock on the dot, he turned up again with his grinning dog and, after a cup of coffee, we settled down in the conservatory to another session of Second World War history.

I continued.

"Our meal that night in the Scott farmhouse was taken in an enormous kitchen, in front of cheerful fire and around a table that was a mile long and covered in a large white table cloth. There were four of us, Ian's mother, his sister, Ina - short for Georgina - Ian, and of course, me. We ate off Royal Doulton china, using sterling silver cutlery, and our wine was poured into Edinburgh crystal goblets. The informality of the occasion seemed a little at odds with the expensive crockery and silverware employed (all well worn). But clearly, this was an ancient household who lived in their own traditional country style, using as normal the best in everything. I sat down feeling thoroughly at ease and among friends".

"We ate succulent, stuffed breast of lamb, which I have always enjoyed. Raised and killed on their own farm, I was told, my hosts adding with smiles that being farmers in wartime was possibly the best possible business to be in. The accompanying potatoes and vegetables, also home produced, were delicious, as was the rich, syrup pudding and the cheeses that followed. With my schoolboy's appetite, I did more than justice to the whole meal."

"Conversation throughout was light, bright and varied. I was reminded many times how similar in appearance and temperament mother and children seemed to be. All the time, I found my eyes being drawn towards Ian's sister, who was an animated conversationalist, her dark eyes always dancing with merriment and vitality. I became aware, too, of Ian's smiling but approving silences and the mother's quiet and gentle understanding of her daughter's 'party performance'".

"Suddenly, Ina addressed me. 'Come on Tom. You're a northerner. What do you know of us Border folk. What does the term 'Border Reivers' mean to you?'"

"I replied that I was hardly a true northerner, having been born only slightly to the north of the dotted line that ran between the Mersey and the Humber. But I was certainly a 'moors person' and the Lake District was well known to me."

"'There you are,' insisted Ina 'What could be more Border country than the mountains and waters of Cumberland. Some of the most famous Border families came from there, Mother's for example.' She then added mischievously, 'Mother's a Fenwick, who were largely English - until she joined us Scotts, that is, and became civilised!' She grinned in her mother's direction. 'But you haven't answered my question about Border Reivers Do you know who they were?'"

"I found myself retaliating. 'I've heard of the term, of course. It means, I believe, Border rascals, or robbers. Something pretty nasty anyway.'"

"Ian's mother intervened. 'You are right there, Tom. In the 300 years between 1300 and 1600, feuding Border families - more than 100 of them - from both sides of Hadrian's Wall, stole more livestock, burned more farmhouses and buildings, and cut more throats than at any time since. There were murders and hangings galore., and even full blown battles involving hundreds of men. In fact, the whole Border area was a violent and lawless place, pacified only when James 6th of Scotland became James 1st of Britain.'"

"I put in with a smile, 'And I bet the Scotts were probably among the worst of them.'"

"'You're right, Tom.' Ina again. 'And rode off over the hills with more virginal maidens than almost any other family. It was sung about in many ballads of the time. A distant relation of ours, Sir Walter Scott, often wrote of the Reivers' adventures in his poetry, which was largely based on the ballads of the 15th and 16th centuries. You may remember learning at school of `The Brave Lochinvar, etc,' the chap who 'came out of the West', pinched a fair maiden and rode off with her over the hills, pursued by the Fenwicks, the Forsters, the Musgraves and others, although they never caught the rascal or recovered the young lady.'"

"'And how did Graeme get into your name?'" I was warming to the subject.

"'Ah, that's something we tend to keep quiet about! You see, the Grahams - spelt various ways - had a beautiful daughter, apparently, in about 1810, who made sheep's eyes at one of the Scott boys and seduced him. Then her Dad insisted on the name of Graeme being added to our own. The Grahams or Graemes, like the Fernwicks, were largely English, although they had family members both sides of the Border.'"

"'And how long have the Scotts lived in this area?'"

"'Oh, Lord! On this farm and in this particular house, for about 250 years. Before that we lived in these same Border hills, certainly since around 1300 and possibly even before then. Originally, the Scottish tribes came from Ireland, and, moving westwards, displaced or merged with the Pictish clans - but you probably know that already.'"

"I put in, 'I've heard of the Percys, the Humes, the Kerrs and others. Did they all come from around here?'"

"'Yes and no. The Percys and Humes were certainty Border families but they were largely in the Eastern Marches. The Kerrs were a local tribe, however. Many of the Kerrs were left-handed, did you know that? Which led to the term Kerr-handed, or Cack-handed, as it later became.' And Ina laughed, 'You see, Tom, when you visit the Scott household, your education is greatly improved.'"

"And so it went on, with bright conversation and many laughs, until the mother finally rose to her feet. 'We farming folk rise early and go to bed early. So, if our gallant guest doesn't object, I shall retire, with the promise to see you all in the morning.'"

"With that she left and our small party broke up."

"I rose early the following day and, going down into the warm Aga-heated kitchen, found it empty. It was a brilliant morning and, deciding to take a brisk walk, I went outside to see Ina in the distance, clad in dungarees and gum boots, carrying a pail in one hand. She waved to me from afar and I returned her greeting before setting off down a wide cow-path which bordered a cheerful-sounding stream. I looked around. The green hills climbed away silently to left and right and the air was like wine. Mmm! It was good to be alive!"

"Returning 40 minutes later - for breakfast, I hoped - I found Ian, his face alight with suppressed excitement."

"'I've just had a 'phone call,' he explained. 'I'm to have another medical in Edinburgh tomorrow and the AOC 13 Group is flying up to Turnhouse to see me. I shall be meeting him at 10.30 am, presumably to discuss my future. This means that I shall be driving up to Edinburgh this afternoon with Mother, who wishes to do a bit of shopping at the same time. So, I shall leave you in the capable hands of Ina, when she has finished her 'jobs' around the farm and has cleaned herself up.'"

"To all of which I agreed, not being in any position to object."

"At breakfast, Ina, suitably scrubbed and with her dark hair tied back with a ribbon, asked me what I wished to do, before quickly making several suggestions, one of which was to take me riding."

"'How are you on a horse, Tom?'"

"I confessed that the last horse I had ridden was a donkey on Southport sands at the age of five. Furthermore, I would have her know that I did not normally cart around riding clobber in my airplane, not even a whip!"

"Not to worry, asserted the girl. A pair of gumboots would do the trick, worn over my usual slacks. After that, all I had to do was hold the reins and hang on, feeding the horse mints every now and then, to keep on the right side of him. Which is what we did, starting off at 2 pm that sunny afternoon."

"'This is Charlie,' said Ina, introducing me to the horse. 'More than a touch of 'Hobby' in him still, despite years of new blood in his veins.'"

"'Hobby?'"

"'Yes. Border-country horses used to be called Hobblers, before they were cross bred with others. They were wonderful creatures, and still are. They are small and tough, bred especially for the hills and bogs of the Lowlands. With so few roads in this area, horses were the only means of transport in the old days. Like Border collies, they were absolutely tireless and were well suited to the terrible weather you sometimes get around here.' She felt in her pockets. 'Here, let me give you some sweeties for him. Later on, when we stop at the pub we're going to, you can give him a pint of beer. If you don't, he probably won't bring you home!'"

"Setting off, with me feeling thoroughly uncomfortable on his jogging, bony back. I had to concentrate more on the horse than on conversation as we walked then trotted together now and then, up, down, and across some fairly steep hills, inhabited only by scores of sheep who gazed at us without interest as we passed. Until after about an hour, and looking down from the top of a steep incline, Ina pointed with a finger."

"'We're going to stop at that pub down there to take a dram or two and give your bum a rest. After that we'll turn for home.' She grinned. 'Still feeling up to it? Not a bit like flying an aircraft is it?'"

"We were the only visitors in the small country pub. The landlord, obviously well known to Ina, greeted us cordially and tried to press food on us but we declined everything other than three pints of ginger beer shandy, one of which I fed to Charlie, who sucked it down gratefully. Then, seated comfortably on wooden seats outside in the afternoon sunshine, I thought it the right moment to question Ina on matters that had been on my mind for some time."

"First, I asked, 'Tell me, why has so beautiful a girl as you not married?'"

"For a moment she looked at me blankly, then began to laugh. 'Why, Tom! You naughty fellow! Are you thinking of proposing to me?'"

"'Not really, though I shall certainly consider it later on. Just at the moment, though, I doubt that my Mum would be very pleased if her 22 year old only son suddenly told her that he was considering marriage. Even to so delightful a person as you!'"

"'And she'd be absolutely right, because I'm far too old for you, young Tom. I'm pushing 29, for heavens sake, and you need a young, nubile beauty to go around with, not a weathered old crone like me. But, thanks for the thought, anyway. I'm flattered.'"

"'But you haven't answered my question. Why?'"

"'Why? Because I run the farm, more or less. I do the books and keep track of all the animals. We have about 800 cattle, sheep and horses. Whilst Hamish, the farm manager, looks after the buildings, the woods, hedges and ditches, plus the arable side, which is the part of the farm that feeds us all.'"

"'And didn't your elder brother get involved?'"

"'No, Douglas, who is a few years older than me, didn't have any interest in farming. After school he went to Edinburgh University, read law, and became a solicitor. He finally ended up a Squadron Leader in the Legal Branch of he RAF when war broke out. No, he was glad to get away and is now overseas in the Middle East.'"

"'And Ian. What about him? I feel I know him so well at times. Then sometimes I find him a stranger. Tell me about him.'"

"Ina was silent for some moments, then in a quiet voice, told me a quite remarkable story about her family."

"'Father was in the Diplomatic Service and was in India when both Ian and I were born. I was about eight when we returned to Scotland and Ian three. You are probably aware that we are all 'left-footers' - Roman Catholics. Both my father and my mother were very devout, but, as so often happens, my elder brother and I somewhat less so. Ian, however, was very much his mother's son and took his religion very seriously. He was a choirboy when young and also an altar boy. He went away to a prep. school in Edinburgh, then on to Ampleforth in Yorkshire, which you may know, is one of two major Catholic public schools in the country.

So, for many years - most of his life, in fact - he has lived in a totally male environment, a sort of seclusion perpetuated when he joined the Air Force'"

"'Right from the outset, he was mother's favourite. Not that either Douglas or I ever resented the fact, because Ian was always a delightful kid - brave, kind, and courteous. And right from the start, mother always wanted him to go into the Church, to become a priest. Which is what we all thought would happen, including Ian himself.'"

"'Then it all changed suddenly in about 1934, when father took us all to London and Ian and I went one day to Hendon Aerodrome to see the RAF Pageant. That day changed Ian's whole outlook on life because he was so impressed by the flying and the gaily marked aircraft, that he came home talking about nothing else.'"

"'For a time mother thought it was only a passing phase and didn't take it too seriously. But when Ian said he wished to go to Cranwell after Ampleforth and become a full-time regular officer, both my parents, but chiefly my mother, became really worried. For the first time ever, she and Ian had words - not exactly arguments, but strongly expressed views. Everything came to a head when she and father refused absolutely to sign any papers to that end, so that there were long faces all around for quite some time. However, when he persisted, it was eventually agreed that he should apply for a short-service commission in the RAF and that, if accepted and following his four year stint, he would then begin studying for the Church. I believe Ian was reasonably happy with this plan at the time, although I don't think he ever really thought it through - four or five years hence is a long time in any young man's vision of the future.'"

"'Well, he started flying in 1937 and was sent to a fighter squadron in 1938 - 72 Squadron as I recall - who were flying Gloster Gladiators from Church Fenton in Yorkshire. He then moved with the unit to Acklington, where they were re-equipped with Spitfires. After that, of course, you know as much about him as I do.'"

"I heard myself asking carefully, 'As his sister, and knowing him all your life, do you really believe that he's suited to monastic life, and that he could tolerate a lifetime of celibacy as a priest? Because he's an attractive chap and I can quite see the girls running after him, and he them, although I've never noticed him thus far being interested in the opposite sex.'"

"Ina responded thoughtfully. 'I've often thought about that, too, If you are asking me is he ' odd ', I'm pretty sure he isn't. . I believe he's naturally shy with girls because he never had much to do with them.' Then with a grin, 'With two domineering females badgering him at home, perhaps that's understandable.'"

"I went on. 'Well, the whole business has now been overtaken by the war, hasn't it? And he's been very successful thus far. Do you really believe he will give up all the action and excitement and go back to being a prelate? Honestly?'"

"A pause. Then, 'Yes I do. That's what he agreed to do and that's what I believe will happen. Knowing Ian intimately, he's not a chap who will ever break his word.'"

"Riding back to the farm that early evening, we hardly exchanged a sentence and I found myself strangely disturbed by Ina's explanation and remarks."

"Ian arrived back with his mother the following day, his eyes dancing. He reported that he was to be posted a month hence to the Middle East, to Egypt initially. Apparently, it was the policy not to employ anyone who had escaped from France, in any squadron flying over the same territory, as the Huns might use the thumbscrews on anyone shot down a second time. He didn't know precisely what he would be doing, or where, but it seemed certain it would be another flying appointment."

"So, the day after, and feeling slightly envious, I said goodbye to the family, and flew back to Tealing. With the happiest memories of them all - especially sister Ina and Charlie, the beer-drinking horse."

This next part of the story of my association with Ian Graeme-Scott, became a little involved and took me quite some time. I'm bound to say, however, Cadwallader continued to listen intently and several times stopped me to clarify points he felt were especially interesting. I had to explain to him that when Ian Scott left for the Middle East, my own career had begun to take off again and that for some months I concentrated more on what I was doing rather than enquiring about Scotty's movements and activities.

I went on with my tale.

"From time to time, I heard of Ian from mutual acquaintances. First, that he had spent a little time at Headquarters, Desert Air Force in Cairo but had then moved to Malta. There, as a newly promoted squadron commander, he had been flying Mark Vb Spitfires, brought to the island on various aircraft carriers including the American USS Wasp. Apparently, he had arrived when Malta was heavily under siege by the Germans, who were desperate to cripple the island's offensive capability against Axis convoys and transport aircraft, sailing and flying from Europe to deliver vital supplies to Rommel's armies in Libya. This would be towards the end of 1942, immediately prior to General Montgomery's successful attack on the Axis Forces in North Africa.. It was an offensive that was to be the turning point in the struggle for the Middle East and a significant factor in altering the whole course of the Second World War."

"I remember this period especially as there were photographs in the national press of Scotty receiving a recently awarded DSO from the hands of Lord Gort, the Governor of Malta, with captions explaining that 'this officer had led his squadron with great verve and determination and has now personally destroyed more than 12 enemy aircraft.'"

"Meanwhile I, too, was commanding a Spitfire squadron and moving around from airfield to airfield in the south of England. I recall being at Biggin Hill when I telephoned Ian's home in Scotland to congratulate the family on his award and to enquire as to his exact whereabouts."

"I was delighted when Ina answered the telephone"

"She was sweetness itself. 'Tom, my dear sweet lad, we all thought you had emigrated! How are you and what are you up to these days?'"

"'I'm not up to anything that should concern you, dear heart, I'm just ringing to congratulate our hero's family on Ian's DSO.'"

"'Yes, we were all overjoyed up here in Border country. Such a pity it had to be presented in Malta and not by the King and Queen at Buck.House. Mother and I went to London for his DFC and had words with the Monarch, which was a great thrill. You must get yourself a DSO, Tom, so that we can all turn up and cheer.'"

"'I'm trying my hardest, never fear. But my second question is, where is our hero now, because I would like to write to him?'"

"'Tom, I wish I knew. He was last flying from either Ta Kali or Quendi in Malta, but I can never be sure, because he really gets around. Did you see the photograph of him on his knees on the steps of Mosta Church or Cathedral? - someone sent us a copy.'"

"'No, tell me about it.'"

"'Well, apparently he went there for Communion one Sunday but found the place locked up. Some ghastly Hun had dropped a big bomb, which fortunately didn't go off, right through the roof. So, finding nothing happening, he went down on his hunkers on the outside steps and was saying his prayers there when the resident priest arrived - someone had told him about Ian being there. Then, after opening up, the priest invited Ian inside where they had a little private ceremony of their own. It was all over Malta, it appears. Quite a story.'"

"'Quite a story, indeed, But what about you? How is your love life these days?'"
"'In the doldrums, dear heart. I'm still waiting for a modern day Lochinvar to ride down from the hills waving his broadsword, then pick me up, throw me over his saddle and ride off with me into the sunset. Alas, I'm still waiting. However, I still haven't forgotten that you have me in mind. That is, of course, if you don't find one of those nubile young maidens I recommended.'"

"When we finally ended our conversation, I saw in my mind's eye Ian Graeme-Scott praying on the steps of that splendid church in Malta. So like him. So very like the chap I had grown to admire, almost to idolize."

The next part of my story introduces two very small developments that occurred during my conversation with Cadwallader ,which, like so many other tiny incidents in life, had an effect quite disproportionate to their importance.

It was at about 11.30 am on that second morning of our discussion, when my wife appeared carrying a tray of coffee and cups.

She said, "You chaps have been hard at it now for more than an hour this morning, so I thought it time I brought you some liquid refreshment. Also, I have a question to ask. Am I allowed to sit in for a bit? You have both been yacking away for hours and I am beginning to feel neglected. Or would I be intruding?"

Cadwallader and I exchanged glances before my guest said brightly, "No, certainly not, Mrs Burgoyne. We would both be quite happy for you to listen in. And also to take part if you have anything useful to tell us. "

I added in explanation, "Perhaps I should explain to our guest that, at the time we are talking about - the latter part of 1943 - my wife was a Flight Officer, WAAF at RAF Biggin Hill, and was pretty au fait with much that was going on. She knew the names and faces of most pilots in Fighter Command, although I'm not sure she knew Ian Scott personally." I looked for confirmation in her direction before adding, "But, it is at this point that I am going to ask our visitor to continue with the discussion, because he could well know more about Ian and his movements than either of us, particularly as I had just been posted to a flying appointment with the Americans and was rather preoccupied at the time."

After which remark, Cadwallader, after nodding, bent down, picked up some documents he had on the floor, studied them for some moments, then launched forth.

"I'm happy to continue but with some diffidence as you were both part of the war at a time I was yet to be born. As I see it, Ian Scott took part in air operations over and around North Africa, flying from Malta, at a time when the Luftwaffe was under heavy pressure, their bombers and transport aircraft being shot down almost by the dozen when trying first, to reinforce, then rescue, the Axis armies in Algeria. He certainly destroyed several enemy aircraft himself during this period and became an acting Wing Commander in the late autumn of 1943. Towards the end of the year, he was placed in command of yet another fighter wing but did not see any action until about April of 1944, when British and American troops were well into Italy, having successfully invaded Sicily six months earlier. However, before I deal with his flying over Italy, there is one period around the beginning of 1944 which I found a little puzzling."

"According to my research, Ian was given about a month's leave, on or about the turn of the year, and apparently came back to the UK for a brief change of scenery - he had then been abroad for more than 18 months. He visited first his family in Scotland then was engaged on a goodwill tour of half-a-dozen cotton mills in Lancashire. The Lancashire Cotton Board had apparently asked Air Ministry to provide a well-known and successful airman to heighten morale by visiting and talking to the operatives of some of their spinning and weaving mills - you know the sort of thing. Ian had then spent two separate periods of a week, doing just that. Well, all his activities when at home, I can account for but I cannot be sure of his movements when in Lancashire. However, I must assume that his time there was taken up entirely by visits to the six-or-so selected mills."

"Anyway, back again in harness in Italy, he did wonderfully well, shooting down another five or six enemy aircraft and taking part in the destruction of innumerable vehicles during the Battle of Monte Cassino, Italy, and in the run up to the capture of Rome. By the autumn of 1944, when he was finally rested, his tally of victories had risen to 20 and he was recommended for the award of a second D.S.O., which he later received."

"Later, after another spell at OTU in Egypt, he was finally brought home and posted to the School of Air Support, Old Sarum, Salisbury, as Wing Commander, Offensive Support Wing. Where,, of course, you sir, were already serving as an instructor and where you met up with him yet again."

At this, our guest looked up, folded his papers and smiled in my direction. "And now, sir, it's your turn. I would now like to hear you story of Ian's brief spell of 11 days at RAF Old Sarum, between 6th and 17th August, 1945."

When Cadwallader had spoken of Ian's rather surprising visit to the UK at the end of 1943 and mentioned Scotty's two-week visit to the Lancashire cotton mills, I found my wife looking in my direction with a query in her eyes, a query which said quite plainly, "Are you going to tell him?" And I felt my own frowning glance in reply, hinting that it was not quite the time to do so.

Within seconds, the moment had passed and I began to explain how delighted I had been to welcome Ian to Old Sarum, and how we had then spent some hours talking about old times and reliving our dramatic flight over France 18 months earlier.

Then a few days later, the Air Marshal School Commandant asked me to fly him to Germany on a quick visit, and we left, flying a Beechcraft Traveller, a Royal Navy aircraft, which was part of the Communication Flight.

Three days later we returned and after an uneventful three hour flight, landed on the grass runway at Old Sarum, to be greeted by the Group Captain commanding the Offensive Support Wing - which I thought at the time was a bit strange. Then, as I stepped out of the aircraft, the Group Captain asked me in rather a tense voice, if I had heard the news. To which I responded with something of a surprised shrug, 'I don't think so. What news?'

"Scotty's just killed himself," came the bald reply. "Took off in the Spitfire XII, did a couple of slow rolls straight off the deck and flew into the grounds of Old Sarum Castle, the silly bugger!"

And I remember just standing there. For five horrible, devastating seconds. Rooted to the ground in dismay. Experiencing a terrible, terrible sadness that was almost a physical blow. Scotty! My friend, the peerless Scotty! How on earth could he have done such a thing? And why? Why? Why, for heaven's sake?

Even fifty years after event, when I spoke of the accident which resulted in the death of Ian Graeme-Scott, very poignantly, all three of us were frozen into a brief period of silence, our eyes lowered, seemingly in respect. Then, Cadwallader broke the silence with a quiet explanation.

"Some years ago now, I wrote to Air Ministry asking for a transcript of the Court of Inquiry proceedings, but they said that they had not kept the complete papers but only an outline of the investigation together with the findings. They stated that Ian had been carrying out low-level aerobatics immediately after take-off, that he had hit the ground with one wingtip, and that he had died instantly as the result of multiple injuries, having been thrown out of the aircraft and landing some 20 yards away from the crash site. Moreover, it appeared that he had not been wearing his seat belt." A sudden fluttering breath followed by a swallowing silence.

"Which is one of the points I want to discuss with you, sir. Because it is something I simply don't understand. Is it really possible for a pilot in a fighter aircraft not to have been wearing his seat belt?"

I found myself hesitating, considering my response. Then I said, "Right. I'll go through the whole pre-flight routine so that you get a true picture of what normally happens. And I have to tell you that I have spent more than 3,000 hours in a fighter cockpit, and it never varies, not with me, nor anyone else I know."

"First, there are invariably two ground crew on hand. One, the airframe rigger, stands alongside the pilot, helping him with his straps; the other, the engine fitter, stands at the star-board wingtip, preparing to remove the battery lead and pull away the wheel chocks.".

"The pilot then gets into the cockpit, where his parachute and dinghy are normally already in place, the dinghy now being too heavy and cumbersome to lug around. The pilot then seats himself on his dinghy pack and attaches the lead from the dinghy to his Mae West, so that if he uses his parachute and lands in the water, the dinghy doesn't float away. After that, he plugs in his parachute harness - left shoulder, right leg, right shoulder, left leg, the metal ends clicking into the parachute release box, somewhere around his tummy button."

"Then there would be his cockpit restraining straps. Once again, left shoulder, right leg, right shoulder, left leg, and so on, these, too, into a small box which had a release mechanism consisting of a lever which has to be turned through 45 degrees to unlock the metal strap-ends. In earlier Spits the straps were secured by a plug and a large split-pin, but the box affair did away with that. The important thing is, the pilot has to make a positive movement with his hand to unlock the box. It doesn't work automatically, nor can it be done by accident."

"After that, the pilot puts on his helmet with his clip-on face mask, and attaches his radio lead, then his oxygen tube, and finally adjusts his goggles - if he needs them. And last of all, he puts on his gloves - cape leather next to his skin, then the silk inners, finally his leather gauntlets. And after all that, the chap alongside him checks that everything is in place, before he jumps down from the wing-walk and the pilot signals to the bloke on his right that he intends starting the engine."

"So, he primes it with about six squirts of petrol into the 12 cylinders, sets the throttle and presses the booster button on the dashboard in front of him. On the Mark XII Spitfire only, he presses another button which fires the cartridge gun that turns the engine over, And, with any luck the big Rolls-Royce Griffon bursts into life."

There followed a short silence.

Then Cadwallader again, "So, you seem to believe that Ian's straps were secured when he started up?"

"If they weren't, it would have appeared in the Inquiry evidence - the rigger would have reported it. But, as we know, he must have said that he handed Ian the straps and they were in position and locked."

"Then, how do we account for the fact that they weren't? After he had crashed, that is."

"That's a mystery that will have to be solved."

"Could the straps have burst?"

"That's hardly possible, they are massively strong. In any case, the lock was apparently in the open position and the straps undamaged, except by the crash itself."

"So it seems Ian must have opened the lock some time later. Purposely."

"Yes. It looks like that, for whatever reason."

"But the fact that he did two slow rolls immediately after take-off, suggests that he knew what he was going to do and that he was aware that his straps were an all important factor. Can you explain exactly why? "

I remember hesitating, then speaking very clearly.

"A normal pilot, even a skilled one, would never expect to do a perfect slow roll immediately after take off as it would be necessary to turn the aircraft over having barely raised the wheels, then push on the control column quite firmly in order to keep the nose well clear of the ground. By so doing, and being upside down, he would then be shot out of his seat. Moreover, there would be more than a chance that an engine fitted with a carburettor, which the Mark XII was, would be flooded briefly because of the negative 'G' force imposed, and would lose power, if only for a few moments. With two slow rolls, the risks would be doubled. If that were so, it might have been a contributory factor to the accident. However, I believe it was reported that the engine was functioning normally when he crashed, which just adds to the mystery."

"Would the cockpit hood be open or closed at that stage?"

"On a Spit, it would always be open on take off. Every pilot normally took off and landed with it open, to enable him to evacuate his aircraft quickly in the event of a crash or an engine failure at low level."

I watched Cadwallader shake his head. "Which really brings me to ask whether or not Ian was sufficiently skilled to carry out such a manoeuvre at so low an altitude. You see, I was given permission to stand on the airfield at Old Sarum and have seen that the Castle stands on a small hill not more than a mile and a half away. Also, I saw that it is in the direct line of an aircraft taking off into the prevailing wind. I am certainly no expert, but it would seem impossible for him to do what he attempted to do in the space available to him. And get away with it, that is. What do you think?"

I answered carefully, "Ian was certainly skilled enough - he was a brilliant aerobatic pilot. But I'm bound to say, what motivated him into taking such a risk, is hard to imagine. If it was pre-planned, it was unwise. If it was not, I can only assume it was either a brainstorm or a sudden rush of blood to the head, caused possibly by the fact that the war was finally over and the future for him was unclear." I found myself shrugging. "It seems, however, that we shall never know."

After that exchange, we talked over that and allied subjects for another hour or so, until Cadwallader stood up and showed signs of wanting to leave.

"You have given me far more of your time than I was expecting, sir, and I'm very grateful. You have certainly clarified a few points in my mind but I can't say I'm any nearer to solving the riddle of my birth, who exactly my father was, and why he was killed, although I shall always have my suspicions. Perhaps if we both mull over the subject in the future, something may emerge that will give us a clearer picture of what exactly happened all those years ago. I hope so anyway"

With that, and much hand-shaking all round, my wife and I followed him and his capering dog outside and accompanied them both to the door of his car. Then, with waves and good wishes for the future, they drove off. And left us both breathing sighs of relief.

Strangely, my wife and I did not discuss either Cadwallader or his visit until the following day. Then my spouse, when serving afternoon tea, brought up the subject; clearly she had had Cadwallader's visit on her mind for some time.

She said, "I remember you telling me, shortly after the fatal accident in 1945, that you had met Scotty during his visit to the Lancashire Cotton mills in the January of 1944, and that you had had dinner with him in company with two of your then girl friends. Would you refresh my memory, because I was expecting you to mention it to Cadwallader and was most surprised when you didn't."

I thought about it for some time before nodding and starting off. "Alright, this is what happened."

"I had been posted as a flying liaison officer to the 9th USAAF over the Christmas of 1943, and had decided to take a fortnight off before taking up my new appointment. My family and I were living then at a place called Monton Green in Lancashire, which is about six miles to the west of Manchester, on the way to Bolton. It was a pleasantly semi-rural place in 1944 and probably still is, although I believe it is now spoilt by masses of motorways running in every direction."

"Anyway, having arrived home, I telephoned a girl-friend of mine whose name was Mimi - Mimi Hetherington, another Border family, strangely enough - and finding her at home, arranged that we should go to the cinema together in Manchester."

"This was a rare occasion as Mimi was then a Section Officer in the WAAF and a Photographic Interpreter stationed at Hemswell, which is, or was, a bomber station in Lincolnshire. She too just happened to be at home on leave, so our arrangement was something of a major coincidence."

"So, you imagine my surprise when in the afternoon of that same day, Ian Graeme-Scott rang my parents at home, to explain that he was on his tour of the cotton mills and was staying at the Midland Hotel in Manchester. Where was I, and if I could be contacted, could he meet me somewhere or write to me at some convenient address?"

"Well, without going into all the details of the many phone calls and conversations that followed, it was finally arranged that Mimi and I, plus Mimi's younger sister, Yvonne - whom I never seen since she was about thirteen years of age - should, with Ian, form a foursome at the Midland Hotel. Here we would have dinner and spend a convivial evening of laughter and conversation - we hoped! Which is more or less what happened."

"I should add here that both Mimi and Yvonne were very attractive girls. Mimi was about my age, a few months older perhaps, and Yvonne was about 19 at the time. She apparently was a VAD nurse, and had been for several years, living with her parents in Monton Green and travelling to wherever she was needed between her home and Bolton."

"Knowing that Ian was often uneasy in the presence of young women, I was not too sure initially how the evening would develop. However, I need not have worried, as although shy at first, he soon became very amusing, having us all in hoots of laughter telling us about his experiences in those cotton mills he had already visited. Apparently, literally thousands of very lusty girls, all wearing head scarves and clogs, gave him 'toffees', as though he were a chimpanzee, talked to him in strange dialects, and insisted on telling him tales he seldom understood, except that they all outrageously rude".

"Well, after I had made my own contribution to the evening's entertainment, Mimi told some melancholy tales about the losses she had witnessed in Bomber Command, particularly when, over one very recent four week period, 300 four-engined night bombers were lost, together with 2,000 aircrew, almost all of them in their early 20s."

"After that, and no doubt wishing to lighten the conversation, Ian brought Yvonne into the picture by inviting her to give us an account of what she did and how she enjoyed her job. Which turned out to be something of a mistake, as it soon became clear that the young woman didn't enjoy her job at all."

"She explained, 'As a VAD, I'm really nothing more than a dogsbody as I am considered untrained and, quite understandably, get all the dirty jobs to do. It is not that I mind much of it. I can cope with all the wee and the poo, but I don't really like being in the Operating Theatres. There, I find I am often asked to carry around all the body parts the doctors cut off. Added to which I don't really enjoy the sight of all the blood and slime, and least of all, the dreadful smell. I've thought of resigning many times, but have always shied away from doing so as I don't want to appear unpatriotic.'"

"At which point her sister put in a trifle scornfully, 'Yvonne is keen to get into the WAAF but wants to start at the top. I've told her that if she does join up, she'll be an ACW plonk and be cleaning officers' boots, or washing aircraft. I'm afraid my kid sister is something of a shrinking violet; she doesn't want to do anything that damages her nail vanish.'"

"At that, of course, there was much laughter and some argument, which went on for some time. Until about 11 pm, when we all stood up to leave."

My wife put in, "And what happened after that?"

"Nothing much. I drove the girls home in my old Morris 10 and I believe Mimi went back to Lincolnshire the next day. What happened to Yvonne, I really don't know, as I don't think I ever saw her again. Mimi married a Frenchman just after the war, as we now know, and Ian, of course, continued his tour of the mills before returning to Italy later. As for me, I travelled down south to join the 100th Fighter Wing of the 9th USAAF, and begin preparing for the invasion of Europe the following June."

"Did the girls comment about Ian and did either of them see him later?" I could see immediately in which direction my wife's thought were going.

"Not as far as I'm aware. They both thought Ian was very attractive but nothing more than that. But, and I have only just thought about it, perhaps I should telephone Mimi and have a chat with her. Her name's now Fayolle, I recall, and I think we have her address and telephone number in our Christmas Card book. She lives in Paris, doesn't she?"

I telephoned Mimi in Paris and she sounded terribly French.

She screamed, "Tommee! Tommee! How wonderful to hear from you. It must be simply years since we spoke. Where are you now and how is your beautiful wife? I've heard from third parties how fortunate you are, with a beautiful wife, a big house and simply oceans of children."

"Mimi, you've been talking to the wrong people! I am well and happily married, yes, but no more than that. Furthermore, my house is adequate but not that big. Anyway, that's not precisely what I want to talk to you about."

"'My dear sweet man, if it's about money, I don't want to know! Henri and I haven't any! We are down to our last million. He's retired now, you know. As an Admiral."

"An Admiral! Good Lord! I didn't even know that he was in the French Navy. And does that make you a Countess or something?"

"Not quite, but something very close. Anyway, what especially do you want to talk to me about?"

"Mimi . . . cast your mind back to January, 1944, when we had dinner one evening at the Midland Hotel, Manchester - you, sister Yvonne, my friend Ian Graeme-Scott, and I. Do you remember?"

"Of course I do. Your friend Ian was such a lovely man. What happened to him? Is he still around?"

"Alas, no. He was tragically killed just after the end of the war."

"Oh, quel dommage! And he was so famous, and beautiful too. Like you, of course."

"Mimi, you are full of flannel! But, this is not about him or me, but about Yvonne. What happened to her, because I never saw hair nor hide of her after we parted that night. She was a VAD nurse, I remember, but she so wanted to join the WAAFs. Did she?"

"She did indeed. And became an MT (Mechanical Transport) driver, driving petrol bowsers, three-ton lorries and staff cars all over the country. She started off at Ringway, Manchester, which was a small grass airfield in those early days. Then she went all over the place. Anyway why do you ask?"

"Yes, but what happened to her afterwards?"

"Afterwards! She married a Flight Lieutenant chap just after the war and they went to live in Malta - of all places! He was a ground type not a pilot, and I don't think the marriage was very successful. Anyway, when she was in her late 30s, she suddenly found she had breast cancer and returned to England where she had one of her 'what'sits' removed, and for a time we all thought she would recover completely. But it was not to be, poor thing, and she died in 1968, when she was about 42. My parents were very cut up at the time."

I paused for some moments, wondering whether or not to proceed with my line of questioning but came to the conclusion that I had to. So I asked carefully, "Tell me, did she have any children?"

A minor shriek. "Sister Yvonne! You must be joking! Having children would have been altogether too farmyard for here. No, I don't believe she ever considered it. I don't think she even knew what went on down there - she was not that sort of girl. In fact, I often wondered why she ever got married."

Another pause whilst I made up my mind. Then: "This is another rather personal question, Mimi. Did she ever have a child out of wedlock? About late 1944, for example?"

Another squeal down the telephone. "Yvonne! What on earth are you talking about? It would have shown, for heaven's sake, although I have to admit, we seldom saw each other at that time. No, my kid sister would never even have dreamt of having a child. I honestly believe she was afraid of sex, afraid of any form of intimacy, in fact. Which was probably the cause of her disastrous marriage. Anyway, why do you keep asking?"

Which question, of course, I felt myself unable to answer, moving on instead to Yvonne's decision to leave nursing.

"I remember Yvonne telling us that she didn't like all the gore and slime of the Operating Theatres and that she often felt sick when going about her job."

"Well, that was certainly true but there were other things as well. For example, she especially resented being shunted about so often, arguing that her pay as a nurse didn't even cover her train fares to and from all the places she was obliged to travel."

"I thought she told us she worked mainly in Bolton."

"Yes, Bolton, but many other places as well. In fact she also did stints in Blackburn, Oldham, neighbouring Irlam, and spent quite a time in Walkden. You know, where the colliery is. The place where they had that dreadful mining disaster some years ago."

I found myself echoing almost stupidly, "Walkden! You mean that small place on the railway line to Bolton?"

"Of course. Is there any other?"

And I found myself shaking my head, quietly and almost sadly. The last piece of the jigsaw? Or was it?

The following day my wife and I were again discussing Cadwallader's visit over the tea table.

My wife asked quietly "So what is your verdict on Cadwallader's birth mother? Was it really Yvonne Hetherington?"

"It looks very much like it. She was very attractive but also a very naive girl and being away from home for the first time, she suddenly found herself pregnant. So, she plucked two names from the air and in an agony of mind, had the child in the John Radcliffe hospital in Oxford - on the quiet, so to speak. Whether or not Ian Scott had anything to do with it we shall never know, even though she named him as the father. She certainly knew him, was clearly impressed by him, and possibly she fantasised about him as the father of her infant, although she got his name a bit wrong. But, she is long gone now, so we shall never be able to ask her."

"And what about Ian Graeme-Scott and his crash? Was it a pure accident or something more complicated?"

"Ah, that's a difficult one as there are so many conflicting factors. However, as I see it, there are two scenarios. The first is that it was a pure accident, in which Ian did nothing more than make an error of judgement"

"Consider the circumstances. Ian had only been at Old Sarum a week and as far as I can recall, had never flown from the airfield. The war with Japan has suddenly ended, the morning was bright and fine - don't forget I was airborne for three hours on that same day. There was no Course in residence, so that he had nothing much to do and his special mate - me, Tom Burgoyne - was abroad, on his way home after whooping it up in Germany. So, he decides to go flying and wanders down to the Communication Flight where there are at least six aircraft for him to chose from. He's not going anywhere special, he just wants to get into the air for about an hour, so he chooses the aircraft he knows best - the Spitfire. But, there are two Spits' available, a Mark V and a Mark XII. So, he opts for the Mark XII, an aircraft, as far as I know, he had never flown before. With a 1,750 horse power Griffon 3 engine, it was a unique type and the last one of only 100 built and formerly used by just two squadrons in Fighter Command. I knew all about that particular Spitfire, incidentally, as I had flown it many time over the past few months and had found it utterly reliable."

"So, we can see him climbing into the cockpit, a smile on his lips no doubt, strapping up, then starting the big engine using his Coffman cartridge gun, before taxying out across the grass to the far end of the airfield. There being no concrete runways, he stops his aircraft in the crosswind position, tests his two magnetos, runs up the engine to clear the plugs, and finally turns on to about 240 degrees and into the prevailing south-west wind. Pointing towards the distant ruins of Old Sarum Castle, standing silently on its rising mound - which I doubt very much that Scotty was even aware of at that point - he opens the throttle and surges across the grass, savouring the sheer liquid power of the raging Griffon engine in front of him. Then, lifting the aircraft off the grass within about 500 yards, he retracts the wheels, and on a sudden whim, decides to give the ground crew a treat by demonstrating how a perfect slow roll should be executed. Turning the aircraft slowly on to its back, before completing the circle smoothly and without any obvious loss of height, he suddenly feels a need to repeat the process. Halfway round the second roll, however, he must have sensed the ground rising beneath his aircraft and probably hastened the manoeuvre, aware that his wing tip was perilously close to disaster. Then, in that single ghastly, horrifying moment before it touched, Ian, the most skilful of aerobatic pilots, probably realised that he had miscalculated and the he was going to crash and lose his life. A second later, the wingtip touched, the aircraft cartwheeled into a chaos of whirling bits and he was catapulted out of the open cockpit some 20 yards away, to die instantly in a small mangled and bloody heap."

Having completed my rather gruesome account of what might possibly have happened, I watched my wife swallow in silence then say rather quietly, "That doesn't explain why, or how, his seat belts were in the unlocked position, does it?"

To which I had to agree. "You're right, it doesn't, and I can offer no solution to that conundrum. But let me speak of the other scenario, which is even more upsetting."

"As I explained, Ian had been with us at Old Sarum for just about a week, but was expecting to remain for another six months. After which, I'm pretty sure he had ideas about going out to the Far East to take part in the fighting there. But the two atomic bombs, dropped in swift succession on Hiroshima and Nagasaki, put an end to all that, as out of the blue, the Japanese surrendered almost overnight. So, his short service commission completed, he was faced with the prospect of leaving the Air Force and becoming a priest; or at least immersing himself in a totally new lifestyle, studying for the Church. Don't forget, his sister Ina always believed he would live up to the promise he made to his mother, who had very fixed ideas about his future."

"Also, and this is very much supposition, is it not possible that Mimi's sister, Yvonne, had been in touch with him? Greatly impressed by Scotty, she knew he was staying at the Midland Hotel and she, of course, lived in the local area. May they not have met again, not once but several times, during his fortnight in Lancashire, and that intimacy had then taken place?"

My wife looked at me with a mixture of disbelief and amusement, but I went on seriously. "Don't forget, we are pretty sure it was Yvonne Hetherington who became pregnant with the child that became Richard Cadwallader, and it wasn't caused by 'a system of mirrors', as was often alleged in our physics text books at school."

"Moreover, if there was intimacy and he did feel that he had committed a mortal sin, if he was indeed sunk in black remorse and there was no Tom Burgoyne around to speak to and ease his mind, is it not possible that he felt driven to the edge of suicide, and that he found himself in that Spitfire cockpit in a state of desperation and despair?"

But my wife was shaking her head. "Yes, but surely there's world of difference between the thought of suicide and the act. He could have killed himself in a dozen different ways, all of them a good deal easier than flying into Old Sarum Castle."

"True. But in his deranged state of mind and knowing his religious beliefs, is it not a possibility? Perhaps he wasn't exactly thinking of it when he started up that Griffon engine, but I can visualize his thoughts and feelings a he slowly taxied his aircraft towards the take off point; the turmoil in his mind created by the end of the war, the commitment he had made to his mother, the uncertainty about his future and other feelings of guilt and remorse about the possible pregnancy. And it is at this point, strange as it may seem, that I can imagine him laying down a challenge to God. 'I will undo my straps and involve myself in great danger', he could be saying, 'so that I may expiate my sins and be given proof that I am still part of your grand design'. Because, you see, Scotty always saw himself as an instrument of God, part of the Lord's overall plan. His religion, you see, would never allow him to take his own life, but he was always willing to take enormous risks, persuading himself absolutely that he was in God's hands and that he would survive if it were so ordained."

But my wife was still shaking he head. "But, no! I still find it almost impossible to believe. Would anyone be driven to do such a thing or think such thoughts?"

"Sweetie, the facts of the accident are plain for all to see. Also, you didn't know Ian Graeme-Scott as I did He was a unique person, a wholesome young man of infinite charm, honesty and faith, and a person of enormous ability and such firm principles. So deeply religious, in fact, that I have seldom come across anyone quite like him."

My wife shrugged her shoulders, was silent for a time, then almost whispered, "And God suddenly decided that Scotty was not part of his future plan?"

"In Scotty's eyes, I dare say he would see it that way. The tragedy, or perhaps the blessing is, not many others of us share his certainties."

My spouse shook her head and sighed in resignation. "Anyway, two further questions. Did you speak later to Ian's family, particularly Ina? And are you going to tell Richard Cadwallader all you know? Because you haven't been entirely frank with him, have you?"

After thinking for a moment I said, "There are too many of us these days who see great virtue in passing on what we perceive to be the absolute truth, no matter what distress it causes others. Cadwallader wanted mostly to learn the identity of his father. That we cannot help him with, as there are too many loose ends. We think we know about his birth mother but even assuming we are right, the girl is now long since dead. Moreover, she died a miserable death, apparently, after an unhappy marriage. Would it really help him to know all that? Are we not likely to be virtuous at his expense? No, my feeling at the moment is that we should say nothing. Later, I may change my mind."

"And Ina?"

"I telephoned her immediately following Ian's death in August, 1945 - you and I had just married and, still in the WAAF, you had gone back overseas, as I recall. She was very sombre, I remember. I asked about her mother and she reported that she had taken it very badly."

"'Mother is very silent and is contemplating going into Retreat. I wouldn't be surprised if she didn't end up in a convent somewhere. The light has gone out of our lives, Tom, it will never be the same around here. Our particular Lochinvar is dead, gone for all time, and I don't know really what the future holds for us.'"

"'And what about you personally?'"

"'Me? I shall soldier on here for a time - the animals and farm have to be looked after. And after that, who knows?'"

"I tried lightening the conversation. 'No one riding down from the hills waving his broadsword, intent on sweeping you away on his saddle?'"

"'Ah, if only! No, I have an obligation to remain. The Scotts have been around these parts for a thousand years. The link must continue. Anyway, the Lord will decide. It was such a pity, though, you couldn't come to Ian's funeral. We missed you terribly and I know he would have so wanted you to have been with him at the end.'"

"'Ina, I just couldn't get away. A new Senior Course was starting and I had duties to perform. I tried, but the top brass was adamant. With the war ending, there is absolute chaos around here. As if peace was that important!'"

My wife than asked, "And did she stay?"

"No, I am since told that she didn't. She married within two years and left. She now has two children, apparently, but I don't know where. Abroad perhaps. Canada and the States are full of Border folk, yearning for the hills."

"And you have never returned, I know."

"Not exactly, no. We have been to Moffat together several times in honour of 'Stuffy' Dowding, but I have never had the heart to go back to the farm. It would be too upsetting. The old order changeth, alas. The Border hills will never be the same without Scotty."

My wife then said a surprising thing. "Do you remember what the King said on the radio at the outbreak of war?"

"I've forgotten. Tell me!"

"He said something I will never forget. Particularly having heard so much about your friend Scotty. It went:

"And I said to the man who stood at the gate of the year, 'Give me a light that I may tread safely into the unknown.' And he replied, 'Go into the darkness and put your hand into the hand of God. That shall be to you better than a light and safer than a known way.'"

My wife added, "I believe it was written quite recently by a woman called Minnie Haskins. So appropriate, don't you think?"

I remember turning away, my mind full of sad memories. Poor, poor tragic Scotty! No, nothing . . . .nothing would ever be the same.

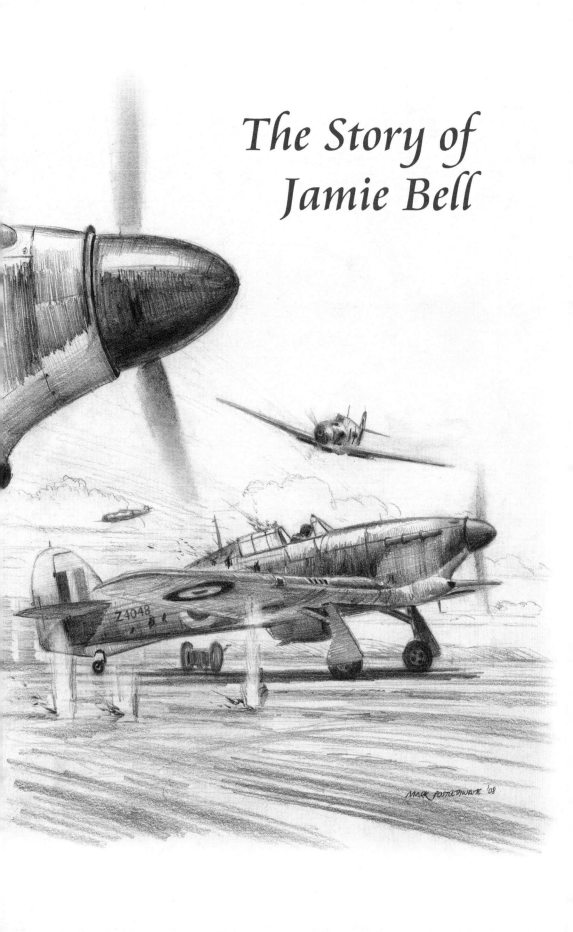

The Story of
Jamie Bell

The Story of Jamie Bell

War for many can be a time of tragedy and despair but also of joy and fulfilment.

It is a tragedy in that it destroys lives and dismembers families.
It is a joy in that it enables many to meet
others they would never otherwise encounter.
It is a time of fulfilment brought about sometimes by
success in battle, and of happiness when friendships suddenly
ignite and burn with an almost incandescent brilliance.
It is also a time of despair when intimate relationships die quickly to
smouldering embers as circumstances bring about death, loss or separation.

This is the story of Jamie Bell, who came into my life in the early months
of 1940 and, thereafter, for more than forty years, made a number
of occasional but dramatic reappearances. Until... well, the events
and circumstances of our relationship are well worth recording.

Again, this story is a little more fiction than fact and the characters
imaginary. The flying passages, however, are based on actual events.

Chapter One

In late April 1940, some three months before the Battle of Britain, I was posted to a fighter squadron flying Spitfires from Kirton-in-Lindsay, a long-established RAF Station in Lincolnshire. I had just emerged from Flying Training School in Scotland and, very wet behind the ears, was a newly commissioned Pilot Officer. I was 19 years of age.

The person I came to know later as Jamie Bell arrived a month or so after me; we were part of an old First World War squadron, reforming. I saw his name in Personnel Routine Orders on the Officers Mess notice board a day or so before his arrival. The entry read 'Flying Officer J.D.G Bell, from 52 Operational Training Unit, Aston Down.'

He arrived with three other young officers, all Volunteer Reservists, who had been in various university air squadrons. The oldest of the group - I judged him to be about 23 - Bell was also the most senior, being a Flying Officer. Although a nice enough chap, I was not immediately drawn to him. The three others were quite clearly younger, noisier, and generally more attractive personalities. At the time, I was not to know that all three would be shot down and killed within six months. Their names, I recall, were Williamson, Healey and Dunn.

Both being in 'A' Flight, Jamie Bell and I found ourselves frequently flying together and soon formed an agreeable coupling. He was a good pilot and a calm and steady partner in the air, if not notably enthusiastic or brilliant. As I had arrived on the squadron before him, I had achieved some sort of bogus seniority, so that I was often the leader during our small forma-tion exercises together. Surprisingly, as he was senior to me in both rank and experience, he never seemed to resent my spurious authority. In fact, he was usually congratulatory when I did something that was either noteworthy or met with his approval. In the air, therefore, we always managed to get on pretty well although, as we were still only working up to becoming 'operational', it didn't really matter very much one way or the other.

On the ground, however, we were less compatible. To put it simply, he was more worldly and altogether `tougher' than me. An only child and a rather gently brought up youth, although physically strong and athletic, I was not a natural 'rough'. I neither drank nor smoked and I did not enjoy the sometimes violent squadron parties in the Mess when uniforms were ripped to shreds and property damaged or destroyed. But, I have to admit, Bell was never especially physical on those occasions although he always seemed to enjoy the hard drinking involved and was a constant pipe smoker.

In fact, it was his wretched pipe that caused the smallest rift in our early relationship. A rather worn out specimen, it had obviously been broken several times, so that he had a piece of sticking plaster permanently wrapped around the stem. Irrationally perhaps, this irritated me to such an extent that I complained about it several times.

"For heavens sake, Jamie," I would say, "Buy yourself a new pipe; this one looks absolutely disgusting."

Usually he would just smile and reply that a new one wouldn't taste so fruity. However, obviously ruffled by my constant criticism, one day he turned on me and snapped: "For Christ's sake stop bellyaching about my pipe. It's the one I enjoy and it's the one I'm bloody well keeping!"

And that was the end of the matter.

Although I was not particularly interested at the time, for some months I did not learn very much about Jamie Bell's personal affairs or what his immediate history had been. Moreover, he never volunteered such information, and as he was a pub person and I was not, the sort of intimate conversations one usually had on such occasions seldom passed between us. One thing I did quite quickly detect, however, was that he had an eye for the girls. Indeed, he seemed to attract them more than I might have expected, as, although pleasing enough a personality, he was not particularly good looking, nor did I ever regard him as an easy conversationalist, particular in the presence of ladies.

However, in the course of time, I did gather that he was from a fairly affluent Midlands brewing family, that he had attended Uppingham public school, and had later gone on to London University to study, of all things, mining engineering. And finally, that he had learnt to fly with the London University Air Squadron.

In short, those first several months in the squadron enabled me to form an easy if not exactly an intimate association with Jamie Bell. He was merely a colleague I liked, I often flew with, and someone for whom I had more than a little respect.

Our squadron was equipped initially with the early Mark I Spitfire. Brought in dribs and drabs from other units, it was mid-May before we had assembled the eighteen that was the squadron's established strength. All had the older de Havilland two-pitch airscrew, and not the constant speed variety which came later, and not all were fitted with pump-driven hydraulics, which enabled the undercarriage to be raised automatically. Moreover, our aircraft had not then been fitted with the new balance weights which made it a little harder for us to apply the elevator. Those early Spitfires were only marginally stable and very sensitive fore and aft, so that we were constantly blacking ourselves out in tight turns or when recovering from dives and, now and then, even over-stressing and wrinkling the wings.

All these and other minor failings, however, did not diminish the glowing opinion we formed of our Spits. Having been trained on much slower biplanes, I found the aircraft a joy to fly and quite thrilling a mount in which to whirl around the sky at speeds I had never before experienced.

And fly intensively we did! Having been granted five weeks to raise ourselves to 'operational' standard, I flew almost 100 hours in one four-week period and averaged at least four or five trips each day - which during the capricious weather of that early summer of 1940, was some going!

Mostly, of course, it was all serious stuff - full throttle height climbs to 25,000 feet, masses of formation flying and dummy fighter attacks, air firing with our eight machine guns, and interception exercises of every sort. But there were periods, too, of relaxation, when we became engaged on so-called 'Sector Reconnaissances'. During these exercises, we were able to fly at very low altitudes around the English countryside, notably the Pennine hills immediately to the west of us, and further north, the glorious crags and valleys of the Yorkshire dales and moors.

Those trips were always enormous fun and, as I mostly flew with Jamie Bell at the time, I somehow came to associate those happy occasions with him. Many were the times we would stream across the hills at barely 50 feet, attacking cars and lorries on the mountain roads and even boats and canoes on the rivers and lakes, frightening the life out of most of their occupants, I have not the slightest doubt.

And all the time, during those carefree weeks of May 1940, a British Army in France was being remorselessly pursued to the evacuation port of Dunkirk and hammered into submission. In that debacle, however, we, as a squadron, were not involved as we were only declared 'fit to take on the enemy' on 1st July, 1940. By this time our Spitfires had been taken from us and replaced with Hawker Hurricanes.

We had only a week or two to acclimatise ourselves to our new aircraft, although we didn't find it much of a problem. The Hurricane was even easier to fly than the Spitfire and in some respects a better fighting aircraft, although rather slower at the high end of the speed range. On the credit side, the pilot sat a good deal higher in the fuselage and saw much more of what was going on around him. Also, the aircraft was less frisky on the ground, the undercarriage being much more robust, and the hood could be moved in the air at all times, which was not the case in a Spit, whose canopy was almost impossible either to open or close above 180 miles per hour. This meant that evacuating a Spitfire at high speed and in times of stress could become a very unpleasant experience. Furthermore, with about 12 gallons more fuel, the endurance of a Hurricane was marginally greater.

Otherwise, the two types were very much the same in that they employed similar engines, had the same armament, and the instrument layout in the cockpit was little different. However, most of our Hurricanes had the new constant speed Rotol airscrews, which were a great improvement, particularly at height. One simply set the required revs and at all power settings and at all heights, the system sorted things out for itself.

But, as we soon were to learn, each type shared one miserable and deadly characteristic; to force-land a Spitfire or a Hurricane in the sea was to invite disaster, as each sank like a stone!

We took up our responsibilities as guardians of the Realm on 1st July, 1940. We had barely been given time to draw breath when we were flung into action at about 4.30 pm the following day. And, as luck would have it, I was one of an intercepting section of three, led by Jamie Bell, who by this time, because of his age and seniority, had been appointed section leader.

We took off breathlessly from our small, all-grass airfield, with me flying No.2 on Jamie's right, and a splendid regular Air Force sergeant named Smithson, on his left as No.3. In this manner, we climbed away steeply towards Grimsby on the coast and, thereafter, on an easterly heading, out to sea.

Some 20 minutes later, we were at 19,000 feet, out of sight of land, and levelling out. Over the RT (radio telephone), a message was passed to us that a `bogy' (unidentified aircraft) had been detected flying south some 15 miles ahead of us. An enemy bomber, for heavens sake! The squadron's first victim, perhaps? The pulses of all three of us must have fairly raced - I know mine did!

That first interception and the events of the following 30 minutes, will remain with me for all time.

I remember us being about 25 miles out into the North Sea, at slightly more than 19,000 feet, and that it was a brilliantly clear day with cotton-ball clumps of cumulus cloud scattered about a few thousand feet below us. In a wide 'vic' formation, we scanned the horizon left, right, and below for signs of the `bogy'. I switched on my gun sight and set the range bars to 60 feet, which was the approximate wingspan of any German bomber we were likely to meet. I then adjusted the intensity of the pink lines of the sight to a comfortable brightness and twisted the gun button on the spade grip of my control column from `Safe' to `Fire'. Then, and not in the least apprehensive, I settled my rump into my parachute cushion - we didn't have dinghies at that stage of the war - and, with a keen sense of excitement and anticipation, stared into the distance, keeping just half an eye on my leader, some 20 yards away from me on my left.

I suppose it was little more than a minute later that I saw the enemy aircraft, a Ju 88, about two miles away, at around 18,000 feet and flying roughly south. It appeared as a single, elongated dark dot, moving quickly against a background of cloud and sea.

Beside myself with excitement, I screamed out 'Tallyho!'- the acknowledged sighting call - and waggled my wings furiously to attract Jamie's attention.

As I had neglected to press my radio transmission switch, he did not receive my almost incoherent sighting message but he did catch sight of my waggling wings, so that within seconds we were in the approved line astern formation and poised to attack.

Sweeping down on the German aircraft, which, by this time had seen us and was taking urgent action to escape into the nearest cloud, we found ourselves closing rapidly, the two of us at the back jumping about to avoid each other's slipstream and that of our leader, and to get our aircraft into the best firing position.

Directly behind Jamie and rocking around in his wake, I found myself screaming pointlessly into my face mask for him to get out of the way and allow me space to open fire, as we were then within 300 yards of the tilting, turning bomber.

But Jamie had other ideas as I saw him straighten up briefly, after which thin trails of dark smoke issued from beneath his wings as he triggered his machine guns. At the same time, streaks of twisting white issued from the rear of the bomber as it fiercely retaliated. Then suddenly Jamie's Hurricane had veered off to starboard and I was faced with the rear end of the bomber less than 150 yards ahead.

With the pink dot and circle of my gun sight swaying maddeningly around my target, I fired and saw my tracer streak out ahead and lay clawing, grasping fingers around the body and engines of the aircraft in front, the strikes flashing briefly like a child's sparkler as some of the bullets struck home.

I surged ahead, still firing, aware that I was tense and shivering with the sheer, savage lust of battle, until the rear of the 88 was within yards of me and I suddenly realised not only that I was about to collide, but that Smithson would be behind me and preparing to launch his own attack.

Then, as I broke away, the rear gunner shot at me and I saw his tracer come in my direction in a swift, flicking stream, so close that I instinctively ducked as the bullets streaked around my ears like angry white wasps. Appalled that my aircraft might be damaged, I shied away violently and glanced quickly down at my instruments, almost expecting to see the pointers registering some minor disaster, my nose meanwhile seeking to detect the airman's greatest nightmare, the terrible reek of smoke and fire. Lord above! That was altogether too close for comfort!

Now some 100 yards on the starboard side of the enemy and flying approximately parallel with it, I saw Smithson finishing his attack and Jamie Bell on the far side, shaping up to make another pass.

The Ju 88, meanwhile, was looking decidedly unhappy with faint smears of dark smoke emanating from both engines. Moreover, there appeared to be no return fire coming from the rear gunner and its speed seemed to be reducing, all this being confirmed when the aircraft began to make a slow turn to the right, which had it heading approximately towards the distant English coast.

At this point, Bell attacked it again from the rear and, as I watched, the right engine sput-tered into a wind-torn smear of vivid red flame, all amid a rolling, bubbling torrent of black smoke. After that, the German aircraft began to lose height in earnest and, clearly in distress, began to head purposefully for England and a possible crash landing.

Then, as we three Hurricanes gathered almost protectively around the limping, fatally damaged bomber, I suddenly realised that we had achieved our first squadron victory and that we would be feted as heroes on our return, if only minor ones. The adrenalin still surging, I was enormously elated and screamed and shouted into my oxygen mask.

But, there proved to be problems.

As we headed for the Lincolnshire shore, an incongruous group of four, with Jamie on the left of the streaming bomber, me on the right, and Smithson behind, I was actually more concerned that the German aircraft might not make a reasonable landing than I had doubts about our own condition and safety. I was fairly sure that my own aircraft was undamaged and that of Sergeant Smithson. However, on impulse, I glanced across at Jamie's Hurricane some 50 yards away, and to my concern, saw a feather of white streaming from beneath his fuselage.

I was on the RT immediately.

"Red One from Red Two. You seem to be streaming a little underneath. Are you by any chance overheating? Otherwise, you may have a fuel leak."

He replied. "Red Two. I appear to be okay at present but there's a smell and taste of sweetness in the cockpit. I may be losing glycol. Can you come across and check my bottom panels?"

Without replying, I slid across and underneath Jamie's Hurricane and it was as I thought and had expected, his radiator or associated pipes had been holed and were leaking coolant quite rapidly.

"Red One from Red Two. You are shedding liquid quite badly. You ought to give a 'Mayday' now as I doubt that you are going to make it to the coast."

There was a brief silence as the significance of my message impinged, after which Jamie responded. "Thank you Red Two. My temperatures are going up now. We'll see this chap to the land if we possibly can, after which I may have to lob down somewhere."

After that, he gave a 'Mayday' message and reported the approach of the damaged Ju 88 and also our own aircraft, giving our approximate position and what we intended to do. Sector Control, who seemed very bucked, responded suitably and said they would alert the Air Sea Rescue Services. Flying alongside the German aircraft and looking into the damaged cockpit, I wondered what the crew there might be thinking - if indeed they were all still alive!

We were some 10 miles from the coast when matters developed rapidly. The German bomber, now down to 50 feet above the water, was limping along, barely maintaining flying speed. The fire had been put out in the starboard engine, the port airscrew was still turning over manfully, but both engines were leaking thin, greasy trails of smoke. Flying alongside it, I half expected it to touch the water with its drooping tail and fall dramatically into the sea.

Jamie Bell's Hurricane had climbed to 1,000 feet so that he could bale out if necessary. He was clearly in great trouble as he had reported that his 'temperatures are off the clock' some time before. Even so, he remained admirably calm and spoke to me quietly from time to time

"Red Two. If I can make it to the coast I will crash-land immediately. If this brute seizes on me before then, I will land in the water and take my chance. Stay with me and direct the Air Sea Rescue people. Get some other aircraft out from the squadron if you begin to run short of fuel. Well done about the Hun, incidentally. Just in case I don't get picked up."

Then, within a minute and in a more urgent tone: "Okay, she's just gone! Seized solid! I'm going down now."

Hypnotized almost by the drama being enacted before my gaze, I watched Jamie's Hurricane float down towards the water. Hold off for some moments with its nose high in the air. Then crash down into the sea.

I found myself flying round in a tight circle my eyes glued to the spot. The aircraft disappeared at once in a chaos of spray, rose briefly to the surface, then tucked its nose down until only the tail remained in sight. Then, in seconds, that too had gone and nothing remained other than a small circle of paler water. Jamie Bell had disappeared! Drowned, possibly! But dead! There was no sign of him. In agony, I continued to fly in a tight circle. Watching. Searching. Hoping.

The 88, meanwhile, had continued to totter on into the distance and out of my field of vision, accompanied by Sergeant Smithson.

Round and round again. Searching still. And praying. Oh, God! Help that man! Please, please God, help that poor, brave man!

Then, joy of joy, when all seemed lost, a tiny head amid the waves. And a glimpse of a yellow Mae West lifejacket. He was out! Floating! Then swimming. And waving even. Lord be praised!

Within two hours, Jamie Bell had been picked up by a boat from Mablethorpe - waterlogged, very sick, but alive. And not as all complimentary about "Bloody Hurricanes, that floated like punctured ducks!"

Twelve miles to the west, the Ju 88 had crashed a mile or so inland. Close to Mablethorpe. The pilot was killed with one other member of the crew. The rear gunner had also been killed, but in the air. One man survived, however, and was taken prisoner by a local farmer's wife. Later, we claimed the tail of the aircraft with its Nazi emblem from the wreck. Which we exhibited for a time outside our 'A' Flight dispersal hut. Our very first victory!

We were to remain at Kirton-in-Lindsay for about two further weeks. Although there were additional scrambles from time to time, which had us chasing about miles out to sea, we never encountered any other enemy aircraft.

Happy that I had been one of the three who had made the squadron's first interception, I was less happy about being shot at by the rear gunner of the Ju 88 and nearly hit - those angry white wasps buzzing round my face had quite unnerved me for a moment. Deciding that I would take any steps to prevent that happening again, I thought long and hard about how I would act in similar circumstances.

Also, the Hurricane's inability to float I found very disturbing. Clearly, crash landings in the sea were definitely to be avoided. On the other hand, even a parachute descent into the water posed serious problems. The Mae Wests, with which we had been issued, were pretty paltry pieces of equipment without any automatic inflation devices, so that the likelihood of having sufficient puff to blow up the wretched things by mouth having been dunked into freezing cold water, was both doubtful and distinctly unappealing. This, too, provided me with much food for thought. Even at that early stage and with the enthusiasm of youth, I decided that there were aspects of combat in fighters that required careful consideration. Indeed they did!

But, there was little time for such morbid thoughts as, in late July, the squadron was sent down south. To another grass airfield, Boscombe Down, near Salisbury in Wiltshire.

Although we remained at Boscombe Down for almost a month, I can only describe our success there as minimal. There were several reasons for this, one being our inexperience, the other being the standard of controlling by Sector, which was woefully indifferent.

At that time, the Luftwaffe was making massed bomber attacks on airfields and aircraft factories in the southern counties, some as far afield as Bristol. The raids were mainly by formations of Heinkel Ills, Ju 87s, and Ju 88s, escorted by long range, twin-engined Me 110s; the single-engined Me 109s had too short a range to penetrate much beyond the coastal fringe around Southampton.

Several times our squadron intercepted major raids in the Southampton area, accounting for several Me 110s and Ju 88s. On the other hand, we failed to intercept other large attacks of 50 plus and more, which was most surprising, not least to us because of the sheer numbers involved.

In fact, for Jamie Bell and me, the weeks were comparatively uneventful despite our being airborne many times and for many hours. Somehow, we always seemed to be in the wrong place or part of the wrong formation. Moreover, for me it would have been entirely unremarkable had I not been involved in the interception of one major raid on the airfield at Warmwell in Dorset.

Attacking a group of Ju 88s from the rear, I threw caution to the winds, forgetting completely the experience gained during my first interception off the Lincolnshire coast. Once again I had to endure, if only briefly, the unpleasant spectacle of streams of tracer coming in my direction, this time from about six rear gunners. But on this occasion they didn't miss and, amid a series of thuds and bangs, I collected a shower of bullets in my engine and wings, which forced me out of the engagement immediately and caused my engine to stutter to a shuddering halt within minutes.

Thankful that I had not been seriously damaged myself, I was obliged to land, wheels-up on a grassy hill not far from the town of Blandford, during which I hit my face on the gunsight and almost broke my shins against the underside of the dashboard. In a good deal of pain and with blood everywhere, I was carted off to the local hospital but was soon patched up and able to return to the squadron the following day.

During that period of several weeks, I have no clear recollection of what precisely Jamie Bell did - except to be around, so to speak. However, I clearly recall that, following my crash-landing and having arrived back at Boscombe Down, covered in plaster and bandages, he met me in the anteroom of the Officers Mess and told me, without displaying the slightest show of sympathy, that I was nothing more than a silly bugger for getting myself shot down!

Jamie Bell was that sort of chap.

Shortly after that incident, the squadron was moved again from Boscombe Down to a grass airfield in Essex on 30th August, which was a Friday.

Our landing ground was little to the north of Romford and was a satellite of RAF North Weald. In pleasant wooded countryside, it was a simple, comfortable, yet convenient base from which to operate. Although we were not to know it at the time, we would remain there for nine months and from its rolling green pastures, climb away steeply a hundred times to take part in some of the fiercest air fighting of the war.

As this tale is not mainly about the Battle of Britain, however, but about Jamie Bell and my relationship with him, I ought to explain that it was the fighting at that time which was to become the main determining factor in the future of both of us. The squadron shot down around 80 enemy aircraft over the 16 weeks of the Battle, but we lost more than 20 friends and colleagues who were killed, injured or horribly burnt, casualties which included both Jamie Bell and me.

From the outset, we found ourselves making up to four or even five interceptions each 18 hour period of duty - our working day started about 4 am and continued until after 10 at night. We lived, ate and slept on the job, so to speak, occupying old First World War huts sited alongside our Hurricanes, which were dispersed around the airfield perimeter, our 'killing fields' being the Thames Estuary, all of Kent and much of West Sussex, as far south as the English Channel.

Throughout those hectic days, I came to know the home counties and the Thames Estuary like the back of my hand and I shudder even now, some 50 years after the event, when I motor through those lovely wooded parts and pass the hospitals of Maidstone, Canterbury, Ashford, Faversham and Leeds Castle. All of these, at one time or another, had received our often burnt, broken and bleeding bodies and restored them to some semblance of normality.

During the 20 or so flying days of September 1940 - a few were ruled out for weather and other reasons - my log book reveals that I was involved in more than 56 interceptions great and small, adding almost 65 hours of stomach churning combat to my meagre total of operational flying hours in Hurricanes. On each day, the routine climbs and interceptions were largely similar but I recall about four occasions being especially stressful, the first occurring on 7th of that month.

The morning started off foggy but developed into a fine Indian summer day, clear, but with broken cloud at about 12,000 feet. We were off several times early on but saw only small formations of enemy aircraft in the distance and did not become engaged.

The big attacks came at around 4 pm when two waves of around fifty bombers each - Heinkels and Dormer 17s - came in over Kent and in the direction of London. They were escorted by a mass of Me 110 twin-engined fighters and a cloud of smaller 109s. Climbing steeply, our squadron of 12 met the bombers at around 18,000 feet in the area of Canterbury.

Our first attack from the front quarter was a wild, breathless affair, which, it appeared, had little immediate effect - there was seldom time to see the result of those first assaults. I remember flying within feet of several light coloured, oil-streaked bombers wearing black crosses, before I, and others, flashed underneath, having fired our guns. Then we were diving away like gannets, the slipstream screaming in our ears and the dust rising in our faces as we were thrown violently against our restraining straps. Below, squarely in my windscreen, the green and brown patchwork of Kent appeared, with a momentary glimpse of broken cloud and the pale wriggle of the far away Thames.

Then in moments, I was climbing, turning, and searching again for the bombers, being surrounded by brown ack ack bursts and fending off attacks from a diving stream of small Me. 109s that appeared from nowhere.

In a frenzy of self preservation, I was pulling and pushing, my sight greying into blackness by the gravitational forces, until . . . nothing! The sky was suddenly clear, or almost so. Except for one small aircraft which was passing in front of me in a shallow dive. A 109! A German fighter! And it hadn't seen me!

To this day, I almost regret what I then did, knowing full well that the pilot was always ignorant of my approach. Chasing after it, my engine straining, I closed sufficiently to open fire. Once! Twice! My eight machine guns making the familiar harsh, incredibly satisfying tearing noise, like linen being ripped. For moments, nothing! Then after several additional bursts, a small puff of debris appeared plus a thin line of - something!

Experiencing a burst of savage joy, I knew then I had damaged him mortally. But strangely, no response. No evasive action. Had I killed the poor chap? Covertly? Not in a sporting way? Suddenly, there was no exultation in my victory. Then, as the aircraft fell away downward slowly . . . tilting. . . . trailing now a grey pencil line of smoke, I watched the 109's descent, oblivious to other aircraft around me. Down . . . down . . . down it fell. Towards the distant ground. Until it was a mere dot and I was obliged to pull away and leave.

Noting that I was down to just under 6,000 feet and conscious of being alone, I climbed as hard as I could. Presently, there were aircraft ahead of me in a formation. Hurricanes! At 14,000 feet, but not of my own squadron! Clearly friends, though, and oh, so welcome!

I joined them at the rear but could not listen to their RT conversation as I was on a different radio frequency. For some minutes I wondered what was going on, then it all became clear. Across our bows, about two miles away and slightly lower, a large formation of Dornier 17s was flying due east, escorted by a mass of Me 109s, behind and above. Obviously having attacked their target, they were on their way home.

The squadron I had joined were clearly bracing themselves to attack. Although I could not hear what was being said, I could sense the tension in the air, not only among the Hurricanes but also among the enemy, who were obviously aware they were about to be assaulted and were preparing themselves for action. In the distance, I watched with apprehension as a small group of 109s broke away, presumably intent on getting behind us. But, ignoring them, and like a cavalry charge with all weapons bared, my companions began their 20 degree dive and, excited beyond belief, I dived with them.

It must have taken about fifteen seconds for us to reach the enemy formation, almost 400 mph registering on our airspeed indicators, slipstreams screaming in our ears, eyes and hands tensed to deliver a flood of tracer and steel in the direction of the enemy. At the same time, from below, a thin, drifting curtain of twisting tracer rose in our direction with deceptive stealth from the bombers as their gunners sought to repel us.

In an instant and for the second time that afternoon, I was through the bomber formation - a flash of black crosses, glinting Dornier canopies, and a mass of oil-streaked fuselages. After which, escaping in an almost vertical dive, the Thames river suddenly appeared close to my right ear and a single column of black smoke rose from the ground in a huge, seemingly motionless column.

Breathlessly, I levelled out, my sight greying, and took stock. I was alone again and out of ammunition, so it was pointless hanging around. But, at 5,000 feet there were balloons everywhere, which obliged me to turn and fly back in the direction of the Thames estuary before crossing once more into Essex.

Only then did I fully recover my breath and feel my heart beat return to normal. My engine sounding glorious healthy, I turned again towards my own airfield, thanking God for my seemingly indestructible Hurricane and its imperturbable Merlin.

As I flew home, smiling to myself, I recall momentarily feeling deeply satisfied that for once I had really earned my corn that day. Four trips, one Hun shot down and, who knew what else? I was glorious happy. But then . . . like a douche of cold water, remembering the

109, there followed a sharp spasm of shame and pity. Murder! Was that not the name for it?

Landing on the grass, the airfield looked strangely deserted. As I taxied in, a group of airmen came running towards me. One clambered onto my wing root. "What happened, sir? You seem to have been in a scrap. Some bullet holes in your tail, I see, and your gun patches have gone."

I threw off my straps, clambered out, and jumped to the ground. "Had a bit of a fight. Two in fact." Then, noticing the Adjutant striding urgently towards me. "Will speak to you later. Just fill me up and check me over, there's a good chap"

Vandenberg, the Adjutant, was a nice man of about 45, who had been in the last war and wore a DFC ribbon - which was unusual for someone who had merely been an Observer on D.H. 4s. As he fell into step beside me he was clearly on edge.

"Thank the Lord you're back, old son. We've taken a heck of a beating. Five down in various parts. Most of 'em baled out but one or two injured, maybe killed. We shall know more later."

I asked, "What about Jamie Bell? Is he alright?"

"Not a word, so far. It seems he's down somewhere, we don't know where. Several landed before you, incidentally, and have taken off again against another raid. It's been quite a day."

Entering our dispersal hut, I began to sign up and hunt for a combat report. It had indeed been quite a day. One of the squadron's worst.

Later it became clear that we had lost seven aircraft. Four pilots had baled out and one had crash-landed. Two others were simply missing, Jamie Bell included.

The eager young Dunn had apparently been killed, dying of burns and shock having been shot down in flames. The admirable Sergeant Smithson, too, had gone. Seriously wounded, it seemed, he had crashed to his death somewhere near Maidstone. And Jamie Bell was still missing. There was no news and no one had seen him go.

As I lay awake in the darkness that night, there were empty beds all around me. Overhead, was the dull roar of enemy bombers en route to somewhere, I didn't know where. Regularly, too, the dull cracks of the ack ack guns in our area, firing their salvos of four, followed by the crump-crump-crump of the shells exploding in the distance. It took me a long, long time to fall asleep. Dreaming of shooting at Heinkels and Dorniers and also of 109s! And of Jamie Bell.

As so often occurred, there was a lull of several days after the excitement of 7th September. The Huns obviously needed time to recuperate and we most certainly did, although replacement aircraft turned up almost immediately. The 10th however, saw us back on the treadmill of racing scrambles across the grass, feverish climbs, followed by hour-long flights, usually uneventful, our usual line of patrol being between Maidstone and Canterbury at 15,000 feet.

Meanwhile, nothing had been heard of Jamie Bell, which had us all suspecting that he had gone for good. This, for me, was an unhappy thought, of course, though, strangely, less so than I had imagined. In fact, I was becoming so inured to casualties, it seemed, that in the silent hours of the night before sleep, I found myself worrying about it. What on earth was happening to me? My friends being crippled and killed all around me and I was hardly being affected.

Then, about a week after his disappearance, a message was received that Jamie was in Canterbury hospital. Wounded, but not seriously. Firing at the bombers, he had apparently been attacked from behind by 109s and forced to bale out. Given another fortnight, apparently, and he might be back with us again, or possibly on sick leave. Glad tidings indeed! We were all relieved and lifted by the news.

On September 11th I shot down a Heinkel 111, one of a large, dispersed formation, which crashed somewhere adjacent to a railway station in the Ashford area of Kent. Later, in my combat report, I found I could not describe exactly where it had fallen. Unbelievably, I was still unfamiliar with the geography of the southern counties of my own country!

September proceeded violently with the squadron experiencing both success and disappointment. There was no let up in the action by day, and the nights were full of the discordant drone of bombers overhead, en route to targets in our own area and beyond. Now and then we would stand quietly outside in the darkness and witness the fiery descent of a Hun bomber struck by an ack ack shell or, less frequently, brought down by the action of a Blenheim night fighter.

Sometimes, too, we were called upon to operate at night ourselves, moving when we did so to the permanent airfields of North Weald or Debden, where there were concrete runways and glim-lamp flarepaths. As one of only several pilots in the squadron deemed to be 'night operational', it fell to me occasionally to be forced reluctantly into the air. I hated it! Day fighting I could put up with, even enjoy the thrill of combat. Fighting at night in a Hurricane, however, had little appeal for me, being waste of time in my opinion.

With dire warnings of imminent invasion ringing in our ears, action by day increased to a crescendo until, on 15th and 27th of that month, the squadron achieved its greatest successes. In days full of incident and tragedy, four interceptions were made on each of those days on raids approaching London over Kent and Sussex, and 30 enemy aircraft were claimed as 'destroyed' or 'probably destroyed'. Sadly, too, the two young officers who joined the squadron with Jamie Bell in May - Williamson and Healey - were killed, shot down by bomber return fire or by defending German fighters. Several other gallant colleagues, too, were wounded, burned, or injured.

Finally, on 28th September, we again roared into the sky bound for Kent – to find the heavens empty of German aircraft. Surprised and suspicious, we patrolled backwards and forwards. But nothing! The enemy had apparently retired hurt. Perhaps even defeated.

Little did we then know that Hitler had called off the invasion of Britain on 17th September. Temporarily, anyway. Our Government may have known of this decision through secret intelligence sources, but they did not choose to tell us, the battling pilots of Fighter Command! In the event, the so-called Battle of Britain went on for a further month, but in a different style and manner, our principal enemy being bomb-carrying Me 109s and their fighter escorts.

It was I recall on 4th October that, after landing from an afternoon sortie over Kent, I was informed that Jamie Bell, having recovered from his injuries, had returned to the airfield in order to pick some possessions before going on sick leave.

Delighted by the prospect of meeting him again, I hastened in the direction of the Officers' Mess, prepared to tease him with the taunt he had levelled at me a month or so earlier, namely, that anyone shot down whilst tackling bombers didn't have his wits about him and deserved everything unpleasant that followed.

When I met him, however, I immediately saw the need to keep such taunts to myself. Uncharacteristically tight lipped, he was obviously still in some discomfort. He had collected a mass of cannon shell fragments in his shoulder and neck. Moreover, he had other unpleasant news to report. Having been obliged to bale out when his cockpit had filled with smoke and fumes, he had landed awkwardly and been knocked unconscious. Then, coming round and finding himself among bystanders, who appeared anything but friendly, he subsequently discovered that his wallet and other personal items had been stolen. In addition to which, and outrageously, all the silk of his parachute had been cut away, so that only a mass of severed shroud lines remained.

Loading his possessions into the boot of his Flying Standard car at the rear of the Mess, his views of some of his countrymen were expressed in the bitterest of terms. Muttering and glowering, he drove off in a cloud of blue smoke, and I did not see him until some weeks later.

Those long days of October - by Government edict we were still on double daylight saving time - we found different but stressful, although there were no large formations of bombers any more, only single aircraft roaming the English countryside, drifting through and between the clouds. The principal threat was from Me 109s, scores of them, each carrying a single 500lb bomb hung beneath the fuselage. Crossing the Channel in droves, there were at least as many again acting as fighter escort. Also, whereas the battles of September had been fought at around 17,000 feet, we were now encountering the enemy at 20,000 feet and above, sometimes even as high as 30,000, at which altitude our Mark 1 Hurricanes were useless.

For us, this lack of performance was a real challenge as the German fighters were much faster than us on the level and considerably more nimble. They could dive and climb away at will and were always able to dictate the terms of combat. Also, it was brutally cold at 25,000 feet, as the Hurricane had holes everywhere around the cockpit, so that many times, after an hour or so at height, we almost prayed that we might be shot down in flames; at least, we argued childishly, we would be warmer for a few brief, if very uncomfortable moments.

Even so, from time to time we did have successes as, during those 30-odd days of October, the squadron shot down at least thirteen enemy bombers and fighters, a total of three being destroyed on the afternoon of 29th October, when a large formation of 109s attacked the airfield at North Weald.

November too, I remember as a month of mountainous cumulus clouds and towering canyons, through which we were obliged to climb in formation each day. We were often dwarfed by their magnificence and now and then alarmed and intimidated when the horizon became totally obscured, so that we found it difficult to decide whether our aircraft were climbing, diving, or on their sides, - most unpleasant and frightening experiences.

It was also a month of incident; a month in which I had a mid-air collision at 18,000 feet and was forced to bale out, and a month when Jamie Bell was shot down yet again and severely wounded and burnt. For him, however, the event was especially momentous as it was to become a major factor affecting the conduct of his affairs in years to come, and, indeed, the indirect cause of his eventual death. And it had all started off so well.

In the first week of the month, we intercepted an attack by Ju 87s and Me 109s on shipping in the Thames estuary and had inflicted several losses on them. Then, shortly after, an Italian bomber force, escorted by CR 42 biplane fighters, was intercepted off the east coast in the area of Harwich and dealt with very severely. Our squadron, however, only caught the tail end of the Italian group and accounted for merely several of the supporting and rescue aircraft.

Recuperating from injuries sustained during my parachute descent, I did not take part in those engagements. Jamie Bell did, however, and was credited with a least a share of the several victories claimed.

Apart from these flurries of action, our days were taken up with constant patrols over central Kent and wearisome climbs and descents through masses of grey murk. We had occasional sightings of single Dorniers or 88s creeping around the fringes of the cloud, ready to drop into oblivion as soon as they saw us diving in their direction.

Higher up, we would frequently run into groups of 109s who would suddenly appear around the edges of massive cloud formations, at which time everyone would be startled into action, turning, twisting, and occasionally firing, such engagements usually brief and inconclusive.

At other times, however, the engagements were rather more decisive and not often to our advantage. The enemy would drop down on us like stones and pick off one or more Hurricanes at the rear of our formation. Such attacks were almost impossible to counter as we seldom saw them coming and even when we did, we were rarely able to catch them during their escaping dives, or remain with them as they zoomed upwards to safety. These hit and run tactics caused us endless concern and real annoyance. How we wished we had a faster, more nimble aircraft! Even so, on the level, and although we were flying a much slower mount, we always felt we could hold our own if only the blighters would 'stay put' long enough to allow us to fight. But, in our more reflective moments, I think even we accepted that, considering their options, why on earth should the Huns do anything different? After all, they were merely exploiting the better qualities of their aircraft when flying over enemy territory. We were playing at home!

It was, I recall, some days after 14th November, the night when Coventry with its beautiful cathedral was bombed into rubble, that Jamie Bell was shot down yet again, this time being hurt rather badly. I remember very clearly lying awake in the darkness that night of the 14th, listening to the continuous drone of enemy bombers overhead until, promptly at 11 pm, the noise suddenly ceased, suggesting that some wretched town further north was in process of suffering.

Several days later, we were on our usual parade over Kent in squadron strength at about 19,000 feet. I remember, too, that it was about 4 pm, that we had had several flights that day, and that I, if not others, was thinking longingly of tea and cake and hoping that this would be our last patrol of the day.

Flying northwards in the area of Maidstone, my thoughts were focused on that welcome cuppa, when there was a brief gabble of conversation on the RT and I looked quickly over my shoulder to see the unwelcome sight of a wriggle of white smoke corkscrewing towards the earth, and a parachute, stationary in the air.

Instantly alert, I found myself wondering how on earth we could possibly have been surprised yet again. Because surprised we had certainly been and the evidence was plain to see. One or more Huns had attacked us from the rear, this time from below, and had shot down one of our two weavers. Almost overwhelmed by feelings of fury, antagonism and shame, with others, I whirled about to confront an enemy who was already disappearing dots in the distance.

Back at base, the victim was identified as Jamie Bell, the other weaver, Sergeant Jury, admitting he had seen the attackers at the last moment but had been powerless to intervene. I was shattered. Poor, poor Jamie! About the third disaster to overtake him in weeks, even if he had been fortunate enough to survive. We immediately took steps to enquire as to his fate and within hours had been informed that Jamie was indeed alive, but wounded and badly burnt. He had been taken to the hospital near Leeds Castle in Kent and every effort, we were told, was being made to deal with his wounds and ease, if not rectify, serious burns to his face and hands. And, no, it would not be sensible to visit him immediately, probably not even within a week.

Ten days later I took the squadron staff car and drove down to Leeds Castle, stupidly without ensuring that he would be there for me to visit. He wasn't. He had been packed off to East Grinstead where a Consultant Physician named McIndoe, a burns specialist, was apparently working miracles on victims of fire damage, particularly among Hurricane pilots. Before I left, however, Jamie's former ward sister showed me photographs taken of his face and hands. I was horrified. His face was a black and raw mass of meat, making his features unrecognisable. I remember looking away feeling slightly sick

We did not see Jamie Bell again until the following March, four months later, when he returned to the squadron, apparently fit to fly again, though not, some of us felt, with quite the off-hand confidence of his former self.

The rôle of Fighter Command aircraft changed radically after that bitterly cold winter of 1940. Until then we had been interceptor fighters defending the nation. On Boxing Day of that year, however, and into 1941 and beyond, we operated over enemy territory as attackers, ranging over France and Belgium on so-called 'sweeps', escorting Blenheim light bombers, or carrying out strafing attacks in sections of two against 'targets of opportunity'. I have to admit that the latter were not tasks those of us flying Hurricanes were any too keen about.

For this reason, it was a short-lived measure of relief when, in March, 1941, the squadron was re-equipped with the Mark II Hurricane, which came as a long awaited if minor blessing. Our new Hurricane was little different from the old model, except that it was fitted with a Merlin 20 engine, which had a manually operated two-speed supercharger, plus several other welcome refinements. This gave us much more power at altitude enabling us to take our aircraft as high as 38,000 feet - if we felt so inclined, that is! Which most of us didn't, it being so cold up there that, with no heating and with draughts everywhere around the Hurricane cockpit, life became intolerable during flights of anything more than 40 minutes. Even so, our new aircraft were certainly a distinct improvement on the old Mark I, although still noticeably slower than even the original German Me 109E. Then, when the newer and faster 109F was introduced later in the year, we were back again to square one.

I mention this as my first recollection of Jamie Bell's return to the squadron came at the time we were experimenting with our new mounts and he took his aircraft to a slightly higher altitude than anyone else. I remember saying to him jocularly that it was because he had probably fallen asleep in the cockpit when the rest of us, who had become so monumentally bored by the time we had reached 35,000 feet, had given up and gone home!

Otherwise, day after day, our operational activities were fairly regular; flights over the Continent on `slow-motion' bomber escort duties and 'sweeps', during which we achieved fewer victories but also sustained fewer casualties than during the previous autumn. And of course, there were the much disliked low level `mosquito' incursions. Everything, in fact, was becoming rather a bore. Until May of that year, that is. When our squadron was suddenly ordered overseas.

The warning notice to 'proceed overseas' came as a not unwelcome surprise. Some of us regarded our duties throughout those early months of 1941 as politically motivated rather than strategically necessary. The Blenheim bombing raids were nothing more than trivial and the low level strafing attacks had resulted in the loss of some of Fighter Command's most experienced pilots, all for no obvious reason or advantage. In short, we seemed intent on pursuing policies the Germans had followed, to their very considerable cost, the previous summer and autumn.

Those early months of the year had also seen significant movement within the squadron. By that time, our original Commanding Officer had left, having been shot down and wounded in the September, being replaced by our senior flight commander. About half-a-dozen pilots from other squadrons had also been posted in to fill gaps caused by our eight fatalities, although a number of those squadron members who had been shot down but only suffered minor injuries, had returned to take their place once more in our line up. Finally, a charmed life and some measure of success had resulted in my being promoted to flight lieutenant and become second in command.

The squadron, in short, had retained much of its original shape and character and its achievements since the previous July had earned it much praise and fame. However, my own advancement and new status caused me some embarrassment as I was by no means the most senior or experienced officer around, and it is a credit to the magnanimity of such colleagues as Jamie Bell and others, that I was accepted without any obvious resentment.

This then was our state of health, so to speak, when in early May, we learned that we would be going to reinforce the Middle East Air Force in North Africa and would be conveyed to the Mediterranean area by aircraft carrier - and flown off!

I have to say that this information, together with the disturbing news that we would be taking with us new but totally outdated Mark I Hurricanes, reduced us all to chilled and uneasy silence.

Again, as this tale is mainly about Jamie Bell and me, I will not give a blow by blow account of our preparations and miserable journey to the Mediterranean on the aircraft carrier, H.M.S.. Ark Royal. Or of our subsequent hazardous flight of almost 1,000 miles at sea level, before landing in Malta in the midst of a major air attack. Or, having arrived in the most trying of circumstances, to learn, to our concern and vast disappointment, that we were to be retained indefinitely for the island's defence.

But, even that blow to our morale was eclipsed when the new Hurricanes we had brought in were flown on to Egypt by the remnants of the squadron already resident in Malta, a unit that had been cut to pieces over a period of months by the Luftwaffe, based in Sicily.

Possessing only the clothes we stood up in, our heavy baggage and ground crews in process of being transported to the Middle East via South Africa, we felt totally abused, isolated, and in a state of mutiny. What on earth were these misguided fools in Air Ministry doing to us?

Malta, and the facilities then available to us, came as great shocks to the system, although they were later to improve.

We inherited nine weather-beaten versions of the old Mark I Hurricane, all without squadron markings, most lacking paint, and one, unbelievably, with a punctured tail wheel stuffed with straw, a spare, apparently, not being available. Totally dismayed, we found our pilots' accommodation and Operations Room on the airfield to be a single, sagging, moth-eaten tent, the primitive communications system a mass of trailing wires and a single wind-up telephone, the whole set-up, in short, a depressing, dog-eared arrangement.

Furthermore, our living quarters in the Officer's Mess were scarcely better, even the food revolting. And all around, was the stultifying atmosphere of breathtaking heat, talcum-powder dust, smells, flying insects - and fleas!

Malta, for God's sake! After the order, comfort and organisation of life at home, it was all vastly different and deeply demoralizing.

But worse was to follow.

Before landing in Malta, we squadron pilots had known little of their `Airships' plans for us, although the enemy seemed to be totally informed. Our arrival on the island coincided with what had obviously been a planned attack, during which my flight and I were obliged to land at Luqa almost without fuel, in the middle of a heavy air raid, and with the ground heaving and erupting in front of us as the bombs rained down like confetti.

Then, three days later and before we had even taken off on our first defensive sortie, three Me 109s appeared over the edge of an adjacent cliff and, in a violent and noisy strafing attack, wrote off five of the nine clapped-out Hurricanes sitting at standby on Ta Kali airfield, our new home.

Having heard air raid sirens wailing in the distance, and in a state of perplexed fury, I had returned from sitting in my own aircraft to the Operations tent and had been angrily telephoning the Control Centre in Valletta to find out what on earth was happening. At which point, the three Huns had appeared at face level, firing at me and the rest of my group who had remained in their cockpits waiting for the scramble order to be given. In an instant, the scream of racing engines and cannon fire filled the air - followed by utter bedlam and chaos!

On my back on the floor of the Operations tent, where I had immediately thrown myself, I had a fleeting glimpse of bullets slashing through the canvas above my head, with me cringing meanwhile, my eyes closed and a grimace on my face, expecting any moments to be killed. Then, in seconds and with a blast of noise that defied description, the enemy departed. Scrambling to my feet, I rushed outside to see the rear ends of the three small aircraft disappearing towards St Paul's Bay - and Sicily!

After a minute or so of shock and dismay, I took stock. Two Hurricanes were already on fire, but in a small way. Later they were to burn spectacularly, with towering clouds of black smoke stretching into the heavens. It was later reported that three other aircraft had also been damaged beyond immediate repair. First estimates, too, suggested that about five airmen had been hit and injured, though none seriously. Thankfully, there had been no fatalities.

Among the pilots, however, there was more depressing news. Sitting in their cockpits, strapped in and unable to move, they had watched, albeit briefly, the 109s approaching at the speed of light, and firing. At least one youth had broken both his legs attempting to escape from the cockpit, another had the parachute beneath him shredded by a cannon shell, a third had had the spectacles shot off the bridge of his nose, and one - Jamie Bell, no less! - had been shot though the foot.

Amid all the smoke, the confusion and the seemingly aimless chaos, he came hopping in my direction. Clearly in shock, he was gabbling, "Sorry about that, old son! Really sorry about that! Always happens to me. Saw the blighters coming but had to sit there and take it. Didn't feel anything, either.. Until I got out, that is. After that it all went numb and I couldn't stand. I just couldn't stand." Then, as I held and supported him, speaking comforting words in his ear, he croaked "Why the hell does it always happen to me? Why, for God's sake? The bloody Huns must surely be tired of making holes in my torso!"

Later, as almost a reflex action, I led our three remaining Hurricanes off the ground in a gesture of defiance - my first flight over the island of Malta. But there was nothing to see. Just blinding sun, space, heat, and clouds of suffocating yellow dust. Lots of bumps in the air, too, and an endless expanse of blue sea.

When I landed an hour later, Jamie and the others had been borne off to hospital. To a place called Imtafa. Until only silence and a dipping sun remained, a brassy, sinking orb. Plus the mosquitos – masses of them! And the stinks!

Malta! And us with just three Hurricanes left! Three! And no replacements! Who would have believed it?

I did not see Jamie Bell until about a fortnight later when I took the squadron transport - an old, camouflaged Austin 16 - up to Imtafa Hospital one very hot and breathless afternoon. He greeted me effusively but it was soon evident that he was deeply depressed. He reported that his injuries had been more extensive than either he or his doctors had expected. A cannon shell had struck his shin just above the ankle and had exploded, scattering fragments everywhere, including the small bones of his instep, a delicate and complicated area, apparently. The ankle would take months to heal, he had been told, if indeed it would ever be fully restored to its normal flexible state.

Encased in a plaster cast he was able to hobble about and, although cheerful enough with the doctors and nursing staff who, according to him, had 'done him proud', he was not at all sure that he would ever fly again, certainly not in the short term. He was pretty gloomy, too, about his future. "Depending on the top brass, I reckon I will be moved on about a month hence; where to I don't know. Not further east, I hope!"

Which, in the event, was more or less true, as he was to leave Malta in the middle of August, although, of course, we were not to know it then.

Meanwhile, the squadron had gradually settled down. But with never more than eight or nine Hurricanes available and 24 pilots to fly them, we were obliged to split the unit into two, one half led by the squadron commander, and the other by me. With so few aircraft available, we were often obliged to travel across to Hal Far, an airfield on the southernmost tip of the island, where 185 Squadron was located. They were almost as badly off for aircraft as we were, so that for a time we were obliged to use each other's Hurricanes in order to put as few as eight or nine into the air. It was a deeply unhappy time, especially for a proud unit such as ours, used to perfection and success.

Operationally, however, we were not too hard pressed. After knocking us for six on that first unhappy day, the Luftwaffe suddenly disappeared, and it was only later that we learned that, in preparation for their invasion of Russia in early June, the Huns had relocated their Sicilian based aircraft to Poland. We now know, too, that they dealt with the Russian Air Force very ruthlessly indeed, causing them catastrophic losses during the first few days of their invasion on the Eastern Front.

Thankfully, in their absence, we had only the Italians to deal with, who proved to be less troublesome adversaries. Using Macchi 200 fighters and Savoia 79 and BR20 bombers, their attacks on the island became almost gentlemanly, occurring mostly at night. Furthermore, by day, they insisted on employing the same tactics repeatedly, which made our interceptions of their daylight raids more predictable and certainly more successful, when compared with our dismal showing against the Luftwaffe.

Even so, we could have done infinitely better had we had Spitfires rather than the slower, out-performed Hurricanes, especially the older Mark Is, whose serviceability was often so poor as to be demoralizing. In fact, the despairing cry from all of us during the several months I spent in Malta was, why on earth didn't their 'Airships' provide us with Spitfires - anything but the out-moded, outclassed Hurricane we were lumbered with.

By the end of July, the squadron had been on the island for more than two months. During that time, we had achieved some limited success in the air but had suffered quite a few casualties, at least one of them fatal. Jamie Bell's health had improved but he was still unable to fly despite the cast being he removed from his leg. Now and then, he would visit us in the Mess at Ta Kali, becoming a little more cheerful with time, but still not quite his normal quiet and agreeable self.
And it was sometime during early August that an incident occurred, trivial in the main, which would always linger in my mind as being responsible in part for changing my former uncritical opinion of the man.

I was in the Officers' Mess having just finished lunch when Jamie sidled in, looked about almost furtively, then came in my direction. Putting an arm around my shoulder - a most unusual gesture from him - he whispered, "What have you in mind for this afternoon?"

Still drinking my coffee, I replied patiently, "Having been up since 4 am and flown three times, I have in mind a spot of `Egyptian P.T".- the then fashionable term for bed and sleep on a hot and sticky afternoon of 90 degrees in the shade.

Looking around again in a most secretive manner, Jamie went on, "Look! I've just been into Valletta, to the British Council Library there, and met this girl. Her name's Florence - Florence something-or-other! Maltese, of course, but very nice. So, I asked her out. But she said no, not unless she could bring a friend. So, I said, fine, bring the fried along, provided she is presentable. Which made me think immediately of you."

I said plaintively, "Jamie, for heaven's sake. I don't want to spend the afternoon walking the streets of Valletta. I want some shut-eye."

"Nonsense, old son! A chap your age should be leaping around like a spring lamb this time of the day. Come on! Get the lead out of your pants!" After his incarceration in hospital, Jamie was obviously feeling excited about the prospects of a day on the town - even bomb-damaged Valletta - with a new female face. Which is how I came to be in the Maltese capital that early

August afternoon, part of a mixed group of four which included two young women I had never before seen in my life. On a stinking hot day, too, and very much a reluctant participant.

The two young ladies turned out to be very toothsome, well brought-up convent educated girls. Florence was about 20, tall, slim and, surprising for a Maltese, fair complexioned and with blue eyes. Her companion, Lilianna was very Italian in appearance, dark and with rather sharp though pleasing features. Both were demurely quiet at first but spoke very good English with attractive Maltese accents, and each was fluent in Italian. Moreover, they soon demonstrated that they were certainly familiar with the English idiom, as they were quick to appreciate our rather juvenile jokes. I found myself quite enjoying their company - as, it seemed, was Jamie Bell!

Not knowing much about Union Club etiquette as regards ladies, we thought it wise not to take them to that austere British establishment, situated as it was in Strada Royalle - I believe the street was later changed to Strada Republique in the Mintoff era. Instead we took them to Monico's and fed them several strong John Collinses, at which they frowned initially then drank them down with delicate enthusiasm, having no doubt squared their religious, alcohol-wary consciences. And all the time, the conversation became more eloquent.

Then, it being stiflingly hot and there being little else to do, we decided to go to the one cinema I knew of on the island, situated in the centre of the town.

I was not too enamoured of this intended move as, having been there once before, I knew it did not possess any air conditioning and that its plush seats were alive with man-eating fleas. Being fair skinned, in shorts, and my sweet English flesh clearly to their taste, I always found the little rascals positively murderous, so that I was invariably bitten into a lump within minutes. Most Maltese, however, seemed quite inured to the little blighters as they, to my knowledge, never complained.

However, everyone was apparently in a happy and relaxed mood when we all sat down in the darkness, whispering and laughing. The programme then commenced, with me half expecting to feel the sharp nip of the denizens of the plush, to be followed by my furtive and, hopefully, well concealed scratching.

Then, within minutes and before even the first `Movietone News' item had drawn to a close, Jamie rose to his feet in the darkness and, with a distant smile and gesture in my direction, left, in order, I imagined, to visit the lavatory.

When he did not return within what I considered to be a reasonable space of time, I began to be concerned. Had something untoward happened? After all, with his game leg, had he tripped and fallen downstairs somewhere? The two girls and I exchanged speculating whispers until I even thought about going out to investigate. But sadly, I didn't, and when 30 minutes had elapsed and Jamie had not shown up, I suspected he had gone for good. Even then, however, I could not bring myself to believe he had left us through choice. Something must surely have happened to him and, in whispered tones, I explained my fears to the two girls.

Two hours later, we three emerged from the cinema into an early evening that was hot and uncomfortably sticky. What did I do now? The normal plan would have been to return to the Monico bar, treat ourselves to several cooling John Collinses, then repair to an upstairs room where there was a small dance floor and a pile of big-band and Bing Crosby records. But with two strange young ladies on my hands, each looking slightly lost and utterly bemused, I was so outnumbered that dancing seemed definitely out.

Pretty though they were and most understanding, I knew then I had to send them away and set about doing so in the most courteous manner I could manage. But, all the time, I seethed inside. Bloody man! What on earth had got into him?

Thirty minutes later, I boarded the ramshackle Maltese bus that would take me to Mosta, the nearest village to the Ta Kali airfield, and the twenty-minute rattling, stifling, garlic-scented journey did nothing to assuage my savage feelings towards Jamie Bell. My anger grew by the mile. If and when I found him, by God I would punch his head!

The Officers Mess at Ta Kali was in a large stone-built house called Torre Combo and to reach the anteroom one had to climb a set of spiralling stone steps. As I trudged to the top, I had a feeling that Jamie Bell would be there.

And I was dead right! Entering the room, where there were about a dozen officers sitting or standing about, I saw him one of a group of four, smoking his pipe with the sticking plaster on it, a pint tankard in his hand. Looking up, he saw me and smiled a quiet welcome. Inviting him across with a jerk of my head, he walked slowly in my direction, apparently at ease with the world.

My voice low but dripping with venom I announced, "Jamie, there are two girls downstairs who would like a word with you."

He stared at me uncomprehendingly. "Which girls?"

My eyes glittering, I said, "The girls we were with in Valletta. The ones you invited. The ones we took to the cinema. Remember?"

He was still staring. "You mean they're here? You're pulling my leg!"

"I'm not Jamie. Like me they want to punch your head. For being so bloody rude and inconsiderate. In fact, I'm tempted to do that here and now." I heard my voice rising and saw people turn their faces in our direction.

But Jamie was equal to the occasion. He put a placating hand on my shoulder. "You're taking this too seriously, old sport. They're only girls, for Pete's sake. And, anyway, they're not really here, are they?"

"No, Jamie they're not. But tell me, why did you get up and leave? Tell me honestly, because at this moment I have it in mind to kick your backside all around this room."

Again his hand on my shoulder. "They were boring me, old chum. They were much too young for me. I had to get away." A sudden grin, "Anyway, you were doing so well on your own." Then, turning away and over his shoulder. "All part of life's rich tapestry, old mate."

And that really, was that. So, I turned away and went to bed.

A week later, Jamie Bell left the Island. He arrived in the Mess one evening announcing that he had been told he was departing that night. In a Sunderland, from Kalafrana Bay. I knew that the Sunderlands came and went regularly, operating always at night because they were so vulnerable. But I had never seen one in Malta, nor did I see one later. Until the early part of September, that is, when I found myself in one, but flying in the opposite direction.

Jamie left after a small party in the Mess. I was there at the time but after the Valletta incident, my farewell was rather muted. His immediate destination, apparently, was Egypt. And at that point, he went out of my life until after the war.

Little did I know at the time when Jamie Bell left Malta, I would be following him in little more than a month.

The reason for my exit was not because I was damaged by enemy action, but that I suffered an engine failure and was obliged to crash my Hurricane in very unpleasant circumstances.

Which is a suitable time for me to give some details of our problems at the time.

Both the Hurricanes and the Spitfires, which came later to Malta, had the engine air intakes situated below the fuselage and between the undercarriage legs. In England, where there is little dust and debris, this arrangement was, and remains, perfectly acceptable. In desert and tropical conditions, however, where there is sand and dust everywhere, such debris was sucked directly into the carburettor of the engine, causing endless problems, the delicate channels, jets and capsules being unable to cope with the considerable influx of foreign matter. Only later did the Mark I and Mark II Hurricanes have fitted so-called Vokes Filters, which had open and closed positions. These cut down, though did not entirely eliminate, the incidence of engine failure resulting from carburettor problems.

During the first two months of my time in Malta, I suffered five engine failures, or what were euphemistically termed malfunctions, when at full throttle, the engine only produced sufficient power for my aircraft to achieve a slow taxying speed during take-off. At such times, a pilot's prayer was always that such malfunctions would happen on the ground and not when the aircraft was just airborne - which happened to be the case on my final, very brief flight.

The other critical factor was Malta itself, which was mainly composed of yellow sandstone, on which a veneer of thin brown soil was spread about in tiny fields, most about 50 yards square and all of them bounded by formidable stone walls.

There were, therefore, no possible force-landing areas anywhere on the island, other than the three airfields themselves - in my day; Ta Kali, Luqa and Hal Far. An engine failure, therefore, frequently resulted in death, a severe injury, or possibly a fatal ducking, if the pilot chose to land or parachute into the surrounding sea. In short, Malta was one of the most unpleasant places on earth to experience an engine problem. And of those, we had plenty in 1941!

On that final flight, I was leading about ten aircraft off the ground in a mad scramble, and was just about 100 feet in the air, when my engine gave a monstrous, jerking cough and the power fell away completely. For an instant, I thought about turning back. This was regarded as a fatal decision to make normally, as it would almost inevitably result in a stall and a spin. Deciding instead to land straight ahead, I remember with a sinking heart, looking directly to my front and seeing only a series of very solid stone walls. Looming! Approaching! Very rapidly! And I will never forget, saying a prayer and closing my eyes.

As my aircraft thumped massively into the ground, there followed a series of crushing, jerking, impacts, with pieces of wall being hurled left, right and over my head. I was thrown violently around the cockpit and was briefly aware of the Merlin engine in front of me being torn from the fuselage and hurled aside. Meanwhile, knowing that 90 gallons of fuel were in tanks in front, left and right of where I sat. I prayed - prayed! - that the aircraft would not catch fire.

But, strangely, at no time was I conscious of pain, nor even of fear. I just wanted it all to end, with me aware of what was happening - which meant I was still alive.

But . . . on it went . . . on! . . . and on!. For all of four dreadful seconds. Which felt like hours.

Eventually, there was stillness. And silence. A silence broken only by the ticking of a vastly overheated engine lying somewhere very close to my face. Cooling down. Plus the reek of petrol. Oh, God! Petrol! And fire! Plus a wet and burning sensation down my neck and on my back. But no fire! Thank God, no fire!

Aware that I was deeply shocked, I realised I was on my side and crushed into strangled immobility. But alive! I had crashed a Hurricane in Malta through several stone walls and was still alive! I had survived!

I suppose I was held in that cockpit for all of five minutes, until some airmen from the airfield arrived breathlessly and tried to free me. They were the maintenance crews of my own squadron, in fact, who had seen me go down.

Finding me tightly wedged in, they pulled and pushed, cutting away my seat belts and parachute straps, before using metal cutters and crowbars. Talking all the time. Reassuring me. Until finally I was lifted free and laid tenderly on the ground. At which point, I remember closing my eyes as all I wanted to do was sleep! Thank God!

After that, an ambulance arrived with lots of feet and other people. Everyone crowding round. "Poor bugger!" I heard someone whisper, and felt like smiling. A victim? I was very lucky, and knew it!

Then another voice - urgently. "He's got acid down his neck and back. From the batteries. Douse him with water. Come on! Where the hell's the water, for Christ's sake?"

Acid? Water? I didn't care and almost smiled. I had crashed a Hurricane in Malta, and was still alive!

It was only in Imtafa hospital that the shock from my accident started to wear off and I began to be aware of my injuries.

I had been badly lacerated in many places, it seemed. I was in some pain, although they had given me masses of morphine, and the battery acid had badly burnt the skin on my neck and back. And rather to my concern and embarrassment, I could not prevent my hands from shaking uncontrollably.

There then followed the usual inspections by a stream of doctors and medical staff, the painting of my entire body with some sort of yellow dye, the prick of many needles, the insertion of masses of stitches and tubes, and my burns being treated. After which, I was carefully laid out on a clean white bed, like a fish on a slab - and left!

Finally, some twelve hours after my accident, I was able to close my eyes and sleep. Thank God! It was good to be alive. In the distance I heard the noise of Merlin engines as my former comrades took off from Ta Kali airfield. I wondered then if I would ever fly again in Malta.

The following day I was shown photographs of my accident. The Hurricane was a terrible mess, with the engine quite apart from the fuselage and lying at right angles to it. The cockpit was horribly bent and crushed, so that it was a miracle I had survived. Thankfully, there were no photographs of me, in the cockpit or lying on the ground. I didn't particularly want to see anything like that.

I was to be in hospital for almost three weeks. My burns and wounds were still a severe irritation but I was not then in pain. After about a week, the AOC, Hugh Pugh Lloyd came to see me. Standing alongside my bed and scrutinizing me with his blue-eyed stare, he congratulated me on surviving the accident and said I would probably be sent home to England. I had been fighting, he said, for more than eighteen months and deserved a rest and time to recover. He would see what he could do.

Which is what happened. Towards the end of September, I was taken across the island to Kalafrana Bay, loaded on to a Sunderland flying boat at night, and taken to Gibraltar. After that, we flew on to England, again at night, where I was sent on sick leave for a month.

Chapter Two

The focus of this story is now centred on my own career rather than that of Jamie Bell, as I only saw him once - fleetingly - in 1946, and after that not until the early '80s.

I should start, however, by mentioning that on my return to England in the late autumn of 1941, I was promoted to Squadron Leader and given the command of a famous fighter squadron flying, first Spitfire Mark 5s, then 9s, from various airfields on the south coast. Throughout 1942 and '43, we flew against Me 109Fs and Gs over France and Belgium, and also against the new Focke-Wulf 190s, during which time we had our successes and casualties, naturally, throughout a period when the RAF gradually gained a marked ascendancy over the Luftwaffe.

Then, after another brief rest, I was attached to the 9th USAAF and flew with them on the Invasion of Europe, flying both P-51s (Mustangs) and also P-47s (Thunderbolts), until we finally reached the borders of Germany in late 1944. At that point, I returned to the RAF as an instructor at the School of Land Air Warfare, at RAF Old Sarum.

Finally, after a brief spell in Burma, the European and Japanese wars ended and I went into the Test Piloting business, flying as part of the Aircraft and Armament Experimental Establishment, Boscombe Down, near Salisbury in Wiltshire.

I might also add that I had met a delightful WAAF Officer when at Biggin Hill in 1943, that we had married at the end of the war, and that we were in process of building a family of three small boys during those first five years of my test piloting career - which, in retrospect, was not the most propitious time to do it!

It was, I recall, on a Saturday morning in late September, 1946. My wife and I, with our new young son of two months, had walked with the pram into Salisbury from our rented home in Portland Avenue, which is on the Coombe Bissett road. We were in the Market Square at the time, watching the farm animals being bought and sold and I remember it especially because the calves were having their ears clipped. This upset my wife rather, because of the hurt being inflicted and the blood that was flowing. I remember, too, looking up suddenly and coming face to face with . . . of all people . . . Jamie Bell! He was standing there on his own, quietly watching the animals, his hands in his pockets.

We recognized each other immediately but I can't honestly say that we fell on each other's necks, although, I admit, our greetings were uninhibited, even effusive.

I introduced him to my wife and we chatted about this and that for a moment or two. I then explained that we were out shopping for the weekend and that my wife needed to buy some essentials. If we allowed her to go about her business, perhaps he and I could go to the White Hart Hotel and reminisce over a coffee or a drink. Jamie agreed instantly and we moved off on our separate ways.

In the White Hart, which I knew very well, I found a table and ordered coffee. Jamie did not demur although I sensed that he would have welcomed something stronger. All the time, I was weighing him up and I daresay he was doing the same to me. He certainly looked older. He would be about 30, 1 calculated, and his face still bore evidence of the burns he had received in 1940 and later. I noted, too, that his hands were still unnaturally white, the skin stretched and scarred, and that he was missing at least one finger of his left hand. When he saw me looking in that direction, he raised his arm and smiled.

"Some nasty German shot it off in Italy, in 1943."

I laughed, but without humour. "My goodness! The Huns certainly had their money's worth with you, didn't they? What was it? Wounded four or five times?"

But he waved away my concern, as though it did not matter. "I've never really bothered to count"

Within minutes he had told me that he was on his way by train to Cornwall and that he had simply broken his journey at Salisbury 'to take another look at the Cathedral'. I replied that I had elected to stay in the Air Force, that I now held a permanent commission, and that I was flying from our old airfield, Boscombe Down.

He had apparently left the Service in late 1945, at which time his family had pressed him to return to the family brewing business. But, as he explained, that didn't appeal to him as he had an engineering qualification and wished take advantage of that. In fact, he was at that moment on his way to the West Country to consider a possible appointment in the tin mining industry.

For an hour we talked easily about this and that until my wife and small son put in an appearance, the pram loaded down with groceries. Just before they did so, however, I asked him if he had married. At this he had hesitated then answered with a smile and a shake of his head, "Not quite!"

To which I replied, rather puzzled, "Not quite! Well, you either are or you're not. Which is it?"

To that, and to my surprise, he gave no direct answer, but said with another smile, "Women frighten me!"

At that point it was my turn to laugh. " Since when? They never used to!"

And that, more or less, was that. After we had all exchanged some further pleasantries, he left to catch the noontime train and, although we agreed to keep in touch, we never did for the next thirty years - when pure chance brought us together again.

One final point is worth making. On our way home that morning, I asked my wife what she thought of him. She was silent for some moments, then answered, "He seemed a bit of an odd-ball to me. D'you know, never at any time did he look at, or even mention, our beautiful new baby. And a chap who is that disinterested, must be pretty bloody strange."

And as she very seldom swore, I knew then, she was very cross with him. And her assessment, too, when I thought about it later, was just about spot on!

For many years thereafter, my career in the Air Force was not only satisfying and enlightening, but also full of travel. My five-year stint as a test pilot took me to Khartoum in the Sudan and also Nairobi in Kenya, where the A&AEE carried out most of their tropical trials. My visits there also enabled me to visit South Africa and other fascinating areas of the 'dark continent'.

A year or so later, I spent three years flying jet aircraft in the Middle East, a time which enriched my life enormously, as I was interested in biblical history at the time. It also coincided with the 'troubles' in that area, so that I became involved the Suez operations of 1956 and, in small way, went to war for the second time.

As the years passed, I ascended the career ladder and attended Staff College, War College, Central Flying School, and several university extra mural courses, becoming an 'expert' in most aspects of Service life. Then, a glorious posting -1 was appointed to the British Embassy in Washington, where I became a pseudo diplomat and found myself a minor British Delegate to the United Nations in New York.

Meanwhile, my family was growing up. My three boys were now teenagers and at public school in England, and life was beginning to take on a new meaning for my wife and me. And all the time, I had only very occasional news of that fast reducing number of friends with whom I had served during the war and immediately after. Also, and as far as I was aware, Jamie Bell had disappeared off the face of the earth.

Then, in the middle 1960s, a change of direction.

As both my wife and I had enjoyed our years in Virginia, I decided to retire from the Air Force and take up a civilian appointment in the United States. I joined a British Consultancy Company working there and I found myself based in an office in State Street, Boston, obliging me to set up a new home in Concord. This is a place of great significance in American history, the town bring about 20 miles into the very pleasant Massachusetts countryside. And there I stayed for some years, returning to England and semi-retirement in Norfolk when the company I was working for was sold to rivals, with whom I had little in common, and for whom, no admiration whatever!

Looking back, it was about this time that a series of minor happenings again changed the course of my life and also greatly extended my interests and relationships.

I had taken up writing in a small way and had been invited by 'Norfolk Life', the local County Magazine, to write an article on the Battle of Britain. This I did and was paid the princely sum of seven shillings and sixpence! A week or so later, the editor telephoned and asked if he could repeat the article in some of the other County magazines his publishing company circulated. I readily agreed and, to my astonishment, found later that it had appeared in more than 20 other magazines up and down the country. Needless to say I was never paid a penny extra for the further distribution of my literary efforts.

There were, however, compensations, as I received letters not only from all over the country but also from overseas - which both pleased and astonished me. One of the letters was from a local author who invited me to call on him as he wished to interview me in connection with a new book he was writing, but also for me to inspect a mass of photographs he possessed in order to identify some wartime faces he could not name.

So, ever willing to oblige, I did as he suggested, called on him and enjoyed a pleasant meal, after which we spent several hours together, discussing the war and many of the personalities I had met and had flown with. It was then I was shown many photographs - most entirely new to me – which included a score taken of my own squadron during the Battle of Britain, and others whilst serving in Malta. These included pictures of Dunn, Healey, Williamson, Smithson and many others. And several, too, of Jamie Bell, in his aircraft and standing alongside. All these pilots, I was able to identify, of course, to the enormous satisfaction of my host.

Then, claiming my attention absolutely, I was shown photographs of several German bombers and fighters we had shot down in September and October, 1940, plus a number taken of our burning Hurricanes in Malta, following the attack by the Luftwaffe on that first dreadful day on the island, with the pillars of black smoke I so remembered rising into the sky. And even more arresting, there were shots of my crashed Hurricane after my accident, with the Merlin engine lying alongside the crushed cockpit. Plus, I was astonished to see, one of me being carried off towards the ambulance on a stretcher, photographs I never knew existed.

It was when we were discussing the names, the fates and the careers of many of the pilots whose pictures had been displayed, that I drew my host's attention to those of Jamie Bell. Having briefly described our adventures over the years, I asked, if at a later date, my new acquaintance ever became aware of where Jamie was, and what had happened to him, I would be most grateful for the information.

Which was how it was left.

It was about a week later that I received a telephone call from my new author friend.

"That mate of yours, Jamie Bell. I now have some information on him. He lives, apparently, in Canada.   Somewhere in the Toronto area of Ontario."

"Canada!" I echoed. "I never imagined for a moment he would ever live there. Do you know where precisely, and what he does for a living?"

"Well, he describes himself as an 'Aviation Consultant'. It seems he mostly acts as a middle man, helping rich Americans and Canadians to buy aircraft. It must be a pretty lucrative business, as about one Yank in ten seems to own a light aircraft these days."

"Goodness me! I am surprised. I had always imagined him to be a mining engineer. But, where did you get this information?"

"From the 'Battle of Britain Fighter Association' for one, but also from other sources. He is a member of the Association, I understand. Don't tell me you are not part of it yourself!"

I replied, almost sheepishly "You're right, I'm not! I am not a natural joiner."

"Well, you should be!" was my informant's laughing reply.. "It's a very worthy organisation indeed, which will help to keep you in touch with all your long-lost colleagues and friends"

I then asked, "One last question. Do you have Jamie's address and know if he's married?"

"I believe so, although I can't be sure. If he isn't, his two children are illegitimate!"

After that he laughed again and gave me Jamie's address in Canada. And also the name of the Fighter Association's Secretary, information which turned out to be priceless and which was to affect both my future and that, indeed, of Jamie Bell!

I immediately wrote off to Jamie's address in Canada, but did not receive a reply for almost a month.

In my letter, I told him of my various homes in Massachusetts and elsewhere, and the many friends I had made in America over the years. Perhaps when my wife and I were visiting the States - which we often did - we could call on him and his wife in Canada, with a suitable warning of course. In his reply, he apologised for the delay but explained that his job required him to travel widely, so that he was often absent for up to several weeks at a time. Being a member of the Fighter Association, he very occasionally came to England to attend the annual Battle of Britain dinner at Bentley Priory and later the Remembrance Service at Westminster Abbey.

The Association was very useful, according to him, as it enabled him to keep in touch with some of the chaps he had flown with. Also, now and then, he used the RAF Club, of which he was still a member, as a convenient 'bed and breakfast' lodging when in London. And yes, he and his wife would be delighted to see me - us - in Canada whenever I - or we - came across. His wife's name, incidentally, was Grace, but on no account was I ever to call her Gracie. Otherwise she was likely to 'thump' me! Which, rather gave me the impression that Mrs. Bell was a bit of a bruiser, which, when I met her later, could not have been wider of the mark. His whole letter suggested that he was delighted to hear from me, and I was equally pleased with his response.

It was almost a year after that interchange of letters, that we made our next visit to the States.

We had a friend in Cambridge, Massachusetts - virtually a suburb of Boston - who had repeatedly invited us across We also planned to call upon others friends in Rochester, in upper New York State, who had become mates of my wife when they had all crossed on the Queen Elizabeth on one occasion. And as Rochester was not too far from Niagara and the gateway to Canada, I thought we might visit the Bells who lived in St Catherine's, a few miles away. So, I telephoned to warn them, but found only Grace at home. She sounded very sweet.

She reported that Jamie was likely to be away around the date I had mentioned, but she would love to meet us both anyway. After which, she gave us directions and sounded quite excited about our projected visit. I came away from the phone strangely pleased about her response to my call. She had sounded quite unlike the person I had visualized.

As there are now no trains left in that part of the United States, we drove through Massachusetts and New York State, first from Boston to Rochester then along the shore of Lake Ontario to the American side of Niagara Falls. There we crossed Rainbow Bridge into Canadian Niagara, and then went on the few miles further to St Catherine's.

Having telephoned from Rochester with the time of our arrival, we were both delighted to hear that Jamie would unexpectedly be around, having returned suddenly from wherever he had been. So it was no surprise when, arriving at the Bell home, we saw them both standing on the front porch, prepared to greet us.

It was a sight that will long remain in my memory, not having seen Jamie for many years. He was smaller than I remembered, and quite stooped. His hair had largely gone, so that he looked much older which, I suppose, ought not to have been a surprise.

His wife, Grace, however, really did surprise me. About the same age, she was tall and very thin - quite a bit taller than Jamie - and even from a distance, both my wife and I noted a rather sad, far away expression on her face. Indeed, I seldom ever remember her laughing out loud - she just didn't seem that sort of person.

Moreover, what we both found a little odd was that she held a dog beside them, but firmly on a lead - a black and white Border collie. Then, as we approached, the dog stood there unmoving and silent, as though deeply suspicious of us. Not at all like normal Border collies, which I always remembered as being very friendly but boisterous. After which, as we all shook hands and uttered the normal pleasantries, I bent down to stroke the animal.

Immediately Jamie warned quite sharply, "Be careful, he'll bite you!"

Instinctively, I drew my hand away as the dog regarded me silently with a suspicious, white-edged eye.

To ease the tension of the moment, Grace added quietly, "Jamie and he don't get on. Rastus bites his master regularly. I don't think he really means it; it's just a habit he now seems to enjoy."

But, that moment of tension was the only spot of uncertainty in what developed into a weekend of great interest and genuine pleasure.

The Bell home was a large, three storied and spacious detached house, built in the American style of white clapboard with a shingled roof. With an enormous basement, which accommodated all the heating, laundry and other household essentials, plus two cars, it was sumptuously comfortable by British standards, with bathrooms and showers everywhere. It was filled, in the main, with furniture constructed of rich American maple and other Canadian woods. And throughout there was the wonderfully satisfying aroma of sandalwood and other exotic scents. My wife and I were greatly impressed. Clearly the Bells were not short of money!

That first meal was a simple, pleasant if not light-hearted affair. Quite informal, we all took part collecting and serving the food, the conversation was agreeable, and even the dog was a quiet onlooker, lying on the floor of the dining room close to my chair. After a time, I dropped my hand and caressed his neck and ears. He showed no sign of aggression and when we moved into the drawing room, followed me and sat down by my side, causing Jamie to look warningly in my direction.

"You'd better watch out," he said. "He could bite you at any time."

I exchanged glances with my wife. "He seems pretty content. He probably knows I like animals." But Jamie's face still registered doubt.

Later, whilst our two wives helped each other in the kitchen and, talking endlessly, walked around the house, Jamie suggested that we might take a ride and visit the nearby Niagara Falls, Which we did. Donning waterproofs, we went beneath the Canadian Falls - as distinct from the American Falls, a few hundred yards away - and got ourselves thoroughly soaked as the water thundered down within feet of our lifted faces, with Jamie explaining this and that and being the perfect host.

Then on our way back in the car, he asked, "Would you care to go to the Muskoka Lakes while you are here?"

When I said with a laugh that I had no idea where the Muskoka Lakes were, Jamie explained that they were located about 100 miles north of Toronto and were a vast and beautiful area of water and islands, where fishing was "out of this world!"

At that, I said that I would be delighted to go, as would my wife. Then, assuming that Grace would be with us, I made some remark to that effect, whereupon Jamie said that, unfortunately, there would only be three of us. Noting my surprise, Jamie added, "Grace has a rather nasty heart problem. She has to be careful what she does and where she goes." Which so took the wind out of my sails that I did not pursue the matter, making a note in my mind, even so, that I would ask further questions later on.

Our journey and brief visit to the Muskoka Lakes will remain in my memory for all time and not only for the interest and rugged grandeur of the place.

We stayed one night in fairly primitive log cabins, situated in some pretty wild bear-infested woods, then took a boat out on one of the larger lakes, even being sufficiently audacious to dip a fishing line in the water - with no result, I may add. But our visit was particularly significant because of one strange, almost worrying incident.

We had pulled our boat to the shore in order to join a group of about 20 youngish people who were enjoying a meal at the water's edge. A log cabin, serving drinks and food, stood under trees in the background. We seated ourselves around a rustic table out in the open, on wooden bench seats that were anything but comfortable. Then we waited until a young girl-student helper came in our direction.   After ordering drinks and food of some sort, we sat back and waited, admiring the scenery and conversing about this and that.

Presently, a small child from a nearby family, drifted in our direction, interested no doubt in our strange English accents. Encouraging the small boy, who was about five, we smiled in his direction and gave every indication of being friendly.

Then, as the child, his face alive with interest, neared our table, out of the corner of my eye I saw Jamie beginning to cringe and draw away.

I then heard him say, "That kid! He's coming for me! He is! Watch him! Send the little bugger away. I can't stand kids. Send him away!"

Amazed, my wife and I exchanged wide-eyed stares. Then we both looked at Jamie, who was retreating into his seat. In another moment, I thought, he will be under the table! Our frowning glances asked each other, is he really being serious? Surely he can't be!

In seconds, however, it became clear that we were witnessing something we had never come across before - a grown man terrified of a small, seemingly likeable child. Then my wife was saying gently to the little boy "Off you go, young chap. Back over there. Chop! Chop! Your parents are looking for you."

For several moments the child stood there, clearly perplexed. Then he turned unsteadily and slowly wandered away.

Around our table, there was dead silence. For about ten seconds. Then Jamie said, almost shamefaced. "I can't stand bloody kids. They frighten me!"

And, strangely, nothing more was said of the incident.

Later, we drove back the 150 miles or so to St Catherine's, if not in silence, certainly without much conversation. Jamie said very little, concentrating on his driving, apparently. I knew all too well what my wife had on her mind. Tactfully, I held my tongue.

When we finally reached home and were greeted by Grace, nothing of the incident was mentioned. The dog, not on a lead now, wandered around us quietly with many sniffs and we both stroked his ears, fussed him, and made friendly noises, clearly to his satisfaction if no one else's.

I remember thinking, Lord above! What a funny household this is.

That night, the last as it turned out to be, my wife and I lay awake in the darkness. I asked her, "What did you think of Jamie's performance today?"

"Surprised and horrified are words that comes to mind." I recognized my wife becoming judicious. "I thought for a moment he was joking, but clearly he wasn't. Actually, his behaviour was much in line with what Grace told me earlier on."

"What was that?"

"That there are all sorts of things that frighten Jamie to death. Dogs, for one. And children. Extraordinary for a chap with a family and one so physically brave. D'you know, he and his son can hardly bear to be in the same room together. The boy lives and works in California and never comes home apparently, much to his mother's distress. Even the daughter, who lives in England now, stays away as much as she can. So sad!"

"Did Grace speak to you about her heart problem?"

"Yes."

"Can't she have something done about it? You know, new valves or bypasses, that sort of thing."

"Apparently not. It's a congenital weakness that only a transplant will cure, and she's not prepared to have one of those. But why do they continue to live in this ruddy great mansion? Sufficient for a family of ten? It must be terribly lonely for her when Jamie's away, which seems to be most of the time." Then she added. "They also have what they call a cottage, did you know that? A couple of miles away and on the edge of Lake Ontario. Jamie spends a lot of his time up there when he's at home. Poor woman! Grace must feel terribly cut off most of the time."

I volunteered, "It appears to be a pretty miserable marriage."

"Well, I'm not so sure. She seems very attached to him, for all his strange, ways. I don't think she'd ever consider dumping him."

"Strange people, women!"

"You're dead right, buster! We're odd! All of us."

I returned from America with mixed feelings. Overall, I had enjoyed our visit; I always did, particularly when travelling by road in the still wild forested grandeur of the eastern States. But my encounter with Jamie and his wife had rather unsettled me. He was not as I remembered him and Grace was altogether different from the picture I had formed of her in my mind.

However, in the months that followed, we continued to exchange letters and I must say, Jamie was a regular correspondent, keeping me informed, and indeed intrigued, with descriptions of his travels and selling successes, not only throughout America but also in the Middle East and beyond. I soon became aware that his brand of Consultancy was a profitable business and that he was certainly not short of energy and enterprise, whatever his personal failings.

I also noted, however, that he seldom spoke of his wife in his letters, except in the most unrevealing of terms, and he never mentioned his family.

Then there came a rather unexpected note from him, telling us that he was flying to England to attend the annual Battle of Britain dinner in September and that he was going on to Germany a few days later. During that interval, he intended to visit us in Norfolk, at which time we could no doubt provide him with what he termed 'a bed and victuals'. There being the slightest, and I daresay unintended element of demand in his letter, it caused his wife to roll her eyes a bit, as she always felt that Jamie's plans took precedence over everyone else's arrangements.

But, we stifled our misgivings and I wrote telling him that we would be delighted to see him again and be able to help in any way possible. Also, I looked forward to joining him at the Fighter Association dinner.

I drove down to Bentley Priory, Stanmore, on the afternoon of the dinner engagement and met Jamie in the Officers' Mess bar that evening. He seemed in good form, chatting happily with many old acquaintances and, sitting next to me during the meal, he seemed relaxed and in good spirits.

I was interested to know the reason for his projected journey to Germany and was tempted to ask him about it, but for some reason, I didn't. We would be together for the next several days, I reasoned, so the subject would no doubt arise later.

The following morning we met again for breakfast before preparing for our journey north to Norfolk. Then, whilst wending our way through the Stanmore traffic, he asked me which route I intended to take.

"I have been away from this country for so long," he explained, "these roads are quite new to me so that I'm lost already."

I smiled in his direction. "I intend going up the A1 to about Baldock, before turning right and going across country."

After a brief silence has said almost diffidently, "Would you be prepared to make a detour and continue up the A1 to about Stamford? There's a place there I want to look at."

A trifle surprised, I readily agreed. "Of course I would. After you had driven several hundred miles out of your way to take us to the Muskoka Lakes in Canada, it would be churlish of me to refuse. Just tell me where you wish to go."

Driving north, we were approaching Stamford, when Jamie said, "If we turn off left about here, I'll probably recognise one or two villages I used to know. Take it carefully, though."

I followed his instruction to the letter so that we drove slowly through several attractive stone built villages and their associated greens. Finally, when I was beginning to tire of looking around, not knowing what I was looking for, Jamie said sharply. "Over there! That big house over there."

I slowed the car down before a large impressive Georgian mansion, standing in what appeared to be about two acres of lawns, shrubs, and mature trees, the whole surrounded by a low stone wall with decorative iron gates.

As I sat there admiring it, I heard myself breathe a comment, "Wow! What a splendid place! Did you know of it before?"

I heard Jamie chuckle beside me. "I ought to. It was mine before I sold it. I inherited it when my parents died."

"You sold it! A house like that! Jamie Bell, you were out of your mind. What possessed you to do such a thing?"

I felt, rather then saw him shrug. "I grew up in it, but with my parents gone, I was uncomfortable in it. Anyway it was much too big for me and I had to get away. I have no regrets. It just wasn't me. At the time, I just wanted to spread my wings and go abroad."

And that really was the end of the discussion. Shaking my head in disbelief, I turned the car and headed east, saying not another word.

Our dinner that evening was a pleasant affair. I was aware that Jamie was very fond of my wife - a fondness not entirely reciprocated, I may add - and he seemed comfortable in the family atmosphere we so clearly enjoyed. He appeared, however, a little on edge, as though he had something important to reveal but did not know quite how to go about it. Although both my wife and I associated his unease with his projected German visit, we took good care to let him make the first move.

This came soon after he was comfortably seated in our conservatory after dinner, with his coffee and a brandy at his side. At this point he suddenly rose to his feet, left us both without a word, then returned moments later with several books under his arm. Dropping them on the small table before us, he explained, "You may already have seen these books, which contain detailed descriptions of the Battle of Britain. But they're descriptions with a difference as they not only give details of all the flights and engagements we took part in, but also the aircraft we shot down, the ones we lost, plus the names and units of all the chaps involved, our own and the Huns" Then, looking mischievously in my direction, "Yours are there, in lights of course, plus most of your victims, as are mine and the rascals who did me in. Which really brings me to what I want to tell you."

Then, addressing me, "Do you remember that flight in November 1940 when I was knocked down over Kent and badly burnt? Well, the blighter who did that was the infamous bloody Galland, and I, apparently, was his 58th victim." Then, pausing as though for effect, "So I wrote to him. Telling him who I was and what happened. And was quite surprised when he wrote back almost immediately - he writes and speaks very good English, incidentally - suggesting that I visited him in Germany, at which time I could also meet some of his Luftwaffe mates who had also fought against us in 1940. If I decided to do so, he could arrange a free flight for me using Lufthansa, and, of course, he and his wife would be happy to entertain me for the whole period I was in Germany."

"So,"- another deep breath - "that's what I did about four months ago, and it turned out to be quite an event."

My wife, clearly surprised, exclaimed, "You mean you've already been to Germany? And this is the second time?"

Jamie grinned. "Dead right, dear lady! And I've brought some photos to show you."

At this, Jamie rooted about in the leather wallet he had beside his chair and produced a large packet of coloured prints, which he spread out on the small table in front of him. My wife and I then examined them with genuine interest and I recognised immediately the familiar faces of Galland, Steinhoff, and one or two other Luftwaffe officers I had met when they had visited England just after the war, although I found myself unable to identify some others by name. There were also in the photographs about an equal number of ladies in formal attire, suggesting that the pictures had been taken at some social gathering or official function.

My wife then asked in a carefully disinterested voice, "And who are the ladies?"

"The pretty one there is Heidi Galland, my host's wife," Jamie was pointing with a finger. "And the one next to her is Helga something-or-other. She's the widow of some Luftwaffe chap who was killed, whether some time ago or more recently, I'm not quite sure."

My wife observed drily, "They all look pretty young to be married to Second World War heroes"

Jamie did not seem to notice her faintly mocking tone of voice. "Oh, most of the blokes I met are on their second or third wife. Hitler's Luftwaffe lads seemed to go in for that sort of thing. As you see, Heidi Galland is a very attractive woman and in her early 50s, I would guess. And Helga what's-is-name, next to her, is about the same age."

"She looks pretty dishy to me, I must say," my wife observed.

Jamie then added, in what appeared to me to be a carefully neutral voice, "Oh, indeed she is. And a very nice person, too. In fact, I hope to be seeing them all again when I get to Germany a few days hence."

At this remark, I glanced up quickly to meet my wife's eyes, and I knew immediately what was going through her mind. Meeting them? - or her?

The following morning, I took Jamie to the railway station in Norwich.

As we parted, we shook hands and he thanked me for our hospitality. Then, as he entered the train he waved and shouted, "I'll write soon and tell you how I made out!"

But he didn't. Not for more than six months.

Jamie's letter when it came, included a batch of photographs. My wife, opening the letter at the breakfast table, read it, then went through the pictures one by one before passing them over to me. All in silence. Then, as I examined each photograph individually, she asked, "Do you see what I see?"

I looked up at her in surprise. "All right, cleverclogs! I see a group of people in motor-boats, fishing on the Muskoka Lakes. Why? Because it says so on the back of each picture. It also says the place is Port Sandfield and the strings of fish they are holding up are freshwater bass. All pretty clear to me."

"Yes, but do you see who is at the end of each line of people?"

I looked again more closely. "No one I recognise, other than Jamie."

"Buster, you are losing your eyesight! The woman on the end of each line is Helga. The 'orrible 'elga. Except, she isn't at all horrible."

For some moments we looked at each other. Then I asked her quietly, "What on earth do you think he's up to? "

In reply, my wife raised one eyebrow. "You are allowed only one guess!"

At this stage of my story, it might be helpful if I described the situation throughout Britain, and indeed my own family circumstances and concerns during the early part of the 1980s.

The war, although by no means a forgotten memory, was more than forty years old. My wife and I were middle-aged and two generations had grown up in the intervening period, only small elements of which were knowledgeable about the Second World War, and even fewer, more than casually interested. War, and anything of a military nature, was unfashion-able among the youth of the '60s, who seemed fascinated only by what they termed 'Love', being 'Way Out', `Personal Adornment', and the ability of 'Flower Power' to cure all ills.

Our own family of three sons had grown up, but we were still in the business of helping to house at least one of them and educate several of our grandchildren. To keep abreast of school fees, the rising cost of living, and a steady stream of stealth taxes, it was small wonder that such extraneous matters as Jamie Bell and his private affairs were not high on our priority list. Even so, the early '80s saw a rise of national interest in the Battle of Britain and other wartime aviation events, stimulated by displays and exhibitions organised by the Imperial War Museum at the old RAF Station at Duxford, and the most excellent RAF Museum at Hendon.

The Battle of Britain Fighter Association began to thrive as well and, despite a reducing number of qualified members, began to attract national and international attention. There were - and still are - annual and much publicised Remembrance Services at Westminster Abbey, and the September dinners at Bentley Priory were always eagerly anticipated by the several hundred Battle of Britain veterans who were still sufficiently mobile to attend.

Such events attracted many former Service members from overseas and Jamie Bell was no exception. He turned up in England, usually in September, at least once every two years, and he wrote his chatty and informative biannual letters to my wife and me, just to keep in touch. He always appeared genuinely fond of us and seemed to treasure our long and mostly agreeable relationship. Also, Grace and my wife established a routine of sending each other flowers now and then, colourful reminders of our past, very pleasant association. And, as time went by, my spouse even showed signs of becoming less prejudiced against Jamie, whom she continued to regard as 'a bit of an odd-ball', and 'not at all reliable'.

For me, however, Jamie always remained a pleasant memory and the personification of the good old days and the many occasions we had flown together over the years. His considerable contributions during five years of war, together with the many wounds and injuries he had suffered, all tipped the balance against the several character failings I knew him to possess. Yes, Jamie Bell was a valued friend, and always would be, whatever the future held.

Chapter Three

It was, as I recall, about June, 1985, when my wife and I received an invitation from a valued friend living in Boston. An author and poet, with a number of distinguished books to her credit, she wished us to be her guests at a very superior literary occasion at Harvard University. However, my wife, being otherwise engaged at that time, it was agreed that I should fly across alone.

I was delighted to have the opportunity. I had enjoyed my several years as a businessman in Boston and the prospect of visiting my old offices in State Street and walking along the banks of the Charles River, watching again the Harvard fours and eights during rowing practice, was more than merely tempting.

Arriving at Logan airport and having hired my usual Budget Rent-a-Car Mercury - I always went for a Mercury, if available - I not only spent a delightful three days at the literary ceremony, but also visited the very picturesque Revolutionary War sites at Lexington and Concord, both within 20 miles of the City centre. Then, having enjoyed myself to the full, it crossed my mind to drive north into Canada and visit Jamie Bell and Grace at St. Catherine's. I then discussed my intentions with my wife over the telephone and decided to extend my time in America a further week or more, provided, of course, my friends in Canada were available.

Happily, they were. Not only did they seem delighted to hear that I was in their approximate area, but yes, I would be very welcome, although Jamie had business appointments in Florida for part of the period of my proposed visit. Not to worry though. Grace would be pleased to entertain me on her own during the time Jamie was away. I was suddenly excited and expectant. Splendid!

The road from Boston, Massachusetts to Buffalo, New York, runs roughly westward through 300 miles of rolling hills of scrub forest and pleasant if ruggedly wild terrain. I always enjoyed the drive through the northern part of New York State as it usually enabled me to make a detour through the area of the Finger Lakes. These were once the home of the five tribes of the Iroquois Indian Confederacy, who had, in the main, allied themselves to the British during the Revolutionary War of 1775. It also reminded me of James Fennimore Cooper, the author of 'Last of the Mohicans', and 'The Pathfinder', two books of colonial times, which had so fascinated me when I had first read them as child. Indeed, I had visited on several occasions, the author's rustic home in Cooperstown, some miles to the south of the Finger Lakes, where the author had lived 150 years earlier.

I was anxious to reach Niagara as soon as possible, however. So I kept to the north and drove through the fruit producing country just south of Lake Ontario, stopping now and then to sample the rich dark grapes, sold at the many roadside halts along the hot and dusty roads. It was a delightful drive in a car that reeled off the miles effortlessly. So that I arrived at the American side of the Niagara Falls several hours before I had expected to, and had only the

Rainbow Bridge to cross before entering Canada. Then, as I crossed the bridge towards the far side customs hut, it was borne home to me how things had changed over the years.

When I had first used the bridge in 1948, the then Canadian Flag, the Union Jack, had fluttered proudly from flagpoles everywhere and the tourist shops were full of pictures and memorabilia bearing portraits of King George and his smiling Queen Now, however, only the new Canadian maple leaf flag was in evidence and the portraits had largely disappeared. Even so, I always experienced that comfortable feeling of `returning home' when I crossed into Canada anywhere, but particularly Ontario.

Despite not visiting the place for several years, I found the Bell house without difficulty. As before, it loomed impressively large and white in its quiet, grassy enclave of obvious prosperity. On this occasion, however, there was no one on the porch to greet me, nor was there Rastus, the unreliable Border collie, who, I was told later, had died some months before.

Jamie answered my ring on the bell and greeted me with a comradely hug and restrained enthusiasm. "Grace is in her room at the moment," he volunteered. "She'll be down in a minute. She's been rather poorly lately, so you may see a change in her."

I grimacing sympathetically, "Is it the usual heart problem?"

"That and other things, yes." Then brightening, "We shall be going out to a meal later on. Would that suit?" Then in explanation, "Grace doesn't cook in the evening nowadays and we couldn't insult you with anything so ordinary as a takeaway".

"Nonsense! You needn't have bothered."

At which point Grace appeared, coming slowly down the stairs. And I was shocked into silence. Recalling her as tall and thin, she now looked like someone out of Belsen. Her hair, as I remembered it a mousy brown, was almost white and I noted that she was obliged to use the banisters to steady herself.

But her smile was still the same. Welcoming and genuine, but above all, gentle.

Approaching, she held out a hand and proffered a cheek. "You have made our day. Such a pleasure to see an old friend again, particularly from home."

Thinking it an odd remark to be made by someone not English, I kissed her and tried to look cheerful.

She added, "Jamie may have told you. We have booked a restaurant table about two hours from now, but we have to drive about thirty miles. So, can I suggest he shows you to your room so that you can freshen up after your long drive." Then the smile again. "I'd do it myself but I'm afraid I'm not very good at going up and down stairs these days"

Five minutes later, I was standing in my bedroom unpacking my few possessions. The room was typically New World, being massive by English standards. It had a polished oak floor with scatter rugs, a huge four-poster king-size bed, and several large pieces of furniture in light maplewood. Flimsy drapes shaded the several windows, there were adjoining bath and dressing rooms, and there was the quiet hiss of cool air coming through the ventilation and air conditioning grills in the walls. And all about was the subtle scent of sandalwood.

I stood for some time, busy with my own dark thoughts. I had been shocked by the change I had seen in Grace, and even Jamie appeared much older than the last time we had met.

However, I decided it would be tactless of me to discuss possible causes immediately without giving offence. But later, when Jamie left for Florida, I resolved to tackle Grace in private.

I was not allowed to use my hire car to take my hosts to our lakeside restaurant that evening, being obliged instead to sit alongside Jamie, driving his large, new Oldsmobile. In the back, Grace sat quietly in one of the sumptuous leather seats and did not take part in the sporadic conversation that passed between Jamie and me.

The restaurant was impressive, a considerable single-storey wooden construction on stilts on the shore of the Lake, a hundred lights shimmering and dancing on the dark waters beyond. Being in the main a fish restaurant, I was happy to order my favourite New England Clam Chowder, then the freshwater bass. To my surprise, both Jamie and Grace ordered swordfish steaks, which I knew would make a heavy meal, a meal I felt unlikely that Grace, in her emaciated state, would be able to eat. Which, in the event, was the outcome. Picking at it fastidiously, she finally left more than half the fish on her plate. Noting it, I carefully kept my eyes averted and made no mention of her apparent lack of appetite.

Even so, the evening passed off pleasantly enough. Conversation, although certainly not animated, was agreeable and continuous, but I sensed that subjects such as Jamie's German visits were carefully avoided, and there was never any mention of family affairs, other than my own.

Finally, I drew the evening to a close by announcing that the long drive had been rather tiring, and my hosts taking the hint, we drove home almost in silence.

During breakfast the following morning, Jamie announced that he intended flying down to Florida early the next day, and in order to catch the 6 am flight, it had been his practice to stay the previous night in Toronto. If it met with my approval, it would help enormously if I were able to drive him to Toronto in the Oldsmobile during the afternoon, before bringing his car back to St Catherine's. He smilingly added that he was aware it was a longish trip, but one well within the capacity of a chap as young and as virile as me. My heart leapt at the opportunity I had so fortuitously been given. I immediately said I would be delighted to, and the arrangement was agreed. Meanwhile, after breakfast, and until the time of our departure, Jamie had it in mind to take me to a local Revolutionary War battle site, as he knew of my keen interest in colonial history.

Which is precisely what happened. We spent a pleasant and instructive morning together before departing for Toronto at around 3 pm. By early evening, I had arrived back to be greeted by Grace with a brave smile and a cooling drink. I was quietly delighted. Yes, this was what I had hoped for.

I detected at once a more relaxed atmosphere in the house. Grace was smiling easily and she was more chatty than usual.

"I thought we might eat at home this evening," she said. "I've found you some Clam Chowder and I've rustled up something cold. After that I want to watch a bit of television as there's a B.B.C. play on tonight I particularly want to see." Then, noting my half-hearted nod of agreement she went on, "Oh, I know by the look on your face that you want to know more about my health and so on, but I don't want to be interrogated tonight. Tomorrow we'll go to the cottage and relax. Then you can ask all the questions you want, although I won't promise to give you answers to everything. And if you enjoy swimming, now's your chance as the cottage is right on the edge of the Lake. Okay?"

It was almost noon the following day when we set off for the cottage. I drove the Oldsmobile whilst Grace sat beside me doing the navigating. Which wasn't a very arduous task as the journey only took about seven minutes.

I was rather surprised by the size and location of the cottage. A single story wooden creation, it was much larger than I had expected and was tucked away in a rather unkempt two-acre garden plot surrounded by middle-sized trees. Completely isolated, it looked quite unattractive at first glance and was in fact, rather forbidding. As we approached, Grace commented, "It looks as though Gloria's gone home, as her car's not here. Gloria's our ' woman-wot-does' - note the English idiom! - who comes in three mornings a week."

Climbing out of the car, we approached the house, which Grace entered without using a key, causing me to ask in surprise, "Do you normally leave the place unlocked?"

"Usually, yes. We don't lock things up in this part of the world." She turned and smiled. "Not a bit like London or elsewhere in the United Kingdom, eh?"

Inside, the cottage was built in the open-plan style, with a mass of living-room and kitchen space, and, I imagined, at least four reasonably sized bedrooms, although I was not shown them at the time. Every opening and window was protected by fly screens. Anticipating my next likely question, Grace added, "Being so close to the water, we get lots of things that bite around here. So the screens are an absolute must and always have to be kept closed." Then standing by the door, she waved an arm "See? The Lake is only yards away and we have about 200 yards of private beach. So, if you want to swim, you will have the place to yourself."

After that, she led me into what she described as Jamie's lair, a room of considerable size. It was furnished with a number of comfortable, cushioned cane armchairs and a settee, several well stocked bookcases, and walls lined with aviation prints and pictures by well known artists; Frank Wootton, Robert Taylor, Michael Turner, and others. And, I was surprised and flattered to see there were several portraits of wartime fighter pilots, including two of me, both by Orde and Kennington.

Turning, I saw Grace smiling at me. "You see how fond he is of you and how proud he is of your achievements."

Feeling totally embarrassed, I was unable to reply but only shrugged.

After a brief lunch, we were seated comfortably on a patio in front of the house, facing the Lake, when Grace instructed gently, "Find yourself a drink. Jamie has a well-stocked cabinet in the far corner of his room. And, before you ask me what I want, I only drink water."

After pouring myself a tall Cinzano and tonic and handing her a glass of iced water, I sat down beside her within touching distance. Then, as she lay there quietly, her eyes closed, I sensed it was the opportune moment for questions.

I started off, "Grace, I don't want to intrude in any way, but you seem so unwell, you sadden me. Although I know you have a heart problem, Jamie hinted there were other concerns. Also, and perhaps I shouldn't say it, there seems to be a strained atmosphere in the house that wasn't around when last my wife and I were here. So, as a long standing friend of Jamie's and as someone who is very fond of you both, is there not something we can discuss?"

For some moments, I thought she would not reply. Then turning, she stretched out a hand and laid it on my arm.

"You're very sweet, but I don't really want to talk about my problems. Please don't be offended, but I find talking about them hinders rather than helps. Also, there is so much to say, it exhausts me just thinking about them."

I fell silent for a minute, in two minds as to how I should proceed.

Then: "All right. Let us take it by stages, then. You've clearly lost a lot of weight. Can you say why?"

A shrug. "Sadly, I have. I'm only about seven stone, now - less than 100 lbs. Which is far too light for someone my size. Also, I'm desperately weak, physically, but that's part and parcel of my heart problem, and there's not much I can do about that."

"Why do you say that, because so much is being achieved these days in that field of medicine?"

"No, but there are other things". A significant pause, "You see, I'm also a diabetic; I now have to inject myself twice a day. And . . . well, at present I'm in remission, having had a cancer operation 18 months ago. Which is why, with infinite lack of tact, Jamie tells all our local friends that I am now 'flying a bit left wing low."

" What! You mean you've had a mastectomy?"

Grace smiled and her hand squeezed my arm. "I thought you might have noticed."

Appalled, I shook my head, wondering what to say. Here was a woman clearly without a future, living from day to day, but surviving without any show of anger or resentment. How on earth could I help? How could I comfort her? I felt myself swallowing. I would try another tack.

"Tell me Grace, is Jamie supportive? How is he taking it all?"

My companion gave an explosive snort. "Taking it! My dear, Jamie isn't taking it at all! Illness frightens him. In fact, Jamie is frightened by pretty well everything - other than getting himself shot in aircraft! He's scared of sickness, children, dogs, family - our family! In short, he can't cope with responsibility. And when Jamie's frightened he simply runs away. Just disappears! Which is one reason he now spends so much time away from his home, and me. And why we seldom if ever see our son and daughter, who simply won't come near him."

I stared at her open-mouthed. Stunned into silence.

Looking back, I often contemplate and am still profoundly disturbed by the bizarre situation in which I found myself in those long drawn out minutes of silence. It was a lovely day, the sun shining warmly, and in the middle distance speed boats carved white furrows across the water, towing water skiers. Children's voices and laughter came faintly to my ears through the trees, and beside me a woman I had only met occasionally, a woman burdened with illness and an uncertain future but the wife of a friend and colleague I much respected and admired, reclined quietly and seemingly relaxed, her eyes closed.

Perplexed and concerned by what I had just been told, I felt there was so much more for me to learn from Grace, about her marriage to Jamie, about their recent past together, and indeed her family's background and history in Canada. Who were they and who was she? How and when had they arrived where they now lived? When had she and Jamie married, and where? Oh, all that and so much more. And also, the immediate future and what it held. If indeed there was a future!

All these questions and a hundred others passed through my mind like the coaches of a slow moving train. But how to go about it? Questions, obviously. But would she respond? As she lay there beside me, still in tranquil repose, it seemed hardly fair to disturb her. But, I hardened my heart and framed my next question with care.

"Grace, can you tell me about your family? A bit about your own history? Because you do not have much of a Canadian accent. Were you educated here, or abroad?"

Opening her eyes and giving a small grin in my direction Grace replied, almost with spirit. "Are you really suggesting I'm not Canadian? If you are you'd be dead wrong because I'm Canadian to the core." Then she laughed - she actually laughed! - the first time I had ever seen her truly amused, which cheered me up more than I can say. After which, she fell silent for a time, then closed her eyes before continuing in a low monotone.

"My family name is Percy, which is still well known in the Border counties of England and Scotland. In about 1695, a junior member of the family emigrated with his young wife to colonial America. They landed in Boston and went to a place called New Towne, which later became Cambridge, Massachusetts. This original Percy was an academic and came to America for the purpose of joining the faculty of Harvard University, which was then about 60 years old."

"About twenty years later, he moved with his family down to Connecticut, probably to join the new Yale University which had recently been established in New Haven. There they stayed, growing in number, until the American Revolution, or War of Independence - depending on which side you were on - started up in the 1760s".

"That war became a bitter struggle, engineered at the outset by smart-Alec lawyers and other malcontents for reasons of their own. It divided the whole population of the thirteen colonies, right down to individual families, into Loyalists and Patriots."

"The Percy family remained Loyalists throughout. When the war finally came to an unhappy conclusion in the 1780s, and with many others of the same persuasion, they sailed north to Halifax, Nova Scotia. Later, they spread out into this part of Canada, my lot finishing up first in the Toronto area, before moving south to where we now are, St Catherine's. We call ourselves 'Empire Loyalists' and still exist as a group to this day, although the term is less fashionable nowadays."

There followed a silence during which Grace lay back with her eyes still closed, so that I half expected her to call a halt to her reminiscences. But, after about a minute, she continued.

"There were four children in our family, three boys and me. We were all born 1918 and after, and I was the third in line."

"In 1937, one of my elder brothers went to England and joined the RAF. He was later posted 'missing believed killed' in 1943, when his Wellington bomber was shot down over

Germany. The other two joined the Canadian Army and were sent to England in 1940, to 'defend the homeland.'"

"I followed later that year, just after the Battle of Britain, and became a FANY, driving ambulances through much of the London bombing that occurred between 1941 and '44. Later, I drove a couple of Admirals around the south of England until we invaded the Continent in June of that year."

"After the war ended, my remaining two brothers up-sticked and went out to Kenya, with many other ex-Servicemen. One bought himself a slouch hat with leopard skin trimmings and went into the Safari-white hunter business, bear-leading groups of visitors around the game reserves and other places. The other began cattle farming on 4,000 acres around Thompson Falls, which is about 100 miles north of Nairobi. Not having anything to do and feeling thoroughly unsettled, I joined my farmer brother and spent a number of very enjoyable years in the so-called 'Happy Valley' part of that fascinating country."

"It was there that I learned to use a rifle, as we had to protect our cattle against lions, leopards and other predators, which from time to time pulled down our calves and took our dogs. And, of course, we shot for meat - antelopes and gazelles mainly, but other things as well".

"Then, when the Kikuyu went mad and the Mau Mau insurrection started, my Safari brother went further south, first to Rhodesia, then after that South Africa. My farmer bro', also gave up and returned to Canada. He now lives in British Columbia, has a family, and is in the fur business."

"About the same time, Jamie and I were married, after a lot of 'this and that', and finally came back here to Canada, because my parents were on their last legs. And in due course, I inherited this house and here we have remained. Which just about brings me up to date."

When Grace described her marriage to Jamie as involving 'a lot of this and that', I remember smiling openly at her remark. At the same time, I realised that if I was sufficiently persuasive, there was much more of a story to come. Moreover, I genuinely wanted to hear in much greater detail what had happened to Jamie after he had left Malta. In particular, I was eager to know how and where he and Grace had met and the state of their marriage over the years, because Jamie was clearly the strangest of characters and the relationship between him and his wife perplexing, to say the least. And so it turned out to be, a story delivered in a flat, low, unemotional voice, as, with closed eyes, Grace reclined in her chair and talked. By the water's edge, during that very pleasant afternoon in Ontario, Canada.

Starting off, she said, "Although I have the happiest memories of those days in Kenya, looking back it was a lonely life for an active and healthy young woman in her late 20s. There were only three white faces on that farm; my brother, who was then unmarried, the farm manager, a South African named Van der Wall, and me. All the others - farm hands, labourers and house-boys - were blacks from the local Bantu tribes. In all there were about 40 men, women, and children. Loyal and agreeable though they were, we had little to do with them and there was not much in the way of day-to-day social intercourse, as our nearest white neighbours were fifteen miles away."

"Once a month, my brother and I would drive into Nairobi for supplies and other essential items, after which we would meet ex-pat colleagues and friends at our favourite watering hole, the bar of the New Stanley Hotel. My other Safari brother would also be there as often as not, his business office being within a stone's throw of the hotel."

"And it was there I first met Jamie. I can see him now, just another chap across the room, in the usual khaki bush jacket, shorts and desert boots. A grin on his face, a pipe in his mouth and a pint of wallop in his hand. I never remember being formally introduced; he was just someone I rubbed shoulders with and with whom I spoke an occasional word above the din of conversation. I knew nothing of what he did at first, although I later learnt that he had a small flying business using a few ex-Air Force single-engined aircraft and one or two bigger twins, such as the de Havilland Rapide. Apparently, he flew from any one of the several small grass strips on the periphery of Nairobi."

"On reflection, there was one characteristic I always associated with Jamie, and that was he was always coming and going. He was never anywhere very long. Sometimes, he was in the New Stanley bar, then suddenly he wasn't. Always entering or leaving. Always grinning. And always with a pipe in his face and a pint of beer in his hand. Looking back, I never recall being especially attracted to him. He was always just a chap who was there! Now and then, that is."

"I saw him at monthly intervals for some time after, until one day I invited him to visit our farm. Or perhaps I should say, Jamie invited himself, offering to fly up and take some aerial photographs of our buildings and surroundings, and talking me into inviting him, which he did."

"I had the boys prepare a landing strip of about 500 yards and Jamie arrived in a small two-seater -1 think it was called an Auster or some such aircraft. Anyway, he gave me a flight, which I thought was great fun, then took some splendid photographs, which I have to this day. He then spent four days with us, drinking us out of house and home, before disappearing southwards in his aircraft, after which I did not see him again for several months. But, I was to remember that first visit for another rather humorous incident - most of us thought it humorous, anyway."

"We had collected at the farm a small menagerie of orphaned animals; a couple of tiny lion cubs, two cheetah totos, several Thompson gazelles and the sweetest and smallest baby elephant. All had been collected in the bush as the result of their parents dying or being shot, either by us or by someone else. When Jamie was being introduced to them, I picked up one of the lion cubs and handed it over for him to inspect and cuddle. Smiling, he took it and held it to his breast, but the little blighter, though small, had all the inbred savagery of its breed and raked his chest with the extended claws of its two back feet, ripping open his bush jacket and scratching him quite severely. With a howl, Jamie tried to drop the little brute, but the cub refused to let go, gripping him round the neck with its front paws and then, adding insult to injury by peeing all over him."

"We, of course, all fell about laughing, but Jamie was not in the least amused and only recovered his equanimity some hours later."

Grace then went on. "In the months to come, Jamie used to invite himself to our farm, arriving when it suited him best. Sometimes he turned up even when we were away in the bush, at which time he would take over the house, put his feet up on the best chairs and pretty well empty our drinks cabinet." A sudden snort from Grace's chair, "No, it was soon borne home to me that Jamie Bell was not a chap to hold back!"

There followed a brief silence

"Then, arriving by air one day, completely unheralded, and with a gleam in his eyes and a set expression on his face, he confronted me and, without preamble, asked me to marry him. I was staggered. I had never considered marriage, certainly not to Jamie, although I have to admit, I had given some thought now and then to having children. I was almost 30, Britain was off-loading its Empire, there were rumblings of rebellion throughout Africa, led by mission-educated, self-seeking black malcontents, and my two brothers were beginning to think of changes. Even so, my immediate reaction was to say 'no', and I did.".

"But Jamie was not to be denied and kept on at me until I finally consented. This brought up a major problem - he insisted that the marriage would have to take place at his home in England. So, three months later, I flew back to the UK in a very noisy Avro York - there were no jet airliners in those days - and met his parents and others in the Bell family home in Rutland, Jamie having arranged to follow me a day or so later".

"Then, literally hours before the day of our wedding, he disappeared."

"Disappeared!" My minor outburst was spontaneous. I could not prevent myself interrupting her almost unbelievable story.

"Yes, disappeared! Did a bunk, or should I say buggered off! He just didn't turn up. Left his mother, family, and me standing there, looking like fools. No, Jamie was doing what I later was to learn he was prone to do when faced with unpleasant reality, he just turned and ran. I simply could not believe it at the time."

"Good Lord! And what did you do then?" I still could not keep amazement out of my voice.

"What could I do, a stranger in foreign parts? Jamie's mother was very sweet and supportive, so I stayed on for a few days, hoping and expecting that Jamie would get in touch. But he didn't, so that there was no alternative to going back to Kenya, which I did. Hopping mad, I may say, and feeling a perfect ass."

Greatly moved by Grace's story, I felt I needed a break. So, I got up, walked about, refreshed my own drink and provided Grace with another glass of water. After that I sat down and prepared myself for another chapter of incident and misery.

"So Grace, what happened after that?"

"Probably what you would expect, knowing Jamie. He turned up in Kenya about a month later, all sackcloth and ashes and with a stream of excuses I did not for a moment believe. Then he proposed to me a second time and swore on a stack of bibles that he would carry the thing through."

I asked, incredulity in my voice, "And you fell for it? What on earth got into you?"

"Well, I had no choice, really. My farmer brother was eager to return to Canada, so that, in effect, I would shortly be out of a home and a job, unless I went with him, of course, which I did not wish to do at the time."

"So you returned to England to marry?"

"Yes, for the second time. But with a proviso, which was that we lived in Canada afterwards. I had no intention of being totally separated from at least one of my brothers. This broke my heart really, because I would have given my eye-teeth for the Bell mansion in Rutland, which I knew Jamie would eventually inherit."

"But he did, and I've seen it."

"Yes he did later, but he gave it away, the halfwit!"

"Gave it away!"

"Virtually. He sold it for peanuts to a distant cousin, who lived in it for a year before selling it on. For a vast profit, I may say. No, in money matters Jamie has always been a fool. He never had to worry about it, you see."

"And did he come back with you to Canada?"

"He did initially, but he was like a fish out of water. So much so that he left almost immediately and tried to get back into mining in Cornwall, then travelled to South Africa to have a go at gold mining there, but found neither to his taste. So eventually, he came back here and went into the aircraft consultancy business. That suited him down to the ground as it meant he could get away from home and wander round the country to his heart's content. A great wanderer is Jamie!"

"And when did the children arrive?"

"Fairly quickly - 1 saw to that! Jamie, true to form, contrived to be away when each of them was born. In fact, as infants they had very little attraction for him and not much more as they grew up, although Debbie, our daughter, claimed rather more of his attention that Robbie, our son. By the age of five, I could see that Robbie greatly missed Jamie's involvement, as his father seldom if ever played little-boy games with him or instructed him in any of the manly sports other than swimming, which Robbie didn't seem to enjoy very much anyway. Then, when the child was eight, Jamie had him sent away to prep. school in Toronto. After that he insisted on packing him off to Uppingham, Jamie's old school in England. So, the poor mite received precious little parental guidance or love for much of his formative years. Then, there followed Cambridge University until he was 22, so it was only at that time we really saw anything of him, when he returned to Canada during the summer vacs".

"And Debbie fared almost as badly. She went to school locally at first before she was also sent back to Cheltenham in England, to complete her education. After Cheltenham she came home briefly but returned to England as she had met a chap there she later married. He is now a schoolmaster at Radley public school, just south of Oxford, where she has since raised a family."

"Meanwhile, Robbie, who had learnt to fly with the Cambridge University Air Squadron, went out to California, took his various civil pilot's licences there, and is now with an airline, flying 747s throughout the Far East."

"So, Jamie's indifference over the years has resulted in our almost total isolation. We seldom see either of our children now, certainly not Robbie, who won't come anywhere near his father, as they can't stand the sight of each other."

At this stage of Grace's disclosures, which had already taken over an hour to recount - 1 have only included some of her story here - I felt I needed another break and stood up to compose myself and stretch my legs. Grace's tale had deeply disturbed me as it painted a picture of Jamie I had only dimly recognised during my more critical moments. And what about his womanising? She had not spoken at all about that side of his life, and, the good Lord knew, it certainly existed! What about his journeys to Germany and his contacts there? The 'orrible 'elga', as my wife was apt to describe her. I resolved to rest a moment then pose the question in my most tactful manner.

I began, "It must have been quite a moment for Jamie, forty years later, to read of the chap who shot him down and so damaged him in November, 1940."

"Oh, it was indeed. And I was glad for him because he had often speculated as to whom it might have been. Then when he learned it was the famous Galland, he felt almost a sense of pride."

"And he went to Germany several times, I understand?"

"By invitation, yes, and he quite enjoyed himself, meeting many of the chaps he had fought against, together with their wives".

"Did you meet any of them?"

"Galland and his wife? No, although we corresponded with them many times. But another ex-wife - a widow called Helga something - yes. She had German relatives in Wisconsin, apparently, and Jamie invited her across when next she visited the States."

"And she came here?"

"Oh, yes. Twice. On one occasion for four days, during which time Jamie took her to the northern Lakes to fish. I believe he sent you photographs of the visit."

I took a deep breath. "And what did you think of her? My wife always refers to her as 'Horrible Helga.'"

At this Grace actually laughed. "Oh, she was anything but horrible. She was surprisingly young, very attractive, and really quite sweet. I liked her."

I then asked carefully, "And it didn't raise any doubts in your mind?"

"Doubts? About him sleeping with her, you mean? Oh, yes. But Jamie has been doing that for years. Everywhere he goes, I reckon he has women friends with whom he beds down. Once, in the RAF during the war, I understand, his Station Commander had to have him posted away after an irate husband had appeared at the camp gates with a shot gun - Jamie had been having an affair with his wife. But" - she gave a shrug - "for the last twelve years I haven't been much of a wife for him, what with my wonky heart and my other more recent problems. I don't approve of such goings on, of course, but I understand. What I find hurtful is that he always lies to me and doesn't ever take into account my health problems and my need for sympathy. I believe he always thinks of me, even now, as someone able to fire a rifle, shoot lions and look after herself. But, sadly,

I'm not that person any more, but one who now needs masses of tender loving care, and I'm afraid I don't get any of that from Jamie."

At which point, looking down at the woman talking quietly and reclining as though asleep in her chair, I felt tears begin to moisten my eyes and was obliged to swallow. Poor, poor unfortunate woman!

I stayed on with Grace at her home in St Catherine's for three more days only. Jamie telephoned on the second day and apologised to me for being kept in Florida, as he would have dearly liked, he said, to have shown me more of the lakes and forests of Ontario.
But, whilst I had reservations about leaving Grace, who was looking very poorly, I felt it best to go. So, I bought a mass of flowers in the town, spread them throughout the house, and tried my best to jolly her along, not that it had much effect.

Finally, as we embraced when saying our final good byes, it felt as though I was holding a bag of bones and my heart turned over. This poor creature was dying on her feet, very bravely and without protest, living from day to day. I was overwhelmed by sadness and had difficulty in controlling my emotion.

So, on the fourth day, I drove my Rent-a-Car Mercury back to Boston, and took a British Airways 747 back to Heathrow and home. Quietly sad and deeply unhappy.

We kept in touch with Jamie and Grace with the occasional exchange of letters for the next five months. My wife sent Grace flowers now and then and received the customary note of thanks in response. Nothing was said of her illnesses and life seemed to be progressing in Canada much as usual, with Jamie away on business trips from time to time. Then suddenly, it all happened.

It was on a Friday, I recall. I had watched the late evening news on television and was in process of undressing before getting into bed. My wife was in the adjoining bathroom and I was bending over a bedside table, hunting for a book, when the telephone rang - we have an extension near at hand.

Wondering who on earth it might be at 11 o'clock at night, and feel slightly irritated, I lifted the receiver.

A voice I immediately recognised as Grace's, said, "Hello?" in my ear. I responded, not too seriously, "Grace my love! It's almost midnight here and we are just getting into bed."

"I know and I'm sorry. But I just had to speak to you." A pause. Then: "Jamie's dead! He's been shot! At the cottage. Someone's shot him!"

At that point, I remember the bathroom door opening and my wife's head appearing. Her lips formed the silent question, "Who is it?"

And me answering, "It's Grace! From Canada! She says Jamie's been shot. Been killed, apparently."

The look on my wife's face was almost comical. "Killed! Jamie? When? How?' Then, "Let me have a word with her."

My wife's voice. "Grace, my love. What's this I hear about Jamie?" A long silence. Then, "Good Lord!" Another silence. Then, "You mean now?" A pause. "All right, I'll see what we can do. Leave it with us for five minutes to think and I'll ring you back You're at home, I take it?"

We stared at each other for some moments, scarcely able to take in the meaning of Grace's message. Then my wife said, "She wants us to go over to Canada immediately."

"Canada! Now?"

"That's what she wants, yes"

"But how can we? With so much arranged next week."

"We can change our plans, though. Can't we?" Then, "Look, 1 think we have to go."

A minute's pause for heart-thumping thought.

"All right. Ring her back and tell her we'll be over as soon as we can. The day after tomorrow, possibly."

Later, still undressed, plainly in shock and with her hand at her throat, my wife asked, "Who d'you think did it?"

I shook my head, deep in thought. Then, "I wonder if Helga or her mates had anything to do with it."

"Why Helga?"

"Well, he's been sleeping with her, apparently, and one of her German mates may have had it in for him."

"Oh, surely not!"

"It's not that far-fetched. You never know with these Germans, particularly the ones in the United States. Towards the end of the First World War, the famous Hun airman von Richthofen was shot down and killed. The chap who was said to have done it, a Captain Roy Brown, was a Canadian who came from these parts. When he came back after the war, his life was made a living hell by would-be German assassins from the States, so that the police gave him permission to go around armed until the day he finally died in the 1940s,"

My wife, still in shock, whispered, "I just can't believe it has happened. That poor, poor woman! What's she going to do now?"

We caught a direct flight to Toronto in the early morning of Sunday, and by the miracle of modern transportation and a five-hour time difference, were in Canada by mid-afternoon the same day.

At the airport, I telephoned Grace, giving our approximate time of arrival, hired a car, and set off on the two-hour drive around Lake Ontario to St. Catherine's.

When we arrived at the Bell home, we were greeted by a buxom black woman who introduced herself as Emily. She would show us to our room, she explained, after which she had prepared a light meal for us. Mrs Bell was sleeping at present but would be down to greet us later. Walking in behind her, the house seemed vast, empty, gloomy and very quiet. I saw my wife give an involuntary shiver.

When first we saw Grace coming slowly down the stairs, clutching the banisters, even though it had been less than six months since our last meeting, the deterioration in her condition was to me most marked and depressing. She looked even more Belsen-like than before and her hair, formerly thick if not colourful, was now a wispy halo of white straying strands. She came towards us slowly and held out both her hands. She whispered, "1 am so glad you were able to come. None of my family is likely to be here for weeks, if at all. And I so need a little support just now."

My wife said "Grace, do sit down and tell us everything. About Jamie, of course, but also about yourself. You look so unhappy and poorly."

Grace seated herself slowly, her hands clasped together in her lap, and I was concerned to note that now and again her whole body shook as though with cold.

"Jamie was found dead in the cottage three mornings ago." She was speaking in a quiet, controlled voice. "Gloria found him when she went in to clean, as she normally does. She then rang me here in a state of absolute hysteria and we immediately called the police. He had been shot in the chest apparently, just once. Probably the night before."

I asked, "Where is he now?"

"They took him away after they had done all the tests they needed and taken the photographs. Then they came and spoke to me."

My wife asked almost indignantly, "Did they consider you a suspect, the silly people?"

"They probably did, until I described my state of health and where I was at the time. Then they asked about the guns we had in the house and I showed them the two Luger automatics Jamie had brought back from the war. Plus the standard Springfield rifle he had been given by the Americans, and a Mauser machine pistol he had obtained in Germany. There was also the 12 bore he used for clay pigeon shooting now and then. They then asked about licences and I told them the guns were Jamie's and that he would have any licences he held in his office at the cottage. Anyway, none of them had been fired for years, and they saw that immediately."

"And have they no idea who might have done it?"

"If they did, they kept quiet about it. No, I was pretty sure they didn't know."

I asked, "Did Jamie have any enemies locally? Or do you think Helga or any of her German friends or lovers may have been involved?"

At this, Grace actually smiled. "My goodness! You really have it in for Helga, haven't you? No, I don't think she had anything to do with it. Or her friends."

"And there are absolutely no clues? No one near the cottage saw or heard anything?"

"Apparently not."

"And the murder weapon?"

"They haven't found one yet, but I dare say they will soon be able to identify it by the type of ammunition used."

My wife and I exchanged glances. Grace seemed almost too controlled and unconcerned and we both sensed it. Did she know something she was not telling us? About her family? About their neighbours? About anything? For around a minute, we all sat there looking at each other. Silently. Clearly uncomfortable and plainly baffled.

Then Grace moved her hands in a quick gesture as though suddenly impatient. "I can see you think I'm holding something back. Well, you're right. I am. You see . . . I'm afraid I did it! I'm the villain. I'm the person who shot Jamie. I'm the one who killed him. I'm sorry, but there it is."

There are very few occasions in life when one is faced with a situation or an event of which one has had absolutely no experience, so that one's immediate reaction is stunned disbelief and tongue-tied silence. I remember on one occasion sitting at dinner alongside a person to whom I had only recently been introduced, who revealed in the most causal of remarks that his twin sister had very recently been hanged, an announcement which reduced me to absolute speechlessness whilst I struggled to find a suitable response. Both my wife and I found ourselves in much the same situation when Grace, in her strangely quiet and unemotional voice, told us very simply that she had just shot and murdered a close friend of mine, a brave man I had known and flown with for more than forty years. The shock of her bald confession was immense and my wife was the first to recover her composure and break the silence.

She said in a quiet voice, hoarse with emotion, "Grace, my dear. Do you really understand what you have just said to us? You have just admitted being a murderer, putting us both in a very difficult situation. Unless, of course, you are intending to tell the police."

"I have no intention of telling the police anything more than I have done thus far" Grace shook her head almost vigorously. "I asked you here today because I wanted you, and only you, to hear my story. To hear exactly what happened, and why. What you do now is your business. It won't really matter to me, one way or the other."

I put in almost desperately. "Grace, please understand. We are on your side. We are your friends, as well you know. We want to help in any way we can. Tell us everything, please."

Which, for the next 30 minutes she did. I have paraphrased some of her remarks, but gist of her tale is as follows.

"I have already told you a little about Jamie over the years. About our relationship, and also about my declining health.

"About two months ago, I felt myself losing a grip on things and went for a series of check-ups. They confirmed my worst fears; the cancer had spread everywhere and I was advised to prepare myself for the worst as I had no more than two months to live. Naturally, I was deeply upset, although it was more or less what I had been expecting. And, of course, I immediately discussed the consultant's diagnosis and my probable life expectancy with Jamie, who dealt with it in his own inimitable way - by looking at me blank-faced, telling me how sorry he was, then going off on one of his 'important' business trips.'"

"So, I was left here alone, with Emily and another daily girl who does the cleaning. Emily, a former nurse, is a good woman; she does all the cooking and looks after me throughout the day, putting me to bed at night before going home. She has a young family of her own and doesn't stay here overnight."

"On the Thursday night - the night Jamie died - 1 had been put to bed and left alone in the house. Jamie, although back from one of his trips, was out at the cottage and had been for several days. He runs his business from there, with his office, computer, files, and other bits and pieces. We both rather look upon the cottage as his domain; 1 seldom go there other than when it is very hot and, even then, only during the day."

"On that Thursday night I couldn't sleep. I remember it was towards 11 pm and I felt utterly lonely and miserable. I don't remember being in pain, it was just that I desperately wanted company and sympathy and the house all around me was dark, quiet, and horribly empty. So, I got up, and still in my nightdress and slippers, walked about and thought about going downstairs and making myself a hot drink. Then, and I don't know why to this day, 1 thought about Jamie out at the cottage. If I drove out to him there, he would at least be someone with whom I could share my misery."

"Making up my mind in an instant, I went downstairs - and again, I don't know why, as I had never done it before - 1 picked out a Luger and ammunition from Jamie's gun cabinet and slipped it all into my bag. Then, I went down to the basement garage, and started up the old Chevvy, which was, and is, my car, but one I had seldom used in the last six months".

"I know you will ask why I took the gun and I will honestly tell you, I don't know. Perhaps it was because I suddenly realised that I would be a lone woman in her nightdress, driving a car in the middle of the night, and presumably very vulnerable should it stop for any reason - although, I admit, I don't ever remember letting such a thing worry me before."

"Whatever the underlying thoughts, I arrived at the cottage and found Jamie sitting in a chair, watching television. He was alone, but I suddenly knew - or sensed rather than knew - that he had been entertaining someone. Getting up, he faced me in surprise and I believe, with some embarrassment."

"He said, 'Grace! What on earth are you doing here this time of night?'"

"And I replied, almost tearfully, 'I came because I was terribly lonely and needed someone to talk to. I'm dying, Jamie, but it doesn't seem to interest you, does it? You can barely bring yourself to say that you're sorry, before you take off again and disappear. I need company and support, Jamie. Don't you understand? Don't you care?'"

"Then, when I saw him open his mouth to argue, I stopped him with a raised hand. 'No, let me finish. Let me get it off my chest. You see, I know you have been entertaining that German woman. You have, haven't you? She's either here now or she's just left. I know that because I can smell her perfume. You also know that I have only days or weeks to live, yet you can t even wait until I go before you are climbing into bed with someone else. I have no family, Jamie, because my children and grandchildren won't come near us because of you. You have lied to me and been unfaithful throughout our entire life together. Right from that first day, you have let me down. You are a brave man, physically, Jamie, but you are an indecisive, untrustworthy rotter, and you ought to be ashamed of yourself'.'"

"At this point, I found myself weeping, the tears blearing my vision. I also heard my own voice as though it belonged to someone else. More than that, I suddenly experienced an overwhelming compulsion to hurt Jamie. To punish him. To strike him. To make him realise what he was doing to me."

"So, with a single movement, I pulled the Luger from my bag and levelled it at his chest, saying. 'Jamie I'm going to die very soon but I see no reason why you should live on, entertaining your string of women. That, and because you have always let me down. Time and time again, Jamie, you have let me down. Ever since the day we first met.'"

"With that and with no emotion at all, I pulled back the safety catch and fired a shot into his chest. Just one bullet, which hit him where I judged his heart would be."

"I saw him stagger just a half step, after which the light faded in his eyes and he crumpled and fell forward to the floor. There, face down, he lay still. Very still. And all I was aware of was the faint smell from the gun. And silence."

At that point in Grace's account, when she described pulling the trigger and shooting Jamie to death, the emotion of the moment was so great that we all appeared to hold our breath and experience a spasm of sheer pain. The next sound I heard was my wife's agonised voice. "Grace, you say you just killed your husband? You shot him to death? How could you possibly do such a thing and how did you feel at that ghastly moment?"

To which Grace answered almost calmly. "I don't think I felt anything. Certainly no regret. I just stood there, looking down at him and feeling numb, all the frustrations of forty years just draining away from me."

Then as though in conversation with us, "I was sure the bang had been heard and waited for a time for someone to turn up. But, no one did, so after about two minutes - it must have been quite that long -1 put the gun back in my bag and walked quietly out of the cottage and back to my car. Leaving him there. Bleeding!"

"It was dark and quiet outside and I'm sure no one saw me. My one thought at that moment was that I mustn't be seen or get caught. Not because I had just shot Jamie, that I was guilty of murder and had to be punished. But that I didn't want the exhausting business of dealing with the police, being involved in a trial, and subjected to all the unpleasant publicity and photographs. I knew that in my state of health, I just couldn't cope with all that. I now realize, of course, that I was wrong and that I should have been thinking of Jamie. But I wasn't. I really wasn't. All I was concentrating on was getting away and not being seen".

"Well, driving back, I took a narrow minor road that skirted the Lake and I threw the gun as far as I could into the water. Jamie had three Lugers, you see, but I knew I could always say he had two. No one knew about there being a third. Back home, I put the car away in the garage very quietly - again, no one saw me, as far as I know. Then I carefully cleaned out my bag and washed both myself and my nightie, dressing gown and slippers. After that, I put on clean nightclothes and just sat in a chair all night, shivering. And waiting for the telephone to ring next morning. Which, of course, it did. With Gloria the other end, being hysterical."

"And that . . . well, that really is about all . . . I think. The rest you know."

As Grace told her story and gradually lapsed into silence, we both watched and waited, staring wide-eyed at her and at each other. Then, as she sagged back into her chair and shook in massive, silent spasms, my wife rose quickly and sat down beside her.

"Grace, you are ill! Let me take you upstairs to bed and we'll call a doctor."

But the woman composed herself, smiled and shook her head "No, just ring for Emily, she will attend to me." Then, rising, "You will want to discuss what I've told you and decide what you want to do. Whatever your decision, it doesn't really matter. I don't care. Really I don't". Then a further pale smile, "Emily will be in tomorrow morning to get you your breakfast. So, good night to you both and thank you for coming. I'm very tired now and need to sleep. It's been a very wearing day."

The doctor did not arrive until the afternoon of the following day, so that my wife and I had plenty of opportunity to discuss our next course of action.

I said, "Have you thought about what we should tell the police, assuming they call, which is more than likely?"

My wife pulled a face, "I've been thinking of little else all night."

I went on. "You understand, don't you, that we are now accessories after the fact, or whatever the legal term is. Which means we can go to gaol if we don't reveal what Grace told us yesterday. Also, we have to decide what we are going to tell the family if, indeed, members of the family turn up. And, how we deal with the press and other media people who will be banging on the door when the whole sordid business becomes common knowledge. And., of course, what we tell the doctor, assuming we tell him anything? And finally, how long we are going to stay in Canada if Grace dies, or remains very ill."

My wife gave a brief grin. "Which question do you want me to answer first? No, I think we wait until the doctor arrives, hear his verdict on Grace, then make up our minds. In the meantime, if the police arrive, we just say we're friends from England who have just arrived and know not very much about anything. In short, we should be like Brer Rabbit and say 'nuffink'. For the moment anyway."

Mid-morning, accompanied by Emily, we went up to Grace's bedroom in a silent column, to find her still sleeping soundly. As she lay there, a still, small mound beneath the duvet, only the rise and fall of her shallow breathing signified life. I looked down at her, trying to visualize the active young woman of past years, the person who was virile and self sufficient, expertly using a rifle to kill game and lions to protect her calves and feed her animals. I was so moved by the sight of her small inert figure, that I was obliged to turn away to hide my distress, only to observe my wife in much the same state.

The doctor arrived in the early afternoon, to whom I explained that we were not blood relations but close friends of long standing, who at that moment seemed to be the only people around capable of making a decision.

After he had examined his patient and rejoined us downstairs, I asked, "If you are able to do so, can you give me your prognosis? Having just arrived from England, it would help us to be able to advise those members of the family who live in distant parts, and also give us a rough guide as to how long we might have to stay here."

After hesitating, the man said, "I take it you know of her condition?" And when I nodded, added, "She's very frail now and usually, with her problems, body functions usually collapse all at once, following renal failure, for example. If that happens, the end could come within days, or she might soldier on for a week or more. One never knows. However, I would suggest that her family is warned immediately, if they don't already know."

I said, "We have been in touch with her daughter in England and she has promised to be here with her two children in less than a week. Her eldest brother, who lives in South Africa, will not be able to come, and her other brother who works in British Columbia, cannot be contacted at the moment. Also her son, who is an airline pilot, is in Australia and can't be with us for some time, apparently. Which rather suggests that my wife and I will be here indefinitely, as there is no one else to look after the shop."

My spouse, who was listening to this discussion, rolled her eyes, hinting that she was already mentally attuned to accepting the inevitable.

The police arrived later that afternoon to interview Grace again, but when they learned of her condition, they took us aside and began to question us in very general terms. However my wife and I - after exchanging meaningful glances - presented straight bats and they left convinced that we knew little that would help them with their investigation. When I asked if they had completed their examination of Jamie's body, they became very evasive, leading us to believe it would be some time before burial arrangements could be considered. So, we deduced that an even longer stay was on the cards if we could not off-load that responsibility.

Suddenly, and to our growing concern, our brief mercy trip to Canada was developing into a long drawn out and very unpleasant task.

Grace Bell died in her sleep two days later.

We were told the name of her solicitor - or what the Canadians call a solicitor - but felt it would be quite improper of us to intrude into the private affairs of someone who was only a friend, even a close friend. So, we decided to wait for the arrival of the daughter and hand over the reins of organisation to her. Which we did, much to that poor woman's shock and obvious disquiet.

Grace's funeral and cremation took place a week later. A brief interment service was held at the local Episcopalian Church, a service which, to our surprise, was attended by over 200 people, almost all of them from the local area. The daughter and her children were there, of course, and the British Columbia brother suddenly turned up out of the blue, looking hot and flustered. There was, however, no one from Jamie's family in England, nor was there any sign of their airline son.

But, for me, the high point of the event occurred later, when, after the service and still in the church precincts, an attractive middle-aged woman I had seen circling and looking in my direction, approached and spoke to me.

"You are from England, no?" Her accent was decidedly foreign. "I am also a friend. From Germany. My name is Helga Schulz and I am visiting. I read about my friend Jamie and his wife. Such terrible, terrible news. I am very sad. But it has been good to see you here, yes? I am very glad!" With that and a pained smile, she drew back with a waft of perfume, and moved away,

When my wife walked up, she asked, "Who was that woman you were talking to?"

Still mildly stunned, I replied faintly, "Believe it or not, that was Helga. The 'orrible 'elga, no less!"

"Helga! Good Lord! She didn't look particularly horrible to me!"

To which remark, I merely tilted my head

With the police reluctant to tell us anything about the release of Jamie's body, it seemed pointless hanging about. The house, formerly so welcoming, now seemed bleak and silent, the large rooms empty and echoing. The buxom Emily had departed, whether temporarily or for good, we didn't know, and even the delightful Niagara Peninsula, with its orchards and warm dusty roads, seemed somehow less inviting.

The daughter, too, with her children, often harassed and petulant, were seldom around, and there seemed little left other than memories.

After a spell of three weeks, therefore, we decided to return to England and driving up to Toronto, caught an overnight flight, finally settling into our seats with sighs of relief. Phew! Thank the Lord for that! What a time and what a ghastly business!

I came awake as our 747, its engines a mere whisper, was letting down through cloud somewhere west of Gloucestershire. In 40 minutes time we would be back on the ground. I glanced at my watch. It was 5.30 am, local time.

As I came awake, a stewardess approached, trilling her cheerful good morning greetings, bidding us straighten our seats and offering us coffee and cold, plastic breakfasts. Beside me, my wife stirred, yawned discreetly, and blinked into life.

She shivered, smiled, then said finally, "Mm! It's nice to be home again, isn't it?" Then: "Sweetheart, if there are any more Jamie Bells in your life, I don't want to know about them. Ever! As that American chap said, 'Include me out!'"

Then, after a moment or two, another question. "D'you think the police will ever find out who did it?"

I smiled. "Did it! I reckon they know already, my love. And always have done. Even the police can sometimes be understanding."

*   *   *